BLOODLINES

ALSO BY T.K. ROXBOROGH

Third Degree

The Ring

Compulsion

Fat Like Me

Grit

Limelight

Whispers

A CROWN OF BLOOD AND HONOUR

Banquo's Son

Bloodlines

Birthright

T.K. ROXBOROGH

BLOODLINES

A Crown of Blood and Honour, Book 2

Published by Thomas & Mercer, Seattle

www.apub.com

Amazon, the Amazon logo, and Thomas & Mercer are trademarks of Amazon.com, Inc., or its affiliates.

ISBN-13: 978-1503946446
ISBN-10: 1503946444

Cover design by Lisa Horton

Printed in the United States of America

This book is dedicated,
with love and affection,
to Jo and David Fielding

Macbeth: . . . they say, blood will have blood:
Stones have been known to move and trees to speak . . .

Act III, Sc 4, *Macbeth* by William Shakespeare

Author's Note

As I said at the start of *Banquo's Son*, 'I have tried as much as possible to draw upon the vocabulary that was in use during the Elizabethan era rather than 11th-century Scotland, as I imagined myself sitting at Shakespeare's desk penning this sequel.' I have endeavoured to source the origins of words, beliefs, practices and anything else of the time I am writing about because I do want things to be authentic.

However, Shakespeare played around with history, as many other authors have, so I make no apology for twisting the facts to fit my narrative. One of my rules in the writing of this series is this: if it existed before 1614 then it is allowed to be used in my writing. This is fiction but I have spent endless hours in books devoted to medieval medicine, Scotland, Norway, Normandy, costume, weaponry, crops, food . . . you name it, I've probably researched it!

So, if there is a historical error, consider it author's licence. Don't tell me flagstones didn't exist in 11th-century housing – I KNOW! But Shakespeare and I don't care. We just want to tell a story and give you a sense of place and pain and pleasure.

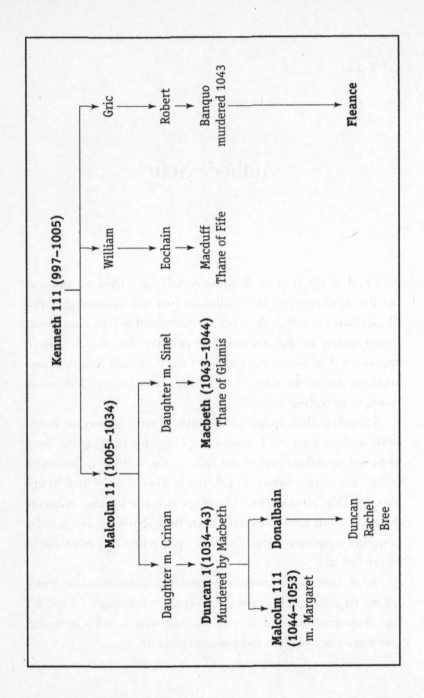

Prologue
Scotland, August 1054

Well?' he asked, pulling the hood of his cloak tightly around his nose to avoid being overwhelmed by the stench from the cauldron and the moist, hot air of the dirty hut.

As one, the three strange women turned from the blackened cooking pot that bubbled over a fire. Each of them held a wooden cup.

The eldest of the three stepped forward, the flickering light from the flames deepening the craggy lines in her face, and she lifted her cup to him. 'Speak!'

Her companion, shorn-headed and tall, mimicked the action. 'Demand!'

The final woman, pale and young, smiled dreamily at him. She put the cup to her lips and took a sip. Then, wiping her mouth, she whispered, 'We will answer.'

Though he was loath to remove the hood, the desire to know the fortunes of his life, the life of the one he loved and his country was greater. He gulped for air under the cloak and then removed it from his face.

The first witch shuffled forward and held the cup to his mouth. 'Drink,' she commanded.

He had seen what they had put into the pot and a fear gripped him. What if this was a trick and they planned to kill him? He looked at the third witch – she had sipped and it had not affected her. He was stronger in body, though she – having connections with the spirit world – might have supernatural protection. So, somewhat anxious, he took the proffered cup, raised it and threw the contents into his mouth. The liquid hit the back of his throat and he gagged, but then numbness came over his tongue and lips and he tasted nothing.

'Tell me – what of Scotland?' he gasped.

The old woman's eyes locked onto his. She took the cup from his hand and shoved it behind her. The tall woman grabbed it and put it on a low table.

The room was quiet, save the sound of the cauldron and the fire – and his laboured breathing. The old witch pursed her lips then closed her eyes. 'She has many enemies,' she said. 'But greater are her friends. Though men will come against her, none shall break her. Though some will inflict wounds and they will fester, nothing will destroy her.'

This might not be good news. To his next question. 'The king?'

The second witch brought her cup and gave it to him to drink. This time he did not hesitate. Without taking his eyes from the hag, he emptied it.

She nodded and began humming. She took his cup back and turned it around and around in her hands. 'Happiness will lose to loss, which will lose to fear, which will lose to rage, which will lose to grief, which will lose to hope, which will lose to happiness.'

'These are riddles,' he cried. 'You have my gold; give me facts.'

'Speak! Demand! We will answer,' all three replied together.

'What of the girl? Will she keep the line alive?'

The third and final cup was handed to him and he drank. Now his whole face felt as if it had vanished. He could not taste or smell or feel, but he could still see.

The last witch stood before him. From within her garments she pulled out a bundle and handed it to him. He held it for a moment, uncertain what was expected. It felt solid and about the weight of the log he'd put on his campfire earlier that day.

The woman stared at him, waiting. Unsure if he was supposed to uncover what was hidden, he began to unwrap the coarse garment. Suddenly, he felt movement between his fingers and he almost dropped it. The dirty cloth fell away and there, in his hands, was the body of a tiny baby boy.

'What is the meaning of this?' he shouted. 'This is madness.'

As if the noise had power to wake him, the baby inhaled deeply, his eyes flew open and he uttered a most painful and piercing wail.

He thrust the child into the arms of the hag and rushed from the hut, the sounds of cackling laughter and the wailing of the infant following him out into the cold dark night.

Chapter One
Glamis Castle, Scotland, April 1054
Rachel

Duncan looked asleep, not dead. Paler than usual but, apart from the blueness of his lips, it looked as if he were dreaming. Deeply asleep. Rachel recognised the familiar stillness she'd observed when they were children and she had stayed awake longer than he. This time, though, there was no soft hush of her brother's breathing. This time he would never wake.

She reached out once more to push aside the thick blond strands of hair that sat lifeless around his face.

When she had left the battlefield, her brother had been alive and laughing, though annoyed he had been injured. When she had left with the badly wounded soldiers, he and Fleance were healthy and strong and well. Victors and victorious.

Who could have foreseen such a different ending?

The thanes had come to the castle and told her how Duncan had stepped forward to challenge Calum, the Norwegian king, just as he released the crossbow bolt – the deadly arrow intended for Fleance, her brother's best friend. She was told he had been hit but had lived – making jokes on the surgeon's table and on the wagon returning home.

Oh Duncan, she thought. *Why did you get in the way?*

She studied the unmoving face. His body had been well prepared for his final journey. The shiny smear of oil on his forehead – evidence of the bishop's anointing – looked like an accidental spill, not the blessed unction intended. The truth was, is, and would always be: Duncan, son of Donalbain, grandson to King Duncan the First, was no longer contained within this empty shell.

Suddenly she was aware that someone else had entered the room and she turned to see Fleance standing just inside the door.

'You are welcome, Fleance,' she said, feeling the dryness of her mouth and the sting in her eyes as she spoke. He hesitated a moment then came to stand beside her. She turned back to stare at her brother. 'My entire life, and his, has been peppered with extremes: late-night goodbyes and angry encounters. Marvellous banquets and rich enjoyment of the best the world could offer. These were all part of the royal house of Scotland. But no one has prepared me for the pain that comes with this.'

He placed a hand on her shoulder and she reached up to grasp it. There was comfort in such a gesture. Fleance cleared his throat. 'Is any man or woman ever ready to face death when it comes too soon?'

Rachel was silent. The question needed no answer. Tears came again, God forbid, but she could not halt them. 'Sorry,' she said, reaching for a handkerchief to wipe her eyes. 'I thought I had no more left.' She tried to smile at him but when she looked directly at his face, she was shocked to see that he, too, was crying. 'Fleance . . .' she began, stepping closer to him. He enfolded her in his arms and she could feel him trembling.

'I should not have let him come with me,' he said. 'It is my fault this has happened.'

Rachel pulled back and grabbed both of his arms. 'No!' she said through her tears. 'This happened because someone chose revenge rather than forgiveness.' She clenched her fists. 'There were other agents at work here.'

They stood, breathing through their own grief and yet holding on to each other. Rachel let Fleance go and knelt down beside the bed. She reached out to her brother but could not bring herself to touch him, knowing that his body was now so cold. Rather, she shifted his hair again and straightened his garments.

'Duncan has always been there to both counsel and tease me. I relied on him to be the . . .' She bit down on her lip. 'He was practical. And I am too, but in a different way.' She looked away but the tears blinded her. 'He was my . . .' What else could she say? 'Duncan was solid and right and good, and I cannot make decisions without him.'

Fleance sighed and knelt down beside her, close to them both. 'Rachel, Duncan became king long before he expected to, but he fulfilled his role admirably and led Scotland well in the fight against the insurgents.'

Yet, she thought, *here he is. Dead.*

She pulled back the sheet and opened Duncan's fine linen shirt to study the blue and violet colours of his wound. Around the hole where the crossbow bolt had entered were angry red agitations. Over the left side of his chest, where his heart lay, was a strange, swollen lump.

'I have never seen such a thing. Do you think, Fleance, that the tip of the bolt was poisoned?'

'Stop it!' He got up and pulled her to her feet. 'Stop trying to work out why it happened. It happened, Rachel. He's dead and no one is to blame except the man who released the bolt and the general who should have known better.' His jaw tightened. 'Me.'

She sat down on the edge of the bed and rubbed her face with her fingers, trying to massage her skull and knead out the thick pain behind her eyes.

'Princess . . .' Fleance said gently, 'there is the other matter we still need to talk about.'

Rachel breathed deeply and turned to him. 'Aye?' She watched as he dipped his head and a faint blush crept over his cheeks. Even with the body of her brother lying cold here in this room, the affairs of the country could not be ignored.

Fleance cleared his throat and breathed deeply before looking her in the eyes. 'I know,' he began, 'that Duncan's final words have been conveyed to you. We need to give some thought to the future.'

So soon? To be dealing with it even while Duncan lay cold at their side? A still, quiet voice whispered, *Yes, even this*. Fleance was right to bring this up now, for they must not delay preparations for the immediate future.

'Only two days ago, I saw my place as the king's sister. I was happy with this and prepared. Today? Now? I am being asked, before I have even buried my brother, to consider my life as the king's wife . . .' The last phrase came out as a whisper and she quickly turned to the wall to avoid his gaze.

She felt him move towards her and sit at her side on the bed. 'Rachel,' he said, 'I understand . . .' He broke off and stood up. 'Lay him to rest and we will think on this again. Soon.'

There was a quiet cough behind them. Rachel stood and turned. It was Firth, the castle's head manservant. She nodded to give him permission to talk.

'We are ready when you are, Princess,' he said, his voice gentle.

Rachel looked back at the body of her brother then turned to Fleance and placed a hand over his heart. 'We will talk more of these plans when I return,' she said. 'Do not think poorly of me, Fleance.

I understand my position in all this, as I am sure you do. Just give me some time.'

As she walked from the room, she pressed her hands into her stomach to try to relieve the ache that pinched and stabbed at her. 'I am ready,' she said to Firth.

More men should have accompanied them to Iona, but with the troubled times and the need to crown a new king quickly, Rachel understood why the entourage was so small. Only the Earl of Caithness and his two sons, as well as a priest and Rachel's chosen attendant, Charissa, joined her and Bree on board the ship with Duncan, now wrapped tightly in a shroud and covered in sweet- and pungent-smelling flowers and herbs.

At first, Bree had refused to travel anywhere: neither with her sister to bury their brother, nor with Fleance who was to be crowned king. Eventually, she gave in, though it was clear she was determined not to make the trip easy for anyone. It was of some concern that the child had not yet shed tears for her brother.

'The grieving will come,' Fleance had told Rachel, his own pain etched grimly on his face.

As if mindful of the tragic cargo held below deck, the sky's colours were soft and the wind almost tender as the ship made its steady way north. Caithness, a ruddy, somewhat silent man, stood on deck watching his sons – young men not much older than Rachel – as they assisted the ship's crew in navigating the waters on their passage to Iona.

Over the next three days they sailed around the top of the main-land and headed south more rapidly as the crew took advantage of the brisk winds that seemed to enliven the sea and clouds on the west coast.

On they sailed between scattered islands, the captain skilfully navigating his way among the rocky outcrops, until they crossed the final channel of water between Mull and Iona, notorious for its swift currents and uncertain winds that could spell disaster for boats smaller than this one.

At last they were able to land on Iona.

Duncan's shrouded body was carried off the ship and up the hill into the village, while the monks said prayers and sang songs with which Rachel was now all too familiar. Bree approached the litter that carried the body of her brother and the men stopped on the path for her.

Rachel watched as her sister, her face unreadable, reached out a hand and touched Duncan's covered head. Bree's hand rested there a moment before she snatched it away, wiping her fingers roughly against her skirts. Then she nodded and stepped back, allowing the men to continue.

Bree now walked beside Rachel, silent and angry. Rachel tried to reach for her sister's hand but the young girl folded her arms in protest. *'Be patient with her,'* Fleance had also counselled. *'She is only a child.'*

Rachel thought on Bree's reaction to Duncan's cold body and she suddenly understood why her sister had first refused the journey: Bree did not want to remember that Duncan was gone for good. Her response to touching the cold body of their brother seemed to confirm Rachel's thinking. The last time Bree had seen him, he had been full of life and strength and determination.

On they all walked, beyond the last low village wall and up the hill past the fields, the thin grass giving way at the edges to reeds that warned the walkers to keep clear of the soft mud underfoot. They headed towards the small group of pine trees that marked the halfway point between the village and the monastery land and, as they turned the corner at the edge of the little field, Rachel could see the first outbuildings of the monastery, above which the sturdy roof of the abbey rose, unmoving, against the grey clouds scudding overhead.

As they approached, the rain began to fall – gently at first, and then steadily heavier, as if the whole island was in mourning for Duncan. Rachel felt as desolate as the landscape in front of her. It should have been bigger. More important. This was the place of kings. Yet sheep nibbled on the grass and there were fewer monks here, at the Scottish birthplace of her faith, than on the mainland.

The sisters stood side by side as Duncan's body was lowered into the ground. Bree was pale and her fists were clenched by her side as the tears at last began to flow.

Rachel put her arms around her sister and pulled her close. Although Bree's body was rigid, she did not resist and allowed Rachel to hold her tight. It wasn't long before Rachel felt the heat from Bree's face come through the fabric of her gown. 'He was so cold,' she cried. 'Rachel, he was so cold.'

'Shhh, bairn. God has taken up Duncan's soul to heaven and left behind the shell. Our brother looks down on us now and is happy and glad.'

Bree lifted her face. 'So why does it hurt me so much?'

Rachel brushed aside the tears that fell down her sister's cheeks. 'Because that is the way of a world that has good men and bad men. And sometimes, before the good men win in the end, the bad men are allowed to do things to hurt others.'

'Not fair!' Bree cried and buried her face in Rachel's side again.

'Aye,' Rachel said, stroking the hair of her baby sister. 'No one has ever said it was fair.'

Caithness came to stand at Rachel's side. 'Princess, we all grieve at the injustice. And we should. Duncan was a great man – as was his grandfather before him.'

Doubtless he meant to comfort her, but his words cut Rachel to the quick with their omission of her father, Donalbain. King for such a short time. Not perfect. But passionate and still her father; killed accidentally some months before.

Was her dear brother to fade in his people's memory in the same way? Rachel looked around her desperately and stepped back from the graveside, reaching her hand out to touch the wall of the abbey. Her fingertips felt the unyielding edges of the stones. They had stood here for so long, withstanding all that the wind and rain could hurl at them over the centuries. And they would remain long after her own life was over.

Duncan would be safe here. Rachel lifted her head and looked, first at her wee sister and then at Caithness, then nodded to the priest by the graveside. Silently, they made their way into the monastery to seek shelter for the night before their return home the next day.

Now to what would await her on the mainland – marriage and an uncertain future. The thought of how uncertain this was filled her with apprehension.

Chapter Two
Scone
Fleance

Blair had hired two torch bearers who would guide them on the trek to Scone. When they arrived, very late into the evening, Lennox greeted them as they trudged towards the encampment.

'We were not expecting you until the morning,' he said as he helped him to dismount.

'Our business was completed at Perth quickly and these fellows,' Fleance said, nodding to the two torch bearers, 'willingly journeyed with us to make the trip less arduous.'

'We thank you,' Lennox said to the two young men, then turned to Fleance. 'Your sister will be pleased to see you,' he said. 'The child possesses a bottomless pit of questions.'

Fleance smiled. 'Yes. I should have warned you.' He patted Willow's rump as the horse was led away. 'Where is she?'

'I will take you to her,' Lennox said, walking towards the giggling sounds coming from a far tent. The torches burned bright and friendly in the encampment and Fleance was encouraged by the familiar faces and sounds he saw and heard.

Morag was, once again, in charge of almost everything domestic. When he pushed past the flap of the tent, he heard her ordering the children to get ready for bed.

The moment she saw him, Keavy rushed over. 'Flea,' she cried. 'I have a white dress.'

Fleance grinned and looked to Morag. 'That is fine, bairn.'

'And Bree's too tired because of the journey with Rachel so Morag said I'm to throw the flowers.'

'Of course,' Fleance said, not surprised that Bree had refused to attend though doubtful it was weariness that caused her unwillingness to see him crowned. Her demands that Rachel stay with her at Glamis might have conveyed the message to the people that Fleance did not have the family's blessings. Thankfully, Bree's reputation of being uncooperative with most people put paid to any mischief the young girl might have caused.

'You need to tell me the stories,' Keavy cried. 'Rachel is not here to explain what we are doing.'

Fleance looked up at Morag. 'I don't understand.'

'She's been nagging me to explain what will happen tomorrow,' Morag said, wearily. 'As if I don't have enough to do.'

'Thank you, Morag. You are a most versatile woman and we appreciate all that you do.'

Morag blushed. 'I'm sorry, Sire. I didn't mean to sound like I was complaining . . .'

Fleance held up his hand. 'I didn't take it that way and my thanks still stands.'

Keavy sat down on the cushions by her bed. 'Flea,' she called, patting the place beside her. 'Come. I have to tell you something.'

Fleance sat beside his adoptive sister and turned to her. 'What?'

'I know that each thing that happens tomorrow has a Sig. Nif. I. Cance.'

'That's a big word, Keavy,' Fleance said. 'Where did you learn it?'

'Preston told me about Sig. Nif. I. Cance.'

'Aye?'

'He said that, tomorrow, when the bishop does all these things, many of them have important meanings.'

He nodded. 'That is true. The men will go to the church and bring out the standing stone and then the bishop will pray—'

'And splash water on you,' Keavy interrupted. 'That's to make you a baby again.'

Morag snorted and Fleance grinned. 'It is like a christening, bairn. It's called rebirth. It means the king starts a new life, fresh and clean from any past sins.'

He watched her taking this in. She frowned slightly. 'Da says sins are bad.'

'Indeed they are,' Fleance replied, the mention of Magness like a stab in the stomach. Fleance picked up her wee hand. 'Then the bishop will take the scented oil and dab some on my forehead, here,' he said putting his finger on the middle of his forehead. 'That's called anointing and it's for protection against evil.'

'You mean bad things like devils and bad spells and witchcraft?'

'Aye.' His legs were beginning to ache from the position he was sitting in. 'I am tired, Keavy, as are you.' As if to confirm this, she yawned. 'We can continue in the morning.'

'But you're not finished,' she said, pleading. 'What happens next, Flea? When do I throw the flowers?'

Fleance then understood the persistent questions. Keavy was nervous and anxious about her role in the ceremony tomorrow. 'All right. I will finish and then it's to sleep. You can count this is as a bedtime story.' He stretched out his legs in front of him and then pulled up his knees so that Morag would not trip over him. 'One of the earls will give the crown to the bishop and he will put this on my head.'

Fleance suddenly shuddered. In the telling of tomorrow to Keavy, he was beginning to understand he was talking about what would be happening to him – not someone else. The reality of the coronation was becoming clear.

'And?' Keavy asked, breaking into his thoughts. 'What does that mean?'

Fleance thought for a moment. 'Well, it means two things: firstly, the circle of the crown is God's never-ending love and the crown itself is like . . .' He thought of a way to explain to the child about sovereignty. 'It's like telling everyone that the human king is doing the heavenly king's job here in Scotland.'

Keavy nodded solemnly. 'That's why we have to do what the king says.' Then her face brightened. 'Is that when I throw the flowers? When you've been crowned?'

'Not quite. The bishop will hand me the sceptre. This means power and it is the last thing the bishop does because here the named king must accept or reject the throne by accepting or rejecting the offered sceptre.'

Keavy put a small hand on his. 'Flea, you won't reject, will you?'

Her question surprised him because no one else had questioned that he might change his mind. Fleance took in a breath. 'No. I will accept.'

Keavy clapped her hands. 'My brother will be the King of Scotland.'

Fleance touched Keavy's face. 'And you will be a princess.' He stood up now, his legs too tired to cope with further sitting. He stretched. 'Then I stand on the stone and I am lifted up and you go before me with the flowers.'

'What if you fall off?'

He laughed. 'I won't. But it is considered a bad omen if the new king cannot balance on the stone.'

'Perhaps you should do some practising,' Keavy offered.

'He won't need to, bairn,' Morag said, coming over and helping the child into the cot. 'He is the rightful king so he will not fall.' She pulled up Keavy's blanket. 'Now, time to sleep or else you will be too tired for tomorrow's events.'

Fleance bent down and kissed Keavy on the top of her head. 'Sleep well.'

'And, you, Flea,' she replied and closed her eyes.

He nodded to Morag who curtsied and then he went out into the dark, the housekeeper's words echoing in his head: *He will not fall. He will not fall.*

Unlike Duncan's coronation, the crowd was small. Lennox, Angus, Ross and Lennox's son were elected to carry the stone. All morning, he had felt a heavy weight, like a presence, crowding into him as if someone was standing too close but, whenever he looked behind him, there was no one. Though he had not dreamt last night, the feeling was caused by the ghost of his father.

Fleance stood in a small clearing with Keavy beside him. The earls had gone to the church and were now returning with the stone, the bishop and the monks following behind. Despite the crowd, he felt terribly alone. He missed the constant companionship of Duncan. All were looking only to him now, but there was not one for him to look to.

The men placed the stone in front of his feet and Fleance put first his left, then his right foot into the carved footprints on the top. The stone was cool but not cold under his bare feet. Fleance looked ahead as the bishop came forward, chanting prayers. He splashed water over Fleance's head and to his right he heard Keavy stifle a giggle. Then, the anointing.

Lennox carried the crown forward and the bishop held it above Fleance's head.

The bishop prayed. '*Oh God, who art Lord of Lords and King of Kings, bless Fleance whom you have called and appointed as King and Lord of these lands and people. Bless him with power, wisdom and strength, his kingdom with peace and light; and may he live long. May yer blessing be on all who rule in his name. May your Spirit bless the waters of sea and land, the fruit of soil and sea, the animals of forest and glen; may your Son's name be praised in every nook and the Cross of Christ victorious over all powers and elements, bless his people with loyalty and courage. Keep our enemies far from us, and the fire of your Spirit warm in every hearth.*'

The monks sang '*Amen*' as Fleance bowed his head for the bishop to crown him. Ross handed the bishop the sceptre who offered it to Fleance. He looked about the crowd and saw Rosie standing among them. He hesitated but a moment before taking it in his right hand. It was final.

As the men lifted him up, it felt as if a huge weight fell from around his shoulders; as if the royal cloak had dropped. But it was not that. It was the ever-present pressure of the morning vanishing, replaced by a new and surprising joy. The procession went forward.

Fleance looked over the heads of those in the crowd. There he was, Banquo, standing off to one side. 'Halt,' Fleance called down to his weight bearers. They stopped and the crowd murmured. Fleance stood high, facing his father, and then lifted up the sceptre. After a moment, his father lifted his hand, smiled happily and, before Fleance's very eyes, faded into nothing.

He lowered his arm. It was finished. 'Proceed,' he said, and they took him to the abbey, Keavy walking in front, throwing flowers.

After communion and prayers, Fleance emerged from the church. On either side, the people formed a line and bowed or curtsied as he went passed. He eventually came to Rosie, Dougal and Rebecca. The two women bowed their heads and curtsied and Dougal bowed.

Fleance put a hand on Dougal's shoulder. 'Never bow to me in your heart, Dougal, because always between you and me, you are Rosie's honoured father and I am Flea, who loves her.'

The older man was silent but he nodded. Fleance stood in front of Rosie and Rebecca. 'I will not forget our times in England. And I will not forget what you mean to Keavy.' He swallowed. 'I hope in the future when our paths cross, there will be fond remembrances.'

Fleance tried to ignore the tears in Rosie's eyes and focus on her smile.

'That is my hope as well, Your Majesty,' she said quietly.

Preston was at his side. 'Sire, we must move on.'

Fleance nodded and with a last look at her, continued towards the banquet tent.

It was late when they approached the castle. The moon was up and a soft mist covered the ground so that, in the reflected light, it seemed as if they rode in snow. Fleance, accompanied by Lennox and his son, rode Willow, who was blowing steam into the night air.

Through the trees, Fleance could see the lights burning in the castle – it was a welcoming sight. Eventually, they arrived in front of the main entrance and Fleance dismounted. A groom ran up and took Willow away and Fleance went to help with Keavy. Morag put the sleepy child in his arms. 'Shall I play for you at the feast, Flea?' she asked, her eyes bright.

'Aye, that would be grand,' he said.

He walked up the steps, into the castle and was greeted by Nurse and Rachel. Nurse took Keavy and he was left standing in front of Rachel. They stared at each other, and then Fleance spoke. 'How are you?'

'Sad,' she replied.

'Me, too,' he said.

Silence fell on them again. Neither moved.

Preston approached. 'Your Majesty, shall I send for some food and drink?'

Fleance's eyes did not leave Rachel's face but he nodded. 'Aye, bring it to the blue room.' Preston left. Fleance felt his shoulders relax. 'Will you join me, Rachel?' he asked offering her his arm.

Rachel stared at his arm a moment and then took it. 'Aye, Fleance. I will.'

He stood alone atop the battlements, watching the first pink rays of a new day spread their fingers over the land. He was Fleance the First, King of Scotland, man of honour, his own man with his own destiny and the power to choose it.

Chapter Three
Glamis Castle, May
Fleance

A ragged line of soldiers and horses made its way up the road towards the castle, a moving column of blacks and browns against the spreading purple heather haze on either side. Fleance heard the chink of shields piled together on a cart, the whinny of a horse as it sighted familiar castle walls at last and the deep grumbling of the metal-bound wooden wheels against the stones on the track.

Something was wrong. The front man put his shield down and the second rider lowered his hood. First one, then another and then another. Every single man's face was smeared with blood and dirt. As they came closer, Fleance was shocked and horrified to see the terrible details: here an arm snapped and hanging useless. There, a bloody, dripping wound.

He was expecting news but not this.

He leapt down the steps and grabbed the bridle of the first rider. 'Report!'

The soldier swayed and almost fell, but Fleance and two of his servants helped the man from the horse and held him upright. 'We were set upon, Your Majesty. After we buried the last of the men from the battle, a swarm of rebels ambushed us as we headed north.' He looked back at the remaining men. 'We fought as hard as we could but many of our number were killed.'

The king's advisor, Preston, arrived at Fleance's side. 'Did you defeat them?' he asked, his face grim.

The wounded soldier's face collapsed. 'Alas, no, my lord. It was we who escaped only with our lives.'

Fleance looked at his advisor and saw his own concern reflected in Preston's face. He gripped the soldier's cloak and spoke firmly. 'You did well and I thank you for your pains.' He stepped back and yelled out to the hovering servants. 'Get these men food and soft beds. They have earned them.'

Preston remained at his side, waiting. 'I know,' Fleance said quietly. 'We must send word to the earls.'

Preston bowed his head. 'I will do it immediately.'

A fire burned uselessly in the hearth of the great hall. It was the end of spring but still the weather offered nothing but cold and damp. Fleance had called a meeting of his senior army personnel as well as Preston and a number of loyal thanes and older earls. They were meeting to consider the latest news of unrest and destruction in some of the outer-lying thanedoms.

Fleance considered the information before him: seven villages attacked by Scotsmen; seven villages devastated to the point that they could not continue to ply their trades.

'Have we men enough to send as protection?' Fleance asked.

Blair, a general and Fleance's childhood friend, shook his head. 'The attacks have no pattern.' He shrugged. 'They happen all over Scotland. There is no warning and nothing is left to tell us who is responsible.'

A loud crunch interrupted the meeting. Fleance turned to Henri, the ambassador from Normandy, who was now sitting sideways on his chair, his legs draped over the arms. Henri was the brother-in-law of the Duke of Normandy and had arrived soon after Fleance's coronation. If the mutterings of Morag, the castle's long-serving cook, were to be believed, the duke's wife, newly pregnant, had grown tired of her younger brother's behaviour in the court. Behaviour he seemed to bring with him.

An apple with a large bite out of it sat in Henri's hand and he chewed noisily. When he became aware that all were now staring at him, his jaw ceased moving and his eyes widened. 'What?' he asked through a mouthful of fruit.

Henri's clear disregard for the seriousness of the problem irritated Fleance. 'Do you not think, Henri, to eat your food in a more gentlemanly manner?' The king caught a look passing between the Thane of Ross and Blair.

'Pardon me.' The Frenchman swung his legs to the ground and stood up. 'I have been thinking and,' he shook the apple at Fleance, 'eating helps me think, so forgive me if I have given offence. But this problem you talk of – I think it is not about looting villages. No. I think it is about you,' he finished, pointing to Fleance. 'This is not random. In my country we call this *la sédition*. The men behind this campaign care little for what they do except that it does damage to you, Your Majesty.'

Fleance frowned. 'I don't understand,' he said. 'We were victorious. We have helped the people to make gains. It doesn't make sense.'

Henri bit the apple again and they all waited while he chewed then swallowed. 'Of course, this behaviour is not known here in Scotland, but it is very bad,' he said. 'The men or man behind this campaign – for him, it is personal.' He finished the apple and threw the core into the fire. 'Have you, Fleance, enemies?'

The atmosphere in the hall chilled. This was the key. Though Fleance knew the thanes and his generals supported him, many others had quietly raised questions about his suitability for the crown. Had even implied the possibility of treachery.

Such questions plagued him. How could he make them all understand the devotion, loyalty and love he had given to Duncan?

How long would it be before he was accepted as the rightful monarch? Tracing the bloodlines, he was rightfully heir. Duncan had chosen him. These two things should be enough. Yet, even here, the whisper caught him off guard: the witches, who had predicted Macbeth's rise to power and untimely end, had also said as much of Banquo. That he would be the seed and father of kings.

But they had also accosted Fleance with weird and confusing proclamations. So strange. So . . .

'Your Majesty?' Blair's question cut through these crazy thoughts. 'What do you say to Lord Henri's theory?'

For a moment, Fleance's vision was clouded by memories of those witches and he had to shake his head. 'I think there is merit in what Henri suggests,' he said, taking a deep breath. 'Scotland's crown has two enemies: my adoptive father, Magness, leader of the rebels who came against us, and Donalbain's former aide, the betrayer and spy, Calum, King of Norway.'

Preston cleared his throat. 'The rebel leader has not been sighted since the death of Macduff and, as I hear it, Norway has troubles of her own.'

'What are these troubles?'

'We have heard the Danes are preparing their soldiers to invade Norway.'

'Again?' Ross asked.

'Perhaps the King of Denmark seeks to strike while he has the advantage,' Henri said.

'As does whoever is attacking our villages.'

'And you are certain it is not Magness?' Blair asked him.

Fleance frowned, thinking of the last time he had seen his adoptive father: angry, determined, but still believing in Scotland. Why would he be behind these raids? 'No man can ever be certain of the secret chambers of another's mind. But it is my hope that with my crowning, he would be pleased with the turn of events.'

'Who else do you suggest, Preston?' he asked. 'Who else might be Scotland's enemy?'

'Your Majesty, there will always be men with overarching ambition wishing to take that which God has not given them by right.' The old man lowered his voice. 'In this room, Sire, you have faithful servants and friends.'

Fleance stared at his advisor for a moment. Though somewhat strange and oily, Preston had proven himself to be completely devoted to whomever he served at Glamis. And, Fleance thought as he surveyed the earls, they too had been faithful and had been since before Macbeth's reign.

Then there was Blair: his friend since boyhood and a fearless soldier. Aye. In this room, Fleance could be assured that he was supported.

Henri leant back in his chair. 'Fleance, I think that it will become clear very soon who is behind these attacks.' His bright green eyes looked directly at the king. 'The enemy is just waiting for a time when you are at your weakest.'

Henri had said aloud the thoughts Fleance had been mulling over these past days. The trepidation he had been feeling was not without foundation, it seemed. Fleance nodded to those gathered and swallowed. It was time to take some action.

'I will not sit idly by like a blind maid.'

The strength of his statement roused all those around him and the room suddenly became animated with movement and discussion. Fleance was not finished, but had to raise his voice over the sounds of restlessness. 'Preston,' he called. 'Do we have enough in the royal reserves to give compensation to all those who have been set upon by these rebels?'

Preston bowed. 'Aye, Your Majesty. We have enough provisions to give some measure of help to most.'

Fleance continued with more confidence. 'Ensure that all those who have lost livelihood are paid damages. If those doing the looting hope to bring down my reputation then let's make sure we look after our people so they can not accuse the king of not making amends. Blair, organise a contingent to go from village to village helping the people rebuild what has been destroyed. Not enough to weaken our defences here at Glamis, but enough to bring swift relief.'

Henri clapped his hands. 'This is good. A wise king indeed. You will force the hand of these rebels because you heal the wounds they make.'

It felt good to make firm decisions. Some of the pressure was relieved by the enthusiasm of his men.

Those who had gathered left soon after, buoyed by firm action. Only Fleance, Henri and Preston remained.

Fleance turned to Preston. 'Was there something else?'

Preston looked over at Henri, who was pouring himself a cup of wine, and then shuffled forward. 'We must call in the princess to discuss the wedding.'

Fleance coughed at the sudden change in direction. He reached for a drink and downed the lump that had risen in his throat. 'You are right,' he said as he looked at them both, for Henri was now attentive to this conversation. Fleance lifted his hands in despair. 'But I had thought we might wait a little longer . . .' He hesitated and then nodded. 'Call her.'

Preston rang a bell to summon a servant and, when a serving boy scuttled into the room, sent him to find Rachel.

'Do you want him here?' Preston asked, pointing to their French guest.

Henri heard. 'Of this matter you are most in need of my advice.'

Fleance thought a moment. The man was a pain in the backside but every word so far that had come from his mouth contained wisdom and truth. Perhaps it was not such a bad thing to have him in attendance. 'He can stay.'

Ten minutes later, Rachel slipped into the room with two gentlewomen at her side.

'Go,' Preston said to them dismissively, and they hurried away.

Rachel cocked her head and raised her eyebrow. 'That was very decisive of you, Preston. I hope you have good reason to pull me away from my sister.'

Fleance stepped forward and held out his hand. '*I* called for you, Rachel,' he said with emphasis. Her demeanour softened immediately. 'We have things to arrange.'

He led her to the end of the table to sit alongside himself, Preston and Henri.

Henri dipped his head at her as he kissed her hand. 'I am so sorry for your loss, *ma chère*.'

'Thank you,' she whispered, looking around at them all.

Damn! Was this too much? She had had only weeks to mourn the death of her brother and now, here they were, about to set upon her with serious responsibility.

Fleance cleared his throat and frowned at the two men who sat with them. *Just be quiet while I begin this*, was his intended meaning.

Preston and Henri both sat back in their chairs. Good. 'Rachel, this is a delicate thing we bring before you, but you and I have spoken of our union.' The princess nodded. 'It is a very important union,' Fleance said. He looked to Preston.

The old man stood up and began to pace the room. 'You, Princess, are from our recent history, part of the royal house of Scotland.' He dipped his head but continued his pacing. 'Fleance's claim to the throne seems, to the people, less clear.'

'But . . .' Rachel began. The old man held up his hand.

'We agree with your protestations, but the people do not understand.' He looked over and Fleance nodded his approval. 'We must give them no doubt that Scotland's future is secure. You both have the bloodline, but the people see yours more clearly,' he said, looking at Rachel. 'Your marriage would be a powerful union and would give the king more credibility because of your line, Princess.'

'And give your people a reason to celebrate,' Henri offered.

Rachel stood and Fleance saw her shaking, but her eyes were on him. 'Is it wise so soon after Duncan's death?'

'It is critical that we do it sooner rather than later,' Preston advised.

'What do you say, Fleance?' Rachel asked, turning to him.

Fleance's heart was heavy with anxiety. 'I do not see any reason to delay. Do you?'

She looked from one man to the other and then curtsied before Fleance. 'If it is the king's will,' she said quietly.

Fleance stood as well and reached out a hand to her. 'I have already said, Rachel,' he answered gently, swallowing the dryness in his throat. 'I welcome you as my queen.' She took his hand and held it firmly, her eyes searching his.

With her other hand, she pushed away a stray curl and looked at him. 'Do you?'

'Yes.'

Rachel exhaled deeply. 'Then that is how it shall be. We must send out the banns.'

Preston smiled. 'Good. This is good news.'

Henri stood now and raised his goblet. 'Excellent.' He lifted it to his lips and drank. 'I congratulate you.'

Chapter Four

With a start, Fleance struggled up out of his nightmare. The bedclothes were wrapped around his legs and he fell to the floor. He lay there a moment, registering the damp of his body and the pounding of his heart. The image of his bloodied friend, Duncan, lingered just beyond his vision and he squeezed his eyes tight to push it away.

Images of the king's death crammed his mind, just as the disturbing dreams he had had after his father's murder had haunted him for years. For some months now, he had welcomed the respite from nightmares and visions. But now this. What did it mean?

Fleance untangled the limp sheet from around his thighs and sat on the bed. Why couldn't the past let him go? Why was he constantly reminded of his loss? These dreams would do him no favours, especially as he had many detractors who would welcome any evidence to use against him.

His thoughts turned to the conversation that had taken place with Preston and Rachel earlier. Fleance knew Rachel cared deeply for him, as he did her. But shouldn't there be more? Shouldn't he feel something of what he had felt for Rosie? A sudden image of

Rosie in a red dress at last year's town fair filled his heart with long-
ing. If only . . .

He shook the idea from his mind. It was never going to be.

But Fleance wanted something else so that it would not feel so
strange to be married to Rachel.

It was not yet midnight. Rachel was like an owl – she often
stayed up late, praying. He might find her and say the words he'd
been imagining these past nights.

He pulled on his breeks and the shirt he had worn earlier, then
went to the wash stand. He splashed the chilled water onto his
face and ran his hands through his hair, and then stared at the face
he saw in the mirror before him. The candle was burning low but,
even in this light, he saw how little he looked like a king: sharp,
light eyes; a dark shadow along his unshaven face; and – what
he didn't want to see – the glowering intensity that spoke of his
disappointment and grief. He went to the doors of the chamber
and pulled them open, startling the page who was waiting on the
other side.

'Your Majesty?' the young lad said, quivering.

''Tis all well. You are not needed yet,' Fleance said, holding up a
hand to stop the boy from moving into his chambers. 'But a parcel
of food and drink would be a welcome sight on my return.' The
page bowed and hurried away towards the kitchen.

Fleance went searching for Rachel.

The castle was quiet but not dark. After his coronation, he had given
orders that, at all times, the corridors be lit. No man, woman or
child, whatever rank, should have to move about in darkness. This
had met with happy reception from the servants, who had been

used to stumbling about to attend to the calls of their former king, Donalbain – often in the middle of the night.

He headed first to the blue room, named for the colour of the walls and lined with vibrant blue and azure tapestries, chosen by Rachel and Bree's late mother, Breanna. Here the family had found a quiet place to gather over the past decade, but Fleance was disappointed to find that the room was empty and the fire almost out. She would be in her chambers, then.

With growing trepidation, Fleance made his way to Rachel's room. He was relieved to see that, under the thick wooden door, a line of light trickled out into the dimly lit corridor. She was awake.

He knocked twice.

'Come,' she said.

He lifted the latch and pushed open the heavy door. Rachel was in her nightgown, sitting on her stool, not yet ready for bed. She looked up and a surprised expression flittered over her face. She stood up quickly. 'Your Majesty?'

Fleance frowned. 'What?'

She smiled, and then frowned herself. 'Sorry. Too formal.' Then she inhaled. 'Fleance, why are you here at this time? Are you ill?'

He stood there, now feeling foolish. How did this woman survive with so little sleep?

Her hair fell about her shoulders and, though the fabric of her nightgown was thick, it did not hide her body. Fleance swallowed. 'Princess,' he said. His voice croaked. He could not take his eyes from her face.

'Yes?'

'I have to say . . .' His heart racing with fear, he stepped forward and kissed her. Rachel's lips were soft but she pulled away.

'Stop.' She put her hands on his chest and pushed him gently. 'What are you doing?'

'I . . . ah . . . I thought it might help if we . . .' his voice trailed off. He could not find the right words to explain what he was trying to do.

'Do not force it,' Rachel said, tilting her head.

Fleance shook his head and took a deep breath. 'Yes, of course. I'm sorry.' A weight lifted from his heart. He chuckled. 'Actually, I am relieved.'

She smiled. 'Good.'

'I feel a bit of an idiot.' He returned her smile.

'Let us talk.' She returned to her seat. 'Fleance. Our union will be good. I trust that. But it is a political one and I am sorry about that for you. Not so much for me, because I look forward to being your wife.' Rachel's words slowed and he understood some of her hope for the future. 'I think we all need something to look forward to that is not as weighty as a wedding.'

'What do you have in mind?'

'We shall have a feast with lots of music and dancing. You could sing.'

'Perhaps.' He studied her for a moment. 'Thank you, Rachel.'

'For what?' she asked.

'For being . . . you. Kind, wise, good. Patient with me.'

'It is not that hard, Fleance. I care for you very much and I know it is your desire that we love one another. Perhaps this might develop?'

Fleance took another deep breath. 'You are honest as well,' he added.

She snorted. '*Blunt*, Morag says.'

'No, that comes from an uncaring heart. Yours is one of the most compassionate I have ever known.'

'Thank you. So, what do you think of my suggestion? We could make some plans now, unless you are too weary and need to return to your chamber.'

'Wide awake,' he said, smiling. 'Let us do as you suggest.'

Suddenly, there was a knock at the chamber door.

'Come in,' Rachel called.

Nurse came through but, when she saw Fleance, bowed low. 'Your Majesty.'

Fleance swallowed and felt guilty – as if he had been caught doing something wrong.

Rachel, it seemed, was unperturbed, more concerned with why Nurse should disturb her so late at night. 'Nurse?' she said.

Nurse bowed at Fleance again, but turned her attention to Rachel. 'Your Highness, Princess Bree is most distraught. I cannot get her to settle. Please come.'

He watched as Rachel gathered herself.

'I will be with you, in a minute,' she said. The older woman bowed once more to Fleance, and then left the chamber. Rachel turned to Fleance. 'Her tantrums have worsened since we returned from Iona.' She pulled up a sleeve and carefully unwrapped a bandage.

'Rachel.' He moved forward and pulled her arm straight. Gouges lined her lovely skin as if it had been punctured by the teeth of a wild animal.

'She did this?' Rachel nodded. 'When?'

'This afternoon. After I told her we were to be married.'

He shuddered at the thought of such ferocity coming from a ten-year-old. 'She is angry and frightened and knows no other way to make herself feel better.' He examined the wound. It was deep but Rachel, as expected, had tended to it with her skill and medicine. 'I think,' Fleance said, 'that Bree needs time away from here. This place,' he said, nodding out towards the greater castle, 'has brought only heartache for the bairn.'

'What can I do?' Rachel cried. Fleance sensed rising frustration in her. 'There is so much to be done at Glamis.'

'The dowager, Margaret, might offer us some hope,' he said. Queen Margaret, the widow of Malcolm, the king who had defeated Macbeth but who'd produced no living heir, continued to align herself with their family. She was wise and godly and pragmatic. Her counsel was not to be ignored.

'You think so?'

'This place,' Fleance said. 'Everything around here reminds her of death: Duncan's and your father's.' Fleance saw her jaw tighten. 'Not that you haven't done your very best, Rachel, but I think Margaret's wisdom and kindness, and distance, may hold some hope for healing the lass.'

She was thinking carefully over his words and moved about the room adjusting fabric and ornaments. Finally she sat back down and looked at him. 'I think you are right, but I should go with her.'

Fleance wondered what Preston might say about this, given their decision to send out word of a royal marriage. And another thought worried him: what if there were troubles in the north as well? 'How long, do you think, will you be gone?'

'A month, perhaps.'

He thought about this. The timing was a delicate thing to bring up. 'Then we shall wait until you return before we set a date.'

Rachel smiled. 'Aye. When we get back from Forres it will be time to look to the future.'

She rewrapped her arm and pulled her sleeve carefully over the dressing. She looked towards the closed door. 'I had best see to the child.' She turned him around and pushed him out of her chamber. 'I will see you in the morning.'

He went to leave but she called out. 'Do not feel guilty that you do not love me like her. Our union will be another story, Fleance.' He stopped and turned to her. She went over to him and reached her hand up to touch his face. 'I will be a good wife and an excellent queen.'

He looked at her for a moment. 'Of course. And I could not wish for a better partner than you.' He took her hand and kissed it. 'Good night.'

———

The next night, late into the evening, after sealing important agreements and signing away small matters, Fleance had given up his free hour before bed to listen to the ambassador from Normandy. Who could refuse such a man?

'Of course, it is not an easy alliance,' Henri was saying. 'But it is an alliance which is the right one. She,' he said, pointing a wavering finger at the door, 'is practical, *non*? You are,' he added, turning to Fleance, 'how we say? Stoic. No more stoic. All good will come out of this union and it will amend all wrongs. Trust me,' he said, and plonked himself drunkenly into a chair.

Fleance swallowed his surprise at the Frenchman's frank words. 'What are you saying, Henri? I don't understand.'

Henri waved his hands in the air. 'Marriage is more than power and passion. It is commitment. I see some of this here in this castle. None of it is easy. Not comfortable or complete, but enough.'

Henri shoved a large chunk of bread, cheese and relish into his mouth. He chomped and smiled.

All the food had been eaten, but Henri continued to lick his fingers and stab at the crumbs. He did not look at the king when he spoke but there was something in his tone that warned Fleance to listen. 'You are royal. And you have lived the life of a peasant. You are intelligent, healthy and strong and a most fierce soldier if the reports are to be believed. *Ayez plus de foi.*' Henri looked up and stared hard at the king. 'Have more faith.'

Then he grinned and raised his goblet, drinking deeply.

'You are a young man and you are a young king. This was all thrust upon you. My sweet father would often tell me that some men are born great, whether that be in status or holiness; some achieve greatness, through great feats or overcoming adversity, and some, whom he considered the poorest of the three, have greatness thrust upon them – often unprepared and ill-equipped.'

He stood and stretched and then came over and placed a hand heavily on Fleance's shoulder. 'I can see, even in the short time I have been living here, that you are neither unprepared nor ill-equipped.' The Frenchman poured another drink and drank some more. He wiped his mouth and smiled again. 'She is a perfect match. Be happy.'

Henri had consumed the full measure of two stands of wine and now he stumbled out to his chamber, leaving Fleance alone in the blue room. The words of the ambassador swirled around in his head. Henri was right. Rachel was a perfect match. She was beautiful, kind, intelligent and wise and just the settled presence he needed. Fleance opened the shutters of the casement at the end of the hall and stared out into the cold, dark night. He needed respite right now.

He took himself down past the grand rooms, out of the castle and around the back to the militia room.

A few hours of training would do his body and his spirit good.

His father's instruction, given during a heated training session, came to him clearly now. *'Men are judged,'* Banquo had told him, *'by their deeds more than their words. Fleance, be a man whose deeds honour his words.'* His father had just reprimanded him for giving excuses as to why he had not completed a task his mother had assigned to

33

him. To Fleance's childish mind, it was a trifling thing. She had asked that he ensure the hounds had enough water for the time that Fleance and his family were to be absent from the manor.

As it turned out, Fleance had forgotten about the dogs in his excitement of their travels. When they came back to Lochaber, they discovered that two of the dogs were so dehydrated that they had to be destroyed.

But this was not the end of the matter as far as his father was concerned. The very next day, Banquo had taken him out with the fishermen. Fleance saw all too quickly how much the men depended on each other.

He had stood on the deck of one of the boats straining hard to help pull in the net filled with fish and, at the same time, trying as hard as he could to obey the command of the captain who yelled instructions. Every man on board the boat did as he was told, even Banquo and, at the end of the day, they came ashore with a bounty of fish.

"'Tis not good luck, Fleance, that this was a fruitful expedition. Obedience to the one in charge reaps rewards. I am Thane of Lochaber. The captain of that boat is below me. But here is the thing: he has been given his place in this world and I, mine. If I should venture into his, as we did today, then I submit myself to him, because this is his world and expertise. Had you, young man, trusted us and done as you were told, your dogs would still be alive.'

That was enough to make him cry. And cry he did, not only for the loss of his dogs but for the suffering he'd caused to innocent creatures. By the time they got back to the manor, Fleance was exhausted by grief and his father had carried him into the house and handed him over to the nurse.

Now, with the cold of night closing in around him, Fleance was faced with a different future to one he had imagined less than a year ago. The advisors, the counsel, the thanes and earls were all right about this marriage. Rachel did know him and she understood the world so well. She was never flustered. She was not Rosie but she was just as remarkable. If he had never met and loved Rosie, he could have fallen in love with this princess and considered himself lucky to have her attentions.

The night turned bitter as the northern winds cruelly raked Scotland, but Fleance kept on with his practice: over and thrust; shield and sword; twist and turn; cut and wound.

The next morning, Fleance's body felt the effects of the late-night weapons practice but his mind was alert. He had given the last of the orders for the distribution of money and goods and labour to the affected villages and, with Blair's advice, had chosen the soldiers who would go from the castle.

There was a knock at the door of the great hall, and a servant entered. He bowed.

'Your Majesty, the princess bids me tell you she is ready to leave for Forres.'

'Thank you,' Fleance said. He turned to the gathered soldiers. 'Wait for my return and then we will ask the Holy Father to give a blessing before you leave.'

The royal litter hung between two large horses. Bree and Morag's niece Charissa were already inside. Rachel stood on the step of the entrance to the castle and regarded him. 'Keep well, Your Majesty.'

He extended his hand and cupped her cheek. 'I regret my suggestion, now, that you go away. I fear I will miss you.'

Rachel arched her eyebrow in a way that reminded him of Rosie. 'Really?' she asked.

'Aye,' he said. 'You reward me with your calm presence and wise counsel.'

She stared hard at him and he felt his face warm under her scrutiny. 'Do not rely so heavily on another, Fleance. We are all mortals and therefore subject to failure.'

Fleance nodded and looked into her eyes. 'You are right, Rachel. As always.' He scratched his head. 'I am sorry but I need you here as well. Deal with Bree but come back soon. If our union is cemented then perhaps we might find peace in our land.'

'I am sure Preston will regale you with advice. Or Henri. Either way, you will deal with it all as you have done in the past: with wisdom, honour and integrity.'

Fleance helped her into the litter. 'Be safe, Rachel.'

Rachel kissed him on both cheeks. 'It won't be long. I will see you soon.'

He stepped back and she settled into her seat. The master of the stables slammed the door closed and the entourage, all too quickly, set off. Fleance watched them pull out of the castle gates. He must now turn his attention to the needs of his people.

His people. It was still difficult to think beyond his own needs and wants. He had barely seen twenty-two summers and yet here he was – king. A title far exceeding any thought he'd ever had both as child and man.

A title thrust upon him.

The litter had disappeared beyond the castle gates. Rachel would do what needed to be done for her sister and for their peace. He had to trust her. More than he could trust himself.

Fleance pulled his cloak tight across his shoulders and stepped back into the castle.

The morning light shone through the large windows of the upper storey and the emptiness of the castle spoke of Rachel's absence. This was the first time Fleance had been at Glamis without Duncan, Rachel or Bree.

He re-entered the great hall and saw that those gathered were in animated discussion. They fell silent at his arrival. Fleance looked out over the men who stood waiting. 'When Princess Rachel returns, we will marry.'

This news was greeted with the expected positive murmurings. Fleance held up his hand. 'But, for now, we have people who need us and we have work to do.'

The next day, word was sent out among the parishes that the marriage of Rachel, daughter of Donalbain, and Fleance, son of Banquo, was to take place by the end of the summer.

Chapter Five
Perth, Scotland, June
Rachel

The sea voyage from Forres to Perth was unremarkable, which was a blessing. The seas were kind and the dealings with people not cumbersome. And, thankfully, the month at Forres Castle had been peaceful.

As they left the town in the royal litter, Bree took her sister's hand. 'Rachel?'

'Aye?'

'Can you tell me a story?'

Rachel looked over at her sister. 'Aye. What would you prefer? A prince battling dragons or a maiden lost in the woods?'

'Mother,' Bree said. 'Can you tell me a story about our mother?'

Rachel paused. Bree rarely asked about their mother. Perhaps three or four times in the last few years she'd asked questions. Mostly, it seemed, she was content with her world. Still, with the sudden death of their father and then dear Duncan, perhaps the child needed more of her life story to help heal the pain.

She tried to smile. 'What do you want to know?' she asked, making her voice upbeat and light.

'Was she nice?' Bree asked.

Rachel laughed. 'Oh, dear Bree, she was wonderful.'

'How?' the young princess demanded.

'She told the best stories,' Rachel whispered loudly, leaning forward. 'Much better than mine.'

'Really?'

Rachel took a moment to study Bree. 'In some ways, you are so like her.'

Bree's eyes lit up. 'Really? Tell me!'

'Well, Bree, you are beautiful, articulate, courageous.' Rachel mocked a frown. 'Opinionated.'

Bree giggled and then was quiet. After a moment she turned to Rachel. 'Do you think she loved me, Rachel?'

The question stunned Rachel. It was written into their history how much this child Bree was desired. Father and Mother rejoiced in the pregnancy despite the worry and anxiety of the state of Scotland. Despite the news that reached them in Ireland about Macbeth and the terrible slaughter he'd carried out.

But how could Bree know this? She had grown up in the safety and security of a Scottish royal household. She had learnt to avoid her father's tirades and she had come to depend on Rachel and the security of her brother, Duncan.

'Well?' Bree asked. 'Did she?'

'Oh, Bree, when Mother learnt she was with child, she was ecstatic. Father ordered a huge feast to celebrate. Duncan and I were younger than you are now, of course, but all of us were so excited. I believe Father thought Mother was sick and about to die, so when the midwives told him she was with child, he was so relieved that he gave a great feast.'

'But she died,' Bree said matter-of-factly.

'Aye, darling, she did.'

'Was she a weak mother?'

Rachel sighed deeply and shook her head. 'No. She was strong. But something went wrong when you were born—'

'So I killed her?'

'Goodness! No! Bree, she was not well, but she lived long enough to give you to us. And for this we are forever thankful.'

There was silence in the carriage but Rachel could tell Bree was thinking, thinking.

'And did she love me?'

Rachel put her arm around Bree. 'Bree, you were a surprise – and a delightful surprise. Mother wept with joy at your birth, as did Father.'

'So why did she die?'

There it was – the question that haunted Bree was the same question that haunted Rachel about Duncan. *Why?*

The dowager's words came to mind. They had spoken often over the last month but always Rachel had tried to grasp at an answer to this question of why.

'This is a dangerous question to ask, Rachel. For, after each answer, another question surfaces just like a weed in the garden. If you depend on knowing the why, a good life, one that makes a difference in this world, will be taken from you just as those weeds drain the goodness from the soil, leaving the plant gasping. If your why is to do with human behaviour, you must look only to the story of The Garden of Eden: why? Because someone had a choice and their choice has caused you pain.'

Instead of offering her own fears, Rachel gave her sister a stock response. 'Bree, life is not kind. Life is hard. We must work with what is given.'

Bree snorted. 'That is so stupid. We are royal, are we not? Can't we demand that things work out better?'

'Yes,' she told her sister. 'We are royal and we need to ensure that this pain does not happen again.'

Bree turned to the maid, Charissa. 'What do you say, Charissa? Do you have more bad things happen to you because you are not royal?'

Charissa coughed and stole a look at Rachel. 'Begging your pardon, Princess Bree, but bad things happen to any rank and sometimes happen on more than one occasion.'

'Charissa?' Rachel was intrigued with her maid's response.

'My grandfather declared he would serve Scotland without arms but my da did not agree and rode against the rebels in your grandfather's army. He was a sergeant in the king's army under the command of Banquo and Macbeth.'

Both names chilled Rachel's insides.

Charissa went on. 'My aunt, our Morag, nursed my da as he died. He was pulled from the fray and brought back to the castle, his wounds fatal.'

'I am sorry,' Rachel said.

'Don't be, Madam. My da was a brave warrior but mindful of his place in the king's army and never challenged those who commanded him. As we nursed him, me and Aunt Morag, he talked. He told us some of the battle. I was only eight, mind, but I still remember my father's last conversation.'

'That must be of some comfort,' Rachel said.

'Aye, it is. The surgeons told us he was to die as his wounds were so bad. We were gathered around and he was talking up a storm, telling us about his childhood and his loves and his thoughts on Scotland. But before he went off, he wanted to tell the tale of his last battle. The one he served with King Duncan the First.'

Rachel was now more interested and turned to face her maid. 'Go on,' she said. She had no recollection that her long-time companion and serving maid was so closely aligned to such a significant event in their country's history.

41

'Well, Da was most upset that some of the war record was wrong.'

'Meaning?'

'Da was most poorly but dead keen to say his piece.' Charissa bobbed her head. 'Begging your pardon at the turn of phrase.'

Rachel waved her hand at her maid. 'I understand and am not offended.'

Bree yawned loudly and snuggled down on Charissa's lap.

Charissa tucked a shawl under Bree's drowsy head. She stroked the young girl's dark locks for a few moments before continuing the story. 'Da said that the King of Norway, Sweno, had surrendered. Da was there when the large blond-headed man put down his weapons and stepped forward, saying, in our tongue, that he gave over his rule.'

The carriage moved on but Rachel was transported back to her fantasies of that time when there were stories told around the hearth about that great battle against her grandfather, Duncan. It was a tale that had excited her back then and exonerated the Thane of Lochaber, Banquo. A great man. A man of honour. Father of Fleance.

Charissa cleared her throat and continued. 'But Banquo, Da says, was mad as a rutting stag, and was not as honourable as the stories tell. Even that tyrant Macbeth tried to stop him. He didn't listen, though, to the Norwegian king's cries. Just drove him through with his sword. Killed him outright. With the body of the king at their feet, Macbeth grabbed my da and threatened him that he must not tell a soul what he had just witnessed. Macbeth told Da that it would serve no good for anybody to tell what had happened and that the dirty Norwegian king deserved to die. That Banquo was a loyal and loved soldier and that there was no honour in recounting this misjudgement on the part of the thane.'

Something stirred within Rachel. Fleance had told her the details of that fatal meeting with Calum on the battlefield that led to the death of her brother. The same meeting where Calum had hurled accusations at Fleance and his family.

And yet there was something else.

Fleance had absolute faith in the purity of his father. All stories and histories confirmed this. But Charissa's father's account cast doubt on the Thane of Lochaber.

She looked over at her sister sleeping and reached out a hand to caress her cheek. Perhaps it would be best not to tell Fleance this story. She wondered how this news might affect his determination and drive to be as good as he thought his father had been.

She turned back to Charissa. 'We will not tell the king of this story.' Charissa blushed and nodded. 'Not that it should stay buried, but perhaps for the time being it is best that this remain in the safekeeping of women. His Majesty has much to worry about with the present times and the past can take care of itself.'

'Yes, Princess,' Charissa replied. 'Forgive me for being so bold to speak thus.'

Rachel reached over and patted her maid's hand. 'You have said nothing for which forgiveness is needed.'

The cabin of the litter rocked from side to side in the gathering dark, and Rachel was ready for home. Bree was asleep, tightly curled on the seat beside her. Charissa sat opposite, upright but with her eyes closed.

The dowager queen, Margaret, had been most encouraging on their visit and Rachel was now more secure in what lay ahead of her than she had been before. Margaret felt confident that Rachel's marriage to Fleance would be a good one – they were both young and they both loved Scotland. Together they would make her great again and the love they would share would be enduring. It would be a great alliance.

'Love takes a number of guises,' Margaret had said. 'This one you will have with the king will bear much goodness.'

Rachel leant back and rested against the walls of the small cabin. During the month at Forres, she had missed the company of the king. It was not Rachel's custom to worry about the unnecessary, about things that were out of her control. She was usually very good at staying content, often seeking comfort in prayer and meditation.

The king had sent two posts and these were generously filled with news of the castle but, more significantly, Rachel sensed a reflection of her own loneliness. Fleance missed her too. So, she was looking forward to seeing him again. She could not yet say the word 'love' when thinking of Fleance, although she cared for him deeply.

Only once had she experienced what she knew to be the love a man and a woman could enjoy. But that opportunity had been ripped from her by the man's tragic death two years before, while fighting for her father.

How strange, Rachel thought. I have not thought about Ewan for months. At the time of his death, she believed she would never be free from the heartache of losing him. But this past year had been a tumult of uncertainty and more unexpected death.

As the night deepened, the boy who rode the rear horse lit the lamps, attaching them to the two side rungs on the cabin, and they walked slowly on into the night. Rachel sighed deeply but

Charissa and Bree slept on. Soon they would be safely back at Glamis.

'Hold!' came a shout from outside. The cabin jolted to a stop.

And then an awful sound: *Thawk! Thawk! Thawk! Thawk!*

The door to the cabin was wrenched open and, out of the black mouth of the night, hands grabbed Rachel and pulled her into the cold air. She heard Charissa and Bree, both screaming and crying.

'Stop,' Rachel cried. 'My sister. My sister!' Rachel looked and saw the bolt of a crossbow protruding from the first rider's forehead as he lay back over the rump of his horse. The rear rider was lying face down in the grass, unmoving. Another of the soldiers lay still on the road. There should have been one more of their company but she could not see him.

Rough hands pulled her down. 'Wait,' she called out, but her voice had no strength. A thick woollen cloth was thrown over her head and Rachel was hoisted up onto a horse. 'Stop!' she cried. 'No!'

Then she heard Charissa screaming and – was that Bree? Too late, because she was already over the horse, which now began to canter on through the night. Rachel tried hard not be sick with the movement; she pressed her head firmly against the animal's flank.

'You are mad,' she screamed. 'Stop now! Stop!'

The speed at which the horses galloped terrified her. *Please take care of the others,* she prayed. *Please keep me safe.* The echoes of her sister's screams and the sight of the dead attendants were burned into her mind. Why was this happening? Who were these strangers?

Rachel tried to lift herself up to speak when a solid blow came from above and she remembered nothing more.

Rachel woke on a tiny, rough-hewn cot. She was at sea. She knew the sensation well for she had many a time made journeys around Scotland. But this time she was not on a vessel from her father's fleet or fitting of a royal journey. This ship was basic, rough, base. Her throat was on fire and her tongue thick.

She looked around. No lantern; no lights. Just the *goosh goosh goosh* sound of sailing into open water. She went to get up and discovered her hands were bound tightly on either side. 'Please,' she cried. 'I need water.' She lay back down, panting.

After a moment of quiet, she heard a deep-throated word: '*Vasser.*'

A guard pulled off her restraints and she sat up. Within minutes, someone brought her a bowl filled with foul, brackish-looking water. Rachel gagged, but understood that it would not go well for her to refuse. It was liquid nevertheless. She sat up and tried to smile at her captor. Then she scooped a cupped hand into the bowl and lifted it to her mouth.

It tasted stale but she drank it anyway. Her stomach twisted in response to the smell but she swallowed quickly to avoid bringing back up what she had drunk. The boy who brought it laid down another container of murky water for her and she smiled her thanks, but the young lad fled through the guarded doors of her cabin.

The water brought another difficulty for Rachel.

No chamber pot was provided. How, then, was she to relieve herself?

Another opportunity for embarrassment. Roused from the quenching of her thirst, she was able to stand. Rachel went up to her guard and looked him squarely in the eye. 'I must relieve myself,' she said. Clearly, he did not speak her language. '*Pissiare,*' she said in Latin.

He looked at her sharply. A word he understood? He went to the bottom of the steps and shouted up to someone on the next level. A muffled response filtered down and then the young boy was back with a chamber pot. He thrust it into her hands and, red-faced, fled back up the steps. Her guard, however, did not leave. She would have to crouch over the pot with a stranger watching.

Consider Him, she thought, *who endured the cross.* Yes, even her saviour had been humiliated. *I have seen more than most*, Rachel told herself. *I have been where few royal women go and I am not ashamed of what I have seen or what I have done. This man will be embarrassed but it is clear that he has his orders.*

Her face burning with shame, Rachel pulled up her skirts and squatted over the pot and, despite the rocking of the boat, and the fact there was someone in front of her, she relieved herself, the hot pee burning her thighs.

She finished. There was nothing she could use to wipe herself and she would not let her captors know how humiliated she felt, so she grabbed her skirt and dabbed herself dry. Then, she picked up the pot and shoved it under the nose of her guard. 'For you,' she said.

The man's eyes flew wide and he grimaced but took her pot and left, holding it in front as if it might somehow infect him.

Later that day, she was hauled to the deck of the ship. The sky was clear and bright but there was no warmth. And there was no sign of land. Where was she and where were they taking her?

Before she had a chance to consider such questions, a large, stocky man yelled foreign words at her. She did not understand and her heart hammered in her chest. *Do not cry*, she thought. *Do not give in.* The man yelled again and, when she did not move, the sailor beside her pushed her to the deck. The rough boards dug into her knees but she refused to cry out.

'*Blaed!*' a voice called. Then, someone grabbed her hair and pulled her head back.

The first slice of the shears shocked Rachel. She had not expected this. Long strands of her thick blonde hair were roughly hacked off and cast aside. Soon, the chill of the wind buffeted her bare skull.

She could not see but knew that her locks had been taken.

Next, she was returned to her cell and stripped naked. Two men stood guard as another pulled her royal garments from her body. She shivered in the cold but knew that it was much more than that. For her entire life she had kept herself chaste and pure, even during her courtship with Ewan, yet now some enemy had taken away her defence. She had been unseen, untouched by any man until this moment, and now here she was stripped bare for all to see. She clenched her teeth and lifted her chin.

If they decided to use her in that way, she would close her mind to it and endure whatever was to be.

Her fear was assuaged when a young boy brought her a rough tunic to pull on. Nothing in the men's behaviour once she was covered suggested they had any impure plans for her.

There it was, then. All remnants of her royal position stripped. All indications of her gender removed. She was Rachel: Princess Royal, betrothed to the King of Scotland but without hair, clothes or title and now in the hands of an enemy.

After four days' imprisonment in the bowels of the ship, she was once more dragged on deck. The bright light of the morning hurt her eyes and the sounds of screaming gulls and shouts of men filled the air. So too did the unmistakable smell of a fishing port.

There were other passengers whom Rachel had not known about. Girls, women like her and some boys, blinking in the daylight. Some screamed; some cried.

Somewhere, she prayed, kinder men had found Bree and Charissa and taken them to safety. It was a thought she clung to tightly.

Rachel was held back. She watched as the other prisoners were herded off the ship and loaded onto carts or marched through the town. Finally it was her turn. With two soldiers holding her arms, Rachel was escorted down the gangplank and onto the soil of an unknown foreign shore.

Chapter Six
Perth
Rosie

The sun had barely been up one hour when Jethro came bursting through the door of the inn, coat wet and flapping. Rosie paused from setting out tables. 'Whatever is the matter, man?' she growled. Jethro, a nice enough lad and a good worker, was prone to excessive outbursts, be it over a leak in a barrel or a dead bird on the threshold or simply a declaration of his love for her. Thank goodness the inn was empty of patrons, the time being too early even for hardy travellers. Such excitement might be a bad sign.

'The princess,' he panted. 'She's been set upon and taken.'

Rosie's mind went into high speed. Which princess? And was Keavy safe? 'Da?' She called to Dougal, who was out the back moving barrels. 'Da, come.'

Within moments her father stumped inside. 'What's all the hollering?'

Jethro leant on the bar. 'We found them on the road. About an hour out of Perth.'

'Who?' Rosie asked, her stomach knotted with fear.

'The two soldiers *and* the driver and his boy. Dead – each with a crossbow bolt stuck into his forehead. The maid and the wee one screaming and crying.' Jethro swallowed thickly. ''Twas a right mess. Dougal, I sent Hamish on with them to the castle and I came back here.'

Dougal, his face grim, nodded. 'Good lad. That was the right thing to do.'

'But,' Rosie interrupted, 'you said the princess has been taken?'

'Aye, she was gone and the wee one screaming that men took her away on their horses.'

Rosie's mother came through to the tavern. 'Hush this noise. We have guests. Or has that slipped your minds?'

Jethro bobbed as was his habit. 'Begging your pardon, Mistress Rebecca, but there has been a monstrous event.'

Rebecca's hand went to her throat as she hurried forward to stand beside her husband. 'Tell.'

Now aware, Rosie thought wryly, of an audience, Jethro calmed and sat at one of the tables. 'Princesses Bree and Rachel were set upon not an hour out of Perth. The wee one and her maid were left but Princess Rachel's been taken. And,' he added, his voice taking on an interesting tone, Rosie noted, ''tis not long till the wedding.'

It was a stab. Rosie, Dougal and Rebecca felt it. That one sentence meant more than Jethro could understand. Rosie closed her eyes for a moment to gather strength. Rebecca moved to her side and put a reassuring hand on her back. Tears threatened to undo her so she took a deep breath and rounded on the young man before her. 'Was Keavy there?'

Jethro let out a sigh. 'No, Rosie. She was not among it all.'

Rosie sat back, relieved that Fleance's young adoptive sister was safe.

Dougal flicked his hand at Jethro. 'Go, boy, and get a carriage ready and fresh horses. You and I must go to Glamis.' Rebecca put a hand on his arm and Rosie saw that her mother gripped him tightly. Dougal looked between his wife and daughter and his shoulders slumped.

Something important had passed between her parents. 'What is it, Da?' Rosie asked.

'Hurry, boy,' he said, waving Jethro out the door. He waited for the young man to leave before turning to them both. 'A message. Which I must pass to the king. I'm sorry for it, for it will add further weight to young Flea's shoulders now this terrible business has happened.'

Rosie shook her head at her father. 'Da, *I* must go to the king.' She looked over at her parents. 'I will go straight away to Glamis. Jethro will accompany me.'

Dougal's face took on his familiar menacing look. 'Lass, 'tis not your place to go—'

She cut him off. 'Let me go to him.'

Dougal's normally ruddy face was grim and Rosie wondered whether the message he had to deliver had anything to do with his trip south last week. 'Aye. You are right. The king will bear it better coming from you than from me, lass,' Dougal said. 'Go pack your things quickly and then I'll tell you what you must say.'

His words filled her with foreboding. Rosie rushed to her room and changed into her travelling clothes. She quickly retied her braid and pulled a cover over her head. They had both made their choice: Flea to accept the throne of Scotland and she to give him permission to accept it. It was his destiny and she knew it. Though she often wept when alone, she loved him too much to deny what was rightly his. For them there was no future. Her head spun. Perhaps now there was no future for Flea and Rachel either.

Even as these thoughts ran through her mind, she pushed a change of clothes into a bag and headed back out the door. As she returned to her parents, Rosie shook herself. *What's done is done. It's done. And it's done without him.*

Da was sitting at one of the tables with Rebecca and waved at her to sit. He had a tankard of warm mead before him and took a long, thirsty drink before he spoke. 'I saw Magness,' he sighed.

Rosie gasped. 'Was that wise?' Rebecca said, her worried expression mirroring Rosie's feelings.

'Well, I didn't go looking for him, woman,' Dougal growled. 'He found me.'

'And?'

Dougal blew his nose and rubbed his nostrils vigorously. 'He asked after Miri and Keavy.'

'He didn't know?' Rosie asked, thinking about the last time she had seen Magness's wife, when she was lying ill and dying back in England. Maybe, as some had said, Flea should have killed him there on the battlefield. Would that have saved the country from this lingering unease? She shook the thoughts from her mind. No point asking useless questions; that was a deed undone too.

'No. I told him Miri died last winter and she'd sent Keavy to live with Flea. I wasn't sure whether he was pleased with that last bit or no.'

'Tell us. What of Magness? What did he want of you?'

'Well, he had no news of his wife and child but he knew a lot, it seemed, about the king and his future plans . . .'

'He kidnapped the princess?' Rebecca asked. 'Our Magness?'

Dougal shook his head. 'I canna see that being his way. He was very concerned with the future of Scotland and how our . . . I mean . . . how the king would manage. He told me, "He's a good boy, our Flea, but his heart is too easily swayed. He doesn't have the stomach to rule our country," he said.'

'That's not fair,' Rosie cried. 'Flea is loyal and honourable. More than can be said for that traitor. And,' she added, bristling, 'Flea's as shrewd as a fox – for that, Magness himself can be thanked.'

Her father reached out a chubby hand and grabbed hers. 'Enough of that, girl. In his mind, he is thinking that his actions are for the good of Scotland.'

Rosie pulled her hand away. 'The man is demented.'

A shadow passed over Dougal's face. 'Aye, you may be correct, but he is a powerful person at this time and has a message for the king which you are to deliver.'

She waited. It would not be a message she'd take any joy in passing on, of that she was sure. 'You are to tell the king the unrest will continue unless he signs a treaty with the rebels. This treaty will give over lands and titles to those who were dispossessed during Macbeth's reign. Magness no longer believes that the old order of kings can do well by Scotland. He thinks it's time for a rule in which the common man has a voice.'

Rosie shook her head. 'But why does he ask for such a thing? Did not King Malcolm call them all home? Did he not give money to the church for those who had suffered?'

Dougal and Rebecca exchanged looks. 'It didn't happen, love. The order went out but, it seems, the church kept much of the money and many, many families came back to nothing. To avoid starvation, they returned to England or Ireland. Magness told me stories of men whose lives were destroyed by the tyrant and then again by the greed of some who serve God.'

Jethro came inside, shaking his head like a wet dog. 'The weather's packed in but I've got the covered wagon so we will stay dry.'

Dougal cleared his throat. 'Thanks, lad, but it will be the lass going with you to the castle. Have you spoken to anyone else of your news?'

Jethro frowned. 'I came straight here.'

'Good. Tell no one what you have seen. I doubt the castle would be pleased if the news the princess has been taken is spread across the countryside. They'll be making Hamish keep his gob shut as well.'

Her father looked at Rosie and she understood his expression. *Keep an eye on him.*

'Give us some time to say our goodbyes, will you, Jethro? Young Rosie will be with you soon.'

'Right.' Jethro stood for a moment, a look of uncertainty on his face. Rosie nodded her head towards the door. He disappeared as noisily as he had come in.

'He's a keen lad, that one,' Dougal said, looking meaningfully at Rosie.

'No, Da. I have no interest in his attentions.'

'He would be a good husband,' her father continued.

Rosie frowned. 'May we not have this conversation again?'

A gust of wind buffeted the building. Rosie stood up. 'Da, I must go now. I do not want to travel the boggy roads in the dark.' She was also mindful that whoever had taken Rachel might still be about.

Dougal gripped her shoulders. 'Rosie, make sure you tell him how serious Magness is. He means to take some control over the governing of Scotland. He has nought to lose now, with Miri dead and Keavy gone to his enemy.'

'His enemy? Flea is like a son to him,' Rosie cried. She looked to her mother and back to Dougal. 'Da,' she said, her voice just above a whisper, 'how can he be thinking such things?'

'Like I said, henny. Our Flea has gone. In his place stands Fleance, the King of Scotland, and against him, Magness, now Scotland's enemy.'

Rebecca came around the table and embraced her. 'Don't concern yourself with Magness and his view of the world. 'Tis not right and we all know it. Guard your heart, love. Do your duty.'

Rosie understood her mother's caution. 'Aye, Ma. I am a servant to Scotland and its king.'

'Take my cloak, girl,' Dougal said, lifting the heavy garment from a peg along the side wall of the inn. He helped her pin it around her shoulders and then opened the door for her.

———

Though it was still early morning, the day was already grey and gloomy, rain falling from the sky. Rosie picked up her bag and skirts and ran the short distance to the wagon. She stuffed her bag under the hides, which were used to keep the weather from the wagon's cargo. Jethro sat impatiently at the front with the reins in his hands. She climbed up on the seat and arranged her skirts. It was cold and she was thankful for Da's cloak, which she pulled across her shoulders. 'Go now, man,' she growled. 'There is little time.'

Time, she thought. Surely by now, Flea would have sent out soldiers to find Rachel. Maybe the princess would be back safe and sound by the time she got there. But a sense of chilled foreboding sat upon her chest. Something warned her that things were not going to be so easily remedied.

Rosie chewed her bottom lip as tears filled her eyes. Why was she doing this? Why should she care what happened to the royal family?

She brushed the tears aside. *Because!* she thought through gritted teeth. Because she loved him so much she wanted the best for him. The best for him at this time was marrying Rachel.

A painful stab in her stomach made her turn away. *Oh, Flea. You were mine. You should be with me.* She took in a deep breath and flicked away the tears.

Jethro pushed the horses at first but, once clear of the river town, slowed them to a steady trot. He did not speak for some time, which gave Rosie space to think about the message she had to deliver and what she might do to assist the king.

About two hours into the journey, Jethro turned to her. 'I heard a rumour about you a while back,' he began.

Rosie looked at him, her eyebrows raised. 'Are you going to tell me?'

He looked ahead for a moment. 'Word is that you were once betrothed to the king.'

In her unsettled state, it took Rosie a minute or two to compose her reply. 'No, I was never betrothed to the king.' This was true in a sense. He had never asked for her hand and she had never given it. Fate had taken over their lives before any of this could happen.

'It just seems you're especially fond of him, and your parents have a familiarity with him.'

Rosie sighed. 'We knew him before he joined the royal household. He spent ten years in England. It's true we once shared a friendship . . . of sorts,' she added.

Jethro nodded. 'I'd heard as much and also that he may not be who he claims he is.'

'Lies!' Rosie spat. 'Our king is an honest and honourable man. He is – and many have given testimony to this, Jethro, so you would be well advised not to repeat such slurs – the son of Banquo, who was Thane of Lochaber, great-great-grandson to Kenneth and so in line to the throne.'

'Fine. Fine,' Jethro glowered. 'Don't bite my head off, woman. I'm just asking.'

'You're a fool if you believe the lies of jealous and suspicious folk who cannot look past rumour and nonsense. Treat a man according to what he does and how he lives his life, not by gossip and idle chatter. Flea was chosen not only by Duncan on his deathbed, but by God Himself. A pox on any person who says different.'

She turned from him but not before she saw a deep red creeping up his neck. For a moment, a wave of regret shuddered over her. She shouldn't have spoken to him like that. But he deserved it, prattling about things he knew nothing about.

Too much damage was done by poisonous words.

Chapter Seven
Glamis Castle
Fleance

It was a living nightmare. Rachel gone; two of the castle's drivers and two soldiers dead; Charissa and Bree inconsolable. Morag, applying all her patience, managed to get the girls to calm down so that Fleance could fathom what had happened.

Dougal's lad was sitting in front of the fire drying off when the king and Preston entered the kitchen. The boy stood and bowed his head.

'What is your name?' Fleance asked.

'Hamish, Your Majesty. I am a servant of Dougal, the innkeeper at Perth.'

The mention of Dougal's name tightened Fleance's stomach. Dougal, a wily old man and opinionated to boot, made no bones about his feelings towards Fleance. Fleance stood tall and motioned to his aide to continue.

'Tell the king what you know,' Preston said.

'We was coming back from here, me and Jethro, when we heard girls screaming. It was deathly dark and it took us some whiles to find them.'

'Describe what you saw,' Fleance said.

'The lamps were out and both riders dead. The two soldiers we found a-ways lying on the ground. The wee one and the maid were holding each other and crying – dead terrified they were. Jethro yelled at them who we were and we took our torches to find out what was amiss.' He swallowed, his Adam's apple bouncing up and down along his thin neck. 'The men were dead, that was clear – they had bolts in their heads.' He touched his forehead in the middle. 'We asked what happened and the maid, she told us that Princess Rachel had been taken. Jethro and I carried the soldiers' bodies to the back of our cart and put the girls in the front with me and I came back as fast as I could.'

'Did they tell you how this happened?' Fleance asked.

Hamish shook his head. 'No, Sire. I take it they were asleep when they were set upon.'

'And your companion. Where did he go?' This was Preston.

'He returned to the inn at Perth, my lord.'

Fleance looked at Preston and inhaled deeply. 'Thank you, Hamish, for your service. Morag will give you a meal and arrange for some lodgings. You must not tell anyone what you know and you must make sure your companion does the same. Is my meaning clear?' The young lad nodded solemnly. 'You may return to Perth in the morning.'

Hamish ducked his head. 'You are most kind, Your Majesty.'

Fleance left the kitchen with Preston shadowing him and went up the main stairs to the great hall.

This story from the groom was incredible and yet, why was Fleance surprised? For years, Scotland had endured tumultuous times.

'Sire?'

Fleance looked towards the voice. Preston stood at the base of the stairwell. 'Aye?'

'We have sent word to the earls that are nearby. They are on their way.'

For a moment, he longed to be back in England, hunting deer. Showing off for young maids – for one in particular. Battling with his adoptive parents about what chores he needed to do.

The weight was almost too much. He'd lost Rosie the moment he accepted the crown and he'd then worked hard to cultivate his relationship with the royal princess. Now, both women were beyond his reach.

Fleance felt a painful twinge in his lower torso. What if . . . ? What if . . . ? 'Do you think she's dead?' he asked quietly.

'No,' Preston answered. 'If they meant to murder her, they would have done it on the road. 'Tis likely they have taken her for ransom.'

Fleance sat down on the top step and rested his elbows on his knees. He thought about all the people he knew; all the men and women he had encountered this past year. Who would do such a daring thing?

'Who have you known, Preston,' he asked, 'who has shown any shadow of disloyalty to this house – other than Calum?'

'Since the death of Macbeth and his supporters, none save your Magness.'

Something stirred in Fleance's memory. 'Have you known none other? Really?'

'None with the power of persuasion and determination that Magness has shown.'

Around a campfire nearly two years ago, Fleance remembered fragments of conversation between Magness and Rosie's father, Dougal.

'For a wanderer, you've got strange loyalties,' Dougal had said.

Fleance had seen the creeping rage in his adoptive father's face. *'An' I've got a long memory,'* he had replied, spitting into the fire. *'Scotland's a hell place for me ever since that bloody Macbeth ruled.'*

Dougal had tried to reason with him, but Magness had insisted that the country was still cursed.

Fleance looked down at Preston who stood waiting for him. 'What have you heard about Scotland being cursed?'

The old man made his way slowly up the stairs so that his eyes were level with Fleance's. 'Some have said that Macbeth's tyranny was so evil it would take generations to be purged from Scottish soil. Some have said that even then, it would not be enough, so great was the bloodshed.'

'What if . . .' Fleance began, an idea rapidly taking shape in his mind. 'What if someone believed that the only way to purge the evil was to get rid of the entire royal line?'

'The wounds are still festering,' Magness had cried. *'Do not be fooled into thinking that Malcolm has been able to clean and clear out the rot. Rather, he has just kept tight a malignant bandage over a festering gash.'*

Preston scratched his chin. 'I have only ever heard this once, from the frothing mouth of a rebel brought in from the battlefield. He was fatally wounded but we had hoped to gain some intelligence from him. Before he died, all he said was that one day a new line would rise up and clean out the rotting house of Scotland.'

In the silence that followed, Fleance thought back over his time with Magness and Miri. 'During the ten years I was raised by my adoptive parents, occasionally I would overhear Magness, and sometimes the men who visited us, saying things about the state of Scotland. I never paid much heed, really, for what does an orphan boy care of politics?'

'What things can you recall?'

Fleance shook his head, trying to remember more detail. 'I know that he was always angry whenever anyone brought up the topic. Not surprising, is it, considering Macbeth had all his children murdered?'

'Many men lost loved ones during that dark time,' Preston said coldly, making Fleance look at him, curious, but the man did not say any more.

'What if, Preston, Magness had been preparing me as the one to start a new line? A line not of royal blood but something completely separate. All those years of training; all those years of keeping me isolated. You yourself said my marriage to Rachel would strengthen the bloodline. What if Magness has taken her to stop the marriage?'

'Is this something you think him capable of?'

Fleance didn't know what to think. Magness was determined, no question about it. And he seemed to have a future political plan as well as the supporters to help him. But to kidnap the future queen? He shook his head. 'I cannot say.'

An hour later, Fleance sat at the great table with his head in his hands, still waiting for the earls to arrive. The room was cold and silent save for the sound of the wind buffeting in the great fireplace and the occasional spitting sound of the torches. Preston stood quietly beside the hearth, waiting as well.

At some stage, someone lit a fire and placed some food in front of him but he was not hungry. The waiting was unbearable. If only the earls would arrive and he could make some decisions – to act rather than simply sit here.

A rap on the door to the great hall made him look up. A servant came forward.

'Your Majesty, there is a young woman who says you know her.' His face flushed red and he looked down. 'She says you will admit her.'

'What is her name, boy?'

'Rosie. Daughter of Dougal, the innkeeper at Perth.'

63

Fleance stood up, his heart beating hard against his chest. 'Bring her to me,' he told the young servant. 'Immediately.'

The page vanished and, for a few painful minutes, Fleance waited until she was brought in. He had worked very hard these past months to remove her from his mind, yet time and time again the memory of Rosie had resurfaced.

She came through the great door, a thick woollen cloak shrouding her head and shoulders and falling to the flagstones of the hall. As she removed the hood, her thick, dark hair fell in soft curls around her face. Her nose, red; her lips, pale; her eyes searching his for the right response.

She curtsied and then spoke. 'I have a message of great importance, Your Majesty.' She blushed then and he felt his heart move.

'Leave us,' Fleance instructed those around him, but held his hand up when Preston moved. 'Not you, Preston.'

Rosie waited while the room emptied of servants. 'Da was found by Magness, Flea.' He flinched at her familiar name for him but tried not to look disturbed by it. ''Tis not good. Magness told Da that the unrest will continue unless you sign a treaty with the rebels – to give lands and titles back to those who were dispossessed during Macbeth's reign. Magness wants an end to the old order of kings, Flea. He says it's time for the common man to have a voice. Unless you enter into discussions the raids will continue.'

Preston's frown deepened with each sentence.

'My suspicions might be proven true,' Fleance said to the advisor. 'Go on, Rosie.'

'Flea, Da says he's possessed, that he's insane, but that he means what he says.' Her words tumbled forward into the space between them and he felt their urgency.

To give himself time to compose a suitably calm response, Fleance went to the table where wine and food had been set. He poured himself a drink. 'Will you have some refreshment, Rosie?'

She nodded and stepped forward. Fleance poured another drink and gave it to her. She gulped down half of it and set it aside. Fleance sipped two mouthfuls of the bitter-sweet juice then turned to her. 'Did he take Rachel?'

Preston bristled. 'Sire, I don't think you should be looking for advice from an innkeeper's daughter.'

Fleance cut him off. 'Thankfully, man, as king I don't need permission from anyone. Rosie here,' he waved his hand towards her, 'has knowledge beyond what we might have access to.' Rosie bowed her head and, for a moment, he felt a long-forgotten tenderness. 'Thank you, Rosie, for your information and your allegiance to Scotland.'

She stood there a moment, looked at him and then curtsied. 'Thank you, Your Majesty, for your audience.'

Fleance gestured to his advisor. 'Preston, you may leave us.'

Preston sniffed and then cleared his throat. 'Sire, I don't think that—'

Fleance interrupted. 'Don't think, Preston, unless I ask you to.' He finished his wine. 'You may go.'

The old man bowed his head and left the room.

Fleance stood before the mantle and regarded the woman before him. 'Are you well, then, Rosie?'

'Aye. Business is good.'

What he wanted to know, but what he didn't want to know. 'And, ah, you have prospects?'

She smiled and his heart ached. 'Flea, I have a few suitors, but I'm not thinking of marrying any of them.' She put her hands on her hips. 'But, man, you have a betrothed to rescue.'

'Rosie, now that Magness has entered the fray again . . .' He motioned for her to sit at one of the chairs beside the table. 'Which is the better king? One that saves his people by fighting against the enemy or one that goes hunting for a stolen princess?' He sat beside her, drumming his fingers on the worn wooden surface.

'And I can't let word get out that Rachel's been taken. It could lead to a second rebellion.'

Rosie reached for his hands and stilled the movement. Her eyes sparkled. 'Flea, I can't lead one of your armies but I can track and hunt well enough. You taught me that much.' She blushed, and Fleance felt his heart skip a beat. 'Give me a companion and we will go search for news of Rachel while you secure Scotland against these rebels.'

He poured another measure of wine. 'That is a generous thing to offer.' He sipped slowly. 'I accept this and I will find a worthy fellow to go with you.' Fleance lifted his goblet. 'In honour of your faithful friendship.'

Rosie took the cup and sipped. 'Thank you for your faith in me,' she said.

They were silent a while, the fire spitting and hissing in the background.

'Am I a bad person, Rosie? I have loved you with my whole self but now I am promised to Rachel.'

Rosie sipped again. 'I think, in another time or place, she and I would be very good friends.'

Tears filled her eyes and Fleance's chest tightened. She had spoken his very deeply buried thoughts: Rosie, Rachel. But he could only be with one of them.

There was a sharp knock on the door. Preston, clearly, was not happy with this meeting. 'Enter,' Fleance called.

The old man came in, trying not to look at either of them. 'Sire, the earls have arrived and are ready for you.'

Fleance sighed. All these men looking to him and relying on him for direction.

He addressed Rosie. 'Thank you for your news and I look forward to meeting with you again.'

Rosie dipped her head and smiled and Fleance caught that look which had enamoured him many months ago. 'Thank you, Your Majesty,' she murmured.

Fleance watched her leave the chamber, her head held high and her back straight. He scratched his forehead, though there was no itch. It was a tic he'd inherited from his father, Banquo. A gesture that signalled facing a worrying situation. Fleance took a deep breath.

'Preston,' he said. 'Tell the earls they may come in.'

Fleance recognised some of those who filed into the great hall: Ross, Angus, Lennox, Preston, his old friend Blair and Henri, looking serious.

The men took their seats around the table and Preston nodded at Fleance. Taking a deep breath, he faced his audience. 'Thank you for coming back so quickly. We have terrible news.' Murmurs reverberated around the room. 'Princess Rachel was abducted last night.'

The room exploded with noise: shouts and cries. 'Men!' Fleance called. 'My friends. Please. Listen. You have been especially selected as wise and loyal, but it is essential that this news go no further than these castle walls.'

Ross interrupted. 'But we must send out word to find her.'

'No,' Fleance cried. 'We cannot send word anywhere.'

Another great rumble of disconcerted voices.

Preston coughed and knocked the table with a mallet. 'My lords! Our king is correct to say such a thing. Think on this: if word gets out that Rachel – both granddaughter and sister of the two greatest kings Scotland has been blessed with these past twenty

67

years – has disappeared, what might the people do to our ruling monarch? What might they say?' He lowered his voice. 'Fleance is our new king. And we honour him.' Many of those gathered crossed themselves and nodded. 'No one else must know what has happened. Though you may feel awkward in yet another change of garments so soon, know that the quality of the cloth is undisputed for those of us with long memories.' No one spoke. Fleance steadied his breath while he waited for the old man's words to sink in. 'We must keep this abduction secret. Those who accompanied Princess Rachel are dead save her sister and the maid. Those who found the lasses have been warned to say nothing of what has happened.'

It was time to rescue the old man. Fleance took a deep breath and addressed the company again. 'This is the reality of the situation and it does grieve my heart to be so blunt: if Princess Rachel was murdered . . .' Grumbling noises emanated throughout the hall. Fleance ignored them and continued with his speech. '. . . then we would have found her. But because she has disappeared, we suspect she has been kidnapped.'

A low murmur flooded the hall and Fleance held up his hands. 'Thanes, earls and those who are close, let us not fall into despair. I have hope that the princess is well cared for and that, in time, I will know the reason for her kidnap.'

He looked about the room but his stomach ached as painfully as if someone had punched him.

Henri stood up. 'Someone must go and find her.' Preston snorted. Henri turned on him.

'What, old man, should you suggest at this time? Let all who care contribute and be not so offended that others may offer help.'

Preston straightened and his face paled. Fleance watched as the old man composed himself. 'Sire,' he said, 'I believe you have better advisors to the course. However, should you think I might be of use, you know where to find me.' Preston bowed stiffly and turned to leave the chamber.

'Wait,' Fleance cried. Preston, stooped low, stopped and faced him. Fleance rounded on Henri. 'Watch the strength of your tongue, man. This is our court, not yours, and we choose who we wish to have as company.' It pleased him to see Henri's cheeks redden slightly. Fleance waited, staring down his guest.

Henri swallowed and bowed his head. 'My apologies, Your Majesty. I have forgotten my place.'

'Yes, but you are correct. We must immediately send trusted servants to bring her home.' He looked around the room. 'This is a course of action I am already considering.'

Ross stepped forward. 'Your Majesty, there is an immediate threat against the crown; these raids.' More murmurs of agreement rustled through the collected men. 'It seems we've scorched the snake, not killed it.'

Fleance nodded. 'Aye, I have had a message which grieves my heart as much as the one which told me of our princess's kidnap: my adoptive father, Magness, is behind these attacks. The ones that Henri here,' he nodded towards the Norman ambassador, 'tells us are sedition. Magness sent word that the raids will continue unless we enter into negotiations with him.'

There was a rumble of anger through the hall. Lennox cried out, 'Scotland will never negotiate with rebels!'

'No,' said Fleance, 'and I do not plan to do so.'

'Your Majesty,' Blair began, 'do you think Magness is behind the abduction?'

Fleance took comfort from the presence of his old friend, now the Thane of Lochaber, a title given as reward for faithfulness and fearlessness in battle. 'I do not know. I thought him a man of honour—'

An angry growl rose from the group. Fleance put up his hands. With courage – he did not know where it came from – he spoke up. 'Yes, Magness is an honourable man. He is also wrong in his beliefs. But how many of us gathered here are blameless for behaviour stemming from ill-conceived belief? I know him better than any man in this room. He is fierce and he loves Scotland.'

The new Thane of Fife stood up, his face contorted with anger. 'No man who loves Scotland would do what he did to our Macduff.'

Others murmured their support but Fleance felt strangely protective of Magness. He held up his hands again. 'Listen to me. Forget conjecture and rumour. Magness, though angry and resentful of his lord, did not kill him. I bear witness to this: it was a lowlife reaver who snuffed out our dear Macduff. Whatever crimes Magness has committed against Scotland, the death of William is not one of them.'

'He's still a madman, Your Majesty.' Fleance did not see who it was who spoke thus.

'Aye, he is and has many in his command. But to take Rachel is something darker again.'

'What about his daughter?' Lennox asked. 'Some think she is her father's spy living under your roof.'

'Keavy is as a sister to me and I am her guardian. She lives under my care and protection at the request of her dead mother. She is no threat.'

Preston cleared his throat. 'The king is correct. Our concern must be for the princess and the defeat of those rebels.'

Blair coughed to gain his attention. 'If it would please you, Your Majesty, but I have spoken to the innkeeper's daughter, Rosie, and she has told me of her desire to help search for Princess Rachel. I have devised a plan.' Blair, light sweat now lacing his brow and top lip, ran a shaking hand through his hair. 'I . . . ah . . . I think . . . it would be, ah, useful to travel in disguise. Rosie and I will go searching for our princess. You should not be distracted from the task of dealing once and for all with Magness.'

The men nodded and someone patted Blair on the back. Rosie must have spoken to Blair on her way out of the hall. Fleance was surprised, but he could think of no braver, more trustworthy companion for Rosie than his old friend.

'Sire?' Angus touched his arm. 'We stand on your pleasure.'

Fleance shook himself. 'This is a possible solution. We need some time to consider the best approach.' He waved towards the wine jugs on the table. 'Refresh yourselves and I will consider the advice given.'

He called Firth over. 'Please find the innkeeper's daughter and escort her to the stables. Preston and Blair, come with me.'

Fleance strode purposefully down the length of the great hall and swept through the gap of the doors opened by waiting pages. He knew the two men followed him and he continued on – down the great stairs, into the foyer, out the front doors into the night and across the courtyard to the stables. Only there did he stop.

He was pleased to see Rosie hurrying in. She looked somewhat startled but smiled at them all.

Blair coughed. 'That was an interesting exit,' he said, going up to Willow and presenting him with an apple. 'Are you going to explain?'

Preston looked uncomfortable and out of place. He stood gingerly against the tack table.

'Of all others, besides Rachel, I trust you three the most.' Fleance regarded them all. 'You have proved to me beyond doubt your faithfulness to Scotland. You have put aside, at least three times, your own safety or hopes and dreams for the betterment of the crown.' He addressed Blair. 'You, my friend, there is no question of your loyalty and I am thankful for your willingness to sacrifice so much for our country.' To Rosie he spoke next. 'Scotland is fortunate to have women such as you. I give you and Blair permission to fulfil your quest.'

The old advisor was fiddling with a worn halter, discarded by the grooms – its tough leather too much for a new bridle. 'Preston? You are from another era. You have witnessed more than we three, though our lives have been painfully marred by events a long time ago. And you are different because you keep so much to yourself. But man, you have honourably proved yourself and your worth and your loyalty. For this, I am grateful.' The old man moved away from the bench and began to tug at his cloak. 'Donalbain trusted you. Duncan trusted you. I trust you,' Fleance said.

Preston looked up and his watery blue eyes filled with tears. His chin trembled. His eyes closed and then he bowed. 'Thank you, Your Majesty. I know I am somewhat different. All my life, people have struggled with me but all the Kings of Scotland, including our beloved Duncan the First, have believed in me.' He wiped away his tears and stood straight. 'Believe in me.'

This strength was what he needed. Fleance took in a deep breath and turned to Rosie and Blair. 'You two will go searching for Rachel and you will travel as married. I will deal with Magness with Preston's help.'

'When shall we leave?' Rosie asked.

Blair stepped forward. 'First light. We cannot delay our search for her any longer.'

'Agreed,' Fleance said. 'Arrangements will be made for your provisions before dawn. Rosie, go and see Morag. She will arrange suitable lodgings for you tonight. I will see you both before you leave tomorrow.'

Both Blair and Rosie ducked their heads then left. Fleance watched as Rosie ran over the courtyard to the kitchen entrance. His heart ached.

'Sire?' Preston touched his arm. 'We should go back to the castle.'

Fleance sighed. 'Aye.' He looked at the old man. 'I would that we were heading to the nursery with the children and Rachel for a good-night story.'

'As would we all, Sire,' Preston said. 'As would we all.'

'They blame you,' Henri said, the signature apple in his hands. 'I hear that your people say you have brought bad luck to the house of Scotland.'

Fleance hadn't yet gone to bed. His restlessness had led him to the militia room where he had spent the last thirty minutes practising with his claymore. Sighing heavily, he looked at his guest. 'Why do you always bring me bad news?'

Henri shrugged. 'I bring you news. Good. Bad. That is not my choice.'

That was debatable, Fleance thought, as he wiped his face and the back of his neck with the towel a servant offered him. 'I disagree. I think you do have a choice and you choose to make my life as difficult as you can.' He felt no anger. Henri had led a privileged life and had the skills and the gold necessary to get him out of whatever fix he found himself in. He could not understand the struggles Fleance and his friends had encountered these past two years.

Henri was surprisingly quiet as they finished for the night. Fleance completed oiling the sword and hilt and checking the scabbard, then put his weapon away.

The apple was finished but Henri, now cleaning out his nails with a knife, was happy to offer comment. 'You have servants for this.'

Sighing deeply, Fleance put away the cleaning things. 'It matters little to me how many fellows I may or may not have to carry my weapons or polish my brooches. So long as I can do it myself and have time to do it, then it will be done by my hand.'

His new companion threw him the now-familiar grin. 'Ah, but that is where you are misguided. You are King of Scotland and as such you have more important things to attend to than the lowly chores which once occupied your time.' Fleance went to challenge this but Henri was resolute. 'There is a natural order for things and God has now determined that you be third from Him. You, Fleance, are divinely appointed and therefore you have the divine right to do whatever you desire. You must be seen more as your country's leader and less as the commoner you were. A kingly manner is more important than being skilled at peeling vegetables, *n'est-ce pas?*'

'You have lived a most privileged life and show no understanding of anyone who does not swirl in your circles,' Fleance argued. 'I, on the other hand, have been given the insight from the God you speak of, to understand how hard, how difficult, how exceedingly painful it is to serve as well as lead.' He was so frustrated he almost wanted to punch something, but that would not achieve any good. 'Henri, your country has been blessed with abundance and good weather. Here, in Scotland, we have been plagued by cold and damp and war. We are a small nation isolated in the north. But to gain access to England, sometimes allies and enemies alike have to come through our land.'

Henri was shaking his head. 'You are too intense, my friend. I was only suggesting a course.'

As quickly as it had come, his frustration left him. 'I understand your intentions, but,' Fleance clasped Henri's shoulder, 'perhaps if you could stop the urge to trace *your* patterns of living and thinking in *my* heart, then you might understand me.' He stared at his French guest a moment then dropped his arm. 'Good night,' he said and walked towards the light of the main entrance, leaving Henri in the darkness of the castle wall.

Tomorrow, Fleance determined, he would put his plans into action. While Blair and Rosie searched for news of Rachel, he would deal with things at home. First he would visit the ransacked villages and listen to the people. Then he would have to deal with the rebels once and for all so that Scotland could finally be at peace.

Blair and Rosie had already readied themselves and left early the next morning before Fleance had a chance to speak to either of them. There was nothing more to be done, so he stood back and watched the wagon disappear in the distance.

Then the messengers came.

The first, a red-faced boy, stammered and stuttered until Preston put a hand on his shoulder and whispered in his ear. 'So please you, Your Majesty,' the boy gasped, 'but I have been given word from the west that there are two villages who have voted no confidence in you since their homes were attacked.' He wiped his mouth and bobbed towards Fleance, clearly unsure what was now expected of him. 'They say that unless you look to make amends, they will not support your sovereignty.'

'Thank you, young man,' Fleance said. 'I will consider your comments.'

The next messenger was an older man with a thick prickly beard, long grey hair and weathered skin. His words did little to reassure Fleance that there would be an easy reconciliation.

'My message is this,' said the man. 'You are a young and ill-equipped ruler and not ready to ensure Scotland is protected. The speaker of the message says, "Give over Scotland to England because all peoples will be saved".'

There were two others who carried similar messages but the final one struck his heart. It was from Ireland.

'Your Majesty, the people of Ireland ask you to stay strong and not succumb to the demands of the English. We have little in the way of warrior power but we will support you if the need arises.'

After this was delivered, Preston moved close. 'This is good news, Your Majesty. Their nation, like ours, has often been plagued by unwanted visitors. Be of good cheer though they may not have the men to aid in any battle.'

Preston's words gave Fleance more determination than ever to go out into the countryside and meet the people. The advisors thought, however, that he should not travel with pomp and ceremony. Fleance agreed. God forbid that his efforts seem insincere to those who had suffered of late. He did not want to add further offence to their suffering.

And so it began – his journey to win over the hearts of his people.

Chapter Eight
Norway
Rachel

Her jailers ushered her onto a cart along with a number of other bedraggled women and children and two baby pigs. Rachel prayed she would not vomit up the bitter gorge that had sat in her stomach since her journey began or, worse, faint, as the cart bounced and jarred along a rutted track in the damp morning.

How was it that she sat among the filth and stench and did not protest? Why was she not calling out, *I am to be the next Queen of Scotland*?

In a flash, a quiet voice pressed into her head: *My strength is made perfect in weakness.* Instantly, she recognised the words spoken by the friar in a service at Margaret's chapel. It was as if God Himself was talking to her. Rachel felt a measure of comfort despite the sharp edges of the boards pressing into her hips. *Yes*, she thought. *If I feel I am unable to do it then God is more able to work through me with his strength.* Another piece of scripture came to her. *Do not be afraid. Do not be dismayed.*

'English?' a dirty young girl asked in a thick accent. She looked no more than fourteen or fifteen.

'Scottish,' Rachel replied, thinking that she probably looked as ragged and poor herself.

The girl smiled. 'Rome,' she said. 'Taken.' She pointed to the two children who sat behind her. 'Ah . . . *frater. Soror?*'

'Brother and sister?' Rachel offered.

The girl beamed and nodded. 'My brother and sister.'

Rachel wondered how a child, almost a woman, and who, given her language skills, had enjoyed some measure of education, could be in this position. Then she almost shook herself: the same could be asked of her.

She tried to remember the Latin she knew beyond the prayers and hymns and tentatively asked, '*Qua sout vestri parentes?*' Where are your parents?

The girl's face beamed and she burst forth with a torrent of sounds and words that Rachel could not understand, though some of them she recognised from Mass.

The girl was desperate and lonely and afraid and she saw in Rachel some hope of rescue.

Rachel held up her hands and spoke a series of questions and comments that only seemed to increase the young woman's agitation. The girl grabbed her hand and rattled off a series of excited short phrases.

Suddenly it was too much, and Rachel turned her head so that her new companion would not see her fear.

The young girl kissed Rachel's hand and pressed it to her cheek. '*Nos es una,*' she whispered. *We are together.* The princess stared at the girl's matted hair and felt a flood of warmth and joy. Rachel turned over the hand that was holding hers and gave it a squeeze. Then she smiled at her and prayed one of the many prayers she recited weekly:

Angele Dei,
qui custos es mei,

Me tibi commissum pietate superna;
Hodie illumina, custodi, rege, et guberna.
Amen.

The girl's eyes did not leave her face but, when Rachel had finished praying, she bobbed her head and whispered, '*Amen.*' Then she added in English, 'Thank you.'

The ragged company arrived at a castle just as the sun was setting. It was cold and the air was damp. The wee boy had begun to whimper about an hour before, which only seemed to irritate the driver, who flicked his whip at the poor horses pulling their wagon.

The piglets were hungry and had been crying most of the journey. Rachel tried to alleviate their anxiety by stuffing her fingers into their mouths to suck, but was rewarded only with cut and grazed hands. In the end, she gave up and put their squealing into the same parcel of suffering as the other things she could not change.

Two thick-set men in armour of a kind Rachel did not recognise came out of the castle to greet them. One of them shouted orders to the driver who, after they had alighted, moved the wagon and its pigs towards a far part of the castle grounds. Rachel, the girl and her sister and brother came forward. The men spoke unintelligibly and roughly pushed them towards the entrance of the gloomy stone fortress.

The soldiers gave off a rank and filthy smell, but the place they guarded had an even more virulent stench. Rachel was forced to stop breathing through her nose because it was so overwhelming. With short intakes of breath she surrendered to the pushing and shoving of these strange men who, with resentment and obvious discontent, moved them down a slimy stone staircase and into hell.

As she was pushed into the cold, dark cell, Rachel recognised the sadness and anger of her guards. These were men who, unlike herself, had probably been pressed into service to their king, their parents unable to afford the taxes or offer adequate labour for the fields. She had seen it her entire life: the system's demands for labour and money and, if this could not be offered, the children as bond slaves. Many became reluctant soldiers or servants in the lord's manor. Never entirely faithful and always bitter.

The place where Rachel was to be housed was cold and damp. Water ran down stone walls thick with algae. In one corner was a rough-hewn hole the size of a large man's fist. In the faint light she saw a drain in the floor of the dungeon that ensured waste was carried away: water, blood, ablutions, sweat and tears. The girl from Rome and her family tried to follow Rachel into the cell, but a guard pushed them on, deeper into the bowels of the castle. The cries of alarm from the young girl tugged at Rachel's heart. *Be strong*, she whispered into the darkness. *Do not give up!*

The ablutions galled her the most. Making her way to the toileting area she was confronted with the spoiled, contaminated waters that flowed over the ceramic tiles. What made it more awful was the knowledge that she would soon be contributing to the stench.

Rachel found a space against the inner wall and squatted. Though the light was dim, she saw she was neighbour to a withered hag and a tiny child. The older woman shuffled over slightly to allow Rachel to set herself against the wall but the child did not respond to the new arrival. She continued to rock to and fro.

The girl was pasty and thin with long, lank hair clinging to her face and shoulders. Rachel's heart ached. Poor thing. She shuffled closer to the young one. 'Hey,' she said. 'Hey.'

The girl turned her head but her eyes did not focus. They were blue, but thick with a white membrane. 'Mother?' she asked.

Rachel breathed deeply despite the smell. 'No. I am not your mother, bairn, but I am here for you.'

The thick, encrusted eyes of the young child filled with tears. 'What did they do? Where is my mama?'

Rachel could not help herself. She reached out and pulled the filthy child to her. 'It will be all right,' she murmured.

———

Rachel's stomach churned and she was constantly nagged by nauseating hunger pains. She longed for fresh air and clean, cold water. She could not work out what might happen to her next. Surely those who kept them captive would not starve them all?

Suddenly she heard the heavy thud of marching, armoured men. And then, there they were in the low light, soldiers coming into their small compound.

The princess stood, feeling ill and anxious. For two days she had suffered diarrhoea and her tunic was stained with her sickness.

Two heavily armed guards pushed their way into her cell and pulled her out, soiled and smelling tunic notwithstanding. Now she was shoved through dank and dark corridors by the two. burly men. In a moment, she was pushed into an alcove and one of them threw a fresh smock at her. They waited and watched, smirking in the gloom as she stripped naked and pulled the garment over her head. She was thankful that her body was again hidden from their greedy eyes.

Then the three of them continued moving on with Rachel ahead of the men, who pushed at her back regularly and laughed without humour. This could only bode ill.

———

Compared with the darkness of her prison, the bright light of the main hall of the castle was dazzling. Her captor sat before her on his throne. His garb was ornate and excessive. He looked at her with a dispassionate eye.

'You!' she whispered, a painful pressure in her chest. Despite herself, tears welled in her eyes. 'Calum?'

He smirked. 'Good morning, Princess. I trust that you have been,' he waved around the large room, 'adequately cared for?'

Rachel tried to appear resolute. She frantically wanted to make sense of what was before her. Someone whom she'd trusted for three years was a betrayer. Yes, she'd heard the stories and heard that it was his crossbow bolt that had brought down her brother, but this was Calum. Trusted, honoured Calum. The man who had been part of her household and who was now sitting before her with a twisted and angry expression on his face.

'Calum?' she began.

'No!' he barked. 'You do not address me this way. I am King of Norway.' Rachel blinked and tried to find in this man some semblance of the aide who had been a constant companion to her father. He studied her for a few moments, shifted his legs and lifted his head. 'Not so high and mighty now, eh, Rachel? Not the future Queen of Scotland? One wonders where your king is. Oh, let me think.' Calum made a great show of putting his hand on his head. 'Oh.' He looked up. 'He has problems with rebels who do not want him on the throne.' He was having fun with her pain.

'King Fleance is well able to solve the problems that confront him,' she said.

Calum stood up and flicked his cloak behind him. 'Yes, it is as you say, but I wonder aloud, Rachel, if our good Lord would approve of your king's resources. I have heard that witchcraft is fuelling your sovereign.'

The mention of God startled her. She looked down, trying to make sense of Calum's words. 'Yes, I see your confusion,' he continued. 'And it is an attitude that would not sit easily on your pure soul.' He lowered his voice and stepped towards her. 'Think about it, Rachel. Where was Fleance when Malcolm died? Where was Fleance when your father died? Where was Fleance when your brother died?'

Her eyes were filled with tears but the guards had tied her hands so all she could do was shake her head to free them from her vision.

'Don't shake your head. It is no use denying it. Your king,' Calum sneered, saying the word as if it was a bitter root, 'has been present at every terrible event Scotland has endured these past twenty years.' He turned from her and began striding towards his throne. 'Think,' he called, lifting his arm to the ceiling, 'about your grandfather, the gentle Duncan.' He turned and spat. 'Were not Fleance and his father present at the castle of the king's murder?'

Rachel whispered, 'I don't understand . . .'

'You are naive, Rachel. That is why you don't understand. The men you have honoured are the very men who are dishonourable. Your father was an idiot! Misguided. Gullible.' He sat down and leant forward. 'Quaintly *stupid*!'

There was a silence in the great hall. Her hips ached and her shoulders stung with the pressure of her arms behind her back. Her scalp crawled with lice and the niggle and twitching beneath her cropped hair was almost beyond her endurance as she stood there, bedraggled, in front of her father's former aide.

'I am sorry,' Rachel said dipping her head. 'I have heard of your pain.'

'*Pain?*' Calum scoffed. 'What say you of such things?' A page ran over and gave the king a goblet, which he drained. 'You,' he said, pointing to Rachel, 'have no understanding of this word.'

His rage reached across the flagstones and punched against her chest. Oh, how wrong he was, but she could see now that the real Calum was not a reasonable man and could not be relied upon.

'Yes,' she said. 'You are correct.'

Her words seemed to give him pause and he shifted in his seat. 'Good.' He nodded to the guard who stood behind her. The man removed a long knife and her heart skipped a beat. This was it, then. It was all finished and now she was to meet her saviour.

Rachel closed her eyes and held her breath, waiting for the fatal wound, but instead the guard used the weapon to cut the rope that held her hands behind her back.

She stood there a moment, disorientated, but was brought back to the present by the stinging in her hands.

Calum eyed her as she rubbed her wrists and tried not to make a show of wiping away the tears on her face. 'Your father always said that you were stronger than your brother. Perhaps he was right.'

She stared at him, uncertain as to what his expectations were. He waved a hand. 'You are an observer, Rachel. Very much like me, I should think.' The comparison chilled her. Never had she felt so far apart from this man. 'Which is just as well because I have plans for you, young princess, and I am pleased that you are now in my possession.' Calum grinned as he bowed low, and Rachel dug her nails into her palms.

He stood again and rubbed his eyes – an action that she had seen so many times before. Did Calum suffer from pains in the head? Was his vision affected? Was there something physical that worsened his mood?

'Are you unwell?' she asked.

Calum paused, tilted his head sideways and studied her. 'My physicians have attended me and are giving me instruction to alleviate the pains I get in my head. Even the monks, when I was in solitude, offered up prayers for healing. Yet, I am still afflicted. It is because the weight of my obligations to the living and the dead press in on me.'

His frankness startled her. For a sovereign to confess to a weakness was a risky thing. Instinct told her to be silent.

He sniffed and coughed, two actions that ignited a tinder of excitement in Rachel. She knew the reason for his suffering: too much of the phlegmatic humour.

'Does Your Majesty drink milk and eat cheese?' she asked quietly.

Calum snorted. 'Does not any man?'

'Aye, but some, it is said, who are superior, should no longer walk as babes and take the milk of any animal.'

He leant forward. Her comment had made him interested, it seemed. 'Go on.'

'Calum, we are the only creatures on Earth who consume milk and its produce as adults.' His stillness encouraged her to continue. 'Calves, foals, dogs, cats – within weeks of their birth they replace their mother's milk with grain or grass or meat. Yet our kind continues to enjoy milk and cheese.'

'As we should because we are not base animals,' Calum snorted.

'Aye, but I have seen that many a man who is strong and intelligent is plagued by symptoms such as yours and when he has removed all milk from his diet has been freed from the head and face pains he has suffered.'

Her words hung in the air of the great hall. No one spoke. Calum regarded her, still frowning. 'And you would offer me herbs and other remedies to poison me.'

Rachel frowned. 'Why would I do that?'

Calum laughed out loud, but there was no humour in the sound. 'Because, like your king, you want me dead.'

She tried to step forward, but was held back by the guards, their hands vice-like against her shoulders. 'Calum,' she said.

'Scotland does not desire your death, even though you took the life of our king—'

'That,' he responded quickly, 'was not as it was meant to be. I had no quarrel with Duncan.' He breathed heavily between clenched teeth. The only other people in the hall besides this king and Rachel were her guards, the page and, standing in the shadow beside a massive thick curtain, another. 'This dialogue is over. Sven,' Calum called and it was then that the shadow moved out into the light. He was an impressively tall and thick-set man with wispy white hair and a tanned face. He stood before Calum and bowed curtly. 'Take her to the wards.'

Sven turned abruptly and walked towards her. The guard gave her a gentle nudge in the small of her back and Rachel found herself moving into step with the giant of a man as he strode past and went out of the great doors.

Once outside, he spun around and studied her. He tapped his chest. 'Sven,' he said, his voice melodious and husky. '*Kom*,' was the next word. She nodded and tried a smile, which had no effect on the tower of a man. '*Bra*,' he grunted and turned again and began stomping down the corridor. With no idea as to what to do next, Rachel followed him. She wondered why he chose to communicate with her in his native tongue when it was obvious from his response to Calum that he understood her language. She tucked the thought away, thinking she would ask him to tell his story.

The further they walked, the colder it became; the light seemed to have been sucked out of the deepening passages. But the diminishing heat and light were replaced by sound and smell – yet more human suffering.

It was not much better than the dungeon she'd come from, except there were no cages or bars. Instead, the dank and dripping walls were highlighted by the smoking torches, which stuck out from either side of the long, narrow room. Prone bodies, some emitting whimpering sounds, lay on rough cots crammed along one wall, the heads of some at the mercy of the dripping wax.

Sven had stopped at the entrance to what was obviously a hospital – but he did not seem to object to Rachel going forward to investigate. At the far end of the room, she could see two people dressed in the habits of a religious order, working quickly and urgently to carry a bowl of something to a man twisting and turning in his bed, his cries plaintive and weak.

As one of the monks prayed loudly, the other tried to pour the liquid from the bowl into the throat of the patient. The sick man protested and struck out. The bowl and its remaining liquid tipped over the monk, who howled in protest.

Immediately, both monks began striking the man with closed fists and angry words. It was a dreadful sight.

'Stop!' Rachel cried, taking a step further. 'Enough!'

Her tone, it seemed, contained something that made both men pause, their fists raised, and turn to her. '*Hvorfor?*'

She turned back to Sven and lifted her hands in a gesture of helplessness. He stepped forward and bellowed at the monks. '*Fordi kongen sier så.*' Rachel picked up a possible translation of the words – king say so – and it seemed to be correct because the two monks pulled back from the cot of the patient and motioned for her to inspect him.

'*Jeg ber deg,*' the poor man whispered.

Her command of Latin, French and German as well as Gaelic and English meant Rachel was able to hazard a fairly accurate guess at the words she knew. *Deg* – beg. *Jeg* – *Je* – I; *ber* – *bein* – be. I am begging.

Assuming the new word she had learnt from Sven meant 'all right', she offered it: '*Bra.*'

Immediately the man settled back against the filthy linen and raised a shaking hand to his mouth. '*Behage hjelpe meg!*' Rachel recognised the word help.

She looked at Sven for assistance. 'Help?'

He nodded. '*Ja. Hjelpe.*'

Rachel went forward and touched her palm to his forehead. It was warm, but not hot, which meant he did not have a fever. She pulled down the grey covering that was pulled tightly over his torso and pulled up the tunic. He was thin but not overly so, and she could see neither wounds nor bruising on his upper torso.

She went to pull down his breeks. All three men rushed to stop her with cries of distress. She nodded. Yes, she could understand their unease. But she needed to ascertain whether her patient had injuries in the lower half of his body. Rachel turned to Sven. Again, she raised her hands in a manner which she hoped he would understand as a question. She pointed at the man's lower half and back at Sven. Was he injured?

Sven asked the question to the monks and they shook their heads. Another round of urgent conversation ensued until Sven put up his hands to stop them. He looked at her and tapped his head and his chest. '*Syk.*'

So, there was a sickness that they couldn't see. The presence of the monks suggested they thought it might be spiritual but there was some energy, some urgency in the man that warned Rachel things were not as they seemed.

She approached his side once again and picked up his hand. It was calloused and broad but the nails were twisted and blue-black. This was not healthy. Then she ran her eyes over his arm and saw a mottled crust on his shoulder. Then another on his forearm and her heart began to race. These sores were not a good sign.

Once before, she had seen something similar on an old crofter who was ailing. The sore had quickly festered and, though she had applied a powerful balm, within a couple of weeks the poor man had had to retire to his bed and, like a grape in the sun, he had shrunk down and disappeared into nothing more than a collection of taut skin and protruding bones.

The man had tried hard to keep up his work but his efforts became half-hearted and it wasn't long before he had taken to bed and could not get up.

Prayers had been given, but the man's descent into the afterlife was swift.

The same was sure to be true for this man. Rachel moved closer to him and knelt down. She grabbed his hands and tried to pour some of her hope into his terrified face. 'Go with God,' she said and tightened her grip on his hands, her eyes filling with tears.

'*Min Gud*,' he said, his eyes wide and fearful.

Rachel looked for Sven who had come to the foot of the cot. '*Ja. Gå med Gud.*'

The poor man clung tighter to her hands and began to cry. The monks moved forward again but Sven growled them away. This man was suffering the fate of many Rachel had heard of who worked all day in the sun, their pale skin no defence against the weather. The sores were so innocuous no one paid much mind to their irritations at first. But when the men, as it so often seemed to be, fell down ill, the rest of the villagers scouted around looking for a cause.

Before Malcolm's death, Rachel had spent some time thinking about such things and their consequences. She knew that many thought these unexplained illnesses were a result of witchcraft. And this was not beyond her reckoning, given her father's attention to the sisters.

But her inner wisdom spoke of more than just simple superstition.

In Latin, Rachel began to recite the prayer for the dying.

The man clung to her, looking thin and pale and ill, his tears running gently down the sides of his cheeks.

As she finished the prayer, Sven appeared beside her. '*Bra mann.*' Good. All right. Right. And Man.

She leant down and kissed the dying man on his forehead. '*Bra mann. Ja.* Good,' she croaked.

As she continued on to survey the rest of the sick, a lightness of spirit settled upon her. She had been sent to save others and, for the moment, that was enough and she was content.

Chapter Nine
Glamis
Fleance

Despite all his posturing about what should be done for Scotland, Henri declined the invitation to travel the country to help make amends. 'It is not my inclincation,' he said, 'to meet your people. Of what concern are they to me?' He folded his arms across his chest and sniffed. 'I am not bred for such things as walking around the countryside patting babies and shaking hands. I am, after all, merely a lord. Not the king.'

Fleance regarded him. Henri's face was flushed red and his feet shuffled nervously. Then it came to him. Though acting staunch and resolute, Henri was afraid. At this moment, Fleance felt more sympathy for the man than he had since his arrival. Now things made sense. Henri did not want to be in Scotland. Did not want to be in this castle. But to hide his uncertainty in the face of the unknown, he behaved in a way that gave offence to many. He wasn't really a coward – more like someone who knew his limitations.

'I think,' Henri continued, 'that my place is here, at Glamis, while you are absent. This means I am able to ensure all goes well, *n'est-pas?*'

It would be an unkind thing indeed, to press Henri to travel with them. 'Perhaps you are right,' Fleance said. 'Your company and presence here at the castle should award the occupants much in the way of humour and joy.'

Henri's relief was palpable and he bowed extravagantly. 'You are most wise, young Fleance,' he said, his face still red.

'Well, mind you keep your attentions to the upper levels of the castle,' Fleance said, staring hard at his guest. 'We rely on you to avoid distraction.' Henri's attentions to Morag's niece Charissa seemed to occupy much of the French lord's time. The last thing Fleance needed was a scandal or a distracted caretaker.

'*Bien sûr!*' Henri replied, smiling widely. '*Mais, bien sûr.* You would think otherwise?'

Well, actually yes, Fleance did think otherwise, but the keen expression on Henri's face stopped him from saying as much. '*Merci, mon ami.* Thank you for your efforts to date and your efforts in the future.' Fleance nodded and then moved from the courtyard to the stables to tackle his next assignment: getting his father's horse, Willow, ready for a long journey at this early time of the day.

He checked Willow's tack – a custom which, he had learnt, frustrated the stable hands, but that was of no importance. They might not like the way he conducted himself around the stables and the horse, but the history he had with Willow dictated a deeper rule – this man and this beast were inseparable. If a spotty young hand thought he should tend the great horse better than the king, then woe betide him. Willow was as cantankerous and uncooperative as any beast – man or animal – denied sleep, food and recreation.

Fleance mounted the horse. In that moment he wondered why it was he had never considered Willow his own. It seemed the animal belonged to another time and another master. Fleance was just a rider.

In contrast to Henri, Preston, without comment or ceremony, joined the gathered party. Fleance acknowledged the presence of his advisor with a nod. Though he had not asked Preston to join them, it was a comfort to know that he would. After all, the man was aged and his body was not in the best of health – despite his mind being sharper and clearer than any in their company.

Before long they set off. The party consisted of twenty strong men – three men from the castle and a small regiment Fleance had secured from his personal guard. Rosie and Blair had set off the day before in their quest to gather news of Rachel, confident that Rosie's contacts in the innkeeping trade would yield much in terms of information about the comings and goings of various ships and boats.

The princess had been abducted not far from Perth. Unless her captors were holed up in some hidden cottage deep in a wood, they were more likely to have escaped by sea.

Try as he might to concentrate on what was before him, Fleance's mind went back to that dreadful day when they were confronted by the blond-haired warrior intent on murder. He had seen the rage in Calum's face and his determination to destroy. Killing Duncan had been a mistake, and Fleance knew that things were not finished for Calum.

Could it have been Calum? To kidnap a royal was a brazen thing to do, especially as it meant sending enemy troops into Scotland. But why Rachel? What benefit for Norway could come from such an act?

Fleance slid his hands forward on the reins to tighten the hold on his horse. Was it Magness, then? Magness was definitely intent on tightening the ropes around Scotland's king. Yet, this didn't feel like something Magness would do. This was a man who had, with a compassionate heart, scooped him up as a lad, half-starved and delirious, and taken him as his own. Yes, Magness was a tough and sometimes brutal instructor. But his loyalties lay with Scotland – a Scotland forever cleansed from the stain of Macbeth's rule.

To Magness it was obvious that this could only be accomplished by establishing a new order. But Fleance shook his head. Could the man who had loved and coached him for ten years be capable of such an act?

She was not dead, of this Fleance was certain, but he feared that she was in danger. This abduction was because of him and this distressed him enormously. He had hurt Rosie before, simply because of who he was. Now, it seemed, Rachel too was suffering because of him.

The first village they came to was settled and quiet. No livestock had been lost but all crops had been destroyed by the rebels. Six families were affected. Six families and thirty-eight mouths to feed. A small place, but their loss was significant.

The party pulled alongside the remains of a field – the scorched earth still emitting a pungent smell. Fleance reckoned that more than just vegetation had been destroyed in this burning. His suspicions were confirmed when he spied the charred corpse of a vole beside that of a lapwing near her blackened eggs.

When they turned their attention to the people, Fleance spotted an older man who was kneeling awkwardly in the dirt. Fleance dismounted and walked towards him.

'Father, would you please tell us what happened here?'

The villager struggled to his full height and Fleance saw that he was not old. In fact, he was the age Banquo would have been had he lived. Yet somehow this man was hindered by an injury that afflicted his body.

'You are wounded?'

'No,' the man replied. 'I am cursed.'

The strength of his words carried across the gathered crowd. 'Cursed?' Fleance asked. 'How so? Have you unforgiven sin?'

The man chuckled. 'Probably. But that is the least of my problems.'

He was obviously the leader of the village because the crowd went quiet. Fleance inhaled deeply and squared with this man. 'What do you mean?'

'Your Majesty, we are ever your faithful servants. Long live the king!' Those gathered murmured a half-hearted mimic of the cry. 'We are an honest people,' the man continued. 'Our community is close and we look out for each other. No hen, nor goat, nor pig, nor ox is lost because we all know where such precious animals belong.

'We have lived these past ten years rebuilding our lives. We honour whichever king our good Lord gives us.' His voice trembled and he pointed towards the blackened crops. 'Why did this happen? We have done nothing to aggrieve those rebels who would seek to aggravate Your Majesty.'

'Thank you,' Fleance said. 'I am most distressed that you have been punished for someone's complaint against me and the house of Scotland.' He mounted Willow once more and sat tall in his stirrups to address the crowd. 'Know this, my friends.' There was a murmur in response to his familiarity, which pleased him. 'No one comes against my people in such a way. No one will bring down the throne of Scotland in such a way. And all Scotland's resources will be used to compensate any man, woman or child affected by this.'

The man stared him in the eye but already the king understood that his words and actions had hit their mark. 'Long live the king,' the man called. 'Long live King Fleance!' he shouted.

The villagers took up the cry and Fleance took great comfort from this support.

'We will give gold to your village leader to ensure that fair compensation is awarded. But do not give power to any man who may abuse his position.' Fleance looked at the faces of the many gathered and took heart from what he saw; he could see that they wanted the best for their community. 'Make sure this gift goes to the right people. If you do not ensure this is so, then your fall from grace is on your head, not Scotland's.'

As he nudged Willow forward, Fleance felt, right to his core, the excited buzz from the villagers. It was so satisfying to have his presence and his words make a difference to others.

South-East Scotland
Rosie

They had travelled for nearly a week. Each time they needed rest or help, it was easy to find. But now Blair and Rosie had been unable to find the remote tavern they had been told to look for after their journey through the forest. What they did find were burnt-out, charred and empty dwellings. In the rain, they peered out from the wagon at the dismal sight before them.

'I do not think we'll be getting a warm bed and belly here, then,' Blair said wryly, his words running together without the usual stutter.

All was silent save for the steady breathing of their horse. Rosie looked through the rain, out over the scarred lands and churned-up road. 'It seems the people who lived here did not give up without a fight.'

Blair nodded. 'Aye,' he said, and flicked the reins. 'We had best continue on, lass, and try as best we can to find a dry bit of shelter against this weather.'

Rosie felt a niggle of hunger. They had only the small snacks she had gathered when they left the last settlement six hours ago. Believing they would find lodgings and supplies further on, Rosie had decided not to worry about replenishing their stores. This was, in hindsight, a foolish decision. 'Do you know the parts further on, then Blair?'

'Aye, I've wandered all over Scotland before and betwixt the troubles. There are gangs of people gathered together around the coast and rivers and good hunting grounds. We may be late in finding folk to accommodate us but we will find them.'

'Late we may be,' Rosie said. 'But pray we be there before I suggest we stop, roast and eat the horse.'

Blair grinned at her. 'My thoughts exactly.' He righted himself and flicked the reins. 'Get on, my beauty, or you'll be supper for us tomorrow.'

The coastal village they arrived at was abuzz with energy and activity and boasted three large taverns – signs to Rosie that this was a prosperous part of the country.

They took a large room to continue their disguise as a married couple but Blair stayed up late to give Rosie time to retire before he himself came in and lay down on the bed he'd made near the fire.

While he was enjoying the hospitality of the tavern – not to mention the quality of the ale – Blair sent word around the villagers that he was looking for information about any suspicious persons who had recently been in the area and that he had gold as a reward for good intelligence.

The next morning, as they were having their breakfast, a young fishing lad was pushed before them. The boy pulled at his hair and attempted a mangled bow. 'We helped a foreign ship into the harbour and gave directions as to the best place to land at Perth. They were dead keen, they were, to learn the distance between the sea and the city.'

'Did they name their business in Perth?' Blair asked.

He shook his head. 'Nay, Sir. He said nothing about the reason they needed the information. Spoke right funny, they did. I understood every word but the tone was somewhat affected.'

'What do you mean?'

''Twas not Irish nor English and their clothes and weapons were strange.'

Blair frowned and scratched his head. 'They were openly armed?' The lad nodded. 'What did they want?' He asked this more of himself than the party that stood awkwardly before them.

The boy bobbed again and swallowed, his Adam's apple moving rapidly up and down. 'I reckons they was scouting, Sir, looking to get a feel for the land. They seemed to be hunting something or someone.' He blinked and looked around him, clearly unsure if he had said too much. 'I hope they weren't planning something wicked, Sir. We just answered their questions.'

Rosie saw at once that the boy was scared that he was responsible for whatever had happened with these strangers.

'What is your name?' she asked, trying to look kindly at the waif.

'Malcolm, Mistress, after the good king.'

She smiled at him. 'Thank you, Malcolm, for what you have told us. It will help in our quest.'

The boy blushed furiously, dipped his head and tapped at his forehead all the way backwards towards the door, until Blair called that he had done enough and the young man, with a grateful glance over his shoulder, fled out into the morning.

'We press on,' Blair said, wiping his mouth with the back of his hand. 'Are you all set, Rosie?'

She nodded. 'I'll gather our things while you pay the innkeeper. Oh,' she added. 'And something for the boy as promised.'

———

Two more days went by and further enquiries were met with shaking heads. No one had seen anything. No one knew anything. Rosie was weary but refused to complain. As they travelled north, she watched Blair as he urged the horse on, grateful for his patience and optimism.

They came to another town further up the coast and stopped off at the busy port to ask the same questions and offer the same reward.

To their relief, a fisherman came forward, but when he told his story their relief turned to dread. 'I had been out just a short time, but I was almost rammed by a foreign longboat. The wash fair near tipped me out but when I righted her I looked north, the direction it was heading, and I swear I saw a woman on board.'

Rosie understood how such a sight would cause fear in a man. These ships were renowned in times gone by for stealing ashore and taking women and boys as slaves. Her thoughts were confirmed when he added, 'I sailed straight back to shore to check the wife and children were safe.'

'What did you find?' Blair asked.

'All as it should be, God be praised. Perhaps I was mistaken and it was merely a lad who looked like a blonde-haired maid.'

Blair handed the man some coins and dismissed him. 'Thank you for coming forward.' To Rosie he said, 'There we go, then. We have lost the cause. She's gone from Scotland and we are in no place to pursue her.'

Rosie stroked her cheek and thought for a moment. 'We could go abroad.'

'No, lass, there is war brewing and I need to be with my king. I will find a messenger to carry this news ahead of us while I take you back to Perth. Then I must hurry to join him.'

The tears did not come but despair sat under Rosie's ribs. Flea would soon know that they had failed to bring Rachel home.

She breathed deeply and squared her shoulders. She would do whatever was needed to bring him happiness. Rosie coughed to clear the thickness from her throat and answered him, 'It seems our future queen has been captured. And our king is about to face war from a rebel force.' She swallowed and continued. 'But,' Rosie added, 'we cannot stop now.'

Blair shook his head. 'Lass, we have lost the chase.'

Rosie lifted her chin. 'Do not be so quick to give in, man.'

Flea's friend blinked and then moved forward. He reached for her hands. 'I cannot give up, Rosie. Though he is my king and commander, I also owe him my duty and my love as a brother.'

Rosie returned his grasp, 'As do I.' She said the words and believed them, but they scoured her heart. They stood there a moment, neither knowing what to do next. She squeezed his hands. 'Why are we here, Blair? We have visited almost every settlement along this coast and our reward has been only bad news and a lot of rain.'

Blair gave her a tired smile. 'I know. We should go back.'

'No,' she cried. 'We have to find out what has happened.'

'But I fear it is not safe for you, Rosie, to go on. Flea is right; Rachel is blessed. She will be alive. Like him, I feel this in my bones. She may not be happy and certainly not comfortable, but she is a strong woman.'

Rosie looked into his eyes and knew the truth of what he was saying.

'Fine,' she said. 'Let us go home. I am weary of this weather and the food. I long for warmth and good broth.'

Blair grinned but there was a trace of sorrow in his face. 'Good choice, Rosie. We are done here and deserve a familiar hearth.'

Two days later. No more news. Nothing more to bring home.

'You are tired, Rosie?' Blair said. 'I have a cousin who lives in a village about an hour west from here. We could call upon his hospitality if you would not mind sharing a bed with his three wee daughters.'

'I would be truly grateful to rest a while, but we have nothing to offer. I was planning on obtaining our evening meal at a tavern in Dunfermline. We surely cannot arrive at his home empty-handed.'

Blair pulled up the horse and the cart came to a rattling stop. The sudden silence was filled with the haunting song of the wind sweeping over the newly hoed fields, the pungent smell of rich earth coming at her on the erratic breeze.

'Aye,' he said. 'You are right.' He nodded towards a forest in the distance. 'If it please you, I will go hunt and bring my cousin a deer or boar.' He frowned. 'I do not want you to think poorly on me that I would leave a maid for a short time.'

Rosie could not help but roll her eyes and laugh. 'I will be fine, Blair. I am well able to discharge an arrow and use a dirk. Besides,' she added, looking behind her and then to the front, 'we are the only travellers on this road.'

Blair nodded and flicked the reins so the carthorse moved on. Ten minutes later, they were close to the wooded patch and he pulled up the horse, applied the brake and leapt off the cart. 'If I find nothing within the hour, I will be back and my cousin will have to forgive my lack of manners.' He attached his sword and picked up his crossbow. 'Phillip owes me anyway, Rosie,' Blair said grinning. 'When I come back, I might tell you why.'

'Go then,' she said. 'And do not be long, for I detest waiting for anything.'

She watched him jog off towards the trees and decided to get down from the cart and walk a bit. Her back ached and her feet felt numb from the hours spent travelling. The horse stood still, his tail flicking with annoyance every few moments at the bugs that sought out his warmth. Poor thing, Rosie thought. She crossed the road into a field not broken up and pulled at the long grass.

Just as she was offering it to him, she became aware of a strange humming sound. At first she thought it a horsefly but could see nothing, and then the noise seemed to reach right into her very core.

Suddenly, the horse jerked his head away and stepped back violently, the cart jerking to the left at an impossible angle. Rosie grabbed his halter but still he stepped back in agitation. 'Whoa, boy,' she said, trying her best to be calm.

Then the noise stopped and the horse stilled. Rosie looked up to see what had changed. Nothing. An unploughed field to the left and beyond it the forest where Blair was seeking a prize to bring to the home of his cousin.

The hairs on the back of her neck prickled and Rosie turned around.

There, before her, were three of the most bizarre-looking creatures she had ever laid eyes on. They were dressed in a collection of men's clothing, skins and skirts. One had filthy, wild, tangled hair. Another, though wearing a dark woollen shift and shawl, looked more like a boy with her short cropped hair. The final woman was deathly pale and was grinning at Rosie, showing a mouth that resembled a dark black hole.

Rosie swallowed with difficulty, terror rattling like small pebbles in her chest. 'Good day,' she said, her voice barely reaching her own ears.

'Hail,' cried the pale one, 'to thee, daughter of Dougal.'

Rosie gasped. 'Do I know you?'

The tall one with the shorn head lifted her chin. 'Hail to thee who holds a king's heart.'

Were they talking about Flea? 'Why are you speaking to me this way?' she hissed.

The third woman, with lashless red-rimmed eyes, put a stained black finger to her lips. 'Shhh,' she whispered and then leant close, the smell of decay and something else now filling Rosie's senses. 'Hail,' the woman continued, so quietly that Rosie was unsure if she was speaking to her or to herself. 'You shall be queen hereafter.'

'Queen? No,' Rosie cried. 'You are mad women.'

'You!' screamed a voice from the distance. 'Get gone, you hags!'

As one, the three women turned, hissing, and then set off over the field at quite a pace. Blair was incensed. 'Keep away from her!' he cried running towards the cart with two rabbits in his hands. 'Go, you. Go!'

Queen? The word hung just before her like the sun's reflected light on a puddle. Rosie blinked and looked around to see Blair behind her.

'Did they hurt you? Are you well?'

She dipped her head and wiped a finger over her eyes. 'What were they?'

'Flea will hear of this,' Blair said, his tone betraying some deep emotion. Fear? Anger? Rosie was not quite sure. 'They are witches.' He threw the rabbits and his bow onto the back of the wagon. 'They are pure evil, Rosie. Their words send people mad.'

He climbed up on the seat. Rosie gave a final look at the quickly retreating figures and then turned to take Blair's outstretched hand. She felt the strength of his grip as he pulled her up to sit beside him. Rosie arranged her skirts and then looked ahead.

'What did they say to you?' he asked as he picked up the reins.

She stared ahead. 'They knew who I was but I've never seen them before in my life.'

Blair released the brake and flicked the straps for the horse to move on. 'They may have heard what our business is.'

She chewed her lip, thinking about the other things they said. Might there yet be hope?

'Rosie,' Blair asked. 'What else did they say?'

'Nothing that made sense.' She looked over at him and smiled. 'Strange ranting. I will think no more of it.'

'No good comes from listening to their poison. This our king has told me.'

They went on in silence, and by the time Blair pulled the wagon up at the home of his cousin, she was dead tired.

⌒

Though Rosie was bone weary, the three children were less of a nuisance than Blair's cousin, who talked and talked and talked.

'So is he what they say he is?' Phillip asked once introductions and meals were attended to.

Blair blinked and looked at Rosie. 'It depends on what you say they say.'

The stout man looked keenly at them over the table. 'I have heard that he is not fit to be our king.'

Rosie, enraged at such a comment, took a bite of the dry bread on her plate and waited for Blair to answer. She was not disappointed at his response.

'You,' Blair cried, pointing his finger at his cousin, 'have no understanding of what is needed to ensure the safety of you and your family.' He put his bread back on the table and took an angry mouthful of ale. His outburst had silenced the room so that when he was ready to speak again, all were listening. 'To think that your king is less than what he is, is to invite a plague upon your family.' Phillip's wife crossed herself and then stared at her husband.

Blair continued. 'The rumours and conjectures that swirl around our country serve only to weaken it.' He looked at Rosie and shook his head. But then he sat up straight and addressed his cousin once more. 'This king is more than worthy of our allegiance.'

In the silence that followed, Rosie attempted to soften the atmosphere. 'So, Phillip,' she said. 'Blair tells me you owe him. What is that about?'

Blair's cousin scowled. 'Yes, I might be expected to owe him, but today we will not talk about this.'

This response sucked all warmth from the room. Rosie felt her face burn with embarrassment. Whatever the situation was between these cousins, it was obviously not a trifling matter. As soon as she could, she excused herself and joined the wee ones on the not uncomfortable cot provided in the back room of the cottage.

Early the next morning, the children awoke and eagerly pulled her from her bed. Although exhausted from a poor night's sleep – what with the twitching and nightmares of her bed companions – Rosie was happy enough to face a new day and continue with their journey home.

Phillip was gone and his wife excused him from the breakfast table. Blair was stoic in his response and it unsettled Rosie. What was going on here?

Nevertheless, both of them were given good provision for their return home.

Later that evening, they found a campsite of merchants whose fire and song welcomed them in. Blair took her arm. 'We are safe here, Rosie. Let us rest for a while.' He put his hand on hers. 'Forget Phillip. The man is angry and filled with a resentment no one can cure.'

'Why?'

Blair frowned. 'His story is not one that I wish to repeat. It began with Macbeth and was affected by Donalbain.' He brushed his hand over his mouth. 'I am ashamed to say that my cousin is not a faithful follower of the crown.'

They returned home along the same road they had journeyed out on. They ignored the burnt-out cottages but enjoyed the hospitality of the standing taverns so that after only a short time, it seemed, they were back at the tavern at Perth.

Blair pulled up the horse and applied the brake. 'Thank you for your company, Rosie.' He blushed and a trace of his stutter returned. 'I have . . . have most enjoyed my . . . my time with you.' The colour of his neck matched his burning cheeks. 'I believe you are a most . . . most exceptional maid.'

Rosie touched his arm. 'And I think you are an exceptional man. I understand why Flea holds you in such high regard.'

Just then, Dougal came out and saw them. 'Thank heavens you are back,' he cried, hurrying as much as his stocky frame allowed. 'You were not successful, then?' he asked.

Rosie allowed her father to help her down from the wagon. 'No, though Blair has sent some news ahead for the king.'

Dougal squinted up at Blair. 'Will you stay with us tonight, son?'

His face still scarlet, Blair shook his head. 'I must hurry to join the king. I will take lodgings at the abbey on the route back to Glamis.'

Dougal grunted. 'As you wish. Thank you for bringing my daughter safely home.'

Blair nodded, then shook the reins, and the wagon moved off.

Rosie watched him go, turning his words over in her mind, her thumb and forefinger gently rubbing the necklace Flea had given her for her last birthday. It was what she did when anxious or thoughtful. Rosie wondered at Blair's reluctance to rest a night.

The answer came to her. Of course he would want to press on and meet up with the army. He had a battle to face.

Fleance

As each new day confronted him with more evidence of the wilful damage done to the land and its people, the growing unease at what Rachel's fate might be threatened to force Fleance to abandon his current task and go and search for her himself.

But his people were suffering and Fleance could almost hear Rachel's quiet insistence that he maintain his focus on them, that he not give much mind to her troubles.

On the tenth day, around midday, a messenger came galloping after the party. A young boy leapt from his horse and bowed low before the king.

'Your news,' Fleance commanded. 'And quickly.'

The messenger lifted his head and addressed Fleance. 'Two posts, my liege, and both to grieve your heart.'

'Well?' Fleance asked, his mouth dry with fear.

''Tis certain, Sire, that the princess is not to be found in Scotland.'

Fleance let out his breath. It was not as he had feared, then – that her body had been found somewhere in a ditch.

The messenger continued. 'General Blair sends word that foreigners were seen out from the coast of the Firth of Tay.'

'Norwegians?' asked Fleance.

'Most likely.'

Fleance felt the blood beating under his suddenly hot face. He turned to Preston. 'I must go to her.'

Preston stepped up to the king. 'Your Majesty, may I suggest that the king's focus needs to remain on the activities of the rebels?'

Fleance considered his aide's words and looked out over the moor, taking in the blackened and smouldering remains throughout the area. There was nothing he could do for Rachel at this moment. If, God forbid, her death was imminent, then leaving Scotland to find her would just expose the kingdom to attack. No, he had to have faith in her to keep herself safe. Saving one at the expense of the many was not wise, no matter how dear the one was.

'We wait upon your leisure, Your Majesty.'

Fleance shook his head and addressed the messenger. 'What is the other message?'

'It is from our spies. A large gathering of men is advancing from the south. Our intelligence tells us that Magness the Mighty has enlisted a stronger army than last time – some of those who have joined him are the English.'

'Numbers?'

The young man shrugged. 'Maybe ten thousand strong and all well armed.'

Fleance chewed his bottom lip. How had Magness managed to secure such a large number of men? The last time the Scottish throne had faced Magness across the battlefield, the rebel army losses had been great, but the royal forces had also lost many men. Each time they went to battle, a fresh army had to be gathered, for many of those who joined with their king were not professional soldiers but men who worked smallholdings and had families to care for.

'We need to strike now,' Fleance said to the small group around him. 'Send out a call for willing men to help defeat this foolishness once and for all.' He turned to the messenger. 'Tell the general the king needs him and as many fellows as he can muster, armed and fit, to take up arms against the insurgents.'

'And what shall I tell him of the princess?'

Fleance thought carefully how to phrase his answer. His decision could be used against him should things turn out for the worse. 'God is with our princess and has blessed her with resilience and a quick wit and mind. Wherever she is, she will be lighting up the lives of all who are with her – even her captors. We ask that the news go out to Scotland's people that the army of Scotland must be strengthened so we can rid our country of these rebels once and for all.' He signalled to one of the pages. 'Give this fellow and his horse refreshments.'

The page bowed quickly and hurried away. Fleance turned from the messenger and walked over to Willow. There was no time to lose. They were a number of days' ride from Glamis. And each day they were not in readiness made it more likely that they would risk losing this fight.

Fleance swung up into the saddle and pulled his cloak around his legs. His horse was tired. So was he. To falter now would mean certain death. He must not show weakness. Margaret had told him that at no other time in history had a king's hold on the crown been so closely scrutinised. Only Macbeth's reign had brought as much division and discussion as Fleance's coronation had.

'Preston,' he called. 'A word.' The old man, head down, shuffled towards Fleance. 'Your advice would be much appreciated.' Preston reached up and grabbed at the rein to steady himself. From atop his horse, Fleance realised how old and fragile this man was. He must take better care of this steward. The man's strange and distant behaviour did not endear him to others, so it was Fleance's responsibility to keep the advisor in good health.

Duncan had mistrusted Preston, but that may have been because of the huge reliance Donalbain had on the man. Rachel confessed she was uncomfortable around him, but Preston had never ever behaved in a way that would be deemed inappropriate.

For the short time Fleance had known Preston, he'd seen him as efficient, discreet and mindful, it seemed, of the past as well as the future. In the absence of Duncan and Rachel, there was no one else Fleance could turn to. He stilled Willow and leant down to the old man. 'What thoughts have you on my decision?'

Preston's watery eyes stared beyond Fleance and the old man's lips twitched for a few minutes before he replied. 'Your Majesty, your decision regarding our princess, though clearly painful and distressing, is the right one. You are correct in your evaluation of the girl.'

Fleance winced at the familiarity of expression. 'Go on,' he said. 'Your thoughts?'

'She is, as you say, strong, determined and resourceful. If it please Your Majesty that I offer my opinion.' He waited again, head down.

'Yes, yes,' Fleance cried, still unused to such servitude.

'If those who have taken her intended for her to die, she would be dead and we would have found her.'

'Wise words, Preston,' he said. 'But should we return to Glamis or strike out towards a southern place to ready for the fight?'

'The king is wisely advised to take the party south and raise men for an army. Make camp and I will send word of a stronghold when one is found. We can send scouts now to find a place until you send the troops into battle.'

'Thank you, Preston. Make arrangements for our men to do this. Send a messenger to Glamis and tell Keavy and Bree the situation, but,' he held up his hand, 'make such pronouncement palatable for children.'

Preston bowed. 'Aye, my liege.'

'Good,' Fleance said. But the argument in the great hall still niggled at him. He could not afford to move in a manner likely to fuel any disquiet. Preston had to ensure the best path was taken, for the canny man seemed to know all things. 'Preston,' he whispered, leaning down along the horse's neck, 'I know that your advice might fly in the face of some who have certain expectations of Scotland's new king.'

The old man looked at Fleance directly, his eyes a watery blue. 'I care not, Sire,' was his whispered response.

Fleance sat up, gathered in his reins and addressed the party. 'Right. We must head south. Two fellows will go ahead to seek out where we will lay our heads until we come against the rebels. May God have mercy on our souls!'

The cry came back, 'May God have mercy on our souls!'

Chapter Ten

Fleance sent word out to all the villages: promises of good provisions and gold for their families in return for faithful service. Magness was keeping quiet and the royal spies fed back information about where his adoptive father was from one day to the next, but not when and where he would strike next.

The building they camped in that night was neglected and cold. The men worked hard to clear out the debris, and one soldier took a cart to a nearby village to purchase fuel, but the meagre amount he was able to buy did little to chase away the desolate and mournful atmosphere of the place.

As Fleance sat before the makeshift hearth, his heavy cloak wrapped around him, he wondered at the situation he had found himself in. A year ago, he was arguing with Miri about chores and dreaming about Rosie. Now, he was facing battle against the one who had saved him as an orphaned fugitive. In the corner of the room of this rough-hewn dwelling, someone else stirred. It was a young lad who had joined them in the last village.

'You are awake?' Fleance asked, his voice soft so as not to disturb the other men who slumbered.

The figure pulled back his hood and faced him. 'Aye, Your Majesty. I can't sleep properly. I keep having strange dreams – maybe some would even call them visions.'

Fleance thought for a moment and then looked back at him. 'If it would help, we could walk for a bit and talk about these visions of yours.'

The boy stood up quietly and Fleance followed suit. They met at the door and the boy waited to allow Fleance to go first. He pulled the door open and the two of them went out into the night. Fleance ordered the guards on duty at the entrance of the building to stay at their posts.

The stars shone brightly and the moon was near full so there was light enough for them to see the landscape before them.

It was bitterly cold. Both shrugged into their large cloaks and stepped out into the night, their boots making sharp crunching sounds as they walked across the frosty grass.

'Your Majesty?' a voice called urgently from the doorway of the shelter. It was Preston.

Fleance stopped and waited for the old man to come outside. 'I am taking a walk with this young fellow. Join us if you wish, but keep your distance as this lad and I need to talk privately. I want to hear his words alone for the time being but I have no objection to your presence.'

'Thank you, Sire.'

Fleance and the boy walked on, leaving Preston some distance behind.

Fleance was pleased to be moving and also pleased to have company. 'You say you have dreams?'

'Aye, Your Majesty. Not often but always when something important is about to happen. Except usually I only know it is important after it has happened.'

'What do you mean?'

They stopped at the end of a copse of trees and turned back towards their dwelling. Preston, keeping his distance respectfully, stopped also. 'Over the years, these dreams have been significant to my family but these last twelve months they have been more to do with you, Sire.'

The boy turned to him and, in the moonlight, his eyes were bright with fear and awe.

'Speak,' Fleance said quietly. 'What do you mean?'

The boy swallowed thickly and ducked his head in deference. 'I saw some things in my dreams last year that I discounted but now that I know your story I see that they were connected.'

'What things?'

'I'm cold, Sire. Can we keep walking?'

For a moment Fleance wondered at the wisdom of walking alone, away from his guards, just to hear this young lad's story. Yet the boy's honest manner made Fleance confident that he would be safe. 'Aye. It's cold. Let us walk.'

'Please forgive my brashness, Your Majesty.'

Fleance waved his hand. 'Information is knowledge and knowledge is power. Do not worry about offending me, but it would be a good start to know your name.'

'Begging your pardon,' the boy coughed. He cleared his throat and stood a little taller. 'My folks christened me Kenneth but everyone calls me Ken. Even as a wee boy I seemed to know things about other folk.'

'Oh?'

'I once dreamt a man would spurn his love.'

Fleance blinked. This was such an innocuous statement. How many men rejected women? But he bit his tongue. 'Aye?'

'But then I dreamt this rejection became a root which grew and grew beneath the earth and sprung up a crop of seven strong plants.'

114

Fleance shook his head.

The boy was silent as they walked back along the path. 'I am sorry that this seems strange but I can tell you of many other visions I have seen.'

Fleance stopped and turned to face the boy. 'I'd like it if you could explain that dream first.'

'It related to my father's brother. He loved a woman from another village and they were to marry and my family were all pleased that such a union was to take place. But not one week before the chosen day, my uncle sent word to his betrothed that he had changed his mind. Her family were so angry they came to our village intent on forcing the wedding to proceed. However, he got word they were coming and fled, leaving my da's family to face the music.'

'Did her father take vengeance on your family?'

'Aye, they did, Sire. They burned three crops that were ready for harvest and set fire to my grandda's cottage.'

'Did your family not go to their lord to seek recompense or even justice?' Fleance asked.

'That they did and their lord was a wise man. He asked of my da and grandda to serve in his army but gave provision for a new home to be built and enough food for one year for the family, provided they found my uncle and made him pay for what he had done.'

Fleance shook his head. 'That is a weighty penalty. Especially as your father's family was ordered to find your uncle.'

Kenneth grinned. 'This is where my dream made sense. Though all these things had happened before I was born, not one year after I'd had that vision, my uncle arrived at our home with his wife and seven sons.'

Seven strong plants.

'And each of the sons was in charge of his own fields ripe with much grain. My uncle, he begged forgiveness from my family and then went to the lord to seek mercy. I do not know exactly what happened after that but some of my cousins went into service for the lord and others stayed on in their own homes.'

'And what about your uncle's spurned betrothed?'

'She married another crofter but produced no children and died before my uncle returned.'

It was an interesting story but Fleance was not entirely sure of its importance.

Kenneth must have sensed his doubt. 'Don't you see, Your Majesty?' Kenneth cried. 'I dreamt what *had* happened and then what *would* happen to my family and it all came true.'

Fleance turned to the boy and stopped him with his hand. 'Many men can look at the horizon and make a forecast about the weather and sometimes these forecasts are accurate. When they are not, they are quickly forgotten. People only tend to remember a prediction when it comes true – forgetting all other times when the visions have been false. I'd like to believe you but, if by telling me this you're hoping to persuade me to take another course, then I'm afraid I can no longer have you in my company.'

Fleance saw the young man's face pale, and then the boy dropped to his knees and reached out his hands towards Fleance. 'Sire, it is not my intention to deceive you. My tale is not finished.'

The king grabbed the outstretched hands and pulled him up. 'Speak, then.'

The boy bobbed and wiped his face anxiously. 'Sire, before I was to leave my mam and da's cottage to serve King Duncan in his fight against the rebels, I had another dream. It was of you – though I did not know it at the time, having never heard of you nor seen you till you came to our village to raise up men for Scotland's fight. But as soon as I clapped eyes on you last week,

116

I remembered my dream and I know that it is a dream that is worth telling you now.'

Though his toes were freezing, Fleance was intrigued. 'Tell me more,' he said.

The boy chewed his bottom lip and frowned. ''Tis not good news I dreamt.'

Fleance smiled. 'The King of Scotland is well equipped to cope with all information. Speak up,' he urged.

'Aye, well, I dreamt I was in a battle but it wasn't me fighting, if you will. And I was with you, though I didn't know it was you. Then I saw a white-haired soldier, angry with you, Sire, shoot King Duncan – I recognised him – and scream at you and then gallop off. I saw the king bloodied but smiling and I didn't make sense of this because it was three weeks before the battle at Kilmarnock.' The boy wiped his mouth again and then looked to Fleance imploringly. 'I tried to send word but was dismissed as mad and,' he hung his head, 'my folks were warned to keep me locked up indoors as I was a menace and would weaken the Scottish fight. Mam and Da were so frightened the soldiers would take me away that this is exactly what they did – kept me locked up in the cottage.'

The hairs on the back of his neck stiffened and Fleance studied the boy intently.

If his words had got through to them, would it have changed anything? Would Duncan still be alive? Fleance blinked again and refocused his eyes on his young storyteller. 'You have been badly treated. I'm truly sorry for what you have suffered.'

Kenneth paused and Fleance saw his face soften in remembrance. A shadow of a smile danced over his mouth. 'My poor Da. I was an embarrassment to him, I think. Mam set me to work with women's chores and it came to be that I was the better

117

cook. I think Da was somewhat alarmed at my skill, me being a boy and all.'

Then the look vanished and he grabbed Fleance's arm. 'But Sire, the dreams have continued and I must warn you that there are dire situations about to befall Scotland.'

Preston gave a shout and began to hurry forward. Kenneth quickly removed his hold on Fleance. 'Begging your pardon, Your Majesty.'

Fleance held up his hands to both of them. 'It is all right. But Preston, join us. Young Kenneth here has news for us.' They waited in the cold for the old man to catch up and then, as a trio, began to walk again. 'What you suggest is what we know. That is why we are going to battle against the rebels. But go on with your story.'

There was a look of dread in Kenneth's eyes. 'I fear, Sire, that more heartache is to come for you.'

Fleance looked into the open face of the young man. Should he tell him about his own affliction with visions and dreams? Would a scrappy lad like this use it against him? No. There was something in the manner of this boy that rang true. He could be trusted. 'Believe it or not, like you, I have been plagued with dreams and visions for many years and I don't feel we should ever dismiss them as irrelevant. But we also can't always know the significance of what we see and dream.'

Kenneth dipped his head again. 'Your words bring me great relief. Thank you, Sire.' He paused and, lifting his head and straightening his shoulders, he continued. 'But I must tell you of my last dream.'

Something in the way Kenneth spoke just then brought on a wave of heat over Fleance's entire body. Despite feeling anxious and uncomfortable, Fleance took a deep breath and tried to appear unconcerned. 'And, what is that?' he asked, striving to keep his voice light.

'Sire, you will be exposed to the worst kind of anguish a man should ever experience.'

Fleance was silent. This boy was no more than fourteen or fifteen years of age – what could he possibly know about *the worst kind of anguish*? These were vague words at best. 'I think I am in need of something more corporeal than this. 'Tis not enough to roast a slug on.' He patted the boy's shoulder. 'But I thank you. Especially for your bravery in revealing such things which many men would dismiss as foolish flights of fancy.'

The young lad raked his hand through his hair. 'Thank you, Sire, but I have not finished.'

Fleance paused and looked back at the face of the boy. 'Oh?'

'I have seen you in a garden filled with blood-red roses and snow-white flowers. No one else was about but you and you had taken a flower of each colour and you held them to your chest. The red rose pricked you and you bled and wept but then the white rose wilted and withered away to dust and this also made you cry. I saw you holding the red rose with blood running down your fingers and I awoke in my bed crying with sorrow for what I had dreamt.'

Fleance looked over at Preston, who was staring intently at the boy, a deep frown etched in his face. Kenneth was a sincere lad, that was obvious, but he was also somewhat strange, Fleance thought, as he studied the earnest face that looked imploringly up into his. Fleance cleared his throat. 'That is a monstrous dream to have, Kenneth.'

'Aye and, to be honest, it took all my courage to come before you with such tidings.'

Fleance laid his hand gently on Kenneth's shoulder. 'I appreciate this courage, Kenneth. Many others would take the easier route by refusing to share such thoughts, especially in the face of warfare and bloodshed.'

They regarded each other some moments before Kenneth bowed his head. 'Begging your pardon, Your Majesty, these visions I have seem to be entirely connected to your fortune, though I know not how or why.'

The king looked at Preston and then back to his young companion. He knew he should not ask because it was as dangerous as asking the same of the witches, but his curiosity was aroused. 'Let us put all such things aside because we have more urgent tasks at hand. What say you? Will it go well for us against the rebels, do you think, Kenneth?'

'You are destined to go to war. Not just once but twice, and one of these will change the course of history.' He rubbed his chin and, for the first time, looked Fleance in the eye without flinching. 'If I could do anything to free myself from the plague of these visions, I would do so.' He looked furtively behind him and then faced the king. 'Your Majesty, I just want to serve my king and country. These dreams are an unwelcome distraction.'

Fleance studied the boy for a moment. 'Aye, but it seems those who control the heavens have other plans for you – and for me.'

His advisor shifted forward. 'The boy's account is fanciful but is not to be ignored.'

'Aye, but at this time of night, things seem more urgent, severe, problematic, don't you think?'

The old man nodded. 'Many a time poor decisions have been made in the early hours of the morning but it appears this lad's insights have some validity. I think we are best advised to keep him close.'

'I agree,' Fleance replied. 'But don't let any others know of his gift. Should others learn he has the sight of future things, it could go badly for him.'

'That is a wise decision, Sire,' Preston said, nodding stiffly to the young lad. 'Come with me, Kenneth.'

The boy looked anxiously at Fleance, who smiled and gestured with his head that this was a good thing. 'Are you coming in too, Your Majesty?' Kenneth asked.

This made Fleance smile further. 'Aye, it is too cold out and I am hoping to take an hour or two of sleep before this new day begins properly.'

A look of relief washed over the faces of Kenneth and Preston, and this warmed Fleance's heart. It seemed there were those who really did care about his well-being.

They all moved off. Fleance was silent as he considered what had just happened. Kenneth had suffered visions, just as Fleance had. The young lad surely had some sort of supernatural knowledge and Fleance was pleased he had chosen to share this with the right person. Him. The king.

Fleance followed the old man and the boy as they, moth-like, returned to the light and warmth of their lodgings. He thought about the dreams – his and the boy's. And those of the witches. Knowing did not necessarily mean being. Could you see into the future and learn of heartache and then in the present stop that pain from happening?

It was a tiresome and vexing question.

'If you can look into the seeds of time and tell which grain will grow and which will not, speak then of me.' This he knew his father, Banquo, demanded of the witches. Was he so courageous as to challenge such things?

As Fleance walked along the glen, Banquo's warning of the danger of trusting in visions and prophecies came to him.

'Sometimes to win us to our harm the instruments of darkness tell us truths, win us with honest trifles . . .'

121

There it was, then. Maybe Kenneth's dreams were just that – trifles; insignificant dreams which held no weight. Though the visions could be true, they were not messages to live life by.

The North Star was shining brightly near the horizon and gave Fleance pause to remember another night many years back, during his training with Magness.

Then, they had studied the stars and determined the course of their hunt, but it was in vain. Though the season was ripe and the word was that deer and boar abounded, when Magness and Fleance had travelled to the wood, nothing came by save a fox and some pheasants.

They had spent days and nights searching for the best prey but it had eluded them.

Before they headed home to Miri and her comforts, Magness had told him a story of his meeting with some other Scots. They had been unhappy with life in Scotland and the current king.

Then, Magness said, they had gathered together in a tavern just south of the Scottish border, a place where men feared for their future. Into their midst came a stocky, dark highlander with fair words and much money. He appeared unafraid of the political state of both nations and addressed them about their allegiances. '*Who might,*' the man had asked, '*be willing to challenge the state as it stands?*'

Magness told Fleance he had felt a thrill of excitement in his belly in recognising a kindred spirit – a man who loved his country but hated the way it was governed. A man who was not afraid to speak his heart despite the danger this might bring to his life.

Fleance had listened intently to his adoptive father's passionate account of the meeting. He could smell the tavern's odour; he could hear the rumblings of its guests and he could almost believe he was there beside Magness.

His tall, dark foster father looked over to him and ruffled his hair. 'Oh, Flea. How beguiled I was to trust in such simple things as truth and honesty among men.' He'd looked then to the fire and was silent for some time before he continued. 'So fresh from our hurt and pain, I willingly spoke up, believing that my companions would join with me. .

'This fellow,' Magness said, 'nodded and shook my hand but when we turned to face the others, they were silent. I said to one, "Are you not in agreement with me, Fraser?"' Magness frowned. 'The man up and left the table and spoke not a word. The others kept their heads down and were silent.'

Fleance recalled the bright light in Magness's eyes as he had gripped Fleance's arm. 'If you cannot remember anything else I tell you, boy, remember this: men use words which come easiest from their mouths. Your job is to decipher how reliable those words are.'

Fleance stared out across the field watching Preston and Kenneth enter the lodgings. That memory of Magness and his fanaticism angered Fleance.

'Damn him,' he thought. 'Damn anyone who chooses to come against us.'

He took a deep breath. 'Scotland will NOT be defeated by sedition and subterfuge. Scotland will not bow down or relent to insurgents.' His face was warm with his frustration and he could feel Duncan's calming hand upon his shoulder. *Settle, man. Take a breath. You will need it.*

'I will face this coward and defeat him and then go north to find my betrothed.' His words sounded more confident than he felt but he could not show weakness. 'Scotland must gird her loins to fight these pests who think they know what is better for the people.'

Unbidden, more words came to him: *Trust your own heart. It, alone, will ensure your hopes and dreams are kept safe.*

Chapter Eleven
A royal hunting retreat, Scotland

Two words Henri had taught him. *Déjà vu.* A repeat of something seen or dreamt. Whatever it might mean literally, for Fleance it meant facing again something he'd witnessed and participated in only a few short months ago. War against a fellow countryman.

'We do not have the numbers,' he said to his leaders. 'We lost some men last year and now we have lost more to the rebel.' Fleance did not like to name him, for that would mean acknowledging his adoptive father was leading an army against him, but he had to face the truth. 'Magness must be stopped for good.'

Ross stepped forward. 'Sire, we have from Normandy one thousand young warriors sent by their king to assist Scotland. They are not yet men, their mothers' milk scarce out of them, but not so infantile that they are useless. For three years already they have been preparing for battle.'

Fleance frowned. 'Taking babes to war is ungodly.'

The earl shook his head. 'Indeed, to their duke it is an opportunity. They train their bairns from an early age and to them, I think, this skirmish is minor.'

'Minor! Are they mad?'

'Aye, very like, but we would do well to welcome their numbers.'

What could be done? How could he use children in battle to solve an old grudge? 'Is there no other option for us?'

The ever-present Preston cleared his throat. 'Your Majesty, Scotland has lost many men these last ten years and we have little option but to agree to any assistance at this time.' The old man stepped close and lowered his voice. 'Sire, we are not in a strong position. The enemy has the upper hand. Proceed with caution.' The advisor lowered his eyes and stepped back behind the men.

Fleance looked about the room; all were waiting for his response to this latest news. So, he had a small army and an angry rebel. His betrothed was kidnapped and his place on the throne doubted by many. He had not been schooled in the art of royal engagement but he had been schooled by the very man who was coming against him.

What are you doing, Magness? Fleance reflected that, although Magness might have saved him once, his gruelling training and his single-mindedness had left a painful scar on the new king. There were very few options, but the one that seemed clear was to fight against the rebel and accept any help Scotland was offered.

'So be it,' he told the waiting lords. 'Send word that Scotland is grateful to Normandy for her generous offer of brave soldiers.'

Preston spoke urgently to one of the court messengers, who bowed deeply at Fleance. 'As my lord directs,' the man said and hurried away from the gathered crowd.

Fleance, his heart heavy and pained, watched him go, and offered up a silent prayer to heaven for the safekeeping of the lads who would soon be appearing across the seas in eager readiness for battle, unaware of what that would mean.

'How many days, then,' Ross asked, 'before we respond to the threat?'

'It depends where we will meet them,' Fleance answered.

'Upon the heath beyond Stirling Bridge, by all reports.'

His heart sank. That was six days' travel and, even if they secured the Norman contingent, there was little time to prepare. But he could not show doubt or weakness. Instead he cleared his throat and addressed the assembly. 'That place well suits the King of Scotland, and we will meet there seven days from this time.'

Fleance knew that Magness would not want to be seen as acting against the natural rules of justice and fair play. He prided himself on behaving honourably in all ways – despite questions that dogged his interpretation of what constituted honour.

———

Fleance had been fifteen when the men had burst into their secluded campsite – seven angry men from Scotland, determined to gain Magness's support for their desire to remove Malcolm from the throne. Miri, Fleance and Keavy had stayed inside the tent but they'd heard every word.

'Duncan has been immortalised but he had no more right to claim the throne than Macbeth.'

They heard Magness spit into the fire. 'Aye, but the people loved Duncan.'

A throaty voice came to them as they huddled. 'That means nought. Duncan should not so easily have taken the crown. He had no political conscience and was as ambitious as any man.'

Fleance had crept forward to look out between the flaps of the tent towards the fire. He saw dark figures standing around, many with their hands stretched out to the heat.

'That may be, but that is what our Lord has determined and any man or woman who chooses to interfere, whether it be by fair or foul means, must deal with the consequences.'

From out of the darkness a cloaked figure advanced. The other men pulled back slightly and Fleance was surprised to see his adoptive father reach for his dirk. Though he did not remove it from its sheath, Magness kept his hand on its hilt.

'This kingship is flawed and should be challenged. A day will come very soon where the line will die out and Scotland will seek another leader. Prepare yourselves for such a time.' The man tugged at the thick cloth that covered his body.

Fleance had not been able to make out the face but felt in his bones that he'd met the man before.

Magness spoke. 'If the people desire action and they are for Scotland then I am for them and will assist your cause.'

This cause had taken six years to go from idea to action, but its slow burn still created an intense fire of rage and destruction. Last spring's battle was testament to this. Scotland had stamped out the fire but, even then, Fleance knew that it had been unable to eliminate every smouldering hot spot.

The king's army marched for five days, gathering men as Fleance and the thanes rode through the villages. He had sent messengers on ahead to warn of their approach and give out the call to arms. Wagons were dispatched from a number of the castles, their cargo swords and weapons, mail and provisions. With each mile they journeyed south, Fleance's chest tightened and by the final day, he could scarcely breathe.

This was only the second time in his life he had faced war and, unlike the last, this time he knew what was coming. This time he could already hear the screams of wounded and dying men. Smell the stench of bodies ripped apart and shattered. See, in his mind's eye, the carnage of dismembered limbs and the look of a man facing death.

They arrived at the agreed camp and Fleance held up his hand to stop the procession. He urged his horse forward and then turned her around to face the soldiers, mounted and on foot, who accompanied him.

'This is our camp. It is a good place, blessed by holy men as they make their pilgrimage to Stirling. Men of Scotland, be assured that the God of our fathers and our kings is with us. We come against men misguided in their hearts and minds. They are angry and determined and are to be feared for the power their passion gives them. But we have right on our side and must defend our home and our place against these foolish warriors.

'You have heard the rumours, but your king says to you now that Fleance, son of Banquo, is God's appointed sovereign.' The men nodded and raised their swords. The gesture grabbed at his heart. He needed to instil in them a burning fury to drive back the rebels and secure Scotland's hold on its own borders. 'Know this, my men' – a murmur rippled through the army at his intimate address – 'from my youth, I have been trained for such a day as this. My father, as you know, was assassinated by the tyrant Macbeth and though I too was a target, I survived so that God's judgement could be executed.'

Fleance hesitated, mindful that there was a keen balance between telling too little and telling too much. 'I thank you for your loyalty to the crown, to God and to Scotland.'

There was a moment of silence, and then cheering and shouting erupted from the men. 'Flea-ance! Flea-ance! Flea-ance!' The noise unsettled his horse, which began to prance and shift nervously.

He pulled strongly at her mouth. 'Whoa. If you cannot cope with this, then you are no good to me in battle.' As if understanding his words, the mare shook herself violently and then stood still, raised her head and whinnied loudly. In reply other horses called back.

'Well, then,' Fleance said, patting her neck. 'It seems you also have comrades to stand beside you. And if I have your allegiance then it bodes well for Scotland.' He lifted his head to the crowd. 'Let us make camp and prepare for the fray tomorrow.'

He swung out of the saddle and stood beside the horse. A page ran up and took the reins, bowed low and took the horse away. Fleance stood there, his stomach twisting with anxiety. He rubbed his palms down the length of his breeks and sought out Preston, who seemed to be completely unaffected by the prospect that they were about to go into battle once more. 'Come, Sire. You must rest a while. Though you will not see the fight in the morning, your men need you rested.'

Fleance shook his head. 'But I must lead my army.'

It was Preston's turn to shake his head. 'You know that a king never goes into the battle on the first day. The people cannot afford to lose their sovereign. You must stay behind the troops and rally them with exhortations and prayers.'

They walked towards the group of boys who were erecting a tent in the centre of what would become their compound. 'But I must be . . .'

'What must you be, Your Majesty?'

'I cannot ask these faithful men to do that which I do not.'

The old man touched his arm and then looked away. 'You are the king and no king must put himself in the way of harm.' Preston stared at Fleance's shoulder. 'This is what they expect.'

'Then that is a waste,' he exclaimed. 'I am an excellent marksman. I know Magness. I can hunt him down and capture him. I know him better than any other living soul.'

'Aye, but there is more at stake here than you know.'

A sudden chill swept up Fleance's back. 'What do you mean?'

Preston now studied his feet, which twitched and scuffed the ground. 'I mean to say that our sources tell us that witchcraft has been used to help the rebel's cause.'

Fleance shook his head in disbelief. 'No. I don't believe it. Magness would never use the dark agents. He hated such meddling and those who sought out their prophecies. Your sources must be wrong.'

'That may be the case with the rebel leader, Sire, but there are other powers at work here too.'

Fleance moved towards Preston and placed his hand under the advisor's chin. Preston looked up and swallowed. 'Preston, as your king, I command you to tell me all that you know.' Fleance spoke quietly but his tone registered with the other man. 'I cannot rule Scotland when my advisor knows more than I.'

'I only desire to serve and protect you, Sire.'

'Not enough! Tell me all or I will send you back to Glamis to be nursemaid to Bree.'

Preston's face lost all colour and, in a rare moment, he looked Fleance in the eye. 'As you wish.' The advisor cleared his throat and rubbed his forehead. It was some moments before he spoke. 'Ah, though you have banished witchcraft, it continues.'

This confirmed a suspicion Fleance had harboured for months – the strange stone monuments randomly placed around the countryside: was there a connection between them and witchcraft?

'And,' Preston continued, 'it seems there is more demand for these sisters.'

'What does that mean?'

'More than just common folk have sought their counsel and this past year I have heard rumours that some of the nobility have given gold for their insights.'

He shook his head. 'Who?'

'No names were offered up but there has been talk overheard in taverns and at the ports.'

Fleance sighed. 'It is not something that can be resolved now. Later we will consider such news. For my part I care little for fools who seek out advice from black-hearted women. We should not set much store in such things.' He made to leave. 'We will ignore the gossip.'

Preston sucked his teeth. 'Sire, it is unwise to do so. The people do take notice of the mutterings and these have affected the mood of the nation. The rumours have spread throughout the country. Every man you see before you will have a mother or a wife who has heard the tales and will pour these into the ears of their men. I advise you that to ignore such things is perilous.'

Fleance was silent. This was worse than he had anticipated. Not only did he have to face the man who had saved his life as a child on a battlefield, but he must also cope with the thoughts and opinions of a misinformed populace.

He looked at the old man, whose head was bowed once again. 'Preston,' Fleance said, taking a deep breath. 'I think your counsel is wise. Let's proceed with our plans for defeating the rebel forces and I will think on what to do in the future about these other matters. This madness is obviously more entrenched than I thought and it will take skill and perseverance to root it out completely. '

The old man dipped his head and then, looking intently at Fleance's left shoulder, declared, 'Your Majesty is ever in God's hand.' He turned then and walked away, his gait awkward and stiff, and for the briefest of moments, Fleance felt sadness for the man. A very lonely role to own, he thought, but one that Preston fulfilled without complaint.

Within the hour, his lodgings had been completed and Fleance, knowing that his horse was safe and well, entered his tent. The canvas hung low and the air within it was cold, but torches were strapped to the three poles that kept the dwelling upright. The moon was high and he had looked forward to retreating into his bed. That was not to be, however, for Blair had returned from his scouting and, though it was good to see him, he had nothing to add to the message Fleance had received days before: Rachel was gone from Scotland.

'It's as in my post to you, Flea,' he said. 'We thought we might find her in Scotland or England but we've found men who swear to having seen a blonde woman on board a foreign ship. I have to say I fear Rachel is no longer within our reach.'

Fleance looked around the makeshift dwelling as he tried to order his thoughts: relief that Blair was here, grief that Rachel was not found and the unspoken question of Rosie's part in all this.

He rubbed cold fingers over his face a moment, welcoming the pleasure of action, knowing it would ease the tense muscles on the side of his head. 'This is a nightmare.'

'Aye.'

'Damn it to hell. They say bad news comes in threes – and I have four to contend with: Rachel gone, rebels terrorising the countryside, a battle and . . .' But he could not say the last, for it was pointless. Instead, he raised his head and looked at his friend. 'Is Rosie well?'

'Your maid is an honourable woman,' Blair began. The possessive pronoun was a jolt and Fleance looked up sharply. His friend continued, smiling. 'I wish I had what you have to bewitch such maids. Then I would have the best wife in the entire world.'

Such opinions were ill-placed and Fleance frowned. 'I mean for you to tell me if the girl is safe, not give me your opinion on her virtues.'

Blair blushed furiously and dipped his head. 'Please forgive my boldness, Your Majesty. I meant no offence. Rosie is back with her parents. Safe but weary, and sad that we could not bring better news.'

Fleance nodded and let out the breath he had been holding. 'There is much to do, Blair.' Suddenly a ruddy-faced soldier burst through the tent's flaps. 'Beg your pardon, Majesty, but we have received a message from one of the scouts that the enemy is moving towards the heath.'

Blair and Fleance looked at each other and Fleance took a deep breath. 'It seems tomorrow we will be at war once more, my friend.'

The next morning, before sunrise, Fleance left his tent and watched as the swiftly moving mist advanced up the valley, muffling the sound of the birds' morning chorus and covering everything in a grey shroud.

His heart fell. Within an hour, he knew, they would be engulfed by the thick grey fog – an unwelcome presence that soaked into every fibre.

Ross appeared at his side and sniffed. 'We're not likely to be effective with this,' he said, spitting into the scrub. 'But neither is he.'

The king nodded. 'This will do little to inspire our men.'

'Don't worry, Your Majesty. Those who serve you love Scotland. And you,' Ross added.

Fleance did not miss the order of the comment. Still, it was to be expected. He was newly king and attended by much speculation, despite proving himself in battle. He tucked his shirt into his breeks and straightened his outer cloak on his body. 'Make the men ready, nonetheless. As soon as this damned fog lifts, we will advance. We know Magness is less than two miles from us.' In fact, in the still of the morning, the sounds of the unseen enemy camp were as distinct as their own: the murmuring of conversation, the noise of the horses, the clank of armour.

Ross bowed. 'As you wish. I will personally go among the men and make sure they're ready.'

What would Duncan have done? Fleance thought. *Would he have been ready to face the man who had brought him up as his own?* Aye, he would have and he would have expected the same from Fleance.

Honour. Such a powerful and loaded word. Because of this word he had abandoned Rosie. Because of this word, he had agreed to marry Rachel. Because of this word, he was about to go against someone who had lost everything – simply because he had lived an honourable life.

He rubbed the back of his neck as he looked around the camp. These were good, good men. Great men. Suddenly his heart was filled with such a feeling of thankfulness that his throat tightened and he coughed with the unexpectedness of it.

It is not about me, Fleance thought, the realisation suddenly lifting the weight of responsibility from his shoulders. He would fight this battle for Scotland, for his father, for Duncan, and for Rachel.

He watched his men preparing for war, going about their tasks with determination. They trusted him and his command as did those closest to him. Yes, from this moment on he would look at himself through *their* eyes and see what *they* saw: a skilled marksman, a man of honour. Their rightful king.

As he tightened the laces on his boots, the fog began to lift as suddenly as it had arrived. Within minutes the way was clear and shortly afterwards, Fleance gave the order for the horn to sound.

Scotland was, once again, at war.

Chapter Twelve
Norway
Rachel

Something had changed. There was an uneasiness, an anxiousness about the place. The men were shouting and the women were silent. Despite her lowly place in the dungeons of the castle, Rachel knew something had happened. Something had gone wrong. Or would soon go wrong.

She stood up, despite the blinding headache that had plagued her for days and, gritting her teeth, looked through the bars down the long dark corridor, waiting for someone to explain.

She was not disappointed. And, in fact, was delighted to see Sven striding through the cavernous tunnel towards her cell. '*Hun*,' he barked, pointing at her, and the guard grappled with his keys before loading the correct one into the lock. The jailer went in and quickly locked the bars behind him, ignoring the pleading cries and supplications of the other prisoners.

'*Kom*,' he said, and she understood directly so pushed herself away from the wall and followed him.

Sven smiled at her and, despite herself, she smiled back. Her prison guard, clearly not happy with such communication, thumped her with some force between the shoulder blades.

God forgive him, she prayed. *He knows no other way but violence.*

At a pace she could barely match, they moved away from the cries of the other prisoners and out of the castle to the wagon that was waiting by the castle wall. It was filled with crates, and two of the priests she'd seen in the castle infirmary were sitting awkwardly against the rail. Sven jutted his chin and uttered something she did not catch, but she understood by his body language that she should join them.

The men eyed her warily and, though she smiled and nodded in greeting, they looked uneasily at each other and shifted their bodies away from her. Still, she was outside and a joy settled over her despite the uncertainty of what was happening. The wagon moved off, Sven riding alongside on a great white horse with distinctive sooty ears.

Despite being late spring, it was cold, and a biting wind came at them with such aggression that Rachel shivered from the blast. However, even this did little to dampen her spirits. She was in the open and revelled in the sights and sounds of this foreign country. Much like Scotland, the land was desolate and rugged, but more populated than her home. They passed many established villages filled with squat, rough-hewn lodgings. These places were bleak and looked inhospitable, their occupants silent as the wagon passed through. *Where are the men?* Rachel thought, her gaze fixed on a dirty wee boy kicking his companion. *I see only women, old men and children.*

'Of course,' she said under her breath. 'They have been conscripted into Norway's army.' *Calum is at war and,* she thought, looking at her two companions on the wagon's tray, *I am to be pressed into service also.* In the back of her mind she wondered who Calum's enemy was.

———

Despite the cold, Rachel was excited at the possibilities that now lay before her. There was work to do. The sight of rudely erected dwellings and the scurrying of people told her that this was the place to bring the wounded.

There was much tension in the air. The priests must have sensed it too, for they sat more upright and regarded their surroundings keenly. Eventually, the horses took them to a long wooden dwelling – tiny by Scotland's standards, but enough to house and protect those inside.

Sven leapt off his horse and offered his hand. Rachel took it and smiled at him and was delighted at the blush that crept up her captor's neck.

Rachel saw the priests lumber off the wagon and trudge towards the makeshift hospital, not even giving her a backwards glance. She hesitated a moment and then, with Sven beside her, followed them.

She was taken to the storehouse and among the food supplies was an area set up with herbs, dried and living plants, bowls of grease and buckets of ground substances – many she did not recognise by sight or smell. A monk approached her and put his hand to her head. She thought she was receiving a blessing and began to kneel, but then he grunted and she looked up. Between his thumb and forefinger was a very fat, very wriggly louse.

This explained the terrible irritation she had been experiencing this past week. Lice. She still had lice, despite her efforts to ensure she was free from the infestation. The monk pulled the hood of his garment over his head and stepped back. This was understandable.

Lice meant disease and illness and often death. She could not work in the infirmary with such an infestation.

Back home, she and Morag treated the afflicted with a reliable mixture of kitchen ash and bacon fat. If she could only make this paste up now, she would be ready soon enough to serve.

However, her companion had other ideas. He picked up a bucket of white powder and another filled with brackish-looking vegetation and went out. Rachel followed him, scratching the back of her neck and trying hard not to be overcome with disgust that, though her hair had been cropped, it still housed the biting, squirming beasties.

They stood beside a barrel of water and the monk took some of the white powder and an equal measure of the dried plant, which he spent some time grinding with a pestle so that it became as refined as the white substance. To this, he added careful handfuls of water as he stirred. Within no time at all, the contents of the wooden bowl were a thick, goopy paste. This, it seemed from the gestures of the monk, was to be applied liberally to her head.

She nodded, took the bowl and knelt down.

With two hands, Rachel scooped up half of the bowl's contents and smeared it over the back of her head and neck, running her fingers through her cropped hair until the back and sides of her scalp were covered. Then she took some more and plopped it on top of her head, massaging it down either side. The smell made her eyes sting and her flesh tingle. She was certain that the living creatures on her head were rebelling and flailing about as they were affected.

The monk squatted beside her, praying. Once Rachel had finished applying the paste, he got up, took the bowl and went back into the longhouse, returning with a fine-toothed comb. He handed it to her. It was almost identical to the ones she and Morag used, and Rachel understood what she must do.

She stood up and looked about for a cloth. He had, it seemed, anticipated such a need, and gave her a clean but stained garment. It would receive the lice and their eggs.

With her eyes smarting and her scalp burning, Rachel began the tedious task of scraping the comb across her scalp. Each tug yielded a thick mass of paste, wriggling lice and clusters of eggs. Over and over she pulled the comb through her short, cropped hair. Sometimes up from the back of her neck, sometimes from her forehead. Each time, lice and eggs and paste were wedged between the teeth.

Only when the comb repeatedly came back with paste alone did she stop. Her arm ached and her nose ran. The monk, steadfast in his attendance, then brought her sweet-smelling soap and a bucket of fresh water.

Rachel dipped her head into the cool water and rubbed the soap over her head and neck. Her fingers scratched over her scalp and even though she had worked tirelessly to remove the lice, the bucket contained many more.

She threw the contents of the bucket out and handed it back to the monk. He hurried off and came back with a fresh bucket and a looking glass, which warmed her heart. Not since Forres had she had a chance to see herself.

After a final wash in the cold water Rachel could see that no lice remained. She took a towel to dry her hair and was rewarded again with the mirror.

Cropped short, her hair was darker. The unevenness of it made her look like Duncan before Morag had cut his mane. Rachel put her hands to her mouth to stop herself from crying out. *This was not the time to think and remember such sadness*, she thought. *Be strong.*

It was only an hour before Rachel was in control of the wounded who trickled in from the sea and wide beaches where, it seemed, most of the battle was being fought. They were taken to one of two places: to be attended to by Rachel and the scrubby boys assigned to her or, if they were more seriously injured, to an adjacent compound to be attended to by the priests and surgeons.

For days she tended men who had horrific injuries to head, neck, sides or legs – deep, bleeding wounds. Men with belly injuries, though often conscious and crying out in pain, would soon join their brothers over with the priests, for there was little that could be done for them. These men were soon joined by those whose gaping wounds had been too long exposed and for whom infection had begun to set in. For some, their exposure to the elements had left little hope of survival.

The wagons waited dissolutely some way off to transport the dead to the pyres.

Rachel worked methodically and it seemed unnecessary that she speak the language of the soldiers. Her calm, steady touch and soft voice worked on their nerves as her balm did on a wound. Although Sven would not speak her language, he understood her commands and needs. Mostly this was to do with dressings or holding bowls as she applied wine to minor cuts and grazes.

That first day did not end for her until well into the evening. No new men had been brought in for three hours and those in their care were as comfortable as she could make them, though the smell of blood and human waste filled the building.

She was in desperate need of some fresh air, so went up to her jailer and tugged his arm. 'Sven,' she said. 'I need fresh air and to rest.' She pointed to the exit. 'Please.'

Sven looked over at the restless bodies, the low light flickering over their painful wounds, and then glanced out into the black night. He nodded and took her arm, his hand so thick and calloused that it scraped the skin above her elbow.

He led her out but his grip was not tight. 'Thank you,' she said and smiled up at him. He frowned down at her and looked away over the land with its sputtering lights and fires and the calls of sentries.

Though she was not certain he would fully understand her, Rachel talked to him anyway. 'Only a few months ago, Sven, I was doing the same I am doing now.' Her guard looked down at her and shook his head, shrugging his shoulders. She moved towards him and took his hand. 'War destroys every side, Sven. There are none who are simply right or wrong. Just the dead and wounded.'

He was uncomfortable with her closeness, but she sensed he appreciated her compassion as he squeezed her hand before dropping it to the side.

The fresh air was helping, though she was exhausted. Unlike when she had worked as a healer during the battle Duncan had waged against Magness, here she could not choose when to take a break. Now she needed her guard to give permission for her to rest.

'I am tired Sven. I need to eat and sleep. Please.'

She looked up at her jailer and immediately saw his alarm. He straightened his shoulders and roughly turned back towards the longhouse. She turned as well and instantly saw the reason for Sven's agitation. There, standing between them and the wounded, was Calum.

'So, Princess,' the king said, coming out of the shadows. 'You have, it seems, political skills to add to your many attributes. Oh,' he added, shrugging on his cloak, 'I do thank you for your ministrations to my men.'

She stepped forward. 'Calum—'

He held up his hand and both Sven and Rachel stopped dead. He barked something in his own tongue. Sven bowed stiffly and hurried away, back into the hospital. Calum stood in front of her, a tall, imposing figure. His face was unreadable in the dim light of the torches. 'I see you think to tell my people how they should live, Rachel.'

Despite her exhaustion, Calum's presence spurred something deep within her. She shook her head. 'It is my truth,' she answered. 'And that, I think, of many who are exhausted by the destruction caused by man's lust for power and wealth.'

He stepped back and looked her up and down. 'It seems, despite my best efforts, I have only changed the outer image. The inner core is untouched.'

'What do you mean?'

'I mean you remain the person you were before my men took you. You seem unaffected by your lowly position. You behave as if you were still a Scottish princess, betrothed to the king and not my prisoner.'

'I am a Scottish princess, betrothed to the king,' she said, surprised at the sudden tremor in her voice. 'I think you have underestimated me, Calum.'

He grunted. 'Not just a healer, I see, clearly.' He came close and tugged at her rough smock. 'You are a political animal hidden in a woman's form. I need to keep an eye on you.' He wiped his mouth and turned to leave.

'Wait!' Rachel cried. 'Calum. What do you want from me? Surely you did not bring me all this way to attend to your wounded?'

'You stupid woman,' he snarled. 'You have no idea what those of us who have to work with the political machinations of our lands put up with.' Calum spat. 'You are a healer. And we here thank the gods for that. But your place in history will be nothing more than a forgotten scandal. It is not you I want as such but your king and with you being here, he will come, fool boy that he is.'

It was a slap in the face. 'This is not so. It is you who are a fool to think so little of Fleance,' she said. Her insolence garnered the expected result. Calum stepped forward and hit her hard against the side of her head. It was sudden and the power of it dropped her to the ground. A blinding pain and white light filled her head before she lost consciousness.

She woke in a dark place. But at least there were no ropes around her wrists or ankles and the straw smelled clean and fresh. Rachel sat up, but her head pounded. Her throat burned with thirst and she spied a bucket, the water reflecting the glimmering light of the moon outside her cell. She crawled over to it and drank down the fresh, cold liquid. After a few moments she sat back down and looked about her. The sounds of the wounded came to her through the small casement. So, she had not been taken back to the castle.

Rachel sat against the wall and sent a quick prayer of thanks heavenwards. She was alive and, apart from the ache in her head, well. Surely the new day would bring a better outcome.

She was given a breakfast of gruel that was hot and clear of infestation. Rachel breathed deeply in relief. Clean gruel would give her strength. After giving thanks, she ate her portion and waited.

It was not long before Sven stood before her cell and beckoned her forward.

'I am sent to bring you to the infirmary,' he said quietly.

At first the shock of hearing her own tongue silenced her. Then she smiled. 'I thought you spoke my language.'

The Norwegian nodded. 'Yes, and many others. Now, come,' he ordered, unlocking the door. 'The battle began early and there is already a fresh wave of injured. You are needed.'

Rachel followed him, somewhat stunned, but also exhilarated by this new turn of circumstances. There were now two people who could understand her: the perpetrator of her kidnap and her jailer.

———⌣———

The sounds of fighting reached Rachel before she even arrived at the makeshift hospital.

There was a monstrous battle being waged on a beach close by. Many young men who were brought forward were taken directly to the priests' enclosure.

Shouts accosted Rachel's ears. A young ensign, deployed with the ships, had fallen into the sea but had been pulled from the water, not breathing. By good fortune, the rough handling of the seamen had got him breathing again, but his way of lying on the cot worried her.

She knelt beside him and put her hand on his cold face. He was alive but only just. Beside him three fellows jabbered on and gesticulated to Sven.

She looked to him, hoping for some help.

But Sven just shrugged. 'He is a favourite.'

It is too late, Rachel thought. She looked him over: blue lips. Been in the sea too long. He was breathing but he was not responding.

She checked him over and reached inside his ears. Dead cold.

Oh dear God, she whispered under her breath. He was on the very edge of death.

Just then, a howling whine split through their concentration. They all turned to see a huge, shaggy dog sniffing the air and whimpering. Again, the men spoke rapidly and Sven translated. 'This belongs to the boy. His constant companion.'

'The dog,' she said, more to herself than the men. 'Here, boy,' she called. The shaggy animal ducked down its head and flattened its ears but came forward hesitantly. Rachel patted the bed. 'Come on,' she called, in a light voice. 'Up! Up!' And then, as the large beast leapt onto the cot, Rachel pulled him close to the body of his master.

Shouts of protest filled the tent but Sven and Rachel were silent as the thick-haired hound settled himself next to the young man.

A priest grabbed her arm and pulled her away from the boy. She could not understand his angry words. 'Tell him,' she said to Sven. 'The animal's warmth will warm the boy and he will recover.' Sven communicated her statement and everyone murmured, some as if they were surprised, others doubtful. 'Unless of course,' she added, smiling, 'they would like to take the place of the dog?'

Sven relayed this and, after a moment of silence, the boy's companions roared with laughter. Rachel gathered up a sheet and tucked it around the young man and the dog.

Sven, who stood just behind Rachel, patted her gently on the shoulder. This small yet intimate gesture startled her and she straightened her shoulders and looked around at him, frowning slightly. He must have realised his error, for he blushed. 'I am sorry, Princess, for being so . . .' he hesitated, searching for the word.

'Forward?' she suggested with a smile.

He dipped his head. 'Indeed.'

'I am guessing it was a spontaneous response to a feeling of pride in a job well executed,' she said.

'It was that exactly,' he replied, his face still red with his shame.

Days passed. Rachel was constantly weary. Her back ached and a dull pain thumped in her skull. The smell from the fires found her everywhere. It was the companion smell to death. Calum's army was being battered and the casualty rate was high. He occasionally came into the infirmary to check on the men, but she wondered if he was there to ensure there were no deserters rather than out of concern for their well-being.

By the week's end, a high-ranking official had taken Sven away.

He had been helping her turn a thick-set man so that she could dress the wound on his back, when the general came in, pointing to a number of the younger or older men who had been working with the injured. When he spotted Sven, his eyes widened and he spoke sternly and rapidly to the guard. Sven responded and pointed at her and, for a few minutes, there was a heated exchange.

The leader barked something that sounded much like a command, and with a heavy sigh, Sven turned his back on her and followed the others out of the longhouse.

Now what was she supposed to do with all these wounded men and no help? Perhaps she could ask the priests to send some women to aid her?

Rachel looked about the cots to check that no one needed her urgently and hurried to the other side of the camp. Another wagon was hitched to a lone horse, its cargo box filled with the death of life and dreams. Even in the cold air the bloody corpses had begun to decay.

She pulled her apron over her nose and mouth and went searching for someone to help the living. The inside of this building, where the very badly wounded and dying were cared for, was gloomy and the smell was worse than in her infirmary. Men cried and screamed or just lay still, their life seeping out of whichever wound they had. The monks, by the look of their drawn faces, had enjoyed little sleep and were systematically moving from cot to cot offering the prayer for the dead.

Should this be a place for me? she thought, as she studied the grim expressions of the cloaked men. Though she had tended the hurt and injured for a long time, it was always with other women as well. This seemed a place reserved only for men – a place where their very souls were being extracted and their bravado and strength taken. Not a thing, she thought, any man would want a woman to witness.

Just then, as if reading her thoughts, one of the monks came up to her and, taking her by the arm, led her outside and away from the sight of the wagon.

In Latin, he spoke to her, *'What are you doing here?'*

'All my helpers have been taken. I am alone with the wounded,' she answered him. *'I came because I needed help.'*

He nodded. *'They took our assistants too, and there is much work to be done.'*

'Can you not spare just one to help?'

He looked thoughtful for a moment, clearly thinking of their joint plight. *'Perhaps if you could help us, we could help you,'* he suggested.

Rachel was startled by this. They had been so antagonistic to her presence before. Perhaps the magnitude of their job was taking its toll. The dead, it seemed, required more work than the living.

She dipped her head. *'I could assist with the final preparation of the bodies.'* His eyes lit up and he nodded. *'This takes time,'* she said, *'but it is a ritual I am familiar with. And I need strong hands to lift bodies and hold men who are in pain and are receiving medicinal assistance.'*

'Wait here,' he said and returned inside. Moments later he was back. *'It is agreed that I will assist you with your work and you will*

spend the rest of the time with our dying.' She swayed with relief and the young monk caught her. *'Are you not well, Sister?'*

'I am tired, that is all.'

A cry from the infirmary caught her attention and she pulled away, lifting her rude garment above her knees so that she could run. When she entered the ward, she was immediately over-whelmed by the smell of fresh blood, its pungent, metallic stench hitting her nostrils.

Down at the end of one row, an older soldier who had lost his leg in battle was thrashing against the stays that she had fashioned earlier to keep him from touching his stump. But the bandages were not as efficient as she had hoped and had worked loose. Blood poured out of the poor man's severed leg.

Rachel rushed to his bedside and grabbed the drab fabric that covered him. She quickly twisted it and wrapped it around his thigh and pulled tight. It was not enough; blood continued to flow from the place she had cut. Looking around, she saw crumpled clothes on the floor and scooped them up, stuffing them at the base of the amputation. He screamed again. 'Sorry,' she cried, hands rapidly stuffing wadding against the flow of blood. Her attempts at restrict-ing the flow seemed to be futile. If only there was another set of hands to help.

She called out. 'Please help.'

Her hands were bloodied but now her patient had stopped screaming and lay whimpering as he looked at her, his eyes taking on the look of a dead man.

'No,' she said. 'You will be all right.' Frantically she kept trying to push wads of cloth into the wound, but it was no use. The bleed-ing continued.

Just then, the young monk burst through the door and came to her side.

'*What can I do?*'

'Pull this tighter,' she said in English. 'It will help to stem the flow of blood.' He seemed to understand what she wanted and tugged hard on the binding. But even as he did this, Rachel's heart told her the man was not to be saved. The monk did as he was instructed, which freed her hands to try to staunch the bleeding, but it was going to be too late. Despite their best efforts, light faded from the soldier's eyes and he became still. Rachel slapped him but even her blows did not discolour his cheeks.

She put her head to his chest, praying she would hear the steady thud of a heartbeat, but there was nothing but silence. His chest did not rise. His breath did not come. He was dead.

Rachel stood back, her heart hurting from the failure to save this soldier. If only she had not left the infirmary. Then she would have been alerted to his predicament earlier.

By instinct, she began to pray, the Latin prayer she had learnt as a child:

> Go forth, Christian soul, from this world
> in the name of God the almighty Father,
> who created you,
> in the name of Jesus Christ, the Son of the living God,
> who suffered for you,
> in the name of the Holy Spirit,
> who was poured out upon you,
> Go forth, faithful Christian!
> May you live in peace this day,
> may your home be with God in Zion,
> with Mary, the virgin Mother of God,
> with Joseph, and all the angels and saints . . .
> May you return to your Creator
> who formed you from the dust of the earth.

May holy Mary, the angels, and all the saints
come to meet you as you go forth from this life . . .
May you see your Redeemer face to face.

There was a moment of utter silence in the ward as if every man there was listening to her. '*Amen*,' she added.

'*Amen*,' the monk responded in a quiet voice. He studied her closely. '*I had heard you were a sorceress and could save men from death*.'

Rachel laughed. '*Then you heard wrong. God has gifted me with healing and knowledge and I have been blessed to have learnt much so far in my life*.' She began to prepare the body, her hands working quickly and silently as she gathered up the soiled bandages and bedding. '*But I have known this since I was a small child: though I may pray otherwise and do my very best, I cannot save everyone*.' Rachel pulled away the tie around the dead man's thigh and picked up the bloodied and useless clothes that had failed to keep the life in his body.

'*Sometimes, even if you are the best person in the situation, it is not enough*,' the monk said.

Rachel reached over and stroked the dead man's cheek. She closed his eyelids and pulled the sheet up over his face. 'Well,' she said in her own tongue, 'here is one more poor man who is at peace, at last.'

Chapter Thirteen
Norway

Finally, Rachel took herself to bed in the small cell lined with straw and coarse blankets. With Sven gone from her side, she had no one to direct her, but it didn't matter. Right now she had to help to save the wounded. The young monk had agreed to watch during the night and promised to wake her should he be concerned. For this she was grateful.

But her sleep was fractured. Her dreams were filled with images of soldiers and their wounds; of trying to escape down a black tunnel, its walls cold and wet, and her flight never-ending; of escaping capture, pursued by a menace much more deadly than anything human.

She awoke then, heart racing, and crossed herself, asking God for protection. A peace finally settled over her and she fell into a deep sleep. Towards morning, however, there came another dream and one so clear and vivid that she would later think of it as a vision.

She found herself alone on the heath, the rain swirling around her. She was drenched and hungry and looking all over for some place to shelter. Peering through the driving rain, she spied a crop of strangely formed rocks. Perhaps here, *she thought in her dream state*, I might find refuge.

It was a relief to no longer have the constant rain on her face. The stones were high and robust and offered relief from the weather. And, surprisingly, they were warm to lean against. Rachel had no sooner rested in that spot than she was visited by three women.

Their faces were indistinguishable, but there was something about them that made her heart race. Perhaps she had been safer out on the heath.

Though Rachel tried to wake, something sinister seemed to be holding her in place.

The women crowded around, smiling and stroking her, cold, dry fingers raking down her face and body. She instinctively knew they meant danger and death. The idea of it hung low around the corners of her mind. Bad, bad, bad. But powerful. Someone whispered. 'True,' she heard. ''Tis true!' With urgency. 'We know. We know everything.'

'So like her father,' said one.

'And her brother,' said the other.

'And husband to be.'

There was nothing alarming about these comments, but they filled her heart with fire. She was unable to speak and suddenly the rain stopped. In the sudden silence all three women stood looking at her.

'Pity,' said one.

'Aye,' said the other.

'A waste,' said the third.

Shouts woke her from her nightmare and Rachel pushed herself up off the straw, feeling more exhausted than when she had first lain down. The words *pity* and *waste* echoed in her head as she pushed her hands through her cropped hair then stretched them out before her.

There.

Bloodied nails.

Rachel wavered. *I have these nails because I have saved lives.* But in her head she wondered about dreams and possibilities. It was too complicated. She prayed quickly, asking God to help her to be ready for the day, whatever that might bring. But remnants of the dream lingered in the corners of her mind.

Sven, her guard, might have gone, but Rachel remained. She knew enough about Calum to know that he would not forget about her. It seemed she was simply one more pawn in some bizarre game he was playing. It angered her to think that she had to sit idly by, waiting for Fleance to walk into the trap Calum had set for him.

The death of the soldier the day before had upset her. She had told him it would be all right, that she knew it would be all right. But it wasn't, and too soon she was helping the monk take the body to the cart that took the bodies to the funeral pyre.

It was just hours later that Sven was brought in. His thick, strong torso was awash with a sea of sweat. Rachel could not get him to focus and searched desperately over his body for the cause.

He had been in a sea battle; this was clear from his drenched clothes and hair. She pulled away the garments, looking for the reason for his fever, and was aghast to see a searing red mark on his chest.

Sven had been stung by a poisonous sea creature. The angry puncture wounds stood proud in defiance; ugly red and purple marks shadowed these festering holes.

She needed to counter the poison that would be charging through his body. The only other time Rachel had been privy to such a situation had been when she was nine.

She and Duncan had been out hunting with the boy who tended the chickens. They pretended to stalk and hunt prey but were only young. Suddenly, the boy cried out in pain and fell, grabbing his foot. Duncan, bigger and stronger than she, threw his arms around the boy's chest and yelled for her to take up his legs. Together, ungainly, desperate, they carried him to the castle.

When they arrived, the old cook lifted the boy from Duncan's arms and took him into the kitchen. Her brother, it seemed, felt the matter dealt with, but Rachel followed the old woman into the depths of the house.

The boy was laid on a workbench and the woman, without hesitation, took her knife and cut out the surrounding area of poison. Then she pressed cloth into the wound and demanded those beside her come forth with a poultice. Within moments this was provided and pressed into the gouged-out flesh of the young boy.

He had lived. And he had lived with a horrific scar, which he proudly showed others although, from that day on, he had never again ventured out in bare feet and had kept a respectable distance from anything resembling a snake, no matter its size.

Rachel wanted to be just like this old woman. To save lives even if it meant scars, for what were physical scars compared to death?

Sven grabbed her hand. 'Are you well, Princess?

His question tore at her heart. 'Aye. I am well but you are not.'

'Better now that you are caring for me.'

Compassion flooded through her. 'Sven, to help you means to hurt you. Perhaps more than a man can bear.'

He shook his head. 'To shake the hand of life is a better thing than to welcome the embrace of death. Do what you must to save me.'

Rachel looked around her. So many injured, and only she and the young monk to help.

She leant forward to his ear. 'I have to do something not seen as appropriate.'

Sven grunted. 'I want you to do whatever is necessary to keep me alive.'

'*Get me some wine,*' she called out in Latin to the young monk.

Rachel bowed her head and then pressed her mouth over Sven's wound, sucking as hard as she could without gagging. The smell of him was overwhelming and she tried not to throw up but failed. Abruptly Rachel turned her head and vomited onto the ground.

The young monk was at her side. Quietly, in Latin, he said, '*If you do it again, then our brother here will be saved.*'

She lifted her head. A hand was offered, which she took. She stood up. 'I am sorry, Sven,' she said, 'for my indelicate stomach.'

Sven sneezed, but it turned into an awful cough.

'*Do what you have to do,*' the monk said.

Rachel took the proffered knife and stood over Sven. 'Forgive me,' she said, then plunged the blade into his chest to remove the poisoned flesh.

For her, it was the smell of his blood she was conscious of, but for others it might have been the sound of his roaring through gritted teeth. The power of Sven's anguished response to her surgery filled the whole room.

'It's done,' she said, panting, her breath coming in and out at the same rhythm as the Norwegian's heaving chest.

He lifted his head a little way off the cot and looked at her with bloodshot eyes. Rachel gave him a small smile and tried to ignore the sight of his tears, which leaked down the side of his face.

She handed the bloody knife to the monk and took the wine. She poured it liberally into the gaping wound and Sven hissed. 'Sorry,' she said absentmindedly, now praying that the wine's healing properties would counter the poison of the sea creature. Rachel's assistant shoved a wad of cloth into the wound to stem the bleeding.

She then went to the apothecary bench, which the surgeons had stocked with various herbs and concoctions standing ready for use, and scooped out an aromatic mixture designed to draw any infection away from vital organs as well as prevent any bad humours from taking hold.

When she returned to her patient, she lifted away the monk's hand and studied her work. There was very little bleeding, which was a good sign. She packed the wound with the poultice and then covered the area with more clean cloths before she wrapped the bandages around his chest.

'Will I live, Princess?' Sven asked, beads of sweat dotting his upper lip and forehead.

She smiled. 'I cannot leave you to die. You are too useful.' But her throat caught with her grief when an image of Calum filled her head. Yes, Sven would survive this, but would he survive Calum's wrath?

Chapter Fourteen
A battlefield near Stirling, Scotland
Fleance

The fury of the soldiers on both sides of the battlefield was almost a living thing. The screaming and roaring as they surged towards each other came at Fleance like a howling wind, buffeting all around.

His men were holding their own against the rebels but each time someone fell, his stomach squeezed painfully, making him clench the hilt of his father's sword tighter. Fleance was at once terrified and exhilarated and if it had not been for the stern advice of Preston, he would have been part of the first wave of soldiers.

How was it that such a dreadful thing could cause his heart to rise in anticipation? Did this mark him as one who fed off the blood and suffering of others? Fleance surveyed the battlefield. No. The surging feeling came about because of his fear, determination and anger at what he had asked of his men.

Still surveying the scene below him, Fleance clenched and unclenched his fingers. He was a puppet, sitting on the rise atop his horse overlooking the carnage, and there was nothing he could do about it.

He saw at the back of the fray, on the rebels' side, a black flag raised high on a pole. Magness's sign. It was like a punch in the gut. Fleance had almost forgotten for a moment who it was he was fighting. 'To hell with him,' he muttered through clenched teeth, as white-hot anger replaced the earlier feelings.

Men were dying and would die because this man had become as deluded as those rebel leaders in the past who had believed they could thwart God's hand. Even Fleance could not turn away from his destiny, much as, at times, he wanted to.

Gathering up the reins, he turned his horse back towards the camp. It would serve nothing to watch the slaughter of men and be unable to save anyone. He rode back up the incline to the camp and swung off the horse.

Fleance shook his head as the grooms took his mount away. This was no way to fight. He was a skilled warrior, emasculated by protocol. Protocol that demanded the King of Scotland should avoid battle, at all costs.

As he entered his tent, a thought came to him. There was only one swift way to end this, and it had to be by his own hand. It was *he* who was to blame for this battle, not the innocent men whose lives were being snuffed out by the minute. If *he* disguised himself and went forth as a common soldier, he would not break any divine rules, surely? Would it be wrong, just for a moment, to remove his royal robes and become simply a man in the Scottish army?

He needed Blair, who was, right now, risking his life once again for his king. Fleance stood for a moment and looked out of his tent. The wind continued to bring him the sounds of death, but to be among it would be better than sitting back like a nursemaid.

Looking back towards the noise and bloodshed, he sent a prayer heavenwards that his friend would survive the afternoon.

The call of the rebel's horn echoed around the hills and the plain and was soon joined by Scotland's reply. The battle would cease for the day. Thank God. With Preston at his side, Fleance stood at the edge of the encampment watching the men who came trudging back up the hill. Wagons had been dispatched to pick up the wounded, dead and dying, but there were also many able bodies and this pleased him.

He spied Blair, face splattered in mud and blood but walking strong and unaided. His friend threw him a weary but happy grin and it warmed his heart.

'We are missing twenty-eight of our number, Sire,' Preston said, matter-of-factly.

Fleance was surprised by the certainty of Preston's tone. 'How do you know this?'

'I counted those who have returned.' Preston looked back down over the plain. 'I suggest that most of them are dead or have feigned death to avoid it. I will send some boys down to find the living.'

Fleance was impressed. Why could he not hold such detail? He scolded himself inwardly. *This is why you have advisors*, his mind said. *To look after details you cannot.* He coughed to excuse his lapse. 'Good then. That is a plan.'

He strode away, back to his tent, hoping that soon enough Blair would find him and share with him all of the day's events. Then, in private, he would tell him his plan.

It was after supper, and Fleance had dined alone except for Preston. The old man seemed in no mood to converse and Fleance's own mood meant that he was more than pleased with this state of affairs. The servants had taken away their dishes and Preston stood. 'Good night, Sire. I wish you good repose.'

'Thank you, Preston,' Fleance said. 'And you, also.' This comment seemed to startle the old man, who blinked twice and then shuffled out of the tent.

Fleance felt strangely isolated and, he had to admit, perhaps even lonely. 'Get me the Thane of Lochaber,' he said to his page. The young boy nodded and fled.

Blair would never question his idea. He had never questioned any of Fleance's plans in all the years they had grown up together. Instead, his friend had found ways of making Fleance's ideas come to fruition. Blair, it sometimes seemed, would move heaven and earth to make the dream work.

Fleance looked around his tent. Nothing here would aid his disguise. He kicked the bundle of clothes beside his bedding. Damn! He would really need Blair to agree with his plan.

And there he was, as if conjured. 'Flea,' he gasped. 'Is everything all right with you?'

'I am to battle tomorrow and I need your help to evade Preston.'

Blair shook his head. 'But the king—'

Fleance cut him off. 'I know – but I am more than just a king. I am a warrior and I am the adopted son of the rebel leader. Who better to be in battle against him than me? I can end this madness, Blair.'

'But if you should die?'

'I won't,' Fleance laughed.

His friend raised his eyebrows and regarded him for a moment. 'Aye, I bet you don't intend to.'

Fleance snorted. 'No, but I need you to do some things, and it will take a great deal of effort to sway the soldiers to follow you when their king is nowhere to be seen.'

Blair rolled his eyes. 'Why do you make my life so difficult?' he asked. But he was grinning, and the two of them sat down to work out a plan.

Two hours later, Fleance ran swiftly over the moor, eyes scouring the ground for dips and rises, or bodies that might trip him up. There was little light because the sky was cloudy. In the distance the fires from the rebel camp drew him forward.

Fleance turned right and began to run in a wide arc around the battlefield. He had confided his plan to Blair, but would not allow the thane to accompany him. He was well armed with his dirk and his crossbow.

It took only twenty minutes for Fleance to skirt the scene of the day's conflict, and then he slowed, creeping up the far right of the low hill that protected the enemy. Though he had been jogging with his body low to avoid being seen against the horizon, he crouched further and paused a moment to take in what was before him.

The camp was quiet but not silent. He could make out men sitting asleep around their fires and, from the shifting shadows, sentries standing almost still. One. Two. Three. There would probably be the same number at the back. Magness would not take any chances.

He was beginning to chill from the lack of movement, so continued his crab-like movement right and upwards, eyes scanning the darkness for a safe place to hide. Magness had selected his command post well, for it was devoid of large vegetation and afforded unobstructed views all around. However, there were large rock formations dotted around the landscape, and it was these Fleance sheltered behind as he made his way forward.

They would not be expecting this. Yes, there were sentries on lookout, but they were to maintain a vigil over the movements of the king's army. And Magness would not be expecting *him*. The rebel leader's words to him the last time they met still stung: *'Miri always said you were from a royal household and to be none other than Banquo's son and under our roof.'* Magness had bowed, a smirk on his face. *'It has been an honour.'* He then mounted his horse. *'You've got a good heart, Flea, but a soft one.'* The compliment was furnished with a withering barb. His adoptive father looked down on Fleance and added, *'You will regret that you let me live.'* He had then turned his horse around and cantered into the fog.

Indeed, Fleance thought, *I regret that I failed to see how far you would go for your own misguided ends. But I have been given a second chance to make things right.*

He paused again, and once more felt the cold damp of the night air. He looked at the dark line that signalled the division between earth and sky and could see that it was close to dawn.

How brazen he was to attempt this plan. That was what would ensure its success – together with his skill with the crossbow. He rested the weapon upon the ground while he used both hands to span the bow. Then he reached over his shoulder, pulled out a bolt and loaded it. He was ready.

The air shifted and he looked up. A rebel sentry had moved closer to where he was hiding and was looking out towards the Scottish army. The man's face was in darkness but there was enough light to create a reflection in his eyes. This was all Fleance needed.

The death was swift and silent. Fleance ran up the short incline and grabbed the man's boots. He dragged the dead rebel behind the rocks and, trying not to make any noise, even though his pulse boomed in his ears, he folded the body into a crevice. He stood back, wiped his face on his sleeve and breathed deeply.

Onwards he continued up the incline, always hedging to the right, skirting around towards the south side of the encampment. He hoped to find cover before the first fingers of light reached out to them.

His feet made no sound on the soft earth and his ears strained for clues as to the movements of the men around him. He had lost sight of the other two sentries, as he was almost at the back of the camp. He reloaded and armed his crossbow and peered into the dark, trying to distinguish the shape of a human being from among the lumps of rock.

There! His breath quickened and he licked his dry lips. The man was doing something with a blade, for it glinted in the dark. Fleance crept closer, keen to spot the mark that would ensure a silent death. The sentry was motionless except for the movement of the blade, but he was facing Fleance. Now to judge the height of the man, for he stood in front of a boulder and there was no light to give a clear sense of shape.

Suddenly it occurred to Fleance what the man was doing: he was using his knife to cut food – whether bread or fruit – and lift the pieces to his mouth. Fleance lifted up the bow and waiting, watched the shimmering flicker of the light in front. Now! He squeezed the trigger and the bolt made a *wuff* as it sped forward to bury itself in the man's head. The blade fell to the ground and the dark shadow crumpled.

In a moment Fleance was up the bank and pulling the guard down to his hiding place. As before, he sought out a nook in the rocks where he could dump the body. Then, he moved quickly back up to the place where the man had been killed, to find his blade. It took some moments of groping around on the ground before his hand found it. A dirk. Long and thin and deadly. Fleance tucked it into his belt and stood up carefully.

From some distance away, the first blackbird started its morning song. Then a thrush, closer at hand. Soon it would be light. Had it been that long since he had left his own camp? Though it was still difficult to see, the black of the night had turned to smudgy charcoal and shapes were now more defined.

Magness's camp was less than twenty yards ahead. Fleance had to find a vantage point before he made the next move. The sun would come up on his right and he was south-west of the camp so would be in darkness for longer.

His adoptive father always rose before the sun to relieve himself in private. It was a habit Fleance had observed for ten years. He doubted the man had slept much this last night. Surely he must know he was to be defeated – if not today, then tomorrow.

But Fleance also knew he had taken a chance by positioning himself at the most isolated part of the encampment. Perhaps Magness had already relieved himself. Perhaps he would choose another place to make his toilet. Perhaps he was already awake and making plans and would soon be alerted to the fact that two of his sentries were missing.

Just as Magness so confidently proclaimed knowledge of his 'son,' so Fleance also understood this man, whom he had loved and worshipped and feared – and now loathed.

Fleance reloaded his crossbow and lifted it in preparation.

A movement to the left caught his eye. Two men walked his way and he saw immediately that one of them was Magness. It was interesting, Fleance thought, that Magness had brought another. Perhaps he was so unsure of the way things might go that he had asked for a guard during his ablutions.

No matter. Fleance would dispatch the companion as soon as they were far enough away from the camp that no one would be alerted. The man who walked with Magness was only half awake, which was useful. Fleance waited. They came forward and, when he could see the space between the eyes, he fired the bolt. The man dropped, dead before he hit the ground.

Magness was some paces ahead and did not notice at first. This gave Fleance the time needed to reload. He stood, his bow charged, and Magness at once realised the situation.

He laughed. 'You really are a stupid boy.'

The insult angered Fleance, but he held the bow steady. 'I have never heard you call me that until this day.'

Magness shook his head. 'Then it is because I have never seen you do something like this until this day.'

'You are coming with me, Magness.'

'Aha!' Magness chuckled. 'You and who else, boy?'

Fleance ignored the insult. 'Me and my weapon, Magness.'

The older man grunted. 'Well, would you be kind enough to let me piss before you imprison me?'

'Aye, but you must do it in front of me.'

Magness narrowed his eyes. 'I would prefer privacy, Flea.'

'And I would prefer that you had not slaughtered six thousand of Scotland's men.' He stared at Magness for a moment. 'So I guess this morning neither of us gets what we desire.'

In the rapidly advancing light he could see red patches appearing on the cheeks of the rebel leader and knew these came when the man was in pain or highly agitated. 'Go on, piss. I have seen worse. Just think of me as that scrawny boy you picked up off the road eleven years ago.'

Magness glared at him. 'That is all I have ever seen.'

The comment was so unexpected that he breathed in sharply with shock. Hadn't Magness always tried to do the best by him? Hadn't Miri loved and nurtured him all those years?

A man's view of his past is tainted by the picture of his present.

This was a truth he'd heard was uttered at the most terrible time in recent Scottish history. And uttered by the man whom all would come to hate, the tyrant Macbeth.

'Then you need a surgeon,' Fleance offered. 'To fix your sight.'

Magness bowed his head. 'I see we have opportunity for some exchange of ideas, but I must piss, so if you would be so kind as to at least turn your head, then I will relieve myself.'

The bow still trained on him, Fleance shook his head. 'No, Magness. I will not even give you this. You are a man, so piss as a man.'

Magness opened his breeks and pointed the arc of his urine within yards of where Fleance stood so that the spray caused him to step back.

And then Magness was upon him and he could not discharge his weapon. The full weight of the man pinned him to the ground, but in his hand was the dirk Fleance had taken from the sentry. Forty-five-year-old warrior against twenty-two-year-old king. Each as strong and angry as the other.

They were now on their sides, face to face, embraced in a fierce struggle. Magness punched at the hand that held the weapon, and the dirk flew out of Fleance's hand.

'Give over, boy,' Magness growled.

'No,' Fleance cried, for he would not relent.

They grappled in the early light and it seemed so familiar – days spent play-fighting under an English summer sun. This, however, was not like their good-humoured wrestling from Fleance's boyhood; this was a fight whose outcome meant the difference between life and death.

The sheer weight of Magness crushed Fleance's chest and Magness's arm held him tightly, but both were too close to each other to effectively inflict damage. They rolled once, again, farther down the hill. The movement separated them for just a moment, giving Fleance an opportunity to lift up his knee and ram it into Magness's groin.

The older man roared with pain but threw himself at Fleance. He seemed almost possessed with an unnatural strength and wrenched Fleance over so that the king was now on his back. 'Give over, boy,' Magness hissed again, his breath rancid and thick. 'I won't save your life but I might give you dignity.'

'I have sacrificed much for what you want to destroy,' Fleance said, twisting and bucking. The effort to hold Fleance still was beginning to weaken the older man. Fleance felt a small shift in the strength of the hold and renewed his efforts to get free.

Both were sweating heavily now, their hands and arms slippery with the evidence of their fight. Both were determined, but Fleance had the weight of a kingdom behind him, and that thought alone empowered and sustained him.

He pulled his right leg out from under Magness, lifted it, and with his knee pushed with all his might against Magness's left thigh. The manoeuvre worked, and he succeeded in shifting the other man's legs off his own.

Now, with this freedom, he was able to pull his lower body around at an angle, twisting and putting the older man off balance so he loosened his grip on Fleance's left arm.

This was all Fleance needed, and he reached out and grabbed his dirk.

Magness, one hand now free, punched Fleance in the side of the head. His ears rang and his vision blurred but the dirk was in his hand and he stabbed at the older man, embedding the blade in his free arm, high on the shoulder.

Magness let him go, cursing, and was distracted enough for Fleance to push him off, leap up, grab his bow, arm it and stand over the man. 'Get up,' he said through gritted teeth. The rebel lay there for a moment, his hand pressing against the flow of blood from his upper arm. 'Now,' Fleance snarled. 'On your feet.'

Magness sat up and looked at him. 'Or what? You will kill me?'

'No,' Fleance answered. 'You will be tried for treason and then executed.'

'Then kill me now.'

'That is not the role of the king.' Fleance lifted the bow and aimed it at Magness's groin. 'Up.'

'And if I don't?'

Fleance's answer was to lift the bow slightly and discharge a bolt into Magness's shoulder. 'Then I will continue to fill you with arrows until you comply.' Quickly, he reloaded his bow and lifted it again.

As Fleance knew it would, the pain almost crippled Magness. His face became deathly white but he stood nonetheless. Panting and sweating, he snarled at Fleance. 'My men will hunt you down before you are halfway to your camp.'

'Oh, I expect so,' Fleance replied.

He pulled a leather tie from his belt and, with the crossbow still trained on Magness, he looped a snare around the hands of the injured man and tied it deftly. The thick arms of the rebel were glistening with blood. Once Magness was secure, Fleance put the bow down and pulled the bolt from his captive's arm. Magness hissed loudly but did not cry out. 'I expect my men to be waiting for us. Move.' Fleance shoved him forward, knowing that the blood loss and pain had weakened him. 'By the way, thank you for teaching me to tie a bind one-handed.'

Rage emanated from Magness, who walked in front. 'Suppose I bleed to death before you bring me to your so-called justice?'

'I have seen you suffer worse. I shall get my surgeon to attend to you.'

'And then you will kill me?'

'No, not me. You have signed your own death warrant and for that I am sad.'

Magness snorted. 'How quickly you have taken to the language of the royal class.'

'What?' Fleance asked, bewildered by the statement.

'Oh, that you "shall have a surgeon attend me". That I have signed my "death warrant".'

Fleance laughed. 'That is unworthy of you, Magness. I would expect you, more than anyone, to appreciate that an effective leader needs to take on the qualities of his surroundings – whatever these may be. I'm as much at home in front of the fire in a small tavern as in a mighty castle. Perhaps this is what galls you the most – that I can find things about any man to admire and be accepted in whatever company I choose, something you could never achieve.'

Magness grunted and Fleance knew his reply had struck a chord.

They made their journey down the hill on the western side of the battlefield just as the pale sun rose above the horizon. Fleance guessed Magness talked to take his mind off the pain. 'I have heard that a man with a pure heart is not a man to trust.'

'Then you have been keeping company with the wrong type of people,' Fleance replied.

Magness snorted but said nothing more. By the time they were on the flat, Fleance could see his men approaching. Moments later, unmistakable sounds of consternation erupted from the rebel camp.

Both men turned and looked upwards.

'Well,' Magness said, 'it seems my men have discovered your wee ploy.' He looked hard at Fleance. 'You had best pray your men arrive before mine.'

'They will, and you had best pray for a fair end to your life, Magness,' Fleance said, pulling himself more upright. 'I have always known and thought of you as a good man. May you not disappoint me in your journey to death.'

Chapter Fifteen

And there was Blair atop his horse and holding the rope of the king's mare. Behind him marched some two hundred soldiers.

'You are a sight for sore eyes, Blair,' Fleance called.

'And you, Your Majesty, have given me no end of grief with Preston and the earls.'

Fleance couldn't help but grin. 'Then we have both been in mortal danger these past few hours.'

Blair shook his head but pressed forward with his horse, a loop of rope hanging from the saddle. He looked at Magness and turned back to Fleance. 'Is this the traitor?'

'Aye.' Fleance nodded to one of the soldiers. 'Bind him well and put him on display. We are about to face an angry audience.' They looked south to where the remaining rebel army was swarming around its post. 'Take him into the battlefield among their dead. Stand him on the back of a wagon and post soldiers ten yards in front on all sides. Then gather all our men but keep them armed and at a distance so that none of the rebel arrows can reach them.' He looked hard at Blair and then at the others. 'The king desires no more death on this day.'

Fleance mounted his horse and looked down at Magness. 'You have thought to know me through eyes that are clouded by all the worries of life, tried to mould me and others in the way you wanted us to go, but you have failed.' He leant forward and lowered his voice. 'I once told a man that if he wanted to know me then he needed to stop trying to know me through his own view of the world.' His voice was now a whisper. 'Magness, I loved you as my father and I thank you for all you did, but you never saw me for who I really am.'

Magness glared. 'And who do you think you are, Fleance, son of Banquo? Who are you in truth?'

'I am who I am. There is nothing else to say.' Fleance picked up the reins and prepared to go into the field. 'Bring a surgeon,' he called. 'Let his hurts be looked at, but do not underestimate his strength. He is a snake in the grass. To ignore this is to invite death.'

He rode swiftly back to camp and it was only a matter of minutes before he was dismounting. Preston was there uttering curses and muttering warnings but Fleance flung up his hand. 'Give over, man. I need food and water now.'

Within moments, this was provided and Fleance ate quickly. Soon he was back on the horse and galloping down to the battlefield.

His men had set Magness on the back of a wagon. His hands were tied, his arms still bleeding, and he stood in the middle of the wagon for all to see. The rebel soldiers had rushed forward but hesitated when they saw their leader surrounded by the king's soldiers. They fell silent and congregated thirty yards back, watching and waiting quietly.

Fleance leapt onto the wagon and stood resolutely in front of Magness's army.

'Rebels against Scotland,' he called. 'This man here, your leader, was my father for ten years.' As expected, a low hum came from the soldiers on both sides. 'I loved him.' Again, there was murmuring from both sides.

'But a year ago my adoptive father engaged some of you to work against our new king, Duncan, who was loved and adored by all who stand on this side.'

He could see that Magness was tiring, for the man swayed before righting himself. Fleance pushed back his shoulders and continued. 'Magness led that revolt and it failed. Magness has led this revolt and he has failed. Magness wants a better Scotland.' As expected, a low, disapproving noisé came from the rebel camp. Fleance held up his hand. 'Your king wants this too. This has always been my desire but your leader has chosen bloodshed to try to make this happen.'

This time, only silence was the response. Men on both sides were listening intently.

'I am sorry for your loss. Your wives. Your children. Your parents.' There! He could distinguish a shifting. 'My father was murdered by Macbeth because that man could not trust in the natural order of things. Your leader,' he pointed again to Magness, 'saved my life. He had lost everything when the tyrant ordered the massacre of all who lived in Macduff's house. He lost seven children. No.' Fleance stopped and shook his head. Then he looked up again, his anger real. 'Magness did not lose his children – they were taken from him by a madman.'

He swallowed to control the rising feeling of sadness. 'Magness believes he is an honourable man.' A roar came forth from the rebel camp and Fleance let it swell and die. 'But he is misguided in rising against the Scottish throne.'

The noise settled and in the clear early morning, as the sun's rays lit up the field, throwing long shadows over the trampled grass, Fleance delivered his ultimatum.

'Your leader is to confess his act of treason. If you want security for your families, then surrender. If you refuse, it will go badly for those you love.'

Silence fell again upon the moor. The morning breeze lifted the hair from Fleance's neck but still the rebels did not move.

A movement from the back of the rebel line caught his attention. A man, dressed entirely in black upon a black horse, moved slowly forward. The rebel soldiers let him pass but they kept their faces turned towards Fleance.

'So sure of your place now, young Flea,' Magness muttered. 'You have taken on more than even you can manage.'

A strange fear twisted in Fleance's gut. Once before, he had seen this man. Then, he had still been a child and still under the tutelage of his adoptive father. This was the stranger who had silenced the men during the night he had crept near the entrance of his tent to hear Magness.

'Soldiers of the Scottish throne,' the black-clad man shouted now over the moor. 'Do not be so easily deceived by the honeyed words of your newly appointed sovereign. He is still an ignorant boy.'

The soldiers grumbled before him and Magness grunted.

The sound irked Fleance but he would not give anyone the satisfaction of knowing this.

'Magness, man!' the stranger shouted. 'We honour you and your sacrifice.'

A roar went up and there was a thundering of stamping feet.

'Shall we engage them?' Blair asked, bringing his horse alongside Fleance's.

'For what? For more to die?' Fleance gritted his teeth and swallowed down the bitter taste that sat in his throat. 'They believe.'

'Sire?'

'They believe their cause is just and honourable. Nothing that is said or done by me, Blair, will alter their minds.'

Blair sighed. 'But we cannot let this linger – this malaise. It sucks life from our country.'

'Aye, it does. But every man chooses his path, and to force a way upon another is wrong and will solve nothing.'

Fleance tried to raise his voice above the swell of noise from the battlefield. 'Those of you who wish to surrender may do so knowing that I will be merciful.'

But the war cries from the rebels only intensified. There was no hope of changing their minds.

Then the sound of a horn rent the air and the rebel army turned away, like a wave returning to the sea, back to their encampment. His men looked towards him – should they pursue or stand firm?

'Wait!' he shouted. 'If any man should surrender, do not kill him. For the rest, do as you are trained to do. Chase them off,' he shouted. 'Send them back to their holes and burrows and hiding places. Go!'

The front row of archers shouted as they went forth. Only a few of the rebels turned and fell to the ground in surrender. But many others were brought down by the arrows unleashed upon them from Scotland's army.

Fleance watched as the black lieutenant galloped off and he was dismayed to see some six thousand men reach the encampment and disappear over the hill southward.

He turned to Magness. 'I am thinking you regard this as a good day.'

Magness snorted. 'Did you not think I would have a deputy?'

Fleance felt a mixture of sorrow and resignation that he had not the power to bring the men back into the fold. 'I did not think—'

'No, you didn't. You are always looking to see the good in people, Flea, rather than the darkness that lurks in most men.' Magness glared at him. 'I wasted ten years.' He spat. 'Miri believed in you but I had my doubts, and now look at you – King of Scotland and as weak and useless as that eleven-year-old starving boy I scraped off the road.'

Fleance could hit him. He could kill him. He could argue back. None of these would be of use.

Blair gripped his arm. 'His words are poison, Flea. You are honourable and righteous and always have been.' Fleance shivered in the early morning – beset by lack of sleep and too much self-doubt. Blair's hold on his arm tightened. 'You are our king. You are good enough. You are a good man.' The last sentence Blair hissed into his ear. 'Hear this, my friend: you are more than good enough and Scotland is better off because you are king.'

Fleance took courage from his friend's words and turned to Magness. 'I am sorry for you, Magness, that you have been so blinded by your grief.' Fleance spoke quietly but his rage caused a hot sweat to wash over his body. 'I am glad that Keavy is safe with me.' It pleased him that Magness twitched at the name of his daughter. 'And that she shall know of a Scotland that is powerful and free from corruption and from men mad with their anger.'

'Burn in hell, Flea,' Magness snarled.

'I may burn for my sins, but these will not include dishonour-ing the role that has been mapped for me.'

It was over. The rebels had failed to overthrow the Kingdom of Scotland once more and those left alive had fled. It took less than half a day to break camp and make ready to march back to Glamis. The wounded had been sent ahead to their villages to be attended to by the local abbots. Though they were weary, there was also much laughter and good-humoured banter between the men and Fleance found himself smiling as he looked over the preparations.

Blair rode up beside him. 'That smile is a sight for sore eyes,' he said, returning the grin. ''Tis been far too long since I have seen you look happy.'

Fleance turned in his saddle, the smile fading. 'I do not think the word happy best describes how I am feeling. "Relieved" and "pleased" sit better with me. I'm relieved that no more had to die and pleased with how my men are behaving.' He looked behind to where the rebels' camp was now an empty site and only faint wisps of smoke from smouldering fires stood as evidence that there had been a small army there just hours ago.

As if reading his thoughts, Blair spoke. 'You can't save everyone, Flea. Though you have good intentions and the heart for it, some cannot survive. And some do not choose the right path.'

Fleance turned to his friend and bit his lip. 'Right path? That is an interesting description of a man's journey.' He rubbed a hand over his face. 'Blair, if I ask others not to read me through the eyes of their own experience, should I not chastise myself for doing the same?'

'That is your problem, Flea. Always trying to do the right thing and say the right thing based on what you think others expect of you.' Blair's face flushed. 'So sorry, Sire, for my forwardness.'

Fleance held up his hand. 'Don't apologise. Say what needs to be said.'

This response seemed to give Blair courage. 'Can you not see it, Flea? You are the most capable and intelligent leader Scotland has been blessed with since before Duncan the First. Though he was a kind king and good, he was not wise. You are. And you are kind. And you have an understanding of the world that many do not.'

Fleance lifted his hand to his head. 'I have had this pushed in my face.' He looked at Blair. 'I did not want this life. I did not want to be king.'

Blair lifted his water-skin to his mouth, took a long drink and then hooked it back onto the saddle. 'Yet here you are, Flea. King.'

They regarded each other as the swirl of military sound and afternoon breeze danced around them. Finally, Fleance answered. 'You have the ability of stating the obvious and yet making it sound like a new truth.'

'Thank you.'

Fleance sighed. 'And you are right.'

Blair grinned. 'I know.'

Fleance leant across the space between them and punched his friend lightly on the arm.

Blair feigned a look of mock horror. 'I am not certain that was a kingly gesture,' he said, rubbing his arm.

Fleance grinned. 'I suppose not, but I feel better.'

'Always, you push the boundaries and delight in this. My entire childhood was spent surviving your escapades. I am pleased to see that you continue in this manner and am pleased to still follow you.'

'You're an idiot,' Fleance said.

'Thank you,' Blair said again.

They looked at each other a moment and then roared with laughter.

Chapter Sixteen
Glamis Castle

Fleance made his way to the prison cells because he could not rest; could not sleep. There were too many questions.

Even though it was a black night, Magness quickly came to the bars of his cell. 'Flea?'

Fleance hesitated. The name knocked at his heart. He closed his eyes and went forward. 'Yes, Magness, it is I.'

The older man cleared his throat and then reached out of the enclosure with a dirty hand.

Fleance looked at the guard. 'Open the doors. I want to speak to this man.' The guard hesitated. 'Your king demands this!' The grimy keeper pulled back the lock, and there was Magness standing tall and proud just inside his cell. The sight of this powerful man placed in the lowest of places seemed such a contradiction.

It was the moment to ask the question that had plagued him for months. 'I don't understand. I have done everything you schooled me to do. Why have you gone against me?' Fleance cried. He shook his head in confusion. 'I have loved you. I still love you. Why have you done this to me?'

Magness straightened, held tightly to the walls of his prison and shook his head. 'It has never been about you, Flea.' The man brushed a hand over his face and then stared directly at Fleance. He breathed deeply and then spoke. 'Thirteen years ago, King Duncan recruited a secret regiment of soldiers to stay inside the castles of the thanes in case there was insurgence . . .' He lowered his head. 'I was one of this army but we failed.' Magness coughed but Fleance saw his tears. 'Duncan understood more than we did but his life was cut short – as was that of his grandson – yet there were many of us ready and willing to take up the charge of creating a better house.'

'This is stupid,' Fleance cried. 'Magness, I am for Scotland just as you are.'

Magness sighed heavily. 'No, Flea. You don't understand. You are part of the old bloodline, one of a line of kings who have never served their people well.'

'How can you say this? Look around you, Magness. Your wife is dead. I have your daughter in my care. I am King of Scotland. Your cause is finished.'

'The only way Scotland can go forward is with a new line, with new rulers. It needs to take a strong player and begin again. For many years I thought it was you but I was mistaken.'

'Are you trying to unnerve me, Magness? Here I am. The one you have trained up. I am King of Scotland!'

His adoptive father shook his head. 'And there lies the trouble, Flea. Scotland's kings with their greed and their hunger for power are the ones who have brought sorrow on this nation. And now you plan to marry Donalbain's daughter. Things will go back to the way they were, no matter how different you think you can be.'

Bitter bile rose up and he had to spit it out. So be it. So. Be. It. 'So you have rejected me for some . . .' Fleance cast around for the words but failed. 'For ten years, Magness, I was your son. You would reject me so quickly?'

Magness's body trembled and he moved away, squatting against the prison walls. 'I had a boy like you, Flea. A good boy. He was coming on seventeen years when Macbeth's murderers culled Macduff's castle. He was my right hand. And then there was Jacob. A serving boy to the queen and best friend to Macduff's young son.' The older man rubbed a hand over his face. 'Shall I tell you how they died?' he cried.

'Magness, don't.'

'They were tortured, Flea.' Magness coughed and then spat out his grief. 'They were barely more than children, Flea! Young men, slaughtered.'

It was too much. 'Yes, Magness. It is as you say, but that horror was long ago. Scotland still grieves for its lost people but those of us remaining have moved forward. We have had to.'

Fleance felt there'd been a shift in the wind. His men had, without voice or movement, given him allegiance. He sat on the throne, but the hard wooden seat and the associated expectation made him feel uncomfortable. The chair was unyielding and too far away from where the action would be: the centre of the great hall. This was where the trial for Magness's life would take place and Fleance was going to be the one who would ultimately decide his fate.

The door opened and Rosie slipped through. The guards stiffened but Fleance waved at them to relax. She looked at the sentries but made her way forward and then curtsied to him. As she stood up he saw that her cheeks were flushed and her nose red from the cold. She tried to smile but he could see that she was anxious.

'Rosie?'

'Your Majesty,' she began. 'I am here to petition on behalf of Keavy.'

His heart sank. 'You know I can do nothing . . .'

'Aye, but you are king and your word is law.' She bit down on her bottom lip and then looked up at him, her eyes red from crying. 'She wants her da, Flea,' she whispered.

'I cannot, Rosie.'

'You can do whatever you want,' she said, an edge to her voice.

He studied her. So young and free. She had the power to ask such things but no authority to carry the weight of what she asked for. He lowered his head and swallowed. 'You are correct, Mistress Rosie.' The formality seemed to hit her with force, for her eyes widened in surprise. 'And what I want is what is best for Scotland.'

The telltale signs of her anger swept across her face. 'So what is best for Scotland means murdering the man who saved you? The man who is father to your sister, Keavy?'

'Magness is a traitor.'

'Yes, he is. But can you not imprison him? Does he have to die?'

'Treason is a capital offence.'

She came forward and knelt down before the throne. 'Can you do nothing, Flea?' He looked over her head to the door of the hall through which Magness would soon be brought. 'Flea?' Rosie called. 'Think on how this will affect Keavy. No one will criticise you for pardoning him. What son can send his father to the executioner?'

The words found their mark but he deflected them. 'Magness is not my father. Banquo is my father.' He squeezed his hands into fists and watched as the blood drained from them. Then he looked at her. 'As king, I can do whatever I wish. As a man who desires all that is honourable and right, I can be guided only by the laws of our land and the tenets of my position.'

Tears filled Rosie's eyes and she sniffed loudly. 'But he is Magness, Flea. He's Magness.'

Here it was, then. A private matter played out in a public forum. This was not about the legality or morality of coming against a sovereign: this was about the man who had been as a father to him.

Fleance swallowed down his own grief. 'I know, Rosie. I know what you are saying, but he is also the rebel leader who came against the crown – twice.' He called a page over to bring water. 'Rosie, he cannot live. He is no longer the man you or I remember back in England.'

The far door burst open and Keavy spilled forth. She fell, picked herself up and ran towards him, shouting, 'Flea! Flea! Don't! Don't kill Da. Please, Flea! Don't kill him.' She rushed to him and fell onto his lap, sobbing. 'Stop this, please!'

Keavy clung to his legs, her tears wetting his robes.

'I cannot, Keavy. Magness has confessed. The law says he must be executed.' Keavy screamed into his lap. He pulled her up and stood her before him. 'I am sorry.'

'But you are king, Flea. You can do whatever pleases you.'

He pulled her to him again. 'No, child. You misunderstand. I am doing exactly what is expected of me.'

Her face was blotched from hours of crying. 'I expect you can save Da,' she cried.

Fleance looked down at her young face and remembered the years of teaching her how to collect the best wood for the fire and the times of playing in the forest and teasing her. He remembered her birth and how protective he had felt when Miri handed her to him the first time.

She had been so beautiful. As she was now, despite her twisted face.

'Keavy,' he said. 'Your da has admitted his crimes and the law is beyond even my power.' He looked over at Preston, who stood in the shadows and nodded. 'He was my da as long as he has been yours, but even though I am the king, a higher authority guides my decision. It is not a trifling thing to try to change the law of the land. Magness must be punished.'

'Can he not just go to jail, Flea?' she sobbed.

'No, bairn. Treason means death, and your father has admitted to this. He will die.'

Keavy pushed away from him. 'No, no, no. This is my da, Flea. Stop it. Stop it from happening,' she shouted. 'I don't believe you can't stop it if you really wanted to.'

If he really wanted to.

Fleance stood up. It occurred to him now why he was feeling such grief. He did not want to stop the execution because he understood completely that it was morally right and just. That it was retribution for the lives of all those who had died this past year because of the actions of this man. Lives on both sides of the battlefield.

Yet he was not without compassion, and Keavy's grief showed him what he needed to do. 'Come, child. Let us visit him.'

Fleance held his adoptive sister's hand as they entered Magness's cell.

The rebel leader was sprawled on the straw in the furthest corner of the room, staring at the floor.

'Da,' Keavy cried.

Magness looked up then and his face immediately softened. 'Keavy, love.'

Keavy clung to Fleance's clothes but when he gave her a gentle nudge, she rushed forward and leapt into the arms of her father. They embraced for some moments before Fleance interrupted.

'I thought it important—' he began, but Magness cut him off. 'Thank you.'

The acknowledgment surprised him. The last time he had seen Magness, the man was a mass of fury and fire. Now, he saw once again the gentle giant of a father he had seen many times over the years.

Fleance pulled his shoulders back and looked Magness in the eye. 'Say your farewells.' He moved out of the cell to the far end of the room and watched as Magness cupped Keavy's face in his large hands before kissing both her cheeks. He could not hear what was said but the language of their bodies spoke loudly of regret. And something else. A strength of purpose. Who knew what Magness said to his daughter? Yet when she looked over at Fleance her expression was one of respect but also something else he could not name: determination? Resolution? Something that he had never seen in her before.

Magness sat down and pulled Keavy onto his lap. The child rested her head on his shoulder. As he spoke, his fingers stroked her hair. It was a scene that Fleance had witnessed many times as he grew into a man. Keavy crawling onto her father's knees to hear stories or to receive comfort.

He gave them the time between supper and nightfall. But finally, it had to be over, no matter how weighted his heart was.

'It's time,' Fleance said, stepping forward.

Magness nodded and pulled his daughter against his chest, kissing her head. 'Go well and go strong, my child. Be not afraid of the world, for you were born after much turmoil and your life will be blessed with triumph.'

He pushed her upright and turned her to face Fleance. 'It was foretold many years ago that your brother would be the king and this has now come to pass. Honour him.' Magness was now looking directly at Fleance. 'I cannot, myself, trust a king of Kenneth's line, but I also know that Fleance is his own man. A good and honourable man. Maybe he will prove me wrong.' Keavy pressed her face into his chest and Magness held her tightly. 'It is all right, child.'

'No, Da.' The child's shoulders were shaking.

'Keavy,' Fleance called. 'This is your last goodbye. Say it now and look to see your father and mother again in heaven.' The attending guards came forward.

The tears spilled down Keavy's face as she kissed Magness for the last time and then turned and ran blindly from the chamber.

Chapter Seventeen

The two men faced each other in silence. Magness, thick-bodied and strong, some grey creeping through the mass of dark hair on his head, eyed Fleance unwaveringly. The king, tall, muscular, had his light blue eyes fixed on the man who had, eleven years ago, given him life and a home and hearth. The man who had equipped him with the fight that always bubbled away under his ribs.

Magness rubbed a hand over his mouth and tilted his head. 'I never expected this strength from you,' he said. Fleance nodded. Magness stared long and hard. 'I did not know I was schooling a boy who would become a king.' Still Fleance stayed silent. 'I see your struggle, Flea.' Fleance gritted his teeth and said nothing. Magness waited, keeping his dark eyes on Fleance, and then turned away. He pushed his hands through his thick mane and then turned back. 'You win. Maybe you deserve to win. Time will tell.'

Fleance raised himself up and addressed Magness. 'I do not need your approval. I was who I would become long before you picked me up from the side of the road.' Magness moved to speak but Fleance held up his hand. 'I am ever thankful to you and Miri for my life but I will never sanction the renegade activities of your supporters.' He stepped forward and lowered his voice. 'I thank you, Magness, for saving me and for teaching me and for being a great teacher and warrior. If only you had put aside your anger and grief you could have been more effective.'

Magness shook his head. 'Flea, when your seed has created babes and you have loved them and played with them and rejoiced with their delight in the world, and then they are taken from you, in such a brutal way, only then will you know my heart.'

There it was. His own comments to Henri came back at him. *'Perhaps if you could stop the urge to trace* your *patterns of living and thinking in* my *heart, then you might understand me.'* Yes, he could understand.

'I am sorry for what is to happen, Magness. Each man chooses paths and gains or loses from that choice. I am sorry for your loss. May God bless you.' He swallowed hard to ensure his grief was not seen and indicated to the guards to reshackle the prisoner and take him out.

Only when they had all gone did Fleance fall back against the wall and slide down to the floor. Then and only then did he let the tears come. Preston and Blair, who had quietly entered the room, both looked at Fleance with pity.

'When will he die?' Preston asked.

'Most certainly before the end of the day,' Fleance replied.

'Has he said anything?'

'No.'

'I see.'

'Thank you, Preston. You may go.' The old man left the chamber as silently as he had entered.

Fleance stood and poured himself some water. Taking a long drink, he walked to the window and looked down to the courtyard where Magness would meet his death.

Blair, who had stayed behind when Preston left, touched his arm. 'Do you want to bear witness or no?'

'I must be there. I don't want to be but what sort of man would I be to order the end of another's life and then hide? He has the right to look on the face of the one who has sealed his fate.'

'He sealed his own, Flea. You are the one charged with making it come to pass. Do not think much more than that.'

'Thank you, Blair. I know it's right that he lose his life. I only wish it had not come to this. Magness would have been a fine general in Scotland's army. He has charisma and passion and loyalty. However, it seems the tyrant Macbeth's legacy still ripples down through the years. He took away Magness's children and now he is the reason behind the taking of Magness's own life. My hope is this: that I can secure some healing with Keavy and ensure that the plague on their house does not continue.'

'Perhaps you should call in the bishop,' Blair suggested.

'Aye, I have thought on that, but my heart tells me that it will be Rachel who heals the hurt.' Blair blushed and he hung his head. 'No, man,' Fleance chided. 'I was not criticising you. She will be found. I know this in my heart. Before Hogmanay, I promise, all will be right again for our country.' Fleance inhaled to steady himself. 'It is time,' he said, and made his way down to the scaffold.

Magness looked magnificent: healthy, well bodied and strong. But the noose around his neck told a different story. The executioner pulled the black hood over Magness's head and tightened the rope. The crowd went silent and then inhaled as one, as he was led to the edge of the platform. Time stood still as they all waited. Then, as if it were nothing at all, Magness stepped calmly forward, out into nothing, and his large body fell. There was one grunt from him as his life was snatched away.

Fleance had seen enough and turned to go. He nodded to Preston, who went ahead and opened the door for him. When he got to the great chamber, Fleance realised he had been holding his breath. He exhaled loudly and then reached for wine. The sharp tang of liquid hit the back of his throat and burned as he swallowed. He welcomed the discomfort, though it triggered a coughing fit for some minutes.

Preston poured him some water and he gulped that down. 'Thank you,' he said, wiping his eyes and nose.

After a moment he was able to breathe steadily again. 'What of those who surrendered?'

'In the stocks.'

'Have the earls spoken to them yet?'

'Aye, and each man has begged for your pardon.'

Fleance poured some more water and drank thirstily. 'What is your counsel, Preston?'

Preston was quiet for a while and Fleance waited, now familiar with the old man's ways: the heavier the situation, the longer it took for him to speak. 'They are young men, bar two. Half of them have families: wives, babes. All of them surrendered on the battlefield.'

He was painting a story for the king and Fleance picked up the brush of the narrative and so continued what Preston started. 'They joined the rebels willingly to fight against the king. Preston nodded, his eyes hooded and hard to read under his thick eyebrows. 'They must be punished.' Again, Preston nodded but was silent.

In his mind's eye, Fleance regarded each of the soldiers who stood now in the stocks, hands, feet and necks immobilised by the crude locks. To send them to their death was too severe; to let them go would give out the wrong message to others who might take up arms against the throne. To imprison them condemned their families to starvation.

'They shall be punished by lashing – fifteen each.'

'I shall send word.'

'Let them be tended to before being sent back to their homes.'

Preston bowed and left the hall, leaving the king in the company of two servants who stood motionless on either side of the door.

Fleance went to the great table and sat. What would he do about Keavy now? Perhaps he could ask Rosie to take her to the inn for a while, until she could come to terms with her father's death.

The muscles in his shoulders still ached from his skirmish with Magness, and he could do with Rachel's healing hands at this moment. His stomach twisted at the thought of her. 'Please be all right, Rachel,' he whispered. 'Please be found.' He could imagine her organising the people around her – whoever they were. She would be strong and steady and content. Not free, but her freedom would come soon, surely. Once this business was finished he would think on how else he could find her.

Suddenly there were shouts and the sound of swords and determined footfalls outside the hall. The doors burst open and Preston, Ross, Blair and two soldiers seemed to tumble into the room. The soldiers were carrying a scruffy fair-haired man between them, his hands tied behind his back and his nose dripping blood.

'What is the meaning of this?' Fleance cried.

The soldiers pushed the man forward so that he fell to his knees in front of the king.

'We found this one trying to sneak into the castle.'

'Sneak?'

'Aye, he was skulking around the back by the kitchens, hiding behind some barrels,' he said. 'Morag had gone out to empty the slop bucket and there he was.'

Fleance looked at the man, who did not look like an insurgent. He was too clean. He was too well attired to be one of those of the lower orders who made their living from undesirable practices. Something was amiss. 'Was he armed?' he demanded.

'No, my lord.'

'What is your business?' Fleance asked the prisoner.

'I have a message for the king,' he said. His accent was thick, foreign.

'Then give it,' Fleance ordered.

'My king commanded that I stay in hiding until this day and then find you and deliver his news.'

'And who is your king?' Fleance demanded.

'Calum,' the man replied. 'Calum of Norway.'

The other men murmured their disapproval.

'What is his news?' Fleance asked.

'He bade me tell you he has your bride-to-be and he will execute her if you do not travel with me to Norway to come before him.'

'It's a trick, Your Majesty,' Ross said. 'A ploy to get you out of the country.' The other men nodded in agreement.

Fleance stood before their prisoner. 'How do I know you tell the truth?' he asked.

'If you will permit me to be untied I will provide you with evidence.'

Fleance nodded to the soldiers and one stepped forward and cut free the ties. The Norwegian reached inside a small pouch that was hidden under his shirt. He pulled out a lock of hair and a necklace and handed them to Fleance. The hair was the same colour as Rachel's and the necklace was like one he had given her after their betrothal was announced. A beautifully delicate gold chain and a solid cross which he had had fashioned especially for her. He turned the cross over and read the inscription: *Above all else, I honour you.* He placed them on the table.

'These prove only that you had her in your custody, not that she is still alive.' But even as he said this, he knew what needed to be done. Whether she was alive or dead, he had to know. 'I have a message, myself, for your king. If indeed Rachel is a prisoner of Norway then we are at war.' He caught a look between Blair and Ross but ignored it. 'Go home and tell Calum that the King of Scotland rejects his demands.'

Fleance nodded to the soldiers. 'Escort him from Scotland.' Then he strode out of the great hall, his heart racing in his chest and his hands sweaty. After a moment, he heard Preston, Blair and Ross striding after him. 'Blue room,' Fleance told them quietly and they followed him down the hall and into the small room.

He rounded on them, breathing heavily. They all began to speak at once.

'We cannot afford another battle . . .'

'The people will be enraged . . .'

'It's a ploy . . .'

Fleance put up his hand. 'Quiet. All of you are correct, but,' he said, a mixture of fear and excitement swirling inside his stomach, 'I have a plan and I need your help.'

Chapter Eighteen
Norway
Rachel

Rachel had given instruction for Sven's care but became busy with the priests, helping to prepare those who were fatally wounded to face their final destination. When, three days later, she lifted back the dressing, she was alarmed to see a clear discharge from the wound. Even more alarming was the foul smell coming from it. *'What is this?'* she demanded in Latin. *'Has nobody reapplied fresh medicine to the wound?'*

Another young monk hurried forward. His Latin was fractured but she understood him. None had attended Sven. His impending death as a result of his injuries was part, it seemed, of God's plan.

Sven's face and chest were bright red and hot to the touch. Rachel offered up a quick prayer and asked forgiveness for the ineptitude of others. She collected up fresh bandages, some wine and more of the poultice, and returned to the feverish guard. *'Give him water,'* she told the monk, pointing to the lidded bucket by the door. He understood her, for he hurried over at once while Rachel cleared away the putrid bandages and poured wine over the infected site.

Sven hissed in pain but did not cry out. Instead, his eyes searched hers and seemed to find comfort in her steady gaze. 'Do not fret, my friend,' she told him. 'It is all in hand.'

When the monk returned with a cup of water, she gave him further instructions. *'Go get a surgeon, for your king's soldier must live.'* The man frowned and said something in Norwegian. He did not understand her.

Despite his ill health, Sven roused himself and addressed the monk, who looked alarmed and hurried away.

'You have me concerned if you believe you need help,' he said, his voice hoarse and cracking.

Rachel took the cup of water and held it to Sven's swollen lips. 'Drink.'

He took a few sips before falling back. She put down the cup and studied the wound. She thought he might recover if the poultice was strong enough. Perhaps the surgeon would offer something else.

The hide flap over the doorway was pushed aside as the monk returned, accompanied by one of the surgeons. The man barely acknowledged her as he removed his cloak and handed it to the monk. Instead he studied Sven's chest. *'You have soaked it with wine?'* he asked in Latin. She nodded. *'And you have readied the medicine?'* Rachel handed it to him. As she would have done, he smeared the mixture into the wound and applied a dressing. *'Have you let blood?'*

'No. I thought it best to wait for your opinion.'

He sniffed. *'A critical technique for any healer. You should have done it first.'*

Rachel ignored the barb and went to get the bloodletting instruments. She would defer to his authority, as was only right, for she had asked him to come.

He made a small incision just under Sven's right nipple and pressed the collecting cup into his chest so that the blood was caught. Rachel studied her guard's face but his eyes were closed. *'Press here,'* the surgeon told her and she replaced his hand with hers over the wad of cloth that pressed into the cut.

The surgeon took the cup and sniffed the contents. *'Do this again in an hour and the infection will be drawn out. He is weak and if we take too much at once he might die.'* He handed her the tools and pulled on his cloak. *'If his fever does not break then he will die; we can only pray that the power of the medicine is enough to help him fight to live.'*

Rachel spent the rest of the day going from patient to patient but found herself constantly returning to check on Sven's progress. As she was instructed, each hour she let his blood flow into the collecting cup and, though she couldn't be certain, by early evening she thought the wound less smelly.

To Rachel's relief then, just before midnight, Sven's fever broke. Though his body was covered in sweat, his colour was returning to normal and his eyes were clear. 'Drink,' she told him again and this time he was able to finish the whole cup and held it out for more. 'This is a good sign,' she said and refilled the cup. 'It seems God has determined that you are to live.'

'For this I am grateful to Him and to you,' he said with a weak smile. This vanished almost immediately when they heard the sound of galloping horses approaching. 'It is the king,' he said, a look of dread on his grey face.

Moments later, Calum came through the door. He was in a state, and seemed to care little that he had entered an infirmary. He shouted at his aides and more torches were lit and placed down each side of the ward. As he paced, he spoke to everyone, occasionally throwing an angry look in Rachel's direction. Sven quietly translated for her. 'He says that many of those he had chosen for his service have failed. We were not overcome but the casualty rate has been too high. We gained nothing by defending our country.'

Under the surging rage of Calum's speech, Sven's quiet voice helped her to understand the king's frustration. 'He has said, "How am I to continue to build our nation if over half the men are dead or rendered useless to me?"'

Calum stopped and stared at them both, panting. He pointed at Sven. 'You,' he raged in English, 'left the girl!'

Sven tried to sit up but was too weak. Instead, he addressed his king lying down. 'Your Majesty, I was commanded by one of your generals to leave my post and go to battle.'

Calum glared at him. 'You took the directions of one lower than me over my *own* instructions?'

'He used your name, Your Majesty.'

Rachel now understood why this interchange was carried out in a language no one else in the room would know. It saved face for the king, because to have any of his commands ignored would weaken his position. Much more so now that Norway had only just managed to defend itself.

Calum rushed forward and slapped Sven across the face. 'Unless the command comes from my mouth, it is a lie.' The king stood back. 'You will be punished for your incompetence.'

He strode out of the infirmary and the effect of his rage brought an eerie silence over those inside.

Rachel turned to Sven but he had already turned his head away. She went to him and put her hand on his shoulder.

'Go,' he said, not looking at her. 'He will kill you.'

'Sven, he is angry. He will get over his anger and come to his senses.'

Sven turned his head to face her and grabbed her hand. 'Believe me, Princess. He has no desire that you live.'

There was something in his eyes that warned her that this was not an idle comment.

'Has he said as much?'

Sven nodded. 'At the beginning, when he was planning your abduction, he told me of his desire to lure your betrothed to Norway and kill you both.' A sudden wave of heat washed over his body so that Sven was again damp with perspiration. Rachel ran to collect cool, damp cloths from a nearby bucket and came back to lay them over the guard's body.

'Thank you,' he said, but grabbed her hand. 'Leave me. The king will have me executed anyway. Take the clothes from one of the dead. They have no use for them now. And Princess, take my horse. Go as far away as you can.' He took his dagger and pressed it to her.

'I can't leave you like this,' she said.

'Please,' he cried hoarsely. 'Save yourself. If you must, teach the boy what to do,' he said, looking over at the young monk.

Rachel called to the young man and, as much as she was able, showed him how to minister to the sick guard. Sven translated for her, telling the boy that the witch would be away for a while to rest.

'But if Fleance is coming?' Rachel whispered.

Sven gripped her hand. 'If he is an honourable king and worthy, then you have no need to fear for him. Save yourself. Go.' Sven swallowed thickly and turned his head but Rachel still saw the tears that ran down his face.

'Thank you,' she said. 'If God is with me, I will make my way south to Normandy. I have friends in the duke's court.'

Sven smiled. 'That is a good plan. I will pray for you.'

Rachel squeezed his fingers. 'I will not forget your kindness.'

To say more would offend his honour.

Rachel slipped out of the infirmary and over to the wagon that held the dead. The blue light of the night made the bodies appear inhuman. She looked behind her to see if there was anyone watching before selecting a man who was about her size. The body was rigid and it took some effort to remove his breeks. They were not soiled, which was a blessing. Almost all, on the moment of their death, voided everything held inside their body: mostly it was, from her experience, faeces or phlegm or blood.

But there was the rare occasion when the corpse had already purged itself and in death lay quietly. Thanks be to God that she had found such a person.

Now the shirt. She took that, but did not take his boots as hers were adequate. She then went from body to body searching for a robe.

Despite the cold, the smell of decay hovered over the wagon and Rachel was about to give up her search when a body toppled off the pile exposing another wrapped in a thick cloak. She gave a prayer of thanks and set to work removing this from the dead man.

With the cloying smell of death permeating the garments, she went into the shadows offered by a small stand of trees, stripped off her dirty smock and dressed quickly. She took the ragged garment and walked quickly back to the wagon, eyes seeking out a place to hide it. It would be a half a day at least before the wagon was taken to the pyre and her dress discovered – if at all – and, even then, it would be unlikely to raise any interest.

Now, to find Sven's horse, tack him and escape without being recognised by the soldiers who lingered around the compound and those who were set to guard the place.

Rachel crept from shadow to shadow, her breath a pale white mist in the cold night air. The horses were corralled between the infirmary and the latrines. She spotted Sven's horse immediately – the huge white beast with black ears. He was against the fence, his large head and neck hanging over as if he were staring at the infirmary.

She wished she knew his name or at least something of his manners. It was too late to go back and talk to Sven. Immediately she crossed herself and offered up another prayer for his well-being. Standing for a moment, while she tried to formulate a plan, Rachel took a deep breath. Sven had warned her that she was in mortal danger. No place now for sensitivities.

This was the time to make good with her skills. She needed to tack this horse: a bridle or a rope at least. All of these were stored in the implement tent to the right of the enclosure.

The tent was guarded.

Well out of the lamplight, Rachel watched the restless young man who stood in front of the entrance. The soldier was jiggling from side to side and suddenly Rachel felt a warmth of humour flood through her. His very actions were like those of Bree when she needed to relieve herself but was too engrossed in her current occupation to heed the demands of her body.

Anytime soon, the young man was sure to take leave of his post. As if her very thoughts made action happen, the soldier quickly looked left and right before he fled in the direction of the latrines.

This was her chance. She ran to the building and stole inside, her hands groping along the sides of the walls searching for what she needed. Within moments, she touched a thick rope and pulled it from its hook. It was heavy and dusty and she suppressed the urge to sneeze. Bridle, she told herself, but a distant cough made her stop. He was coming back.

She backed out the way she'd come in and bolted to the dark shadows that had hid her before, willing her breath to quieten. Just as she got her breathing under control, the soldier resumed his post.

The rope was rough and weighty in her arms but it was all she had. She would have to take the horse using only this. She crept around to the corral and was relieved to see the huge animal in the same position, his dark eyes reflecting lights from around the camp. *Please, Lord*, she prayed. *May he be the mirror of his master.*

Rachel walked silently towards him, her hand was outstretched. She made a low clucking noise. The horse turned his head slightly and regarded her. There was something in his expression that spoke neither of fear nor welcome.

She placed one end of the long rope over his neck and took the other and worked a series of loops and knots so that a basic halter rested over his ears, around his nose and under his neck. She then slipped another knot under his chin to make the loops secure. Then, slipping through the gap in the fence, she pulled him towards her as she moved among the sleeping horses towards the gate.

Sweat was trickling down her back and between her breasts. The horse nudged her and stood back in alarm. He had smelt the death that clung to her body. Clucking again and pulling firmly on the rope, she continued forward to the gate, opened it and led him out.

His hooves made echoing thuds on the hard earth, but just then, a chorus of laughter erupted from a nearby camp. The shouting and mirth filled the night air and Rachel took the chance to quicken her pace so that very shortly they were hidden in the woods.

She grabbed a handful of his mane and swung herself up onto the horse's back. Startled, he shifted nervously under her weight, but her soothing noises and the firm pressure of her thighs reassured him. She urged him forward, keeping the rising moon to her right as she glimpsed it through the trees.

Before long, the forest became less crowded with trees and she was able to urge the horse to a faster walk. He was thickly built and well fed and surprisingly comfortable. And incredibly sensitive to her instructions.

As they settled into a rhythm, Rachel evaluated her predicament. She had no clothes save the ones she was wearing. No money, no food and no clear idea where she was heading.

When she was nine, and still exiled in Ireland, she and Duncan had got lost. They had gone hunting in early autumn, taking a path that they had not used before. Within an hour, a thick mist had rolled in but still they trudged on. 'We must get above this cloud,' Duncan had said, turning to his left and walking up a bank. 'Come.'

She had taken his hand and they had scrabbled up the hill for about ten minutes until they broke through the thick white mist that engulfed the countryside.

'It looks like we are surrounded by a white sea,' she had told her brother. 'And we are standing on islands.'

'Huh,' was all Duncan said, before sitting down on a dewy hump. 'We will have to wait this out. It would be foolish to go into that sea of yours to try to find our way home.'

Rachel had lifted up her skirts a little and sat close beside her brother, shoulders and legs just touching. She remembered the security she had felt from the strength and heat that radiated from him.

Much later, the mist seemed to tire of its brooding and gradually dissipated, rewarding the watching children with a clear view that stretched out below them for miles.

Yet, the problem remained: they did not know where they were and which way home was. And it was getting dark.

'Hungry?' Duncan had asked.

She had nodded but then grabbed his arm, stopping him in his tracks. 'Mother says if ever we need anything, all we are to do is to ask the good Lord.'

Duncan's eyebrow lifted and he shook his head slightly but quickly changed his expression. He must have seen the shadow of doubt wash over her because he nodded. 'Aye. We must.' He took her hands and they knelt down in the grass. 'Will you do the honours, then, wee Rachel?'

All these years later, she could still picture them there, alone, children in a vast wilderness, before the Creator asking a simple thing: 'Dear Lord, please take us home and please can we have something to eat? Amen.'

With renewed vigour they had walked briskly towards the setting sun, hand in hand. A long time later, when the sun had set but there was still light enough in the sky, they had stumbled across a plover's nest filled with a late clutch of four eggs. These they ate greedily.

Next, as they crossed a valley, they were rewarded with a brook that was happily bubbling over rocks. There they took a long drink of fresh, cold water.

They were both still quenching their thirst when the sound of horses and the sight of torches filled the night air. It was Preston and the stable hand. Their rescue party had come to find them.

Later, when she was in bed and recounting her story to her mother, Rachel told her about the prayer.

'Aye, lass,' her mother had said, stroking Rachel's hair. 'Our Lord reminds us to consider the lilies of the field and the birds of the air. God takes care of them, so how much more will he take care of us? Never be afraid to ask Him.'

It was her mother's words that resonated in Rachel's heart now. Though her plight might seem bleak, there was always hope.

In front of her were danger and possible death.

Behind her were danger and certain death.

She had no other choice but to hope that she would escape both danger and death and make it to safety.

Scotland
Rosie

Ma had asked only a few of the locals back to the tavern for the night. Jethro was there because, well, it was part of his job and because he was almost part of the family. The castle had agreed that Keavy could spend some time with them and she had insisted that Princess Bree accompany her. This caused no end of consternation from the castle (and, indeed, from Ma) but the dowager Queen Margaret herself had given permission and had sent word that she would be most pleased to be accommodated in their large suite.

They had chosen to delay the celebration of Rosie's birthday until she had returned from the business for the king. Da had encouraged young Blair to attend and it was a comforting thing having him standing there among the other guests.

'All set then, lass?' Dougal asked as he placed another barrel of ale under one of the trestles. 'It's a good gathering, mind, with us only here a short time.'

Rosie's heart sank. Before they moved north to Scotland, every birthday there had included a wonderful group of girls with whom she'd spent her days. Now, confined to the tavern and lately travelling with Blair, Rosie had been less free to cultivate friendships. Most young women her age were married and had two or three children. She could feel their pity that at her age she was unwed.

Though if Ma or Da had any say, Blair would be roped in to wed her immediately, and if he were not willing – 'I'd flay him for any reason he gave,' Dougal had growled – then there was the ever-eager Jethro.

Rosie watched her father and Blair lift the roast pig onto the huge platter laid out on the table. The younger man was pleasing to look at. He was strong. He enjoyed life. And, she knew, he wanted her. But his touch made her cold and she could do little more than see him as a cute puppy who would one day grow into a most disagreeable and laborious dog.

She did not feel so inclined to celebrate this birthday. Her parents always made a big thing of them. Perhaps the loss of all their other children made the recognition of her own birth and life that much more important.

'They love you very much,' a soft voice beside her said. It was Queen Margaret. Rosie curtsied low, her face red and blotchy from embarrassment at having her thoughts apparently laid bare before the dowager queen. 'There, child,' the dowager said. 'Do not be alarmed. I am here to honour a young woman who means so much to our king and his sister.'

'Thank you, Your Majesty.' Rosie said, baffled now as to the protocol.

'Rosie, dear, I am an old woman and what I desire most is that the people of this wonderful nation know that there is a God who loves them.' Her eyes twinkled, but Rosie saw tears. 'When we have embraced our fate, then we will be at peace.' The small woman took her hand and Rosie was delighted at the smoothness of her skin. 'Shall we go forward and sample what your mother has prepared?'

The two of them walked towards the tables laden with food. Keavy and Princess Bree came running through the small gathering and the princess fell into the dowager's arms. 'Aunty,' she cried. 'Isn't it wonderful?'

Queen Margaret smiled. 'Aye, wee Bree. Birthdays are always great moments to celebrate. No matter whether boy or girl God has chosen a day for a child to be born. This must always be remembered by those who love the child.' She looked over at Rosie and nodded. 'Now,' she added, taking Bree's face in her tiny hands. 'A good princess should be able to assist at any important feast. Go find Rosie's mother and say that you are now free to help her.'

A cloud passed over the young girl's face and she frowned. 'But I am a princess. Why should I serve?'

'The King of Kings washed the feet of a prostitute, Bree. We must live by His example.'

Princess Bree screwed up her face. 'I'm not washing anyone's feet,' she said.

The dowager leant forward and took the young girl to the side. 'Jesus says, "If you do this for the least of my brethren, you do it for me."'

Bree struggled free. 'I don't know what that means.'

Keavy stepped forward. 'It means, Bree, if you want to rule you need to understand how everyone you rule lives. Easy.'

White fury filled the young girl's face. 'Not easy at all if you are a princess.' She stood with her hands on her hips.

'Yah. Easy if you are not thinking about how important you are.'

The princess flew at Keavy and the two small girls were suddenly rolling around on the ground.

Rosie threw herself into the kerfuffle and pulled Keavy, panting and crying, over towards the side of the tavern. The dowager had similarly extracted the princess and was moving her into her suite.

'You've gone and done it now,' Rosie said. 'Keavy, what is wrong with the friendship you have with this poisonous girl?'

Keavy's tear-stained face lifted up towards the older girl. 'She is my friend.'

'Yes, but she is also nasty.'

'Not to me. Well, not often.'

'Fine. But please. Ma and Da have worked hard for this celebration. Can you not at least try to keep your friend under control?'

Keavy pressed herself into Rosie's skirt. 'I love you Rosie and I love Flea and I love Da and I miss Ma and I love Bree and I love my horse.'

Amid the fracas, they had all forgotten that the lass had lost her mother before her father was executed. Rosie's heart winced at their negligence. The child was now an orphan.

Rosie put her arms around the small girl and pulled her close.

———

What a pleasant evening it had been: great food and drink and friends who did not mind that there was Scottish royalty among them. By the time the moon had reached its zenith, most had gone home. Jethro still lingered. Blair had gone two hours ago. The dowager and the young girls were tucked into bed in their lodgings.

'Rosie,' Dougal called. 'Come inside now. We have something to present to you.'

Obediently, she moved into the inn, excited but anxious of what might happen now.

To her surprise and delight, Dougal was less affected by the ale than usual. Ma stood close to him as they waited beside the bar. 'Tonight,' Dougal began, 'we celebrate my daughter's birthday. We celebrate it today because on her actual birthday she was wandering around Scotland for our king.' The remaining guests laughed, but Rosie felt a sudden stinging hurt.

Da was correct but she and Blair had not been wandering: they had been searching. And how they had searched.

He pulled something from a box that had always sat among his personal possessions. 'Come here, girl,' he said. 'I give you, in recognition of your birthday, this brooch. It was given to me by my father and his father before him.'

Dougal pinned it to her dress and turned her around to face the crowd.

Everyone cheered and clapped and, shyly, Rosie thanked those who had organised her birthday party.

Rosie held the brooch in her hand, amazed at its beauty, and wondered about its worth. It was beautiful and the stones resembled rubies, amethyst and jade. Red, purple and green. How on earth did her father come to possess such a thing? It was sure to be worth a lot of money. Why hadn't he sold it before now?

The brooch, along with Flea's necklace, lay on her dresser. She fingered the ornate emblem. She'd seen nothing like it in Scotland or England. Perhaps it was Irish? She picked it up again and went quietly out of her chamber.

She made her way to her parents' room and knocked gently. She waited a moment, listening to the sounds of her father getting out of bed and coming to the door. He opened it and, when he saw her, his frown evaporated. 'Rosie, love. What's wrong?'

She peeked into the room and saw that her mother was sitting upright in bed, kneading her hands. Rosie was instantly contrite. 'Oh, Ma. I am sorry I did not make time to do this tonight.'

Her mother waved her away. 'Lass, I am not so useless that I can't rub ointment into my own joints. This has been your day.' She patted the bed beside her legs. 'Sit and tell us why you've come this late of the evening.'

Her father settled himself back into his side of the bed and pulled the covers up over his chest. 'Yes, what is it you have on your mind?' He looked at his wife and winked. 'Were you going to tell us you've chosen a suitor?'

Rosie shook her head. 'Please! Let's not talk about that!' She hesitated. 'Da, this gift . . .' She held out the brooch. 'How did you come by such a precious piece?'

'Ah, now, wee Rosie, there's a story there to warm your heart and make you believe in the power of true love.' He grinned and Rosie wondered if he were teasing. 'That gem belonged to my grandpapa and he gave it to my father who gave it to me. My grandpapa died before I was born but my da told me that he had loved a lass so much that he was willing to leave behind his family and run away with her to another country.'

Marriage was always seen as a respectable thing to do. Rosie spoke her mind. 'Why would he need to do this?'

'Seems his parents did not want him to marry his love.'

'Why?'

Dougal shrugged. 'I don't know that part of the story, lass, but I do know that my grandpapa took his love and fled, settling here in Scotland. My father told me his mother's father was a blacksmith and, when they came to Scotland, Grandpapa became a wainwright and did very well for himself.'

Rosie pulled a blanket over herself. The late night air was cool and she was beginning to shiver. 'Were they happy, then, Da?' she asked.

He nodded. 'Aye, so said my father. He told me once that as a wee lad, he had come upon them cuddling and kissing in the workshop. He told me that he wanted to be just like them.' Dougal leant forward and grabbed for her hand. 'Most marry for a reasonable transaction. Some marry because they need to, to save face. A few of us marry because we are fortunate enough to find the one who will love us and whom we love.' He let go of her hand and leant back onto his pillows. 'My grandpapa loved his wife; my father loved his wife; I love my wife.' He looked at her with tears in his eyes. 'I want you to be a wife who is loved. Soon.'

Rosie lowered her eyes because what he was saying spoke to her heart. Sure, Jethro was a keen and constant suitor. Blair had hinted their union would be desirable and that he would indeed be pleased to wed her, but how could she? How could she join with either of these two men when her heart was locked away for another?

'Yes,' she said. 'Thank you for a wonderful story. A restful night to you both.' Rosie stood up and, swallowing back her emotion, let her parents go back to sleep.

She placed the brooch in the top drawer of her dresser, removed her dress and put on her nightgown. As she climbed into bed, Rosie wondered if she would be the one to doom her father's legacy of love. She blew out the candle and settled down into her covers. *Please, God, no*, she thought. *I want to be like them.* As she pulled the blanket over herself, she was rewarded with the image of the one she loved losing the crossbow competition and winning her heart not so many months ago.

Chapter Nineteen
Norway
Fleance

The arguments had gone on for hours but Fleance won out in the end – he would travel to Norway alone. Preston and Blair had insisted he stay until a proper rescue party could be organised, but Fleance was insistent. Calum would expect this and would be on the lookout for any significant numbers travelling from Scotland. A lone traveller would attract little attention. This would give Fleance the element of surprise.

Now weak from seasickness, he was not so sure of his decision. As he stumbled down the gangplank, he had to pause and empty his stomach one more time. Sailors behind him laughed but he no longer cared whether anyone thought him strong or brave. What he cared about was firm land, fresh water and a place to lay his head while he waited for his body to cease fighting against the solidity of the earth. Then he might be ready to eat again.

The gold in his purse pressed hard against his thigh and he sought a tavern in the port to buy a bed and time to recuperate.

Preston had given Fleance a few phrases in Norwegian that he thought essential:

> *A bed for the night, please.*
> *I am not armed.*
> *Bring me your best dish.*
> *Where is the toilet?*

'A bed for the night,' was the only thing he needed to say to the rosy-faced innkeeper's wife, who took one look at his gold and then took him to a small, cold room off the brewery. But the cot had clean bedding and the room was quiet. She poured fresh water from the jug on the table and passed him a drinking vessel, which he drained thankfully. Once he had crawled into bed, she blew out the one candle and closed the door, leaving Fleance to a welcome night of rest and stillness.

The pale northern sun hit his face in the early hours of the morning. Fleance sat up and his stomach protested. He made it to the chamber pot in time to drag forth the last remnants of a dreadful sea journey, then sat back against the wall and looked around. The pains in his stomach slowly abated, and five minutes later he was able to stand and begin dressing.

There was bread, some fruit and some sausage beside the water jug. The innkeeper's wife must have brought these in during the night. But rather than feeling alarmed that he'd been so completely unaware, Fleance was thankful for her thoughtfulness. His instincts told him the inn was a simple and safe place. The children playing out front, the smiles of the patrons. All told of a safe and happy community.

The fruit and sausage were bypassed but the bread was welcome.

Fleance still felt queasy and another night in this place would help him gather his strength, but Rachel had been a prisoner long enough. He must move on and keep going north. There was no time to linger.

By mid-morning, all traces of the seasickness had left him and Fleance was pleased that he had kept the fruit and sausage from the inn. By midday, he was keenly famished and ate everything he'd brought with him.

Preston had told him that the king's castle lay five hours by cart from the sea port of Stavanger. Heavily disguised as a crofter, the Scottish king had walked about two miles before he was picked up by a farmer late in the afternoon. As the farmer's wagon rolled on, Fleance was surprised at the feeling of excitement that came with his mission. To be free to focus on a single task without all the protocol was a relief.

The farmer started up an animated conversation with Fleance, who smiled and spoke in French: *'I am not good at your language.'*

The old man smiled back and shrugged his shoulders but seemed to content himself with chatting anyway. Fleance settled back against the walls of the cart and took in the sights, sounds and smells of this land.

How similar the country was to Scotland. The same grasses and rocks; the same sense of wildness and exposure to the elements. Unforgiving. Cruel. Fleance could appreciate Calum's determination and resilience. It was much like his own. Being born to a life lived in an inhospitable climate brought challenges that tested any soul. Food, shelter, warmth and security were hard-won in a place like this.

Hours later, the old driver shoved him awake. He jabbered foreign words, the tone of which told Fleance this was the place he had asked for. In the fading light, Fleance saw the castle beyond the trees. He smiled at his host and pressed a coin into his hand to complement the three he had offered at the start of their journey. The driver smiled and jabbered something while unknotting his kerchief to add the coin to the others.

Fleance jumped down, shrugged his rough crofter's cloak tighter around his shoulders and ran into the woods.

There would be sentries. Preston had spent some hours describing the recent history of the country and its current issues. It was not a kingdom that slept easily at night. Despite Preston's language advice, no one had anything to add to help him on his mission.

As in Scotland, the castle was surrounded by an impenetrable wall. Inside, life would be chaos: cooks, butchers, smiths, maids, servants – all called to wait upon the royal household. He would, at the start, present himself as a man ready to work in the stables.

Fleance strode down the main road into the castle grounds, but he did not get within twenty yards of the entrance. A torrent of words rained down on him from the sentries who stood atop the walls.

His French was limited but that was what Preston advised he stick with. While Fleance looked, a cluster of men rushed him, their swords and arrows menacing.

He took a deep breath so he would not trip over foreign words, and spoke, *'I am a poor man,'* Fleance said. *'Wandering far from my native Normandy. I only seek a place to sleep and honest work so I can make my way in the world.'*

He was employed, not in the castle but in the troughs. He had not yet heard anything of Rachel. Yet in the short time he had worked in his position he had discovered that Norway had recently fought a great battle with the Danes and was now licking its wounds, though it had not lost. There were many angry mutterings spat out among the men and women who serviced the castle.

Two days after his employment began, Fleance decided to strike out and search for Rachel. At midnight, with the full moon illuminating the dark sky, Fleance crept towards the main part of the castle and entered through the kitchen. The cook was snoring before the fire and seemed so deeply asleep that to wake her would be a crime.

Just yesterday, he'd spied Calum coming from the main door of the castle and talking to some soldiers. Surely, if what the Norwegian messenger said was true, Fleance would have seen Rachel by now. It was imperative to find if she was actually being held within these walls.

How was he to know if Calum was bluffing? What if Rachel had already been killed? A chill swept over him at this thought.

He should not think on such things. It was better to convince himself that she was here, well and safe, or, better still, had escaped.

The kitchen reminded him of Glamis. The placing of utensils was similar and the spotlessly clean bench was a telling sign. This was a cookhouse ruled by a fierce woman like Morag.

If this castle was like many he knew in Scotland, a stairwell down to the prison cells would be nearby. Fleance assumed Rachel would be a prisoner. Why else would her abduction be carried out in the manner it had if not to take and keep her captive?

Fleance eased open the door that led to the main building and peered through a small gap. Despite the dormant atmosphere of the kitchen, the hallways of this castle were populated by guards and sentries. They were dozing, as was to be expected at this time of the night, but he could not make his way out without being seen.

Silently closing the door, Fleance pulled himself back against the kitchen wall to consider his options. Moments later, however, the door burst open and three men rushed through. For a moment, they did not see him – they seemed intent on raiding the cook's supply of food – but there was nowhere for him to go and it took only seconds before he was spotted.

They seized him, shouting and pushing and eager to ensure Fleance understood his transgression. The food was forgotten as they tumbled him out and along the corridor and up a flight of stairs into a long dark hall.

———⌣———

Calum came through a side door and regarded Fleance. 'I knew you would come,' he said.

'What honourable man would not?' Fleance replied.

The King of Norway snorted. 'That is an interesting word you use – honourable. I think you and I have different definitions.'

Fleance was standing before the king, his hands tied securely behind his back with two guards, left and right. 'Where is Rachel?' he asked.

Calum gave him a sly smile. 'We will get to her in due course, but right now I have other business to attend to.' He shouted something in his own tongue to the guards.

Fleance was dragged away. 'Calum! Wait. Tell me where she is!' he called out, but Calum did not respond. The guards hauled him out of the castle and pushed him into a low wooden dwelling. Through cracks in the door he could see that the men remained in front of the hut, keeping watch.

He sat down on the damp earth and put his head in his hands. *Do not give up hope,* he told himself. *It is not finished and will not be settled until I find her and bring her home.*

Hours later, Fleance was hauled from his prison. A rough cloth was stuffed in his mouth and his hands were tied before he was taken, once more, into the presence of Norway's king. 'It has been a most interesting night,' Calum said. 'Not one, but two visitors from Scotland. I think this latest arrival will interest you,' he smirked, and Fleance was bundled to a side alcove where he could not be seen from the main hall.

There was a banging on the great door and the servants opened it to reveal another, more elaborately dressed guard and – Preston! The guard came forward with the old man and bowed low in front of Calum. When he stood up, he spoke rapidly in Norwegian and gestured often at Preston.

'I am most surprised to see you, Preston,' Calum said in English. 'Are not all Scots enemies to Norway?'

'You of all people should know that is not the case,' Preston replied calmly.

Calum chuckled. 'Yes, I do. And for their support, Norway is most appreciative.' The two men regarded each other a moment. 'I did not think to see you again.'

Preston bowed his head. 'Begging your pardon, Your Majesty, but I feel some urgency in bringing you warning that you are in danger.'

Calum's eyebrows shot up and he tilted his head. 'Oh?'

'Aye. That young upstart, Fleance, is on his way here now to unseat you.'

Fleance, though gagged and bound, felt fury flood his whole body. How dare he? His own trusted advisor and counsellor. How long had he been deceived by this traitor?

Calum took a sip of his wine and pursed his lips. 'How came you by this information? Hmm?'

Preston straightened his shoulders back. 'This past year I have been his advisor. He is a most uncooperative and unwilling sovereign – he is led by his heart and has little understanding of how to take the right path.'

Fleance was tightly bound, but his fury gave him a wild surge of strength. He wanted to leap forward and slit the throat of this unfaithful man. He struggled grimly, but was pushed back by his jailers.

'This is a fair summation of the youth.' Calum smiled. 'But what of your part, Preston? I have always taken you to be something of a man who says yes to anyone who should suggest a certain political point of view.'

Preston smiled meanly. 'Of course I am a yes man. I have been advisor to this family for many years. Do you think I would stay in my position if I argued with the one who pays me gold?'

A servant topped up Calum's cup. 'Would you care for some refreshments, Preston?'

The old man bowed. 'Thank you. I am most obliged by your hospitality.'

Calum roared with laughter but Fleance heard no mirth in the noise. 'Hospitality. You are too polite, old man! But nevertheless, I welcome you and I am eager to hear your news.'

A page, in response to Calum's signal, came over to Preston with goblet and jug. He gave the advisor the cup and then poured a generous amount into it. Bobbing low, he scuttled away. Preston took a sip and smiled at the king. 'Very nice. Made here in Norway?'

The king snorted. 'We can't grow grapes here. No, made in Scotland. Ironic, don't you think?'

Preston coughed and cleared his throat. 'I do not want to seem rude, but I think it important I give you my intelligence as soon as possible so that you may be prepared.'

Crossing his legs, Calum tilted his head and stared at Scotland's counsellor. Fleance was certain he was enjoying this game. 'What have you to say to me? Preston,' he said, 'I think you are a spy.'

Preston did not blink. 'I am.'

Calum paled and looked to his guards, who reached for their weapons. 'Don't worry, Calum. I am no threat to you. I am a spy against the wheedling, ineffectual sovereign of Scotland. Like the rebels who joined you and the many others who came together against the crown, I am one who does not desire to see this bastard king continue his illegal rule.'

The eyes of the Norwegian king were unreadable. His jaw was taut and his face pale. He was angry, Fleance realised, but there was something else: fear? Annoyance? Frustration? 'Come on, old man. I am busy. Tell me what you have come to say.'

'The King of Scotland has come to Norway in disguise, determined to destroy you.'

Calum raised his eyebrows. 'Why should I believe you?'

Preston appeared to flounder. 'I, like Norway, am determined to rid Scotland of its king. I admit that I love Scotland but I see no other way to unseat this usurper than to appeal to you, Your Majesty.'

Norway's king was silent and Fleance longed to break free and speak.

'What say you then, Preston, about Fleance? What threat is he to me?'

An audible sigh came from the old man. 'Be warned, Calum. He is a crafty devil. Skilled in combat and not easily subdued. His plan is, and I heard this myself, to come here, rescue the maid and kill you outright.'

Again, rage surged through Fleance. He had never said such things! Preston was poison.

'Take care,' Preston told Calum. 'He will be here, somewhere, in disguise.'

Calum roared with laughter and the sound echoed around the chamber.

If he had his crossbow right now, Fleance would kill Preston dead. *I am a fool. A fool,* he thought. *I had learnt to trust this weasel and this is my reward.*

Calum flicked his hands and suddenly Fleance was pushed into the middle of the hall. Someone untied his binds and he ripped the gag from his mouth and immediately fell upon his advisor.

'May God strike you dead, you traitorous bastard,' Fleance raged. The attending guard punched Fleance across the face so that he fell to the ground. 'Curse you, Preston,' Fleance muttered, his lips swelling from the blow. 'I will never forget your betrayal.'

Calum clapped his hands with delight. 'Oh, this is good! To see Scotland's troubles played out in my own court.' He grinned. 'Good. Good.' He called to the men before him but his eyes were fixed on Fleance. 'This man, Preston, is for us. Give him what he needs. As for the spy, treat him as he deserves.'

They hauled Fleance away while Preston stood firm in front of the king.

'Come, old man.' Calum stood up. 'We have much catching up to do.'

The king walked to a door at the back of the room and the guard gave Fleance a rough shove as they headed in the opposite direction.

⌣

Angry men grabbed him and spat foreign words in his face. He was hauled before a dark and scarred man who was the guard of the dungeon. Apparently, his crimes were recounted and Fleance was pulled once more into the blackness. The dungeon was deep within the castle and took some time to reach, although the smell of human misery greeted them long before the sight of lumpy dark shapes crowded behind bars and stockades. There was a rustle of straw and bodies, and their appearance seemed to awaken those in the cells. All too soon, moans and cries and shrieks came at them along with skinny outstretched arms.

The guard hit out at the prisoners, which only served to increase the wailing. Fleance tried not to focus on the painful thudding that was pulsing through his skull. Instead, he took in every detail of his surroundings, mapping out his whereabouts. If he were to get out of his cell, he would save time knowing which way to go to avoid the guards.

At the far end of the low-ceilinged prison, one man was in a cell by himself. He stood tall and proud – unlike the misshapen and broken beings Fleance had passed. His face was in shadow until the guard's torchlight flickered over it.

The man wore the scabs of a recent assault: a crusted wound above his right eye and a painful-looking lump on his upper lip. He was also swaddled around the chest with a dark bandage, which Fleance guessed was coloured by old blood. The guard unlocked the cell but the prisoner inside did not move when Fleance was roughly pushed through the open space of the door. The King of Scotland turned to face his jailer. 'Food and water?' he asked, hoping that the Norwegian would understand him. The guard relocked the cell and turned away, taking with him the only light.

In the suffocating darkness and cold, Fleance reached out to find a place to rest. His hands were gripped by another.

'Sit here,' the man said in accented English. 'It is away from the sewers.'

'Thank you,' Fleance replied, allowing himself to be guided by the hands of this stranger. Though the cell was cold and damp, the ground was dry and free of rubbish.

'I am Sven,' the man offered. 'I was a soldier in the king's army.'

'Was?'

'I betrayed him.'

Fleance was silent for a moment. 'Then you are destined to die, I think.'

'Yes, and I go gladly, though the sin I committed against my king was a virtue in God's eyes.'

His curiosity piqued, Fleance shifted and faced the man who joined him against the wall. 'Pray tell, what did you do?'

'I left my post and disobeyed an order. An action all know is punishable by death. But I am at peace because I saved an angel.'

Fleance chuckled. 'Angel? In this place?'

'Yes,' Sven said. 'She was the most beautiful and generous woman I have ever met.'

'But why did you need to save her?' Fleance asked.

'Because, if I did not, then she would die.'

Despite his pain and the hunger that gnawed away at his stomach, Fleance was surprised that such a man would care so much for a woman. 'She must have been important to you.'

'I am nothing,' the man offered. 'But I am a man of honour.'

'And an educated one, I suggest,' Fleance said. 'A foreign soldier speaking another language is a rarity.'

'To be rare is to invite condemnation.'

'So you are condemned twice over?'

The rustling sound beside him meant Sven had changed his position. Moments later he replied. 'Yes, as are you.'

Fleance paused to consider the gravity of his situation. 'Can we escape?'

'No.'

'So, what happens to us?'

Despite the darkness, he could see Sven's profile and understood the man was thinking. 'I will be executed in a few days. You, I do not think the king is finished with yet.'

Fleance leant into the prison wall once more and welcomed its coolness against his back. He was sore and hungry but his wits were intact.

'This woman,' he said. 'What is her story?'

'Like us, she was Calum's prisoner.'

'A slave?'

'No, though she was brought in with slaves. The others were kept together and guarded, but he singled her out and appointed me her solitary keeper.'

'What was she to him, do you think?'

'They knew each other but he seemed to take great delight in humiliating her.'

Fleance's heart began to race and he leant forward. 'Describe her.'

In his quiet voice, Sven continued. 'Very tall for a woman. Her hair had been cropped and she was dressed in sacking, but still she held herself as if she were a queen.' Fleance's hope and fear bubbled up in his chest. 'And,' the soldier added, 'she was a healer and when the fight came, she was taken to help the wounded.'

Fleance leant forward excitedly. 'The woman you have described is my betrothed.'

Sven smiled. 'So I am in the presence of royalty.'

Bitter laughter spilled over Fleance's swollen lip. 'Royal I may be, but because of me, her father died. Because of me, her brother died. Because of me, she was kidnapped and brought here.'

The prisoner's hand found his arm and gripped him. 'Be of good cheer, my friend, if you can,' he said steadily. 'She is not here. Four nights ago, I gave her my horse and blade and told her the way to her freedom. If the gods are kind, she is now close to her allies. It was her desire to go to France to seek sanctuary with William of Normandy.'

Fleance fell back against the wall. Thank God that Rachel was gone from here. He could only hope she survived the journey to the Norman court. Knowing that she was alive and that she had wits enough about her to survive her ordeal lightened his heart. And another familiar feeling burned in the pit of his stomach. It was what he always felt when facing an opponent intent on his death. It was a feeling he relied upon to provide strength and cunning in the face of danger.

'This is welcome news. Scotland will hear of your bravery and sacrifice.'

The man grunted and removed his hand from Fleance's arm. He leant back and rested his shoulders against the wall again.

'Are you injured?'

'I was wounded in battle and your betrothed saved my life.'

Fleance didn't know what to say. Her ministrations had been in vain.

As if reading his thoughts, Sven spoke into the darkness. 'Had she not healed me, I would have been unable to help her flee. Even more so, I am here to pass on the good news that she was alive and well when I last saw her.'

'Thank you,' Fleance said. 'It is of some comfort to imagine that she is now safe.'

'Yes, she is safe.' Sven had not finished. 'But you are not.' He put his hands under his armpits, for a numbing chill was filling the dungeon.

A moment later, Fleance did the same. Despite what his companion might say, Calum had misjudged him. While he still breathed, he would not give up the fight. Too many had sacrificed too much in these past years.

They pulled Fleance from the dungeon later in the afternoon. He was thirsty, hungry and angry. Angry at their treatment of him but also angry with himself for being captured. Angry too with how upset he was now that he knew the truth about Preston. *What a fool*, he berated himself again.

He was brought back into Calum's hall and pushed down again in front of the throne where Calum sat with a smirk on his lips. Preston stood remotely to the side and did not look at him.

'Rest well, did you, Fleance?'

'Most interesting company you have in your dungeons.'

'I hope you enjoyed your time with Sven. He was a good soldier but he disobeyed an order from me. As I'm sure you will understand, sometimes a king must make difficult decisions regarding one of his subjects that will benefit the whole. I cannot let such behaviour go unpunished or I will have trouble in my ranks.' Calum spoke conversationally, as if they were both seated around a banquet table and not as they were: one king on the throne and the other battered and bruised at his feet.

'It must be irksome when those whom you try to control insist on behaving out of their own free will and against your wishes.'

Fleance's voice was hoarse from thirst. 'On this point I do agree with you, Calum.'

Calum raised his eyebrows. 'How so?'

'Sven is a good soldier because he is honourable. To go against your sovereign is to invite certain death yet he did so willingly because he obeyed a higher authority.'

The King of Norway's face clouded momentarily and then he smiled, though there was no warmth in his eyes. 'I am the highest authority.'

'Are you saying you are higher than God?' Fleance asked quietly.

'I am saying that I am God's representative here – as you were in Scotland.'

The past tense rankled but Fleance let the insult fall between them. 'And it must annoy you that you allowed Rachel to slip from your grasp.'

Calum looked at him coolly. 'The girl is of no consequence to me now that I have you. She has served her purpose and she was most useful while she was my guest.' His last word dripped with sarcasm. 'What say you, Preston? Has our prisoner guessed at the reason for his incarceration?'

Preston moved slowly and looked at Calum. 'I would say he was too stubborn and foolish to have even the slightest idea.'

Calum laughed. 'Indeed.' He looked hard at Fleance. 'I told you once before that I have been given a task passed on to me – to avenge my father's death. Until I fulfil his wish, I cannot be free to go forward with my life.'

Fleance shook his head. 'Come on, Calum,' he said softly. 'You are mistaken to believe my father had a hand in your father's death.'

At once, Calum was on his feet and sweeping towards Fleance. The young king had no time to prepare for the stinging blow that knocked his head back, and he toppled sideways, his bound hands unable to protect his face from the hard floor of the castle.

Norway's king stood over him. 'It is you who is mistaken. You were not there, but I have spoken to men who were.'

Banquo had spoken little to his son about what had happened in the battle between Scotland and Sweno, the King of Norway, except to say that one of Scotland's thanes, Cawdor, had fought alongside Norway to defeat Duncan's army. Later, as stories of the battle were repeated, all Fleance learnt was that his father and Macbeth had been instrumental in the victory over the foreign army.

Something, a doubt, a worry, moved in his mind. Why was Calum so determined? Was it more than misguided loyalty to a dead father?

He struggled back up onto his knees and looked up at Calum. 'Punishing me will serve no good,' he said.

'"The sins of the fathers shall be visited upon the children."' Calum sneered. 'If I cannot avenge my father's murder by killing your father, I can do it by killing you.' He turned on his heel and went back to his throne. 'What would you advise, old man?' he said to Preston.

Preston frowned and cleared his throat. 'Sons must live out the paths and legacies their fathers have created.'

Calum grunted. 'Exactly.'

Fleance's heart fell, for Preston's words held truth. Was he now to fail to be the man his father had wanted him to be?

'You will remain in this hall until dawn,' Calum told him. He lifted his chin and turned his head to one of the men standing at the door. His eyes seemed to shine as he shouted out an order to one of the soldiers, who ducked down in response before quickly disappearing from the room. 'You may say that by your death, I achieve nothing. But your death will satisfy my father's command and I will be free to look forward once more.'

The doors banged opened and the soldier returned, dragging what looked like a squat wooden crucifix.

'Bind him,' Calum ordered.

Fleance was pulled to his feet and the ties that held his hands behind his back were severed. He rubbed his wrists, welcoming the tingling feeling in his hands. But this was short-lived and he was pushed up against the post with both arms stretched out on either side. His arms and wrists were secured and another strap was tightened around his middle.

Calum came forward and stripped off his outer garments, laying his chest bare. Every part of the man was honed muscle.

Calum flexed his fingers and held out his hand to a guard and spoke a word in Norwegian. The man passed him a thick-handled axe. 'I was fifteen when my father was murdered.' He smashed the blunt end of the axe into Fleance's belly. 'It was a shock. Much like this, I would think,' He struck Fleance again and then danced away. Fleance tried to regain his breath but was rewarded by a sharp pain under his ribs.

'So how is my torture helpful in avenging your father's murder?' Fleance gasped.

In response to the question, Calum came forward and struck him three times in the face. The pain from the vicious blows blurred his sight. His nose was now bleeding and his head was throbbing.

Calum shook his head. 'It doesn't. Only your death will do that. It does help me to see you suffering, though.' Fleance fell forward against the ties that bound him. 'Use the time you have left, Fleance, to curse your father who brought this on you.' Calum looked at Preston. 'Come, I have further questions for you.' Preston bowed and followed Calum and the others out of the hall.

When the door slammed behind them – a deafeningly ominous sound – Fleance was alone with a solitary guard to watch over him.

The leather bindings were tight and, though they did not cut off feeling to his hands, the skin was rubbed raw by any movement Fleance made.

His throat burned and, despite licking his lips, they remained dry and chafed. His swollen face sent a pulse of pain at regular intervals down his jaw and into his teeth. His vision was still blurry and the beating had left him dizzy, unable to clear the fog from his eyes.

Calum would kill him in the morning, of this Fleance was certain. The mad rage Calum had shown confirmed that no amount of reasoning or pleading would change the outcome. He had been a fool to come here. With his life snuffed out, who was there to take the throne and lead his people?

The buzzing in his head made it hard for him to think. Who was next in line? Feverishly, he tried to think through a sea of faces. One of the earls? Perhaps. They were good men. But what of those he would leave behind? Keavy, Rachel, Rosie, Bree. What would happen to them?

The thirst was undoing him. His tongue now felt like it was made of rough bark and scratched the inside of his mouth.

His chest hurt if he breathed too deeply and he wondered if it was his body protesting at the way he was bound or if Calum had caused serious damage.

He thought about his father and a deep sadness welled up inside him. He had made a mess of things, thinking he could sneak into this enemy stronghold, rescue Rachel and ride off into the sunset like a king in one of Rachel's fairy stories. Now he had put everyone he cared for in a hopeless position.

It was getting harder and harder to stay awake. The constant pain and his utter exhaustion caused Fleance to slump forward, ignoring the pinch of the ties against his raw arms. He no longer had the strength to stay upright.

He closed his eyes and tried to concentrate on the sound of his breath, which rattled in his ears. Maybe it wouldn't be long before he passed out and was free from this suffering.

The murmuring of voices stirred him and he lifted his head. In the shadowy light, two tall figures shimmered and wavered before him. Fleance tried to focus as one of the figures appeared to float away. The other, who came towards him, was dressed in a hooded robe. A memory flickered and his heart skipped a beat. Rachel. His prayers were answered.

But when the hood fell away, Fleance jerked back. It was not Rachel come to mend him but the traitor Preston. 'What do you want?' Fleance hissed, though the effort split his lips further.

'I kept telling you that things are not always as they appear to be.' Preston lifted a chalice to Fleance's mouth. 'Drink.' As if reading Fleance's mind, he added, 'It is not poisoned, I assure you, Your Majesty.' Water spilled down the sides of his face as Fleance gulped down the cool liquid. Then, to his surprise, Preston began to cut loose the leather straps that secured him to the post.

'I am sorry to have deceived you and also apologise for some of the things I have said in this castle, but I needed to assure Calum that I was a traitor.'

'You are,' Fleance muttered.

'No, Sire. I followed you here to ensure you lived.' The second strap was cut and Fleance's arms and hands began to tingle and sting as he flexed them. Preston poured more water into the chalice and offered it to Fleance, who sat down in relief and drank the cup empty.

'Do you think you can walk?' Preston asked, taking the chalice from him.

'What are you doing?'

'Saving the life of my king.' He pulled out a small satchel, opened it and took out some dark bread and sausage. 'Here. This will go some way to restore you.'

Fleance accepted the food and ate it, looking around nervously. Was this all another of Calum's sick jokes?

'Don't worry about the guard,' Preston said. 'I told him to wait outside as I had some business with you – part of Calum's torture.'

In the darkened hall it was difficult to make out Preston's features and Fleance could not trust himself – or Preston, for that matter. Perhaps this was no more than a hallucination or worse, part of a great ruse.

'We haven't got much time, Your Majesty.' Preston appeared flustered. 'Yes, at first, I shared some of Calum's disquiet about you, but this past year I have watched you live your life with honesty and integrity. And there is something else I can see from the way you think and the decisions you make. You are young, but you will be one of the greatest kings Scotland will know. Of this I am certain.'

'I still don't understand,' Fleance said, rubbing his sore wrists. 'Why did you follow me to Norway? You had your orders.'

'Aye, Sire, forgive me for disobeying them but I knew my duty was to protect you. Had your plan succeeded, you would never have known I followed you. But when you were captured, I had to infiltrate the castle to try and stop harm coming your way.'

Fleance was not entirely convinced, but here was Preston offering him food and water, and he had released him.

'One league north of the castle grounds, there is a black mare tied behind a copse of trees. Take her and ride east until you get to the sea. There are many fishing settlements. Choose one where the men are older and take passage on a boat across the Skagerrak Strait to Denmark.

'Head south, Fleance, and ensure you make your way to Henri's brother-in-law, William. There you will find sanctuary.'

'And you?'

Preston removed his cloak. 'Take off your shirt,' he said. He dumped his great cloak to the floor and began pulling off his own tunic. He handed it to Fleance. 'Put this on, and this,' he added, picking up the cloak. 'Give me your shirt.'

Numbly, Fleance did as he was told, still lost in his pain and confusion. But soon he was dressed in Preston's clothes and the old man handed him a bag. 'Here is a water-skin, more food and a small sum of gold.' He then stood with his back to the post and raised his arms. 'Now tie the straps.'

'What are you doing?' Fleance asked. 'Are you mad?'

'No, but I am old. And if this act secures your future as king, then I have done my duty.'

'When Calum discovers this, he will kill you.' Fleance began to tie the straps around the old man's arms, moving as if he was in a dream.

Preston closed his eyes. 'Aye, he will.'

The water and the food had begun to take effect and his head cleared. Fleance frowned at the man. 'You had me fooled, Preston. Back home I had begun to rely on you, and your betrayal here was a deep disappointment. I thought I had betrayed Scotland by trusting you.'

Light caught the old man's eyes and, looking closer, Fleance saw tears. The advisor looked at him directly. 'I beg your pardon, Your Majesty, but you can be read too easily. If Calum did not believe your shock, he would have killed us both.'

233

The king stood back. Remarkably, in the low light of the hall, Preston could have been any man.

'At a better time, old man, you could have joined the court players.'

Preston chuckled but there was deep sadness in his tone. 'Wake the guard and say these words: *Jeg er ferdig med ham, men han er fortsatt i live.*' Fleance repeated the phrase. 'You will be telling him that you are done with the prisoner and that he is still alive. And then: *En god natt til deg.*' He waited while Fleance uttered the line and then he nodded. 'Good. This means that you also wish him a good night. Keep the hood well over your face. He will assume you are me and that I am you.'

Fleance stepped back and regarded this man with whom he had never felt completely at ease but who had never once given him poor advice. His heart heavy with pity, Fleance addressed his advisor. 'Preston, thank you for your sacrifice. I will make sure Scotland never forgets your great bravery and courage.' A quiet sob escaped from the old man. 'Is there someone that you wish the castle to contact and take care of?'

Preston looked up, startled, and then he smiled – such a smile that it almost undid the king. 'I have a niece. She is coming up fourteen. She lives with a family on the outskirts of Dumbarrow Forest. Her parents were killed by Macbeth. I have been her bene-factor for many years. If you could see your way to take care of her then I will die happy. My sister, God rest her soul, would be pleased.'

'Consider it done,' Fleance said. 'Her name?'

'Ina Drummond. She is a bonny lass.'

He came towards the old man and put his hands on the out-stretched arms. Swiftly he kissed Preston on each cheek. 'Bless you, Preston. One day, I will enjoy our reunion in heaven.'

Fleance stood back, pulled the hood over his head and walked towards the great doors, whispering to himself the words his advisor had given him, trying hard to blank out the quiet sobs that came his way along with the smoke and light of the torches.

Still not completely convinced that he wasn't about to be set upon, Fleance warily prodded the sentry. Deepening his voice, he said the phrase Preston had taught him. The Norwegian stumbled up and rubbed his eyes and muttered sleepily something that seemed not unpleasant. Just as he was to make his way down the corridor, Fleance remembered the other phrase.

It was like a magic potion, for the man grinned and thumped Fleance heavily on the back, then he was gone, back into the great hall and as Fleance fled out of the castle, he hoped the dozy guard would not see that anything was amiss.

True to Preston's word, the mare was quietly dozing in the dark shadow of a group of trees. Fleance wondered when Preston could have arranged this, for not only was the animal tacked but there were further rations of food and water. The horse was skittish and unhappy to be on the move at this time of the evening but the full moon and the road, soft and quiet from recent rain, gave Fleance courage to follow his advisor's words. He headed east. The moon, a swollen ball of light, was now descending to the west. In several hours she would be almost below the horizon.

Despite his own urgent mission, Fleance couldn't shake off the feeling of regret that he had left the old man behind. He could almost smell and hear what would happen when the advisor was discovered: his blood being spilled and his screams filling the hall. Preston, who would be sacrificed for his king's survival.

The fishing village Fleance came to was already alive with noise and movement as fishermen came ashore with their night's catch. Seagulls squabbled and flocked just above the masts of the boats. Fleance watched from the road on the hill before he descended into the township. His eyes scanned the young boys and older men who worked methodically to offload barrels of fish from their fishing boats. Further up the coast, he spied a man tying up his boat. The man's casual movement and the lack of seagulls around his vessel caused Fleance to watch him for a time before tugging at the reins of the horse and making his way down to the wharf. With any luck this man was a trader or traveller willing to accept gold for passage across the sea to Denmark.

By the time Fleance had covered the short distance through the village to the northern-most pier, the man was carrying supplies back to his boat. When he saw Fleance he stopped, put his load down and stood waiting.

Fleance dipped his head in greeting and spoke a few words in Latin. The man frowned and shook his head. Fleance tried French but it seemed this was not a language the man knew either. He spoke in his own language and it was Fleance's turn to shake his head. He pointed to himself and out over the sea and then pointed to the man. 'Denmark.'

The man grunted but nodded. Fleance reached inside his bag and pulled out the purse of gold Preston had given him. He pointed to the mare and held up two coins. The man nodded some more, picked up his load and walked towards his boat. '*Kom!*' He called over his shoulder. Fleance was at a loss to know what to do with the mare.

'What about the horse?' he asked.

The man turned once more, sighed then lifted his head and let out a high-pitched whistle towards some scrubby cottages further up the hill. Suddenly, a small body came flying out from one of them and bounded down towards them.

He was a small child, about nine or ten years of age, very thin but with bright eyes and a too-large mouth. The man spoke quickly to the boy, who faced Fleance with a look of both surprise and delight. He came towards the horse, clucking and cooing, and held up his hand. The mare stretched her head down to him and blew softly into his open palm.

'She approves,' Fleance told the boy. He looked back at the man. 'Thank you.' Fleance handed the reins to the boy and went to the saddle to remove his belongings. 'Go well, girl,' he told her as he patted her neck. Then he walked after the man, following him onto the boat.

By late morning, Fleance could see that the Danish coast was closer than the Norwegian and it was not long before he spotted other small boats as the features of the low-lying port became more distinguishable.

The Norwegian boatman came over and stood nearby. He lifted his arm and pointed. '*Hirtshals*,' he said. Fleance recognised the name. Preston had told him of the main trading ports between Norway and Denmark. Hirtshals was the Danish port often captured during the earlier Viking raids.

Within the hour, the boat had docked and Fleance said his farewells to the strong, quiet man who had brought him across the strait.

Now, he needed a horse, some supper and a bed for the night, which were easy to find in the bustling sea town. After a tasty stew with delicious dark bread and a refreshing tankard of ale, Fleance was ready for sleep.

Immediate danger was past, but still Fleance placed his dirk under his pillow before closing his eyes and waiting for his body to stop feeling like it was still on the boat, swaying to and fro.

Chapter Twenty
Rachel

Rachel sold Sven's horse at one of the coastal villages for a worthy sum. The beast's strange colouring attracted interest and there was furious bidding among those who had the gold to spend. Then she bought a passage on one of the Norwegian trading ships that was loaded with logs and destined for Denmark. For her own safety Rachel maintained her pretence as a young man. Later, after they had landed on a sandy beach in Denmark, she slipped away into the village to find directions to an abbey that would give her sanctuary.

Before the sun had all but disappeared, she knocked on the door of a small church. A woman not much older than herself welcomed her in and Rachel was accommodated for the night.

She was finally free from threat and obligation.

As she lay on her small cot, Rachel gave thanks for the small mercies afforded over the past few days. Tomorrow, she would set out for William's court and hoped that her belief in the kindness and generosity of mankind would help her on her way.

A few days later, she arrived in Normandy at the manor of the duke, William. Her ragged and filthy clothes and cropped hair unsettled the royal guard and it was only her knowledge of French and certain key facts about the duke's brother-in-law that convinced the gatekeeper this strange visitor was worthy of being presented.

The key facts? Henri's predisposition for women, wine and apples.

Finally Rachel was given entry into William's court. Matilda, William's wife, was clearly the one who had insisted on her admittance, and she fell upon Rachel with cries of alarm and questions about Henri's welfare. The duchess decided it was critical Rachel be presented to the duke, even though she was filthy and still wearing men's clothes.

William stood in front of a roaring fire, one long arm behind his back. In the other hand was a letter he was reading. Though he was not much older than Rachel, he looked like one who had already lived a lifetime. His hair was thick and dark but touched with strokes of silver at his temples.

Matilda took Rachel's arm and gently pulled her forward. 'William,' she said. 'It is Princess Rachel of Scotland.'

William held up a hand to silence them and continued to read. They waited in the quiet of the hall, though Rachel would sooner have lain down in front of the great hearth and slept for a week. Just when she thought she might actually enact her daydream, the duke finished reading the letter, folded it swiftly and held it out to a serving man. He said something quietly and urgently in French, but Rachel did not catch the meaning.

'My apologies, Princess. It was a difficult letter to understand and it was a matter of great importance.'

'My liege,' she started, bowing low. 'I beg forgiveness for my attire and the manner in which I present myself.' She lowered her head and waited.

'I have seen worse,' William said, and it was with relief Rachel saw that this man was impatient with ceremony, for there was a lightness in his tone. 'You are a friend of *mon beau-frère?*'

'*Oui, votre beau-frère est très cher à moi et ma famille,*' she said, so exhausted she wanted to sit down right then.

'*Oui, oui. Très bien.* And why are you here in my court?'

A simple question which undid her.

Rachel swallowed thickly but the tears were still in her eyes. She took a moment to compose herself. 'I was abducted from Scotland and forced to serve the Norwegian king.' There was a visible shift in their demeanour. 'No. Not like that. He did not debase me in that way,' Rachel said rapidly. 'It was because of old wounds and the desire for revenge that this happened.'

William nodded. 'Revenge is something I understand. It has been a hard-won battle to secure my position against aggrieved barons who believed I was too young to be given what I was entitled to.'

Rachel continued. 'Indeed. I commend you for your fortitude.' The duke smirked. 'What I mean is that you did not give up your rightful cause.'

William and Matilda exchanged looks. Then he leant forward. 'I believe that if you are right, then you are right. Do not let any man or woman pull you from your path.'

She was silent for a moment, thinking on the anger in his words. He was correct.

'Thank you,' she said. 'Your wisdom comes at a time that helps my mind. But let me tell you more of my story.'

The duke waved his hand and smiled. 'It is one, I am sure, we all will enjoy hearing. Go on.'

'I escaped when I learnt my life was in danger and have spent days making my way to you,' Rachel said.

'Why, specifically, to me?'

'Because you are my hope and also Scotland's hope, I trust.'

William looked to his wife in such a manner that it reminded her of Bree when she had worked out a plan to get up to mischief without being caught. 'Then I say welcome, fair Rachel, to our court. I am certain my dear wife will endeavour to see that you are provided for before we discuss the politics you speak of.'

Matilda stood up. Her swollen belly spoke of impending childbirth but she seemed unconcerned with her condition. She went to Rachel and took her hand. '*Venez avec moi,*' she whispered, her soft hands caressing Rachel's. This was a most kind offer and Rachel swallowed deeply, following Henri's sister through the many corridors to a warm and light room. 'Please sit.'

Rachel fell into a chair, sick with hunger and weariness.

'*Mon Dieu.* You're exhausted! You need sleep and food,' she cried, and with relief Rachel understood that Henri's sister was aware of her exhaustion.

'*Oui, madame,*' she whispered. 'I am tired and hungry. Please help me.'

Henri's sister, shorter than her brother, but stronger in voice, barked out orders to her servants so that in no time Rachel's terrible clothes were pulled from her body and she was pushed into a steaming hot tub of sweet-smelling water, where kind hands swept all traces of her ordeal from her aching body. Then she was helped out, dried completely and tended to in a manner more suited to the next Queen of Scotland, dressed in fine sleepwear and given a tasty supper to warm and nourish her.

She had slept a full day and a half but was now invited to William's table. The maids dressed her kindly and again she succumbed to their ministrations. They clucked over the state of her hair and so combed the uneven locks back and secured them tightly against her scalp. Next, they inserted beautiful shell combs and then laid a soft silken veil over her head, attaching the edges to the pins just behind her ears.

Rachel studied herself in the mirror. One could almost believe that her long hair had simply been tucked away. Without the abundance of curls around her face, she looked somewhat thinner and undernourished – perhaps she was.

The tables were simply dressed and the party a smallish group. Rachel was introduced to the others around the table and her story was briefly told.

Between servings of tasty dishes, William and his wife asked her questions, polite in their manner, but clearly impressed with her tale.

'Henri has written of your skill and fortitude. I think he is a little intimidated by you.'

'No.' Rachel shook her head. 'He should not be. I adore him and his effect on our home. Henri is lovely and a welcome presence in the castle.'

'All the women think so,' someone murmured. Everyone heard, and there were knowing smiles and quiet laughter.

William wiped his mouth. 'He told my wife that the King of Scotland will gain not only a beautiful wife but a useful consort. We have heard you are somewhat of a healer.' He raised his eyebrows at her as he took a sip of his wine.

'Yes, that is a gift the Lord has blessed me with,' Rachel said, embarrassed by the endorsement.

'Indeed,' the duke said. 'And a blessing to be shared with your brethren, it seems.' He coughed politely. 'I wonder how you would feel about sharing some of this gift with my wife, for it is a subject in which she takes much interest.'

Matilda gave her a keen look. 'I would be most grateful for any knowledge you have.'

'Of course,' Rachel said, surprised but excited at the prospect of sharing her knowledge. No one had ever shown much interest in how her medicine was administered.

The warmth of the room and the richness of her food were beginning to make her drowsy. There was something tugging at her thoughts. So overwhelmed was she that she was safe and warm, Rachel had forgotten about those back home. 'Can you arrange a post to get to Scotland to tell Fleance I am safe? And the children – they will be worried for me.'

'But I thought you had not yet had children?' Matilda asked.

Rachel shook her head. 'My young sister, Bree, and Fleance's adoptive sister, Keavy. Her mother died last year and her father has disappeared. He was a rebel leader in the battle at Kilmarnock.'

'Was this Magness the Mighty?' William asked.

'Aye. He was also the man who adopted Fleance.'

'He is dead,' William said, a hard look on his face. 'He came against your king not two weeks ago, so we have heard. He was captured by Fleance and executed.'

A burning wave rushed over her body and an image of Keavy flooded her thoughts: her long braid swinging from side to side, her face lit up with joy as she chased Bree down the corridors. 'Poor Keavy,' she said quietly. And poor Fleance.

'I admire a man who acts honourably and is not swayed by emotion,' William continued. 'I like this king of yours. I think he and I are somewhat alike. It is not for the king to tolerate insubordination in any form. No one should go unpunished.'

Those at the table stilled and Rachel was overwhelmed by a sense that a great and terrible thing was being remembered.

William had just bitten into a thick piece of bread, but frowned and waved his hand towards her.

When he had finished his mouthful and cleared his throat, he spoke: 'I am sorry, Princess, for you have endured more than any woman of your status should. At first light I will send my hardiest messenger to go south to the French coast, secure passage across the channel and ride north until he gets to Glamis and your king. No more than seven days.'

'Seven days!' Rachel exclaimed. 'So long . . .'

Matilda came to William's rescue. 'What my husband is trying to say,' she said with a smile, 'is that the sea between our country and yours at this time of year is sometimes most inhospitable.' Rachel's heart sank. 'But, my dear, all is not lost. It will mean we get the pleasure of your company and,' she looked at William, 'as William says, no more than a week.'

Is there no quicker way? Rachel thought, but she said, 'I thank you for your generosity.'

William placed his hands on either side of his plate and smiled kindly at her. 'We will get news to your king and he will receive it with much joy. Within the week he will know you are safe with us and ready to return to Scotland.'

Rachel relaxed further into the chair. It was not such a long time after all. Soon the children would know she was safe and Fleance would not be forced into some rash heroic act.

'Thank you,' she said again as she brushed the last remnants of the feast from her skirts.

A servant filled William's goblet, which he then raised in front of him. 'I toast Scotland, her king and her future queen. And a toast to all men – and women,' he added, nodding his head to his wife and Rachel, 'to be able to take their place as predestined by God.'

They all drank.

William, it appeared, was not finished with her. 'Stay and honour us with your company.'

The duke finished his meal and the guests stood as he and his wife took their leave. 'Come, Rachel,' he said, offering her his arm. 'Join us, if you please, in the room we regard as our sanctuary.' She looked at the others gathered, who smiled but looked away. This was a very important and personal request, it seemed. Though exhausted, Rachel stepped forward and took William's arm.

Rachel was surprised at her reaction now she was so close to this man. He was shorter than her, but how wonderful he smelled. And his confidence was so attractive. No wonder Matilda loved him.

Perhaps it was the wine. It may have been the heat and the exhaustion but she blurted out, 'Matilda, your husband smells so good.'

Both of them roared with delight and Rachel wondered if she were drunk. But William still held firmly to her arm and steered her towards their destination. '*C'est bien, mon amie.* Bless you. My wife will be most encouraged by your comment.'

———◡———

The Duke and Duchess of Normandy's sanctuary, it turned out, could be called a rainbow room, for it was filled with exotic prints, startling colours and gilded artefacts. Rachel saw that one of the wall tapestries was very similar to one that hung in Glamis great hall. She pointed to it. 'We have something very similar to this.'

Matilda stood beside her. 'It is very old,' she said. 'It was a gift to my great-grandfather, who was himself the great-grandson of Alfred the Great, King of England. My father gave it to us as a wedding gift.'

William snorted. 'To remind me, I am certain, of my bastard line and your royal one.'

Matilda shook her head as she made her way to a chair. She eased her thick body into the soft cushions and ignored her husband. 'It is a sore point with William that my father and I at first did not wish to accept his offer of marriage.'

They seemed so comfortable with each other that Rachel wondered at this comment. 'But you seem so in love,' she said.

'Indeed,' William agreed. 'I love Matilda with all my heart.' He went over to his wife, picked up her hand and kissed her gently on the inside of her wrist. He sat in the chair next to her and signalled to a servant, who came over with a tray of wine. The servant offered the refreshments to Rachel, who shook her head. She needed to be alert to fully appreciate the conversation.

'What is your story?' she asked, her curiosity piqued.

'I am surprised you have not heard it,' Matilda said. 'It was quite the scandal.'

Rachel shrugged. 'We were somewhat preoccupied with all the troubles at home.'

William sighed. 'Yes, these past few years have tested us all.'

'To our story?' Matilda said, looking at her husband. 'Which version shall it be?'

William grinned. 'You always make me out to be a bully.'

'And you always make me out to be a snobbish wench.'

'You were!' he declared.

'William, William,' the duchess chided. 'You paint the wrong picture for the princess. I had not met you. I had only heard that you were, ah, a somewhat determined young man.'

'True. And I was determined that you would be the best match for me.'

Rachel interrupted their almost private discussion. 'Pardon me, but how did you know this to be true?' Their looks flustered her. 'What I mean to say is, how did you know Matilda should be your wife?'

William rubbed his jaw as if thinking on her question. Then he reached out to Matilda and held her small hand in his massive one. 'The first reason was practical. I needed to marry into the royal house to secure my position. It was as frankly political as that. Secondly, I had known not only of her beauty, but also of her intelligence and strength of will. I desired a companion who would complement my leadership skills. But finally, it was her refusal and her response to my anger that secured my determination that she was the best woman to become my wife.'

'What happened?' Rachel asked, amazed at the honesty with which the duke was recounting the story.

'I pulled her hair,' he responded with a cheeky smile. 'Have you not heard that when a boy likes a girl, he always pulls her hair?'

Matilda laughed and hit her husband lightly on the arm. 'Tease. Yes, Rachel, the brute actually did pull my braids and pushed me to the ground.' Rachel gasped in horror. 'I know. A terrible thing. So I did what any self-respecting, well-bred woman would do.' She paused, her eyes twinkling. 'I stood up and, despite my stature, kicked him soundly and firmly in the private parts!'

Both roared with laughter and Rachel offered a smile, but did not see why it was so funny. Still, they seemed not to mind that their relationship started off in such a manner.

William, still chuckling, drank some more. 'You are shocked?' he asked.

'Yes, but more because of the tenderness I see between you now.'

'And you are thinking about your engagement to Fleance?' Matilda asked.

'Yes, I am. I would like the companionship and affection I see here.'

'Do you not love him?'

Rachel paused, trying to put the right words together to explain her feelings for Fleance. 'I love him as I should,' she said carefully. 'And I am very fond of him. He is a good man with a great heart and he has made a promise, as did I.'

William drained his goblet. 'There is no shame in marrying for honour, Rachel. Nor for politics.'

'And love?'

The duke snorted. 'This is a word stolen by women to bring themselves misery in a vain search to have a life filled with the unobtainable.'

'Do not speak so harshly, William,' Matilda chided. 'I know you love me as I do you. Do not seek to discourage her.' Matilda patted the cushion on the floor beside her. 'Come, Rachel. Sit beside me.' Rachel did as she was instructed; she sat carefully beside the duchess and allowed Matilda to take her hand in hers. 'Love may already be waiting in the home you make as man and wife, or it may need to be invited in. It does not matter so long as you both keep it at the centre of your hearth and tend to it and nurture it. Before you know it, you will wonder how you ever did without it.'

Rachel stood up again and straightened her skirts. 'Thank you, Duchess. I would very much enjoy some time in chapel,' she added.

The couple exchanged a look, but William nodded. 'After all you have been through, Princess, such a time would be most beneficial. But I recommend a visit tomorrow, as our sanctuary is very cold at this time of night.'

The next morning Rachel was up early, having had a dreamless sleep. She found that the chapel was, as William warned, bitingly cold and she almost turned back. As she hesitated, a choir of young boys spilled in from the back, dressed in matching garb, and then arranged themselves in formation at the back of the altar. A monk went down the sides of the chapel and reignited the torches, which had gone out. Within moments, the light brightened and, though still cold, the atmosphere became a lot more welcoming.

The rustling of their clothing settled and another man came through a door, a staff in his hand. He walked somewhat tentatively but there was an air of confidence in his manner. *He must be very old*, she thought. Dressed in priestly thick robes, the choir master halted and stood before the singers, with his back to the congregation, and raised his arms. Every one of the boys had his gaze fixed on him. Fascinated, Rachel observed the interesting position of the fingers of each of his hands. The man tilted his head to the right and a young boy opened his mouth and offered one pure note. The choir shuffled almost imperceptibly and then the man tilted his head to the left and another child offered up a deeper, fuller tone. The master's arms were still for the briefest of moments and then he flung them outward and the boys sang forth with such a pure pitch of sound she could easily have believed they were angels. Such heaven on earth came from these voices.

Rachel crept forward and sat in the row three from the front.

The choir master turned slowly, his face now in full view, and she saw that he was blind. The mottled pale scars on his face could not conceal his affliction. Nodding as if knowing there was an audience, he turned back to his charges once more. 'Again,' he commanded and in that moment, Rachel's world dissolved.

The choir's voices filled every space in the chapel and she was winded. They sang on and on and her knees trembled. Surely she had misheard. Surely it was not who she thought it was.

They finished their song and for a brief moment fidgeted in their gowns but were clearly pleased with what they had done.

'Very good,' the master said, and many smiled broadly. 'So, we shall do it again.' He lifted his arms and Rachel recognised those pale fingers. They sang once more but she could no longer hear the music. Tears of buried hope and grief welled up with a realisation that Ewan was alive.

———

She had only been sixteen, but the handsome young captain had caught her eye immediately. Ewan had enlisted six months earlier and, though he was the second son of the Thane of Monteith, he desired more action than his father's estate allowed and so had joined himself to Donalbain's small regiment.

In a rare moment of hospitality, Donalbain had hosted a feast after a particularly rich harvest and was in good spirits. Rachel sat next to Ewan and the evening had disappeared as they talked long into the early hours of the morning.

Along with her brother, Duncan, she had taken the journey to Monteith at the request of Ewan's mother. The visit, though entertaining and enjoyable, was cut short when they were called back to Glamis.

The day after their return, Ewan had approached her father and asked permission to marry Rachel. To her surprise Donalbain had agreed, but first the regiment was needed down at the English border to help the king's army quash the border reavers, who were wreaking havoc on the surrounding villages.

Rachel said goodbye to him the very next morning with a promise from him that when they met again, there would be rejoicing. Alas, this was not to be. Three weeks later, when the regiment returned, Ewan was not with them. He had fought bravely and sacrificed himself for his king, she was told.

She had grieved privately for nearly two years – only her brother Duncan sensed the depth of her loss. There had been so many things she had wanted to tell Ewan, and she felt such sorrow every time the sun warmed her face or she heard the pretty sound of a young bird – things she knew he had loved.

This past year, she had spent more time thinking on the future than mourning her own loss. So much had happened.

He had died, they told her, from his wounds, which was honourable for a soldier. What she could see now for herself, however, was that he was very much alive.

The choir had finished and, unlike their sombre entrance, their exit was noisy and boisterous. Ewan stood still, his staff in front of him.

Rachel moved out of her pew and walked up to this man who had taken her heart two years ago.

'They sound beautiful,' she said to his back.

He spun around and this allowed her a closer look at his injuries. The healer in her saw what the surgeons had tried to do. His eyes had been rendered useless, but not damaged so much that they needed removing. He was able to open and close his lids but his eyes saw nothing. Despite herself, Rachel was impressed. 'You must be very pleased.'

He frowned and gripped the staff tighter. 'I thank you for your kind words, Madam.'

'Ewan?' she offered and he froze.

'Who are you?'

'Do you not know me, even now?' He hesitated and swallowed but with such difficulty that Rachel felt sorry she had confronted him. ''Tis Rachel, Eb,' she said, offering the endearment.

Ewan's hands were shaking and it made her uncomfortable that she was upsetting him so.

'Why are you here?' he choked. 'What are you doing in my chapel?'

There was such anger in his voice, she stumbled back. Then she shook herself and gritted her teeth. 'I could ask the same of you, Ewan Boyes. I was told you were slain in battle and I mourned your death. Yet, here you are, alive and well.' She could not help but allow the anger in her heart to well up.

Ewan was silent, his hands twisting around and around the top of his staff, and then a wave of emotion washed over his face. 'What could you expect from me, Rachel? I was no longer worthy of your hand and I could not ask you to marry an invalid. Scotland became a cold, unkind place for me, so I came here and sought our Lord's instruction.' He touched his eyelids and dropped the staff. 'What good would I have been for you, Princess?'

She could understand why he might ask such a question, but that did not stop her from responding with the words she had stored away for so long. 'What good, Ewan? I loved you. You were the only other person who made me feel safe in this world.' She swallowed down her disappointment because it would serve no good now. 'Duncan is dead,' she whispered.

'Aye, I have heard.'

'He adored you.'

Ewan sighed, 'And I, him.'

She tried to swallow her grief but it remained stuck in her throat. 'He was honourable in his death.' But her alarm at his presence had only added to her agitation. 'Yet, Ewan, I am surprised that you have moved so far from those you loved.'

'I am loved by God,' he said.

'Meaning?'

'I have committed my life to the church and I aim to do my duty in such a way as the Lord requires of me.'

She shook her head but then realised he would not see this. She was determined not to succumb to useless platitudes. 'Tell me, Ewan, with honesty, were we in love?'

'I believe so. I am sorry that you suffered,' he sighed. 'I did too, knowing that another man would soon claim you as his own. But I am content that I have now found where our Lord wants me to be, and this is my place.' He moved away from her and nodded towards the crucifix above the altar. 'I made my choice as to whom I should love and I do not regret that choice, though I acknowledge the pain that has come with it.' His cheeks flushed red and he turned his unseeing eyes towards her. 'I am happier now than I have ever been and this happiness affirms that there is a great plan in place. My desires for you, and perhaps yours for me, will not be satisfied – but there are others who will enjoy such contentment with the paths we choose now.'

'I am glad you have heard from God, Ewan, and that he has chosen to bless you with such insight.'

Ewan laughed. 'I believe you are being sarcastic, Rachel.'

'No, and not bitter either, but perhaps frustrated – perhaps disappointed – that God decided to keep me out of the knowledge of his great plan.'

They stood there in the silence of the chapel and Ewan's face took on a familiar grin.

'If ever I understood how a mortal might know the creator God, I thought it was you who would be first in line.' His mouth dropped and he reached out for her. Rachel grabbed his hand and delighted in the familiarity of its touch. 'He has prepared you, Rachel, for what you must face. He has not overlooked the desires of your heart.' He squeezed her hand. 'You have been chosen to be part of whatever is to be the history of Scotland. I am not part of that plan but I am part of something he has mapped for me. It's just that we are not to be together.'

She had one last thing to say. 'I believed with all my heart that it was the right thing for us to be together.'

He pulled her up sharply. 'Really? Who can say? We thought it the right thing at the time, but we were young and knew little of the wider world. God has determined that we follow different paths and you, so I have heard, must take your place as the next Queen of Scotland. This is far removed from the life I could have offered you, Princess.'

He might as well have punched her. Rachel tried one more time. 'I loved you,' she said, her throat thick with emotion. 'You must know me well enough to realise rank and position mean nothing to me. I missed you so much. One word from you and I would be at your side tomorrow.'

Ewan stood firm. 'I will never love anyone as I have loved you, Rachel. But our Lord has given me another task.' He chewed his lip while Rachel's mind was filled with a whirl of all the things she had longed to tell him – yet now, none seemed important.

The choir master continued. 'As painful as it is for me, you deserve so much more that what I could give.' He reached over and stroked her cheek. 'This man, Fleance, I hear is a good man and worthy of your love. Do not be held back by ghosts of the past.' He smiled. 'I am happy, Rachel. This . . .' He gestured around the chapel. '. . . is my life. It means much to me. No one can have every hope and dream, but I am blessed that almost all my hopes and dreams are satisfied in my vocation. Only the fact that I do not have you is a reminder that life is never perfect.'

He bowed his head. 'It is an answer to a prayer that I have met with you again, Rachel, and learn that you are well and as strong as

I remember. Grasp hold of this new path the Lord has given you. Do not look back.' He lowered his voice. 'Looking back only serves to make your going forward crooked. Peace be with you,' he added.

Then Ewan, with his staff, made his way back out of the chapel, leaving her with a feeling of disbelief. And something else. Was it relief? That he was alive? That she did not have to hold on to his memory anymore? That she was free to love another as she had once loved him?

Chapter Twenty-One
Normandy
Fleance

Fleance had lost count of the days. Was it five, six nights since his escape? And five more since he had left Scotland? Had Blair and Henri been able to keep his departure from the people? Who knew what news awaited him when he returned home. But Blair and Henri and the thanes were resilient enough to hold back all questioning arrows, thank God.

He knew that he could not relax until he was safely in the grounds of William's palace. The horse he'd bought was strong and steady and gave him some sense of comfort. Peasants working in their fields helped him on his way, pointing him in the right direction, offering food and, twice, a welcoming hearth. Before long, he saw the Duke of Normandy's home set against the horizon.

The horse plodded on and seemed to share his weariness. There, in the distance, were some women in a garden but Fleance was searching for the main entrance to the courtyard. His stomach ached and his jaw was sore. He had managed to avoid aggravating his split lip but it irritated him nonetheless. Every time he leant forward, his bruised chest reminded him of Calum's beating. He wished he had sought out a surgeon earlier.

He raised a hand in greeting to the two women who were standing among the plants of a well-kept herb garden watching his approach. One was tall and one very short. They were dressed in the manner of the court: colourful gowns with intricate embroidery on the hems and sleeves, and elaborate headwear. Both carried baskets overflowing with all manner of greenery. The shorter one was with child.

The tall woman suddenly gave a shout, dropped her basket, picked up her skirts and came running towards him.

'Fleance!' she called out and he pulled up the horse. 'God be praised,' she cried as she scrambled over the low stone wall. 'What are you doing here?'

'Rachel?' he said. 'Oh God, Rachel!' He dismounted, his legs unsteady from so long in the saddle, and turned just as she threw herself into his arms. Pain raced through his body but he held her tight regardless.

'Sorry,' she said pulling back, grimacing. 'You are hurt.'

'Aye. Somewhat.' He gave her a wry smile.

'Look at you, Fleance. Your face alone tells a story.' She touched the side of his face and traced the bruises ever so lightly.

'At the hands of Calum,' he said.

'Calum? I don't understand.' She looked back down the road as if she might see the very man himself coming behind.

'He has not followed me.' They stood in silence a moment, there in the lane that led to the duke's home. 'Come here,' he whispered. He opened his arms to her and she approached, gently this time. It was such a relief to hold her. 'It is so good to see you are safe,' he said, his voice breaking.

Just then, the other woman arrived. 'Rachel?' she said, interrupting them.

'Duchess,' Rachel said, turning but still holding on to Fleance's hand. 'May I introduce you to Fleance, King of Scotland. And, Fleance, this is Matilda, Duchess of Normandy.'

Matilda held out her hand, which he took. 'You are welcome, Fleance, though I am most surprised to see you so soon. My husband only sent word three days ago that Rachel was here.'

He shook his head. 'It is a very long story.'

Matilda handed Rachel the basket she had dropped. 'I look forward to hearing it. But for now I will hurry ahead and make known the news of your arrival.'

They followed after her, hand in hand, walking slowly, for though strength was returning to Fleance's legs, it was still uncomfortable to move. After such a dark time, to feel the warmth of the sun on his shoulders, the comforting rhythm of the horse's hooves striking the ground beside him, and the relief at finding Rachel almost as he last saw her filled him with joy.

'So, that is Matilda?' he said. 'She has a way about her that is very much like Henri.'

'She does!' Rachel agreed, with a smile. 'But not so direct with her words. Her heart is as generous as her brother's and I have found her company most enjoyable.'

'What is her husband like? I have heard stories about him.'

'Well,' Rachel hesitated. 'He is not quite what you would expect.'

Fleance was intrigued. 'Is this a good thing or not?'

Rachel squeezed his hand. 'I will not prejudice your judgement. Currently I am of two minds. He is very ambitious and, I gather from a little of what the maids have said, he can be quite ruthless. But perhaps that is needed to be an effective leader.'

He did not respond, but it was a truth that he was coming to learn most painfully.

⌣

In Fleance's eyes the interior of the palace was stunning, used as he was to the bare interiors of his own castle. Exhausted, he could not help gazing in awe at the tapestries and painted walls and ceilings. It reminded him a lot of Malcolm and Margaret's castle at Forres. Rachel interrupted his wonderment. 'Would you like to refresh yourself first, Fleance?'

'Aye, that would be good, for I warrant I look more like a sewer rat than a king.'

She eyed him and grinned. 'A handsome sewer rat.' Still smiling, she led him into a side room that had a basin and water. 'Would you like me to find some fresh garments for you?'

Fleance looked at her directly. 'That would be most kind, Rachel.'

'I will return soon and take you to where I can more easily attend to your injuries.'

'Thank you.'

Rachel left him, closing the door after her.

There was a single cot pushed hard up against the wall and a side table at its head. At the end of the bed were two folded linen cloths. In contrast to the ornate corridor on the other side of the door, this room was simply furnished and looked as if it would be more suited to an abbey than a duke's palace. He found the idea of it puzzling and decided he would ask Rachel about it later.

Fleance stripped off his filthy tunic and winced as his ribs protested. *Damn Calum.* He poured water into the basin and splashed his face and the back of his neck. He took the small portion of soap and rubbed it between his hands, then washed his chest, face and neck. The cloth came away filthy so that, by the time Rachel had returned, the basin was filled with black water.

'The duke himself has offered you a set of his own clothes. I hope you are not too offended at the fashion,' she said.

There was a polite knock on the door and a servant entered, speaking to Rachel in French. She smiled and handed the dirty clothes to the servant. 'You can burn these,' she said to him in English. He bowed stiffly and went out again.

In this time Fleance had pulled on the tights and shirt. He was struggling to pull the tunic over his head when Rachel came to his aid. 'It would be easier for your healing if you did not make all this movement, but for the sake of appearances you had better appear fully clothed while we walk through the palace to the healing room.'

'I do not disagree.' He paused in his attempts to get the tunic over his head. 'Can you help?'

'Sorry.' She blushed.

'Why are you apologising?'

'These tunics are designed with open sides that are drawn together with ties,' Rachel said, removing the garment, which was tangled around his head. 'Lower your arms.' She tugged away at the tunic and then came to him and laid the fabric over his head and pulled the ties on each side together. 'I should not have even let you attempt this.' He let her minister to him, enjoying the company of someone who knew and understood him well.

'There,' she said. 'Now we will try these shoes.' She knelt down and helped him into the black leather slippers. 'How do they feel?'

He wiggled his foot. 'A bit tight but I think I will manage. Just don't burn my boots,' he said pointing to the muddied pair that he'd placed beside the bed. 'By the way, Rachel, explain this room to me.'

'I know. Is it not strange?' She picked up his boots and handed them to him. 'This room is a sanctuary for anyone who comes to the manor in need. The duke does not care if they be friend or foe but that they have asked for help renders them worthy of a space to rest and recuperate.'

'How many times has the room been called upon?'

They moved out into the corridor. 'I do not know, but it makes me feel more kindly towards my host that he has decreed such a thing.'

Despite the sting on his lips, the pain in his jaw and the relentless ache of his chest, Rachel's comment disturbed him. He reached for her arm and pulled her to face him. 'Are we safe here?' he whispered.

'Yes. But he is a very determined and strong man. A man who plays and fights hard.'

'Can we trust him?'

They had reached a doorway. 'Yes, I believe we must.' They went in, but Rachel was not finished and closed the door on the servants who had trailed them. 'We need to be alert, for he does not suffer fools and hates those who break protocol.'

Despite its being summer, the air was cold, and there was a fire in the hearth. The room was cluttered with instruments, pots of various shapes and sizes, rolls of bandages, herbs and plants hanging from a drying rack and, thankfully, a number of stools next to a long table holding a pile of linen, a jug and some cups.

'Take a seat here, Fleance. I need to remove the tunic and shirt and then I can begin to make you feel better.' She removed his garments and he heard her gasp. 'Oh dear, Fleance.'

'What?'

'Your injuries are more severe than I think you know.'

'Yes,' he said. 'I am tired and beaten but not broken.'

His words stilled her movements. Rachel pushed back her sleeves and began to unwrap the wimple on her head. She paused. 'Fleance, I am afraid you might be in for another surprise.'

A fleeting twinge of worry went through him. 'What?'

She let the fabric fall from her head and the sight of her jolted his heart. All her beautiful long hair gone, her head now covered in unevenly cropped curls. She stood before him and he looked her over, then reached out to touch her hair. 'What happened?'

Rachel blushed but looked him directly in the eyes. 'Calum thought to dishonour me by stripping away all that I had that was royal.' She tapped her head. 'Even my hair.'

'I'm so sorry,' he said.

'Don't be. It will grow back and I will have the satisfaction that he did not win.' Her chin trembled but he watched her swallow and lift her head. 'Now tell me, what of Scotland? And what events led you to battle again with Magness? And why do we meet here at the Duke of Normandy's palace? Why on earth did you leave Scotland?'

So many important and hard questions. 'I will start with your last question, as it is the easiest one for me to answer. I came to rescue you.'

She looked up. 'Did you not think to send someone else? Why did *you* come?'

Her response surprised him. 'What else should I have done, Rachel? I am the king! And you are to be my queen. What sort of sovereign would leave his bride to the unknown? What sort of man would I be had I not tried to find you?'

'A wise man who knows that the crown which sits on his head offers the people hope of a safe and prosperous future.' Her mouth set in a line, she searched for what she needed.

'Rachel, you are as much a part of Scotland's hope as I – perhaps more so. And I need you. I need your care and calm and wisdom.'

'Did no one counsel you against this?'

'Of course they did, but there had been no news and I needed to know . . .' He could not finish the sentence. Could not say out loud the real fear he had felt after the Norwegian spy had been captured. That she was dead or worse. 'Aye, but I had no choice. I needed to get to Norway and then find you.'

'Surely Preston . . .'

The mention of the name brought a lump to his throat and he looked away from her.

'What? What is the matter?' she asked.

Fleance took her hand in his. It was smooth and pale against his tanned and battered knuckles. 'Rachel, Preston followed me to Norway.'

She shook her head. 'What for?'

'To save my life,' Fleance said.

Rachel picked up a bottle of clear liquid and poured some onto a soft cloth. Then she began to dab at the cuts on his chest. 'I do not know what to say about that. He is the strangest creature a royal household could ever be troubled with.'

Fleance understood her ambivalence. 'Yet he loved the throne of Scotland.'

'That is true,' she said, nodding, but looked at him sharply. 'Loved? Why "loved"?'

'I believe Preston to be dead by now.'

'What do you mean? What happened?'

'When I saw him at Calum's court, I believed him to be a traitor. I was so angry.' He recounted the moment of shock and horror at seeing his advisor in Norway. He told her the story of his beating and of meeting Sven. 'But I was wrong about Preston. He saved me, but in doing so probably sacrificed his own life.'

She leant back against the table. '"Probably"? I don't understand what you are saying.'

Fleance breathed as deeply as his hurt ribs allowed. 'He followed me to ensure my safety and when he saw I was not safe he came to my rescue. Rachel, Calum had me tied to a cross after he had beaten me and then left me, intending to come back in the morning and finish me off.'

'I did not realise you had been so close to death,' she said, now looking grim.

'Yes, and I did not welcome it. I thought about how my father would be disappointed in me. That he had lived his entire life without blame, always pursuing honour over glory. Always determined that he and those around him live their lives without fault.' He could feel the familiar grief welling up but swallowed it down.

Fleance told her what Preston had said in those moments when he was getting down from the crucifix. Even now, as he relayed Preston's praise for his leadership, it felt hollow. 'Perhaps I was a coward to let Preston take my place.'

She put a hand under his chin and lifted his head so that he could see right into her clear blue eyes. 'You are nothing like a coward,' she said gently. 'Listen to the story he told you. You had no other choice, Fleance. What good would your death have achieved? How would Calum's murder of you help our nation? Nothing and none to these questions! Preston was strange at times – we never knew where we were with him, and he was difficult to talk with – but he was right to do what he did. God bless him for what he did. Preston died that you might live because, like us all, we know your life is essential for Scotland.'

Her words were like the soothing water Miri had often poured into his eyes after a long night hunting. Made of boiled salted water and witch hazel, it was a balm she used regularly on travellers who had journeyed through dry and dusty roads. 'You think this is so?' Fleance asked.

'Yes. And though I am sad for the old man, he was right in what he did.' Fleance sank back onto the stool. 'You cannot save everyone,' she added.

Her words bit into him, though he recognised the truth of what she said. 'I am my father's son, Rachel! I am king of my people and I have this constant nagging in my head that tells me I must try.'

'There is no dishonour in trying and failing.' She stroked his cheek and smiled. 'Now, your wounds need attending to.' He was stripped bare to his waist but was not cold. She pressed firmly at the purple and brown bruises that covered his upper body.

Fleance gasped each time she touched a particularly tender part. It hurt so much at times that he could feel his gorge rising. 'What are you doing?' he hissed between clenched teeth.

'Fixing you,' she said. She straightened and he was bemused at the expression on her face – it was a look he often observed in farmers studying a sick ox or horse. 'You have either cracked or broken ribs. Whatever the condition, it requires me to strap you tightly.' Rachel gathered the bandages. 'Lift your arms out, please.' He did as he was told, though it pained him. Then she pulled the bandages tight around his chest.

At last, he could breathe better, but the dull ache stayed with him. 'Rachel, you are an angel.'

'I'm not done,' she said. 'Now to this face of yours.' She worked on him silently, her sure fingers cleaning his wounds and applying some type of concoction – Fleance knew it was not her usual balm, for it smelled terrible.

'What is that?'

'Hmm, sorry, but it is all I have been able to make with the limited resources they have here. Still, I expect it will be almost as effective. Are you going to answer the rest of my questions now?'

The healing room, as she called it, was warm and filled with light, but Fleance shuddered, suddenly hearing and seeing and smelling the battle. 'Have you heard news from Scotland?'

Her hands stilled and he could hear her breathing. 'Aye.'

'That I killed Magness?'

'I have heard the news that he was executed for treason,' Rachel said. 'I know how much he meant to you, Fleance, but you did what a king must do. Even William said as much of your decision. My grandfather had to contend with traitors he'd loved and respected. This is the way of kings.'

'But my father would have acted differently. Of this I am certain.'

She had finished with his injuries and began wiping her hands on a towel. 'Do you know this for sure, Fleance?' she asked quietly, not looking at him.

Fleance stiffened. He sensed an insult, a challenge. 'Yes. Absolutely.'

Rachel went to the basin and washed her hands. There was something in the way she conducted herself that unsettled him. What was she hiding?

She came over to Fleance and sat down next to him. 'Listen to me,' she began. 'I say this because I care about you.'

'It does not feel to me that this is going to be pleasant.' He stood up slowly and went over to the long table and poured himself a tankard of water.

Her eyes followed his hands as he finished the drink. 'Fleance.' He watched her bite her bottom lip. 'You have to stop trying to be exactly like your father.'

'What? Where did this notion come from?' he asked, returning to sit beside her once more.

'What I mean is, stop trying to replicate the idea of who you think your father was.'

Fleance shook his head. 'I cannot understand why you are saying such things. You did not know my father.'

Rachel breathed slowly and then straightened her back. 'No,' she said. 'That is true. But I know you.' She stood up and walked to the window. 'I have heard a story about Banquo that I think you should hear.'

'It's not a good story, if your demeanour is a guide.'

She nodded. 'I have heard a story about what happened on that battlefield.'

He frowned. 'What? What battlefield? The one I've just been on or the one where your brother was killed or . . . ?'

She held up her hand. 'The battle where Banquo and Macbeth were victorious over Sweno.'

'What about it?' He saw the look in her eyes and understood then that this was no joke, no prank.

'He was a good man,' she said, the concern in her face clear. 'But I think Calum has been right all along, Fleance,' Rachel said quietly. 'I think your father *was* the man who murdered Calum's father. Banquo did slay Sweno.'

'No,' he cried. 'That cannot possibly be true.' He felt the blood pounding in his ears.

'Can you please hear out what I have to say?' She returned to the stool. 'Your father was so incensed by the battle . . .' She stopped and put her hands on his.

It was his turn to stand but he moved too suddenly and immediately flinched at the pain in his ribs. How could he make sense of the picture she was trying to paint for him? He looked at her sitting there, grim-faced with her uneven haircut, and it came to him. Of course. Why had he not thought of it before? 'Rachel,' he said steadily. 'I do believe Calum has used some magic to make your mind diseased.' The image conjured by his words softened his heart.

She shook her head. 'No! He has done no such thing.'

'Rachel. Dear, dear Rachel. You have been through more than any woman should have to endure. Calum is a clever man but angry and dangerous. He has filled your mind with poisonous stories.'

She returned the grip he had on her hands, but her lips formed a determined line. 'It was not Calum who told me the story.'

The worry he had felt before the battle, at the idea that there were those against him who still held sway over the people, returned. He dropped her hands and folded his arms across the thick bandages that covered his chest.

She continued. 'Charissa told me the history of her father, who served Scotland under my grandfather Duncan. He was a sergeant in the king's army under the command of your father and Macbeth.'

Fleance watched her face for signs of madness but, apart from the cruelly cropped hair, she was the same Rachel he had said goodbye to all those weeks ago. He would listen to this story and then make a judgement.

Rachel continued. 'Charissa's father was pulled from the fray and brought back to the castle, his wounds fatal – though Morag tried to save him. The surgeons told them he would die and before he went off, he wanted to tell the tale of his last battle. And as they nursed him, Charissa and Morag, her father talked. He told them of the battle, Fleance.' Rachel's eyes bored deeply into his, leaving him nowhere to hide from the truth of what he was hearing. 'Charissa said her father was most upset that some of the war record was wrong.'

'I don't understand . . .' he faltered, in a last desperate attempt to stave off the slowly dawning realisation of what she had to tell him.

'Charissa's father was desperate to say his piece,' Rachel said. 'Fleance, this is what she told me the night I was kidnapped. Sweno had surrendered. Charissa's father was there and he saw this large blond-headed man put down his weapons and step forward saying, in our tongue, that he gave over his rule. But Banquo, in her words, "*was mad as a rutting stag, and was not as honourable as the stories tell*". Even Macbeth tried to stop him. Banquo wouldn't listen to the king's cries. Just drove him through with his sword. Killed him outright.'

Fleance stood up and walked over to the table, the firelight flickering on the bruises on his hands as he leant them gingerly against the surface, seeking the unyielding certainty of its smooth, polished wood. 'He can't have,' he cried. 'He wouldn't have. That was not my father.'

Rachel followed him, turned him round to face her and held his arms, her eyes looking straight into his, into the very centre of his soul. 'Charissa had no need to lie.'

'How old was Charissa when she was told this?'

'Eight.'

Fleance nodded triumphantly. 'How could you possibly believe the memory of a little child recalled so many years later? She was too young.'

She touched his face. 'Were you too young, Fleance, to remember what happened to you when your father was killed?'

It was hard to think standing up. The pain from his lip and his chest made him seek the stool again. He stared at her but was ever aware of the pain that came with his breathing.

A look of concern clouded her face, and the line of her mouth softened. 'Can I get you something to ease the hurt?'

He shook his head impatiently. 'No. Don't distract me. Go on with your fairy tale.'

She breathed out slowly and Fleance saw the expression Rachel wore when she was dealing with Bree at her most difficult moments. *Careful, man*, he cautioned himself.

Rachel continued. 'Your father, good as he was, was still a man, but, like all of us, I believe, still capable of doing a dishonourable thing.' She stood right before him, tall and strong but with tears in her eyes. He turned away. 'Look at me,' Rachel said softly. 'Fleance. Look at me.'

He brought his head around and looked up at her. 'I don't believe this is a fairy tale,' Rachel continued. 'Charissa said her father was ordered not to tell a soul what he had just witnessed. Macbeth told her father that it would serve no good for anybody to tell what had happened and that, in his words, "the dirty Norwegian king deserved to die". That Banquo was a loyal and loved soldier and that there was no honour in recounting this misjudgement on the part of the thane.'

'You expect me just to accept a story from a maid who never met or knew my father?'

'Perhaps not, but it rings true, for it is very like the things I have seen in the way men treat others. I feel it in my soul that the story has merit,' she said. 'I don't want to give this to you but I care for you too much to leave it buried with the bones of an old soldier. Do not throw away what I have to say to you.' Rachel stared at him. 'Do not dismiss me so.'

'I am not dismissing you,' Fleance offered. 'I am merely suggesting that you have been through a very difficult time and that you may not see things as they really are.'

'Fleance, stop it! Has there ever been a time when I have lied to you or led you astray?' She put both hands on her hips and looked hard at him.

The room seemed suddenly lacking in air. Fleance touched his lip, which had begun to bleed again and was throbbing.

He stood up and reached for her discarded towel to stem the blood. 'Well, you have my attention, Princess.' His own disquiet was unsettling, for he had to acknowledge that what she had said about her trustworthiness was true. This was one of the many reasons he knew that choosing Rachel to be his queen was good not only for the country but for him personally. 'But please, if you will, could you give me some moments to digest what I am hearing? This is a heavy meal for any man.' This was true – her words sat like stone on his stomach.

'Of course,' she said. 'Shall I leave you?'

He nodded. 'Aye.' Rachel stood up and went towards the door. 'Can you arrange two things for me?' he asked.

'Certainly.'

'That I be brought a small meal and then have an audience with the duke.'

'These are easy things to arrange,' Rachel said. 'Fleance, I am sorry. I could have kept this from you but I believe that I have . . .' She paused and he watched as she gathered herself. 'I am not sure of it exactly, but I believe that I am to you as a mirror. You need someone to reflect who you really are so that you can go on to be all that God wants you to be.'

What was she saying?

'I'll be back soon. Think on my words, my dear friend, for they come from a heart that loves and cares for you.'

Her sudden absence made the room even colder and Fleance reached over and pulled the tunic around his shoulders.

Was she right? In all the months he had known Rachel and in all his conversations with Duncan, at no time was her word ever doubted. Fleance had seen her stoic manner on the battlefield. And though she was hurt beyond measure at her brother's death, still she had rallied. Preston's words came to him then. *'She is, as you say, strong, determined and resourceful.'*

Again, it appeared the old man was right with his observation. He had not wanted his king to go abroad. He had believed that Rachel, if she was still alive, would make her own way home. And he had been right.

So, then, the view of his world was shifting. He *could* choose to disregard Rachel's story, but in his heart of hearts he guessed that she could only have spoken the truth. What then was he to make of this story of his father? If it were true, then Calum was justified in his actions. If false, then there were people spreading lies and rumours about the quality of his bloodline. Such stories might weaken his position and be used to bring down the throne of Scotland.

Fleance rubbed a hand across his face, feeling the coarse bristles of more than a week without shaving. *I must look a mess*, he thought.

All these years he had measured himself against his father. All these years he had made decisions based on what he believed was Banquo's wisdom. How old was his father when he went to battle for his king? If his figuring was correct, not ten years older than he was now. Ten years. It was a magic number. Ten years he'd spent with Magness and Miri. Ten years before he'd begun his journey home to find the person responsible for his father's murder.

He stood in front of a small looking-glass hanging over the basin. 'If I am not the son of the man I thought he was,' he said quietly to his image, 'then what sort of man am I to be? Who is Fleance?' It was not his father's ghost that haunted him but a fabricated spectre drawn from his own insecurities.

Thirty minutes later there was a quiet knock on the door. It was opened before he said anything, and Rachel came through. 'May I come in?'

'Yes.' He rubbed his eyes, feeling bone weary. 'May I tell you my thoughts?'

'Of course,' Rachel said as she walked over to the stack of firewood and placed two logs on the fire. Then she sat gracefully on the stool and faced him.

The fresh wood caught the flames, which spat and crackled. He watched as the glow lit up her hair. Despite the crudeness of the cut she was still a beautiful woman.

He took a deep breath and began. 'All my life I have tried to please my father. Every year. Every moment. Much of this, in my head, has met with some sort of disapproval. Not from him, but from a fictional counsel whose opinion I have worried about.'

'But you can't live like that,' Rachel said.

'I know. I know this.' Fleance shook his head and squeezed his eyes shut. 'I know!'

'So what is the struggle for you?' she asked.

He clenched his fists and turned to her. 'I want to do the right thing – to be a good King of Scotland!'

'You are, Fleance.' He could hear the insistence in her voice. 'You are a good king.'

'But if I carry this history, how should I walk in the way of kings, knowing that my father was a murderer? What am I supposed to do with this information, Rachel? How is this to help me lead our nation?'

'I don't know. But you must find a way! All this does not make your father less than what we all know he was – a brave and honourable man.'

She studied him for a few moments, closed her eyes and then looked up at him. 'I think Banquo was a man who did what he thought he should do. I know he was a great man and I understand that he carried on his shoulders knowledge of dark and terrible things. He was considered the best, as a general and a thane. My grandfather loved him like a son.' She took his clenched fists in her own hands. 'He was everything else you believed him to be, Fleance.'

She pressed on. 'But he was a man, as you are. And no man can be perfect. That time, on the battlefield, he did the wrong thing. It might have been the only misjudgement he ever made – but he did it. Someone saw it, remembered it and handed it on.'

He was silent for a moment, remembering the last time he had seen the ghost of his father, remembering how a weight, like that of a heavy cloak, had fallen from his shoulders. It was a feeling he was experiencing now. 'When I was at Scone,' he said, 'I saw my father in the field.' Rachel frowned. 'It was an illusion,' he added quickly. 'Once the crown was on my head and the sceptre in my hand, I suddenly felt the heaviness I had been carrying for so long fall away.'

'That was good, wasn't it?'

'Yes, but these past months I have pulled an even heavier burden onto my back. I have filled the pockets of the royal clothes with rocks and stones, picking them up along my way rather than letting them lie or throwing them away or handing them to others who are better suited to hold them.'

'Where are these rocks now, Fleance?' In the silence that followed her question he could hear the sound of palace life continuing outside the room: children's voices, footfalls in the passageway and, somewhere, the cry of a baby. Normal life that seemed too far out of his reach.

'This information from Charissa has helped remove the biggest rock. What you need to understand is that I have spent my life,' he said, 'living up to a standard that I thought my father wanted.'

'That is good. Banquo was a good man. To measure yourself against him is a worthy notion.'

'Perhaps when I was younger and still becoming a man that was so, but today you have shown me what Blair, Preston and even

Duncan tried to get me to see.' He covered her hand with his. 'What is it that makes us truly grow up, Rachel?'

She thought for a bit. 'Time. Opportunity. Loss.'

'Yes, each of those pushes us on our way – but I can see now that it is the point at which we make decisions for ourselves rather than worrying about what we believe other people would think of those decisions. That is the point at which we start to become adults, Rachel. Those decisions that we make are born from our own wisdom, understanding and beliefs.'

'It is very hard not to want to please others.'

'I am not glad that I learnt something terrible about my father.' Fleance paused and swallowed – but continued before Rachel could say anything. 'But I can see why you told me. You could see that the burden of my imposed expectations was suffocating me.'

'You are not angry with me?'

He stood up, grunting. 'I am sad but also resolute.' He touched her face gently. 'We will be a strong partnership, Rachel, and will lead Scotland well.'

She took his hand and kissed the inside of his wrist. Such a tender gesture and a small one, but it spoke a promise of their future together.

Chapter Twenty-Two
Normandy

Fleance was led past the palace's great hall, down a long corridor and towards the west wing. The servant spoke with the attending footman at the door of the room to which Fleance had been summoned. The finely dressed young man bowed and then opened the doors with a flourish to admit him.

'Sire, I present Fleance, King of Scotland,' the servant announced first in English and then in French.

Fleance was surprised by the design of the room. Three of the four walls were fitted with arch-shaped glass casements set deep within the recess of the stone, but the afternoon sun streamed in, creating a feeling of warmth and contentment.

His bleak mood lifted as if the room itself was an antidote for his battered heart.

The Duke and Duchess of Normandy, William and his wife Matilda, sat in identical chairs in the light-filled room. They both rose as he entered.

William bowed and Matilda curtseyed, and then William came forward, kissing him on both cheeks. 'Welcome, Fleance. We are delighted to finally meet you. Rachel has told my wife much of your situation and I myself have heard stories of your bravery and wise politics in these troubled times.' The duke gestured to another chair. 'Please, if you are able to, take a seat.'

The deference to him was somewhat unnerving. He moved stiffly and was conscious of the injuries his face had sustained. The left eye was healing but was still smudged purple and yellow, and the eyeball itself had burst a vessel so that half of the white was blood red. Not the ideal look he would desire when meeting a foreign dignitary.

The duke spoke to a diminutive maid who stood almost invisibly beside a heavy drape. 'Would you ask the princess to join us? I am certain she will be most pleased to be with our guest.' The girl bobbed quickly and went out.

'Rachel will join us?' Fleance asked, almost afraid that William was talking of someone else. To have her here now would allay some of his nervousness.

William smiled. 'But of course. I know you two have already enjoyed being reunited.'

Matilda broke in. 'It would not be wise to discuss the state of affairs without her here. As the future Queen of Scotland, her woman's intuition is as valuable as a man's decisiveness.'

Fleance nodded, relieved. This would be the first time that he was fulfilling his role as a political leader outside of Scotland. To have Rachel's understanding of Europe's long history of feuds and alliances would be most welcome.

Much of the past twelve months had been taken up with Scotland's domestic problems and concerns. With William sitting across from him, Fleance was reminded that it was time he gave thought to the future of Scotland beyond the current trials and troubles.

While they waited for Rachel's arrival, the servant poured them each a drink. Fleance was glad to have something to do with his hands, for it seemed neither the duke nor the duchess had anything to say to him at this time, busy as they were giving quiet instructions to various servants who stood in attendance.

The waiting, though not unpleasant, made him restless. As Fleance sipped the fruity wine – the taste a lot tarter than he was used to – he watched William converse with a rotund older man dressed in fine clothes with unruly grey hair. The interchange reminded Fleance of how Preston conducted himself whenever he'd offered advice of which he thought Fleance might not approve: the slight blushing of the cheeks, but also the determination of the jaw, suggesting an awareness of the delicate position of telling one's superior what to do when convinced that the advice was the best course of action.

Duncan had once pointed out to Fleance the mannerisms of a nobleman's advisor: the physical tics, the skill with words and languages, the canny ability to anticipate when to speak and when to be silent.

'Watch what the old man does now,' he had murmured during one of the many meetings Fleance and Duncan had witnessed last year. *'He will sidle up to Father, hesitate, blush and then do that thing with his face where he lifts his chin.'* Both he and Fleance stopped what they were doing and watched as Preston cleared his throat, moved to the side of Donalbain. *'Your Majesty,'* he had said, a blush creeping up his neck and over his cheeks.

Duncan had jabbed Fleance in the side. *'Told you,'* he whispered.

Donalbain did not look around but waited as his advisor leant even closer and spoke quietly into the king's ear. Donalbain had nodded and Preston moved away, almost into the shadows again.

'See,' Duncan said. *'That's how the best ones work: slipping in and out of view, making their lords believe the ideas are their own.'*

It had been different with Fleance and Preston, however. Though Preston was always somewhat uncomfortable, he had lost that sense of nervous fear he had displayed around Donalbain.

This advisor was different, in his way, with the duke as well. Though he was in servitude to William, the duke had an easy way of responding – in much the same way an older brother might argue with a younger sibling.

Fleance could never have considered Preston in that way, but he had very quickly learnt to trust the old man. A wave of sadness swept over him. Who should he choose now to be his trusted advisor? Who was there back in Scotland to offer advice and counsel now that Preston was gone?

It didn't help to dwell on such things, so he turned to study the duchess, who was excitedly giving instructions to her lady-in-waiting. How similar she was to her brother, Henri. Like him, she had thick dark hair, which at this time hung prettily around her face. There was the same slightly upturned nose as Henri's and the grey eyes that now and then looked over to Fleance not unkindly.

She was a very attractive woman. And the affection with which William regarded her seemed to transcend more than her outward appearance. The almost habitual looking over at his wife, as if reassuring himself that she was comfortable and in agreement with whatever he was saying, reminded Fleance of the brief time he had seen Malcolm with his Margaret before Malcolm had died.

I want that, his heart whispered. *That is what I want for Rachel and me.*

The duke's advisor bowed and left the room. William smiled broadly at Fleance. 'I am surprised at how quickly you received our message.'

There it was again, the suggestion that he had somehow been summoned. 'I did not receive a message from you,'

The duke frowned. 'Strange. I thought that was why you had come.'

Fleance shook his head. 'We searched everywhere in Scotland for Rachel after she was kidnapped, but could find no trace of her. We did not give up hope and did not believe she was dead. Then my soldiers captured a Norwegian spy who delivered to me the message from Calum that she would die if I did not go to Norway.'

'You fell for such a ruse?'

'Not directly.' William raised his eyebrows. 'I sent word that I would not come. That I did not believe the claim but that if it were true, then Norway was once again at war with Scotland. However, I left Scotland in the hope that I might bring her home without any more bloodshed.'

Another servant offered the duke some sweetmeats. He took a portion and chewed them thoughtfully, his head tilted to one side as he listened to Fleance. 'But she was not there, no?'

'That was some kind of relief. I was told by a condemned man who had been her constant guard that he had helped her to escape.'

'And we have been most delighted with her company. Is this not true, my love?'

Matilda smiled. 'Such a head on her shoulders. If she were a man, she would be a worthy ruler.'

William turned back to Fleance. 'But it did not go so well for you, it seems?'

'I was captured and tortured. Calum thought he had gained what he had long desired: a chance to exact his revenge for wrongs inflicted a generation before.'

Both duke and duchess raised their eyebrows this time so, as quickly as he could, he recounted his adventure.

He had only just finished his tale when Rachel arrived. Both men stood and William kissed her hand and guided her to another chair. 'We were talking about your king's adventures and I am certain you will have some thoughts on the matter as well.' He signalled for a cup to be brought to her. 'But enough of this now. Tonight we may speak of politics and the future but for now, tell us the plans for your nuptials and your story of how it came to be that you, Fleance, are King of Scotland and Rachel is to be your queen.'

———

Fleance appreciated the reason for the feast. It was a celebration for the reuniting of Scotland's king and his future queen. It was a celebration that there had been triumph over adversity.

No longer dressed in the duke's clothes, but in garments that sat more comfortably on him, and accompanied by Rachel who looked outstanding, her chopped hair hidden behind a mirage of silks and strings of pearls, they made their way to the great hall. His one small regret was that he didn't have his crown to denote his position as King of Scotland.

Rachel put her hand on his arm. 'Remember what you told me, Fleance, about the power of the opinion of others. Think on that and you will not be dwarfed by these men.'

He gave a short laugh. 'Do you read minds as well? I was just now missing my crown – the first time I've thought on it for many a month. But what you say is true. As I understand it from Preston's briefings, no one in power has been without tribulation. I think many of the men in this room have suffered at least as much as we.'

Rachel nodded. 'Yes, and perhaps more.' She took in a deep breath. 'But I believe we are but small players in the game that these ambitious men play. Scripture warns us to remember that we have two ears and one mouth. I suggest we listen more than we speak if our country is to stay secure and in safe hands.'

They stood before the doors of the great hall, and then, with a trumpet sound and a shout, they were announced: Fleance, King of Scotland, and Princess Rachel, daughter of the late King Donalbain.

As a couple they moved into the room and took their allocated places at the high table of the banquet hall. With relief he saw that Rachel was only across and one down from him, which meant she would alert him to any problems.

The King of France had not been invited. Last year's attempt by Henry the First to oust William from power had met with a crushing defeat by the duke's men. William would not admit King Henry onto his lands. Though William had petitioned to the pope for a Truce of God agreement, the French would not agree, so there remained an uneasy truce between the two leaders.

It was a magnificent feast and many dignitaries were present. Though many times William had raised his goblet to Fleance and Rachel, both knew the gathering was an opportunity for the duke to hold court with those he considered essential in his plans for the future.

This Fleance had learnt from Rachel, who had translated the gossip she had gleaned from the palace servants, who told a sobering tale of a man determined to gain what he believed was rightfully his.

A few years before, the Earl of Wessex, Harold Godwinson – an important man, since his sister was married to King Edward of England – had been shipwrecked along the coast of Ponthieu and promptly captured by one of Normandy's counts. William had demanded that Harold be released into his care, yet it seemed the Englishman went from being a clear enemy to acting like a friend and the man was pressed into service to fight one of the many battles the Duke of Normandy was embroiled in, this one against the Duke of Brittany. The story was that Harold had saved two of William's young soldiers who were caught in quicksand and sure to lose their lives. This had pleased William and after they were victorious in battle, he had presented Harold with a knighthood and arms.

Whether it was to show his genuine gratitude for William's support, or whether it was to try and get back to England as soon as he could, none could be sure. But it was recorded that Harold had sworn to the duke that he would support William's claim that King Edward had promised him the throne of England, should the opportunity present itself.

Fleance remembered listening to Macduff and Ross discussing this story and deriding the earl for making promises over which he had no control.

Now, observing how everyone present behaved in such a deferential manner towards the duke, Fleance wondered if there was more to the story than those at home in Scotland knew.

The next course appeared and distracted him from his thoughts. His stomach turned when he saw what was being put before them. A peacock had been cooked but made to look like it was still alive. Fleance remembered the cooks at home squabbling about the best ways to roast fowl and beasts and then make them appear on the lord's table as if they had just stepped out of the forest.

The feathers of this bird were shiny and beautiful, but he passed when the servant offered him a piece. Across the table, Rachel was smiling at a thin, watery-looking man beside her as he leant forward. 'Have you killed any game, my dear?'

She did not miss a beat. 'Fourteen animals. Ten of them chickens, two pheasants and two peacocks.'

Those around them erupted with laughter.

'Forget the pheasants and peacocks. Chicken is the best,' someone offered. There was more raucous laughter. *The wine is working its magic*, Fleance thought, though his heart was pleased that the content of discussion had lightened.

'Agreed,' said a young baron to his right. 'I would rather a boar than a deer. A goat than a stoat.'

Suddenly, they were looking to him to offer something to the conversation. He cleared his throat. 'Our cook can make a stoat taste as good as a rabbit and make a rabbit taste as good as a lamb.'

This must have carried down to the end of the table, for the duke spoke. 'Your Majesty, is your cook a woman?'

Fleance nodded. 'Aye, she is.'

'Is she married?'

'Widowed.'

William paused a moment. 'Tell me your terms and I will take her from you.'

Fleance laughed. 'She would be most pleased with your interest but I can attest that this feisty woman intends never to leave Scottish soil.'

William leant forward. 'Good,' he said, but his tone silenced the room. 'Keep her. A servant who is that faithful is a servant a king can never afford to lose.'

Rachel spoke then. 'Without Morag, our family would have been lost. She is not royal and not educated but she has loved and cared for us always.' The room stayed quiet and she lifted her chin. 'Especially during the dark times of Macbeth.'

The room was now filled with mutterings and the shaking of heads.

Matilda added her voice to the discussion. 'Love and faithfulness, Rachel: these qualities are more valuable than anything.'

Fleance watched as Rachel dipped her head and continued with her meal.

An hour later, much more wine had been consumed and Fleance longed to find the right time to retire. But William was not finished. 'How are things in Scotland? We have received word that you have gone to battle and quashed rebel advances twice in less than a year.'

'True, but we have finished with that business. The leader has been executed.' Fleance said the words plainly but they stung.

'But until we change the hearts and minds of the people who serve us,' William said, 'change them to believe that with loyalty and faithful allegiance they will always be rewarded, then we as rulers will continue to struggle against insurgence.'

'Only God can change a man's heart,' Rachel said.

The duke studied her a moment, his lips pursed. 'No,' he said, shaking his head. 'I disagree. If given a choice, what man would forego land and prosperity as payment for his unconditional loyalty?

'Even to an evil man?' someone called out.

Rachel seemed undeterred. 'The church teaches us that God chooses His representative on earth. And we must all give our allegiance to God. It follows then that all must give their loyalty to the crown and pray for their sovereign to be protected from evil. The cause of much of the unrest in countries is men who choose to ignore divine teaching and think only for themselves and not for the greater good.'

William wiped his hands and mouth. 'The peasant who ploughs the land of one of your thanes gives allegiance to him because his food and accommodation are provided for. Your thane gives your king allegiance because he has given him land. The thane's peasant has no thought of King Fleance, for they do not see their livelihood coming directly from his hand. Why should they put down tools and take up arms for the king?'

Fleance's stomach burned with an indignation, the source of which he could not name. Was it that he felt belittled by all he had done for his people already? That William's words identified something he himself had sensed when he had gone among the villagers?

The duke did not wait for Fleance's response but went on. 'Think on the two battles Scotland has fought. The enemy armies were led by a man you would expect to be loyal to you. Yet he had no respect for the crown.'

Fleance carefully put down his goblet and turned so that he was directly facing his host. 'I suggest that you are simplifying things, William. We all have choices to make. Some are as inane as whether to have ale or mead. Others are whether to choose what your head knows to be right even if your heart protests. Not even a king can compel an individual to serve his life in allegiance. Such loyalty must come from that man's sense of duty.'

'Perhaps. But I know that one can compel a man more effectively with fear than with love. Is not our obedience to God motivated by our fear of spending eternity in damnation?'

'I cannot speak for every man. I am compelled only by what I know to be honourable,' Fleance said.

Matilda coughed, laid down her fork and smiled at the guests. 'I believe what the king has told us has been evidenced many times in recent history. Perhaps not to do with war, but there is one story my mother told me when I was a child.' She tilted her head to Fleance. 'Tonight your words were as if my *maman* was telling me again the right way to live life regardless of my feelings – always with honour and always as is my duty.'

The only sound now was the rush of the fires in their hearths. No one was eating or drinking. All eyes were fixed on the duchess.

Matilda picked up her goblet and took a sip. 'Some of you seated here may remember the story of that Welsh prince.' A few of the much older guests nodded. 'My mother told me he was a fine man and very much loved by his people. He had three sons – all handsome, kind and also beloved by those who served them. The prince had secured good matches for his sons, but one night the second son came to him to say that he did not want to be hand-fastened to his father's choice. Rather, he was in love with a maid from the village.' Her words caused a slight stirring around the table and

Fleance felt his heart begin to quicken. 'The prince, so the story goes, was sympathetic to his son's dilemma and they talked long into the night.

'When the prince finally retired, he was pleased that he had helped his son come to his senses and slept soundly. The next morning, however, his manservant woke him with the news that his son had disappeared during the night.

'No one had seen the young man leave. The prince sent out his men to find his son but both the young man and, it was discovered, the maid, had vanished.'

Matilda took another sip and then dabbed her lips with her cloth. 'The prince, we are told, was heartbroken. But his sorry story did not end there. His eldest son was killed in battle and the youngest, though obedient to his father's choice of wife, was unable to produce an heir.' She frowned and Fleance watched her intently, for it seemed this story was one she held tightly. 'The second son chose love over honour; he chose feelings over his duty and that choice broke not only his father's heart but the lineage of his ancestry.'

'Was he ever found?' Rachel asked.

Matilda shook her head. 'Never seen or heard of again. Not then and not even now. There are rumours he lived a simple but happy life.'

'A cautionary tale,' said the old man beside Rachel. 'The young need a firm hand to guide them to make decisions that benefit all in the years to come rather than satisfy wanton desire in the present.'

'Hruump,' William coughed, and he and Fleance regarded each other in the silence that followed. The duke then picked up his goblet and signalled for it to be refilled. 'Thank you, my sweet, for this evening's lesson.' He looked again at Fleance. 'I do not think we are in disagreement, Your Majesty.' The title was said with emphasis and caused a chill across Fleance's back. 'We want the same things from our people and to live in a land free from siege. Yes?'

Fleance nodded. 'It is my hope.' He stood then. 'Please excuse us, but the princess and I are due to return to Scotland in the morning.' All at the table stood as the two of them made their way out of the banquet hall. Once the doors were closed behind them, Fleance let out a great breath.

Rachel tucked her arm into his. 'You were wonderful, Fleance. You speak so wisely. Unlike many of those in that room, there is no pretence with you.'

He squeezed her hand. 'Thank you.' They walked towards their chambers in silence but soon he pulled them to a stop. 'I am not yet ready for bed. Would you accompany me for a walk around the gardens? All that wine and smoke and talk has filled my head with straw.'

She smiled. 'I would welcome that.'

The half-moon gave adequate light as they made their way down the path to a stone bench beside a plot of sweet-smelling spring flowers. 'What did you think of the duchess's story?' she asked.

'I thought it was sad. I think the son did the wrong thing.'

'I thought so too – that it was sad, but sad for everyone.'

He moved closer to her, took her hand and carefully spread his fingers out so that they lined up against her smaller ones. Then he folded them over so that their hands were entwined.

Rachel put her free hand over their entwined pair. 'Are you afraid, Fleance?'

The question surprised him but he guessed at her meaning. 'I think getting wed is likely to make even the bravest soldier anxious.'

She shook her head. 'Not afraid of getting married. Afraid of the cost of your duty.'

'No. I am not afraid.' He stroked her fingers and looked back at the palace, ablaze with a thousand lights. 'One might say that I choose you, Rachel, out of duty, but this is not a bad thing. It honours you that I choose you as my queen – and that is no hard choice; it honours the promise I made to Duncan and it honours the Godly requisites for a royal marriage.' He paused, listening to the sounds of music and laughter floating towards them on the night air. 'These acts of honour are the seeds of love.' Fleance rose. 'Rachel,' he extended his hand, 'I am ready to return to Scotland.'

She came close and leant her head against his chest, sighing wearily. 'As am I.'

They walked back to the palace in a companionable silence. Though, like Rachel, he was weak from exhaustion, the thought of returning home with her beside him ignited a happiness he had not felt in a long time.

Chapter Twenty-Three
Off the coast of Scotland, August
Harold

The Earl of Wessex was woken by the knock on the cabin door. 'Come,' he called, sitting up stiffly in the tiny cot. His manservant entered with a jug and a towel. 'Good morning, my lord. The captain says the tide has turned and we are to make our way up the river.'

He lifted his legs out of the bed and stood up, remembering to keep his head low. He touched the bruised spot on his head where he'd banged it on the low ceiling the day before. 'When does he anticipate our arrival at Perth?'

The servant poured water into a washbowl and set down the jug. 'Mid-morning. We have secured lodgings for two nights as per your wish, and then we shall be in Glamis before the week's end.'

The earl scratched his chin and then dragged his fingers through his beard, enjoying the slight ache this caused his skin. He longed to stretch. 'Has Lady Edith arisen?'

'She has indeed and is already on deck.'

He splashed water on his face and dipped his hands into the bowl again, scooping some more water to run through his hair and beard. The servant handed him the towel and the earl rubbed his face and the back of his neck.

'I will have my breakfast on deck as well.'

The servant bowed and went out.

When he had finished his morning ablutions and had dressed, he left the cabin and climbed the ladder to the upper deck. He saw his wife talking with his sister and went up to them, kissing one and then the other on the cheek.

'How did you sleep?' he asked them.

'Without my king beside me,' his sister said, her face reddening, 'it is very difficult to relax properly.'

He nodded politely, thinking about his brother-in-law, the King of England, and the way he treated his queen. Rumour was that she was still a virgin and that her husband was punishing their family by ensuring that his wife produced no children. 'I am sorry to hear that, sister.' He turned to Edith. 'And you, my dear?'

She smiled. 'I have the same complaint, my love. I shall look forward to resting in a proper bed with you beside me.' She took his hand. 'But enough of that. Let us eat. This sea air brings on such hunger.'

The three of them sat at the bench that had been arranged just for them and enjoyed their breakfast as the ship travelled up the estuary towards Perth.

While the two women chattered about tomorrow's wedding, his thoughts turned to the plans he had made for this visit. His advisors had given him intelligence about the King of Scotland, but he needed to find out for himself more about the man he would give his allegiance to when the time came.

He also wondered at his own king's decision to send the queen consort rather than journey to the wedding of Fleance and Rachel himself.

The passengers disembarked and their party was supported by five of the King's Guard. It was the first time he had been to Perth and he was impressed at the living hum of the place. He had sent ahead two of his house and they greeted them now with a carriage that would take them to their lodgings.

The queen had been invited to the Thane of Angus's manor and she went off with the guards, calling behind her a promise of reuniting at the wedding.

'Poor thing,' Edith said quietly as they watched her make her way out of the town.

He leant over and nibbled her on the neck. 'It is only that you feel sorry she does not enjoy a man's love. Hmmm?'

She pressed herself close and took his hand. 'Perhaps. And that there are no children.' He gently traced his nose up her slender neck and she giggled. 'You are tickling.'

'Good,' he murmured. 'And I hope to do more when we are established in our room.'

The room was more than adequate for their needs. They were accommodated in a cottage at the back garden of one of the largest taverns. The well-cared-for plants and flowers partly obscured the small house but light filled their chamber.

Later that evening while Edith was sleeping, Harold got out of the bed and dressed silently. As he turned to leave, he pulled the covers over her bare shoulders. She smiled but did not open her eyes, a look of happy satisfaction on her face.

He tucked his blade into his belt and went out. Two servants stood guard outside the door to the cottage. Harold nodded to them and waited for them to carry out their orders. One man handed him a flaming torch. He looked up at the sky a moment. Heavy, grey

clouds were rolling east, pushing ahead fine mist and beginning to
blot out the moon and stars. The storm would be over the town in
less than an hour. Shrugging himself into a cloak, he wondered if
this was an omen.

———

The forest was cool and black and the light from the flickering torch
threw up strange shadows against the tree trunks. Harold listened
intently for the signal and was rewarded by the sound of a night
bird. He stopped, dug the end of the torch into the soft earth,
cupped his hands to his mouth and returned the call. Immediately
the answer came back and then he spotted a shifting light ahead.
He grabbed his torch, went forward quickly and came to a small
clearing where two horses and one of his secret and most trusted
advisors were waiting.

'Good evening, my lord,' Nathanial said. 'I trust the voyage was
not unpleasant.'

'It was adequate,' Harold said, handing his servant the torch so
that he could mount.

Nathanial handed him a large woollen cloak. 'I suggest you
remove yours, Sire, and put this on. That way you are more disguised.'

The earl nodded and unhooked the elaborately jewelled clasp
that kept his cloak closed and flung it off and over the branch of
a nearby tree, startling the horse so that he was almost unseated.
Nathanial was quickly beside him. 'Sorry, my lord. Would you
prefer the other horse?'

Quickly gathering his wits, the earl shook his head. 'No, this
will do.' He put the other cloak on. It was long, even for him, the
hem reaching down past the tops of his boots. 'You have located
them?' he asked, putting his hand out for his torch.

Nathanial gave it to him. 'Yes. It will take us an hour's ride.'

He squeezed his thighs and was pleased that the horse moved off. A well-trained animal was as valuable as an obedient and well-trained soldier. 'The weather is coming in,' he called over his shoulder. 'Let us hope tonight's business is finished before we are caught in it.' He waved his advisor on.

Nathanial mounted swiftly and retrieved his own flaming torch, which stood sentinel-like in the middle of the clearing. Then he trotted past the earl and set a steady pace for them.

Only when he was certain they were past the last of the crofters' cottages did Harold relax. He moved his horse forward so that both men rode side by side. 'How did you find them?' he asked, his voice low.

'They build signs to show where they have been and to point to where they will go. My spies scouted the area and came across a new structure four days ago. We have been monitoring them and it is clear they are settled.'

'And they know of my arrival?'

'Yes, but they do not know who you are, just that you have paid them well.'

The earl shifted in his saddle. 'This might turn out much better than I had hoped,' he said. They continued to ride on in silence until a strange light could be seen ahead. Both men pulled up their horses.

'This is the place,' Nathanial said.

'I will go alone,' he said, dismounting while holding high the flame. 'If I have not returned in thirty minutes, come for me.' He took a deep breath to steady himself and then strode towards the light coming from a run-down barn-like enclosure.

'Well?' he asked, pulling the hood of his cloak tightly around his nose to avoid being overwhelmed by the stench from the cauldron and the moist, hot air of the dirty hut.

As one, the three strange women turned from the blackened cooking pot. Each of them held a wooden cup.

The eldest of the three stepped forward, the flickering light from the flames deepening the craggy lines in her face, and lifted her cup to him. 'Speak!'

Her companion, shorn-headed and tall, mimicked the action. 'Demand!'

The final woman, pale and young, smiled dreamily at him. She put the cup to her lips and took a sip. Then, wiping her mouth, she whispered, 'We will answer.'

Though he was loath to remove the hood, the desire to know the fortunes of his life, the life of the one he loved and his country was greater. He gulped for air under the cloak and then removed it from his face.

The first witch shuffled forward and held the cup to his mouth. 'Drink,' she commanded.

He had seen what they had put into the pot and a fear gripped him. What if this was a trick and they planned to kill him? He looked at the third witch – she had sipped and it had not affected her. He was stronger in body, though she – having connections with the spirit world – might have supernatural protection. So, somewhat anxious, he took the proffered cup, raised it and threw the contents into his mouth. The liquid hit the back of his throat and he gagged but then numbness came over his tongue and lips and he tasted nothing.

'Tell me, what of Scotland?' he gasped.

The old woman's eyes locked onto his. She took the cup from his hand and shoved it behind her. The tall woman grabbed it and put it on a low table.

The room was quiet, save the sounds of the cauldron and the fire – and his laboured breathing. The old witch pursed her lips then closed her eyes. 'She has many enemies,' she said. 'But greater are her friends. Though men will come against her, none shall break her. Though some will inflict wounds and they will fester, nothing will destroy her.'

This might not be good news. To his next question. 'The king?'

The second witch brought her cup and gave it to him to drink. This time he did not hesitate. Without taking his eyes from the hag, he emptied it.

She nodded and began humming. She took his cup and turned it around and around in her hands. 'Happiness will lose to loss which will lose to fear which will lose to rage which will lose to grief which will lose to hope which will lose to happiness.'

'These are riddles,' he cried. 'You have my gold; give me facts.'

'Speak! Demand! We will answer,' all three replied together.

'What of the girl? Will she keep the line alive?'

The third and final cup was handed to him and he drank. Now his whole face felt as if it had vanished. He could not taste or smell or feel, but he could still see.

The last witch stood before him. From within her garments she pulled out a bundle and handed it to him. He held it for a moment, uncertain what was expected. It felt solid and about the weight of the log he'd put on his fire earlier that day.

The woman stared at him, waiting. Unsure if he was supposed to uncover what was hidden, he began to unwrap the coarse garment. Suddenly, he felt movement between his fingers and he almost dropped it. The dirty cloth fell away and there, in his hands, was the body of a tiny baby boy.

'What is the meaning of this?' he shouted. 'This is madness.'

As if the noise had power to wake him, the baby inhaled deeply, his eyes flew open and he uttered a most painful and piercing wail.

He thrust the child into the arms of the hag and rushed from the hut, the sounds of cackling laughter and the wailing of the infant following him out into the cold dark night.

Nathanial was waiting, as he expected, when he jogged up to the horse, panting and out of breath. He'd dropped the torch and almost stumbled over the uneven ground as he fled.

'My lord?'

'Let us get out of this place!' he cried.

'Are you well?'

He didn't answer for a moment because he was still trying to make sense of what they had offered him. 'I am not sure even you would be able to unravel the riddles. Are you certain their gifts are genuine?'

'Most certain. Their predictions have never failed. As far back as the reign of Duncan the First, those hags have offered men who sought it unearthly knowledge, intelligence that has proved true over and over.' Nathanial was quiet for a few minutes. 'But Sire, we need to take great care with what they have given you. There is a parchment, some eight or nine years old, on which a priest has recorded their mutterings and how they were fulfilled.'

'A bizarre thing for a priest to do.'

Nathanial snorted. 'He was burned at the stake for consorting with witches. But his writings were smuggled out of Scotland and I was able to acquire them.'

'Acquire?'

'With your gold,' Nathanial said, a hint of a smile in his voice.

'Then my gold has been well spent.' Harold inhaled deeply. The effects of whatever it was they had given him were wearing off and he felt the beginning of a deep-seated and painful headache. 'Tell me of these writings.'

'They told of the death of Sinel, Macbeth's father, before he died. They prophesied that Macbeth would become the Thane of Cawdor and that he would be King of Scotland. They foretold the death of the priest who believed he would be saved by God – and they warned two kings of traitors in their midst.'

'What prophecies, if any, are there of Fleance?' This was his burning question.

'When the child was young, they said he would be king. And he is king.' They were coming now towards the town. In the distance, small beacons of light flickered, so they went on quietly.

Famous for his sense of direction, Nathanial led them back to the very spot where they had met. They dismounted and Harold winced as his stiff legs jarred against the impact of the ground. He retrieved his jewelled cloak and replaced it with the one his advisor had given him.

'We will talk tomorrow,' the earl said. 'I want some time to ponder this knowledge before I offer it to you as well.'

Nathanial bowed his head. 'Certainly. Now, take my torch,' he said, handing it to the earl. 'I will be able to find my way to my camp. It is not far from here.'

'Thank you, Nathanial. Once again, you have proven yourself most valuable.'

'It is my duty, my lord. And my honour.'

He clasped a hand on the man's shoulder. 'When things I am putting into place come to be, you can expect to be rewarded handsomely for your faithfulness.'

'Thank you. It is a hope I shall hold dear to my heart. Good night.'

Harold turned around and picked his way carefully through the forest until he was back at the cottage. The guards, though obviously weary from their vigil, were nonetheless alert to his arrival.

He handed them the torch and stole through the door. Undressing quickly, he then climbed into bed beside Edith, pulling her warm body to his own. 'You were gone?' she murmured.

'Not for long. Go back to sleep,' he said, kissing her forehead. She buried herself into his embrace and was immediately back asleep, breathing softly.

But not he.

He lay awake the rest of the night turning the riddles over and over in his mind. It would not be until he arrived at Glamis that he would be able to learn more about whether Fleance, King of Scotland, was friend or foe.

Rosie

Perth was crowded with folk who had arrived to see the royal wedding – the first in over twenty years. The tavern was full and Rosie, who had given up her room to guests, rolled away the bedding she had used and placed it under her parents' bed.

She had not slept well last night. Da was a fierce snorer but it was her thoughts that had kept her awake. Tomorrow, Flea would be wed.

Only four days before, they had received the royal invitation to attend the wedding. A solemn young man from the castle had called upon them demanding an audience and then pronounced that they were all welcome, not only at the wedding, but at the feast afterwards. Oh, and could Dougal ensure there were enough barrels of wine to accommodate the number of guests?

Da was pleased, as was Ma. Rosie went to her room to lie down.

'I do not want to come with you,' she protested. 'You have Jethro to help you with the labour.'

'If you are to take up the management of this business, lass, then you must know all parts – including the drudgery of delivery.'

'Da,' she said quietly. 'It is a day before his wedding.'

Dougal snorted and removed some litter from behind the counter. 'Aye. 'Tis.'

Why was he doing this to her? 'What good will I be there today?'

Her father stopped fussing and glared. 'Because this needs to end now. You need to see that this is over.'

Rosie shook her head. 'It makes no sense at all. Who knows if he will even be there? What do you expect to happen?'

He leant against the counter and looked at her. 'I don't expect anything, child, but I do hope that today might bring a stop to your foolish hope.'

Was Da right? Was her hope foolish? Perhaps if she saw Flea once more before he wed she could ask him herself.

Rosie slipped from the wagon while her father and Jethro unloaded the barrels of ale and found herself wandering towards the stables. Was it only last year that Flea had brought her here and explained his story? Had promised her that he loved her and that they would be together soon?

'Rosie?'

She looked up at the sound of his voice, remembered, and quickly curtsied. 'Your Majesty.' She had forgotten how handsome he was. 'Blair,' she added, inclining her head to Flea's companion. 'Are you well?'

'Aye, R-Rosie. It is good to see you,' Blair stammered.

The three of them stood in awkward silence just outside the entrance to the stables. The rain that had threatened all morning now began to fall intermittently, with large wet drops landing on them all.

Flea offered his hand. 'Let us take shelter a moment.' The sound of his voice settled over her like the warmth of a south wind and his touch brought her body alive.

Only when they were safely inside the stables did he let go of her hand. The absence of his touch almost made her cry out. Instead, she pulled back her shoulders and took in a deep breath.

As it was mid-afternoon, the horses not in use were dozing in their stalls. The stable hands were taking supper before they began work again. Rosie, Flea and Blair stood just inside the door and stared out at the frantic activity of Dougal and Jethro as they tried to avoid getting too wet.

For a moment, they stood ill at ease. Should not the king speak first? Rosie listened to the sound of the rain now thrumming on the thatch overhead, echoing the sound of her own heart as she struggled to calm her breathing. Oh, how she was glad of the poor light: it gave her a chance to swallow the tears that had threatened to rise up and to regain some much-needed equanimity that had fled at the unexpected reappearance of her beloved Flea.

'Is Dougal well?' Flea asked eventually.

'He is, and growing fatter and richer as each month draws to a close.'

'And Rebecca?'

'Scotland's weather worries her joints more but she is happy that Da is happy. And Flea, she is very much looking forward to the wedding.'

As soon as the words were out, Rosie felt the cutting truth of them. For weeks she had overheard Ma talk to patrons about the royal wedding to the point that Rosie had stopped thinking of it as Flea's wedding.

Somewhere behind her in the gloom of the stalls, a horse shifted in its straw and she heard Blair greet Willow fondly.

There was a pause before Flea spoke. 'He is in love with you.'

'Yes,' she sighed. 'I know, but he's not the one who has my heart in his keeping.'

He frowned. 'I . . .' Her statement had unsettled him.

'Why did we ever meet?' she asked quietly.

'What are you saying?'

He was clearly thrown off balance by this, which gave her courage. 'Why did I have to meet you and love you? I still love you, Flea, and always will. Please tell me you feel the same.'

Flea cleared his throat and dipped his head before responding. 'No, Rosie, I don't feel the same. You must know now that anything that was between us is in the past.' He looked over their surroundings and then leant forward. 'You must put it behind you.'

What? Had she read the signs all wrong? This is not how she imagined this conversation might go. Rosie grabbed his hand and pulled him into the shadows, feeling her temper rise. 'How can you say that?' she hissed through gritted teeth. 'This is *just like* that damned time in England.'

'Rosie—'

'No! Don't bother speaking now. At this moment I care little of who you are. You will hear what I have to say. I listened to your talk of honour and your father . . . but what is this now? You have played me for a fool. You begged me to believe you with talk of love.'

'You must understand . . .' he began, shifting his feet, colour draining from his cheeks.

'I haven't finished.' She could not stop the angry tears that came now, but to hell with it. Let him see them. 'I believed in you and

303

what you stood for. I have made sacrifices for you, only for you to turn and . . .' The tightness in her chest was making it difficult to find the right words. '. . . *belittle* what was between us.' She flicked away the tears. 'Before your coronation you told me you would always love me . . . Was that a lie too?'

'Y . . . Your M . . . Majesty?' Blair had come forward.

'Go back, Blair. You need not hear this conversation.' Fleance inclined his head and with a shaking hand, waved Blair away.

Blair blushed scarlet and gave Rosie an anguished look before he lowered his gaze and hurried out of the stables.

'Coward,' she cried, not caring now who heard. 'How easy it was for you, Flea, to tell me that you loved me when you did not have to honour such a declaration. You just hid behind the garments of royalty and what it demanded.'

'I am sorry, Rosie, that you feel this way.'

He reached out a hand but she pushed it away, shaking her head. How he had changed. Through her tears she looked into his face, searching for the man she believed him to be. He could not meet her gaze and looked down, his hands fisted at his sides. 'Well,' she said, trying to steady her breathing. 'I spit on your union. I curse your seed. May you suffer as you have made me suffer.'

Just then, Henri came into the stables. 'Fleance. We have been looking all over for you.' Then he saw Rosie. 'Ah. I see.' He tilted his head at the king. 'Shall I come back another time, hmmm?'

'A moment, Henri,' Fleance replied before once more turning to Rosie. 'I am sorry, Rosie . . .' he began, but a cry from outside drew their attention.

'Goddam it, boy. Pick up your bloody feet.' Dougal's angry shout echoed around the courtyard.

'I must go,' she said, and pushed past him, making her way towards the doorway.

'Wait,' she heard him say, but her rage spurred her on.

The rain stopped and the wind picked up. A barrel had fallen from the cart and smashed on the ground and Da was giving orders for Jethro to clear the mess.

Rosie lifted her skirts and walked to her father's cart. She looked down and the necklace Flea had given her for her birthday, sitting just above the neckline of her dress, caught her eye. A fresh wave of rage flooded through her. She stopped, grabbed the delicate chain and pulled fiercely.

It broke and, just for a moment, she looked at it shining in the light. Then, taking a deep breath, she straightened her shoulders, lifted her head higher and went to join the others, throwing the necklace to the ground as she went forward.

It was finally over. As she climbed up on the wagon and looked at the imposing walls of the castle, she finally understood her place in this story.

But from now on she would be the one to determine her own course. She would no longer be a pawn in any man's game.

Chapter Twenty-Four
Fleance

He sat mesmerised by the swing of the necklace. What a stab in the heart it had been to see Rosie toss it away. Such anger and hurt and rage.

The door to the room opened slowly and Fleance looked up. It was Henri.

'Come in,' he said, looking away again.

Henri stepped inside and closed the door but did not move further into the room. Fleance looked back at the necklace, replaying the scene again in his mind. He had expected her to be hurt but had forgotten she had a temper to match his own.

'How goes it, Henri?' Fleance asked, still staring at the chain.

'I am well, my friend,' Henri smiled. 'Unlike you, I suspect.'

Fleance put the chain down on his knee and rubbed his face. 'I had to do that to her.'

'Yes,' Henri said. 'Your general has told me of your . . . conversation with the maid.'

Fleance scratched the bridge of his nose but could not contain the deep sigh that now escaped. His thoughts were only of Rosie. 'She would never have got on with her life,' he said. 'I had to speak to her that way.'

There was a rustle of cloth as Henri came forward and placed a hand on his shoulder. 'I know. But perhaps the price is too high, no?'

Outside the window, muffled shouts and men's voices were a reminder of the important celebration tomorrow. 'Has she gone?'

Henri removed his hand and stepped back. '*Oui.*'

'Did you hear her say anything more?'

'No, but your general was there to offer her some comfort before she left. He is fond of her, yes?'

Fleance breathed in deeply and swallowed, then leant back in the chair. 'Yes, yes, I think he is. This is for the best,' he added. Henri nodded but remained silent. 'She is better off without me in her life,' Fleance added.

'That may be so, my friend,' Henri replied, pouring them both some wine. 'But are you better off without her in yours?'

There was a rap on the door and it opened to admit Firth. 'Your Majesty, the Earl of Wessex and his wife have arrived. They are in the great hall.'

'I will be there shortly.' Firth went out.

A moment later the door opened again. It was Rachel. 'Princess,' Fleance said, nodding. He turned to Henri. 'I will see you at supper.'

Henri bowed quickly. 'I look forward to it.'

After he had left, Rachel walked over to where he sat. She smiled but there was a look of worry in her eyes. 'Is something amiss?' he asked.

She frowned but still regarded him. For a moment her eyes flicked away and then she looked at him directly, her expression serious. 'I know a little of what happened this afternoon in the stable.'

A pebble of irritation shifted in his chest. 'Which is?'

'Fleance,' she chided. 'Please don't be obtuse.' She tilted her head and studied him. 'You are upset?'

He nodded. 'Yes.'

Rachel came close and took his hand. 'Will you tell me?'

What should he say about Rosie? As Fleance tried to work out what and how much to say, he stood and guided Rachel over to the chairs, where they both sat.

They both settled with Rachel looking at him expectantly. *No*, he thought. *I will not hurt another this day.* 'I am upset, Rachel,' he began, the story solidifying in his mind. 'Because I was the cause of another's pain.' She sat there, still and attentive, her hands folded in her lap. 'I had to tell her the truth,' he said, wincing inside at the lie.

'Which is?' she asked softly.

'That I no longer love her.'

Rachel's eyes widened. 'Is this true, Fleance?'

He willed his heart to slow as the lie began to quicken his pulse, making his hands sweat.

'Aye. I told her it was over between us: the first flush of young love. It is like a mist that evaporates when the heat of the sun is upon it.' He licked his lips to remove the dryness he felt.

Rachel shook her head. 'That is a bitter, bitter herb for any woman to taste.'

Fleance was unable to remain still in his seat. Abruptly he stood and began to pace the room. 'For that I am sorry.'

'This is a hard thing for you, Fleance, the day before our wedding.'

'Not any harder than many things I have had to do these past months.'

She stood and came close to him, putting her hand on his cheek. 'Your strength is a blessing.'

Her hand was warm on his face and the gentleness of her touch comforted him. 'As is yours,' Fleance said and lifted his own hand to cover hers. It was good that she saw his pain but not the truth behind it. *Pray God that over time my pain will wilt away and be replaced by the joy of this new union.*

———

The hall was already filled with guests and harried servants were scurrying to and fro to bring drink and food to those gathered. The doorman rapped his mace on the floor and the noise abated. 'Fleance, King of Scotland, and Princess Rachel, daughter of Donalbain.'

Those gathered clapped politely while Firth hurried forward. 'The earl is most keen to meet you,' he said.

'As am I him,' Fleance said, smiling. He looked over and saw Margaret, who was in animated discussion with the two youngest royals of the castle, and they exchanged looks. Fleance grinned and turned to Rachel. 'Your sister and mine are keeping the dowager busy, it seems.'

Rachel looked over at the young girls and let out a deep sigh. 'For this I am thankful. A night without Bree's antics is a good night.'

A handsome man and his pregnant wife came forward. 'Your people seem pleased with this union,' he said.

Fleance was startled. 'As am I.'

'Forgive me,' the Englishman said, holding out his hand. 'I am Harold, Earl of Wessex, and this is my wife, Edith.'

Fleance nodded. 'And also the King of England's sister. Welcome and thank you for coming.'

Edith curtsied, even with her protruding belly, smiled and looked to Rachel. 'You are a stunning creature,' she offered, coming forth to kiss Rachel on her cheek. Then she looked at Fleance. 'And you are a very fortunate man.'

Harold tapped him gently on the shoulder. 'Indeed you are.'

Fleance caught Blair's eye. To touch a king without invitation was unusual.

Blair came to his rescue. 'Begging your pardon, but the king has some other guests to meet.' The earl and his wife bowed their heads and shifted away. Rachel broke off and went to join the wives of the Scottish thanes and earls who were seated at the other end of the hall.

Fleance and Blair moved to join Henri. 'Did you not think it strange,' Fleance said to them both, 'that he accepted the invitation when he has never shown interest in Scotland before?'

'Aye. My instincts tell me he has sensed you are more than England has given you credit for,' Blair said.

Henri nodded. 'He smells like a rat with a garland around his neck.' He shrugged. 'Though in his home country, he is well loved by those he leads. Maybe they like rats.'

All three laughed at Henri's quip but then Fleance nodded his head towards the guests. 'He is right at that, though. The people are very happy.'

'And why should they not be? You are Scotland's hope. With Rachel as your queen, the people see a settled today and tomorrow.'

'Word has come from all over that the people of Scotland bless this union,' Blair said.

Fleance was moved by the passion in Blair's voice. 'For this I am grateful.'

'Good. So be at peace, my friend and my king.'

Epilogue

The weather was perfect. A beautiful, light day with only a delicate breeze. It was cold, but all gathered had known to wrap up warmly. And for a wedding, nothing could be better. One could hear the music before the procession came into view. A joyous sound of drums, strings and trumpets. The crowd began to quiten down from their informal conversations and the sounds coming from them were laced with a keen anticipation.

The groom's heart began to race and he took deep, steadying breaths to calm his nerves. Coming up the incline towards the church, the bride and her cart were accompanied by a colourful band of musicians and dancers. In front of the bride's cart, the musicians played and danced. Behind the players, all could see young maids scattering flower petals before the horses' hooves. They were dressed in ornate costumes and danced and giggled before the cart. They did not understand the solemnity of the occasion.

On either side, a contingent of armed and decorated soldiers marched, keeping the enthusiastic onlookers at bay. A gaggle of interested folk lined the path to the church but only a few were admitted to the area immediately below the steps.

The groom, smartly attired but clearly nervous, stood outside the building, beside the taciturn bishop appointed to the role of minister for the nuptials.

Even from this distance he could see his bride was beautiful. Her hair floated free around her face, and her bright white gown fluttered around her legs so that she had to lean forward and hold the material firmly down.

The procession pulled up in front of the church and servants ran to the side of the cart to help the bride down onto the pebbled walkway. The musicians stepped back and the young maids, smiling coyly at those gathered, also moved to the side.

The bride stepped off the cart and arranged her skirts. So stunningly beautiful. The cloth of the white silk gown, embroidered with thick gold edging, hung close around her figure.

The groom felt his heart skip. Had it been so easy to forget what a striking woman she was?

Finally, she was here. The crowd voiced their appreciation but he had eyes only for her as she walked towards her husband-to-be.

'You are well?' he whispered.

She smiled and nodded. 'Are you?'

'N . . . now that you are here.'

She laughed out loud at his reply and gently touched his arm.

Outside the church, she stood before him, smiling, and he could barely pull his eyes away from her face to turn to the bishop and follow the man's instructions.

The bishop stood on the uppermost step of the church and held up his hands. This silenced the crowd.

'I am obliged by the decrees of the holy church to ensure the following before I bestow blessing on this union: that the partners be of equal and free rank and that they give their consent to marry.' The old man looked at them both and they nodded. 'You may begin the vows.'

The groom turned towards the bride and took her hands. With a steadying breath, he spoke. 'I, Blair, give my body to you, Rosie, in loyal matrimony.'

'And I, Rosie, receive it,' she answered.

Acknowledgments

Thanks to Vicki Marsdon, Katie Howath and Josh Getzler – all of whom helped me to hang in there with this story and pushed me to make it better

Jo Fielding. Goddess divine. Also, I like my inversions, thank you very much. Blessings to you for your 'there, there' support. Those emails; those 'call, continuity, and complain' comments – you are one in a trillion. Applause to Jo.

David Fielding: forget your prodigious title at the uni – it's the times around your dinner table when you said, 'You do know, don't you, that . . . ?' That rocked my writing world. Actually, NO, I DID NOT KNOW. Damn and blast that it made me scuttle back home and change my story details. But this story is better for those questions. A gentleman and a gentle man. Hence the reason this book is dedicated to you, David, and to Jo Fielding.

Thanks to Adelaide Dunn for writing the first draft of the Iona segment. Lovely.

To Lyn and Chris Wainwright: thanks for the retreat and the love. Lucky me that you guys came into my life! The babes: Imogen, Danielle, Dannielle, Laura, Penelope, Flavia, Annie, Imogen, Aimee and, remotely, Kato – go, you sure things. Thanks. And really, and you know what I mean by this: thanks so much! And to your parents who offered prayers; for this I am grateful.

My friends who know and understand what we were going through while I was writing this book: thank you thank you thank you. I was not a faithful friend at this time but I appreciate your support during my tears. But most of all, I give thanks to my God that my husband and children were sustained during this very, very hard time.

About the Author

T.K. Roxborogh lives in Dunedin, New Zealand, and has been an English and Drama teacher since 1989. Born in Christchurch, she spent the first twenty-five years of her life living around the country, experiencing everything from tobogganing on the slopes of Lake Ellesmere to scuba diving in the Bay of Islands. Now an award-winning author, she has published works across a range of genres: novels, plays for the classroom, Shakespearean texts, English grammar books and adult non-fiction. She spends most days juggling teaching, studying and writing, and, with her husband, runs around after their family – both the two-legged and four-legged kind. Roxborogh loves reading, watching movies and TV shows, and staying in her pyjamas for as long as possible.